EVENTUALLY BLAKE

A. K. STEEL

Eventually Blake
Copyright ©2021 by A. K. Steel

All rights reserved. No part of this book may be reproduced or transmitted in either electronic, paper hard copy, photocopying, recorded, or any other form of reproduction without the written permission of the author. No part of this book either in part or whole may be reproduced into or stored in a retrieval system or distributed without the written permission of the author.

This book is a work of fiction. Characters, names, places and incidents are products of the author's imagination. Any resemblances to actual events, locations, or persons living or dead is purely coincidental.

The author acknowledges the trademark status and owners of products referred to in this fiction which have been used without permission. The publication and use of these trademarks is not authorised, associated with, or sponsored by the trademark owners.

Published by A.K. Steel

Edited by Contagious Edits

Blurb by Contagious Edits

Cover Design by Opium House Creatives

ABOUT THE BOOK

Their relationship was doomed from the start. Too bad nobody told their hearts.

Blake Donovan is looking to start over. He's more than just an ambitious builder; he's the heir to a criminal empire... and his dad is looking to collect. When you've been raised in a family where love is a weakness, it's impossible to let someone in. But then a one-night stand with a sexy stranger leaves him wanting more than he ever thought possible. He knows he's not the right guy for her, with a past that could destroy them both. He should just leave her alone, but he can't help himself, and when he sets his sights on something he wants, he doesn't stop until he gets it. And this time, he wants her.

When aspiring artist Indie Martin's long-term boyfriend rips her heart to pieces, she retreats to her local pub, hoping to numb the pain. When she bumps into the intense and irresistible Blake, suggesting a night of fun to help forget her hurt, it's an offer she can't refuse. She gives him a fake name and takes off before he wakes up; that way there's no risk of getting invested in someone that will only break her heart. Too bad Blake has other plans. Suddenly, he's everywhere, embedded in her life with no hope for escape. She knows she should run from him... but love isn't about being smart.

Their romance is bound to fail before it's even begun. Friendships, felonies, and family secrets... there are no limits to the obstacles they will face.

PROLOGUE
BLAKE

I'm walking through the busy dance floor of my new local pub with my mate Fraser. It's a Saturday night and the music is blaring with some band I have never heard of on the stage. They must be a local favourite because the place is packed.

We're on our way to the bar to top up our drinks. Then, as we push our way through the crowd, a girl calls out to Fraser from behind us. We both turn to see who's calling him. Another pretty blonde. She wraps her arms around him in an embrace, and I decide to leave him to it. Must be someone he knows from high school. This is Fraser's hometown, and he seems to have a lot of fans. We've only been here for an hour and this is the fourth girl to throw her arms around him, like he's famous or something.

Me, I'm not a local. I don't know anyone but Fraser and a couple of the new boys I hired to work as part of my building crew. Fraser and I only moved to Byron Bay this week, to set up our new business. It's been a really long week, and tonight we're finally celebrating our hard work. I turn back towards the bar, a little too quickly, and feel a thud on my chest. I glance down to see a cute brunette smiling awkwardly up at me, her red drink running down the front of my pale blue button-up. Damn. The sticky liquid quickly absorbs through my shirt.

"I'm sooo sorry. Did I mess up your shirt?" She wobbles a little in her extra-high heels. I can see why she wears them, she's tiny. Even with the heels on, she's only up to my chest. Her pretty eyes blink up at me through thick black lashes.

I reach past her and grab a napkin from the bar, dabbing the wet spot where her drink connected with my favourite button-up. "Don't worry. It was my fault. I wasn't watching where I was going. Let me get you a refill. What are you drinking?" I ask, offering my most charming smile. This girl is cute, and it's a happy coincidence that we literally ran into each other. She's dressed in a short, silky-looking, emerald-green dress that matches her eyes, which haven't left mine since we ran into each other.

Her pouty red lips give me a sideways smile. "Vodka cranberry, thanks."

"Vodka cranberry and a Stone and Wood," I tell the bartender.

The pretty brunette downs the remainder of her spilt cocktail, setting it down on the bar, and takes the fresh glass from me. As she takes the drink, her hand brushes against mine and I get this strange feeling running through me. I can tell she feels it too because she pulls back quickly, looking at me with a questioning gaze. Her eyes roam over me, and I wonder what she's thinking. She looks down to her drink, throwing it back and draining the red liquid in her glass. She places her empty glass on the bar, signalling to the bartender for another.

I'm not quite sure why I'm still here at the bar. I've done the right thing, replaced her drink. I could just move along with my night, get back to whatever it is the other boys are doing. But there's something about her, more than the fact she's hot. She looks sad or angry... I can't read her well enough to know which, yet. Curiosity has the better of me. I want to know why, why she's in a bar all alone, sculling drinks like there's no tomorrow. "You on a mission to get drunk or something?"

She takes a seat at the bar and I move a little closer to her. It's hard to hear with the music still pumping through the air. She tilts her head to the side, watching me as she fiddles with the large hoop earrings she wears. "Something like that." She turns back to the bar and picks the next drink up, cradling it in her hand, swirling the liquid around, some of it sloshing over the side onto her hand. She flicks out her tongue, slowly licking it off. Her emerald-green eyes watch me as she does.

And, fuck, there is something in that gaze of hers. She's naughty, I just know it. I get an image of her on her knees in front of me. Her red lipstick smeared. Her tongue running over my hard cock, licking my orgasm off after I've fucked her mouth. This night just got a whole lot more interesting.

"You might want to slow down a bit, if you don't want to end up with a mammoth hangover tomorrow. You're only tiny. I can't imagine you can drink much," I tell her, taking another sip of my drink.

"I can drink plenty, don't need you looking out for me, thanks, Dad." She giggles, pushing me on the arm, the movement causing her to wobble on the bar stool. I rest my hand on her knee to steady her, so she's doesn't fall.

I'm close enough to smell her perfume; she smells like

summertime. "Okay, but when you wake up tomorrow in my bed, with your head thumping, don't say I didn't warn you." Let's see what she thinks about that.

My mate Fraser talked me into coming out tonight, to get my head off Lexi, and I can't think of a better way to forget the fucked-up situation with my ex than a night of hot-as-hell sex with this cute brunette.

She looks up at me, her eyes narrowing. "Who said I'm ending up in your bed tonight?"

I drop my head so I'm almost whispering into her ear, "Me! I've been talking to you for a while now and there's no friends or boyfriend in sight. There's only one reason a girl comes to a bar by herself... she's looking for a drunken hook-up. Tell me I'm wrong."

"That's very presumptuous of you. I could be waiting here for someone. Maybe my friend is just late," she says quietly.

"And is that the case?"

She sits up a little taller, reaching down and removing my hand from where it is still resting on her knee. "Well, no. But I'm not looking for a drunken hook-up either." She pauses for a moment. "I just needed to get out of my apartment for a while and have a drink. It's been a long day." She sighs, looking down into her drink. She's definitely sad.

I pull up a bar stool next to her, giving her a little space, but I'm not ready to give up yet. I have a feeling about her, that she's someone I want to know. "Are you okay?" I ask.

Her sad eyes rise to meet mine. "No, not really. My boyfriend of nine years is moving his stuff out of our apartment as we speak, after dumping me out of the blue. I couldn't stay there and watch him. How pathetic would that be?"

Shit, that's a bit fresh. "I'm sorry. That sucks." I pause for a minute. "I just realised, I don't know your name."

She looks at me, nibbling on her bottom lip, hesitant to answer.

"I could just make up a cute nickname for you, like cupcake or shortcake."

She eyes me over, not looking impressed.

"I know, I have it, I'll call you pixie."

"Pixie?"

"Cause you're little and cute."

She giggles. "You're not calling me pixie. My name is Violet."

I hold out my hand to shake, and she places her hand in mine. "I'm Blake, nice to meet you, Violet. I'm sorry to hear about your boyfriend leaving. Who would leave someone as beautiful as you? What a dick."

She offers a little smile, then shrugs. "We've been together since high school. He felt like he was missing out on a more exciting life. Wants to travel the world or something, try new things. Truth be told, I think we just drifted apart. Wanted different things, you know," she says quietly.

"Yeah, I do. I was dragged out tonight by my mate." I point him out in the crowd. "I just broke up with my long-term girlfriend as well. We wanted different things. She fell in love with my best mate, at the same time as she was in love with me. Wanted to try a polygamist relationship. I didn't!" I laugh; it's not funny, but maybe my shit love life could distract her from the pain she's in tonight.

She chokes on her drink, spluttering, trying to catch her breath. "Umm, wow, that's not what I was expecting you to say. Each to their own, I guess. I can almost forgive you for your shit pick-up lines tonight. Now I know what you're going through." She giggles.

"Thanks. I thought I was doing all right. You're still talking to me." I bump her arm with mine playfully.

She rolls her eyes dramatically. "What? By telling me I'm going to wake up in your bed tomorrow morning?"

"That wasn't a pick-up line. Just an observation. I'm taking you home tonight. Sounds like it's what we both need, take our minds off our shitty breakups," I offer with my most charming smile.

She looks me up and down slowly as if assessing me. Then looks down to the drink in her hand, gives it another swirl, then empties the contents of her glass. "All right, take me home, let's see what you've got."

I throw back my beer, leaving the empty bottle on the bar. I hold my hand out for her to take and she places her hand in mine. She smiles at me as we walk out of the pub.

That escalated quickly. Here I was thinking she was about to tell me I had no chance in hell. We walk past Fraser on our way out, and I wave to let him know I'm leaving and not to come home anytime soon. He's busy with the blonde and couldn't care less.

We both hop in my ute that's parked out the front. It's just a short drive to my house a few streets over.

"A ute, hey. What do you do for work?" she asks, buckling up her seatbelt.

"I'm a builder. My mate and I have just moved here from Newcastle to start up our own business together. He's an architect. What do you do for work?" I ask as I take off up the street toward my house.

"That's pretty cool. Must be hard work, though, setting up a business. I'm an artist, mainly psychedelic pop art kind of portraits. If you even know what that is." I smile and nod like I do. "I sell some of my stuff at the local markets." She shrugs.

I glance over at her. "Yeah, I can see it, you look like an artist."

Her gaze is on the road in front like she doesn't trust my driving, so she has to watch the road for me. She tilts her head to the side, looking over to me. "Do I? How's that?" Her brow wrinkles as she says it.

I shrug. "I don't know. You just have that free spirit kinda thing going on. Someone who doesn't follow what society expects of them, makes their own path, that kind of thing. Would I be right?"

Her lips curl to one side. "Oh, I guess that's me. It's because of the tattoos, isn't it?"

I let my gaze roam over her again; I'm going to have an accident if I don't watch the road, but I can't take my eyes off her. "Nah, it's just your vibe. I'd like to see where that trail of flowers leads to, though."

"I'm sure you would," she says, running her hand over the intricate, detailed flower art etched up her arm. I ache to run my hands over the same path and wonder if the pattern stops or continues along her body under where her dress sits.

I pull my ute up out the front of my house—somehow we made it home in one piece. The light shines through from the streetlight, highlighting her beautiful features, her heart-shaped face framed by her chocolate-brown hair, just short of shoulder length. Her long fringe almost hides her pretty almond-shaped eyes. She's an absolute stunner. Why did she agree to come home with me?

"You going to stare at me in your car all night or are we going inside to fuck?" she says with a cheeky smile.

"I was just admiring how striking you are, Violet."

She rolls her eyes. "Enough with the flattery. I'm already at your place. You know you're going to get lucky."

"Not why I said it." Does she hate the way she looks or just doesn't know how to take a compliment? I hop out of the ute and walk up the path to my house. She follows carefully on the uneven driveway in her extra-tall heels.

I open the door, flicking on the lights, and she follows me in. "You want something more to drink?" I offer.

She shakes her head as she walks around the living room like she's doing an inspection on the space. "Nice place. You have pretty good taste for a guy. Is this a real *Eames* chair?" she asks, running her hand along the black leather lounge.

"Thanks, but I can't claim it. My housemate and business partner, Fraser, is an architect with an excellent eye for trendy furniture, and yeah, it is the real thing." I go to the kitchen and pour a scotch, taking a big swig, then walk back into the living room.

She sits on the chair, running her hands over the leather. Fuck, she looks sexy. "Lucky you. Is he around tonight, this friend of yours?"

"No, back at the bar we just left. He won't be back for a while, if at all." I sip my drink.

"Good." A smile crosses her face, and she stands up from the chair. She slowly crosses back over the room, closing the gap slightly but still keeping her distance. "Now that you have me here, what are you going to do with me, Blake the builder?" Her teeth bite into her bottom lip. My cock twitches with appreciation. It's so hard it feels like I'm going to split my pants if I don't get to fuck her soon.

"Make you forget what you ever saw in your ex, and you can make me forget why I was ever with mine."

"I like that plan," she whispers, her eyes twinkling with desire. She stands before me. Her silky dark green dress catches the light, looking like water rippling over her curvy body as she walks towards me, stopping just out of my reach. She drops one strap off her shoulder, then the other, and the dress slides down her body, pooling in a pile on the floor.

She's breath-taking, standing there in nothing but her incredibly high stiletto heels and lace panties that match the colour of her dress. With her perfectly perky tits on full display, her pink nipples harden in the cool night air. Her flawless, tanned skin is silky smooth against the contrast of the intricate flower pattern which runs up her arm and across her chest on one side, stopping just before her breasts. My hands ache to touch it.

I place my drink down. "Forgotten." I can barely remember my ex right now. All the blood has rushed to my cock. My brain is no longer operational. Violet is a fucking goddess, and I'm going to fuck her every way imaginable before the sun comes up tomorrow.

I stalk her, closing the gap between us. I reach down, lacing one hand through her hair to the back of her head, and the other moves to her lower back, pulling her into me. Her skin feels just how I imagined, soft and velvety under my touch. I bring her lips to mine, kissing her slowly as my hands run over her bare skin. I'm desperate for her to touch me.

Like she can read my mind, her hands skate over my chest, fumbling with the buttons on my shirt, tugging at the fabric until she has undone each one. She runs her delicate hands over my chest.

Our kiss intensifies to a frantic need as I swipe my tongue through her open mouth. She lets out a little moan. My hands roam over her body, reaching her breasts and cupping them, plucking her hardened nipples. She pulls back for air. I plant kisses down her neck to her chest, moving lower to take her nipple in my mouth, sucking as much in as I can. My teeth graze her skin.

She whimpers. "Blake, that feels so good." Her hands are in my hair, tugging at the strands, pulling my head back up to meet her greedy lips.

Our kiss is so intense, I don't feel like I have just met her, she's too familiar. I sense that, without me knowing until this very moment, this is where my lips have longed to be my whole life.

As we kiss, I guide her hand to my belt. She makes quick work of unbuckling it, pushing my pants to the floor. The look in her eyes is pure sin as she slides down my front to her knees. She hooks her thumbs into my boxer briefs and pulls them down, letting my cock spring free. Her hands explore my length as she looks up at me with those sparkling green eyes, drawing me in as she opens her pretty mouth. And, just as I imagined earlier, she licks the tip of my cock, tasting me. She grins up at me, her face giving away every bit of how excited she is by how I taste. She licks again, swirling her tongue around the top, then down my length. I shudder, it feels so good, and I want so much more of what she has to offer. "Violet, that feels fucking amazing," I groan.

She smiles up at me again with a sexy-as-fuck smile, then parts her red lips, taking me in her mouth. She slowly sucks my length, taking her time, as she watches me. It's the sexiest thing I have ever seen. She slides back and forth up my length, swirling her tongue when she reaches the tip. She's driving me crazy.

I feel myself getting close. My hands go to the back of her head, lacing my fingers through her wavy hair as I pick up the pace. I pull her into me, fucking her pretty little mouth with deep, fast thrusts. Her wild eyes look up at me, watching intently as I lose control.

"Fuck, Violet, I'm going to come," I groan in warning. I shove into her one last time as I feel my balls tighten and I release into her mouth. She drinks it down, licking her lips, a sexy-as-fuck look on her face. She's a vixen, a creature of pure sexual perfection. I want to taste her, make her come apart in my hands.

I reach down and pull her up to her feet. She wobbles a little, still wearing those impossibly high heels. I pick her up in my arms and she's light as a feather. I walk her over to the leather lounge and drape her over the smooth cold fabric. I position myself at her pussy, spreading her legs wider, tearing away the lace fabric of her panties to get to her sweet spot.

She's one hell of a hot sight, her hair wild, her body on full display. Her pussy is glistening wet and ready for me. I trace my finger through her slick folds, and she arches her back. "So fucking wet for me, aren't you, Violet? Ready for me to fuck you all night, fuck you so hard you'll forget why you came into that bar tonight."

She looks up at me and nods, her cheeks flushed. "Yes, Blake, fuck me all night. Make me forget."

I push two fingers into her tight pussy and watch her head fall back as she moans in pleasure. She's so responsive to my touch and it's driving me insane. I want to be inside her, but first, I want her screaming my name. I run my tongue up the inside of her leg to her core, licking and tasting as I slowly fuck her with my fingers. I circle my tongue around her clit, sucking it hard and flicking my tongue over it, as she moves around against the leather, arching her back, rocking her hips to meet the thrusts of my hand. I continue pumping my fingers as I taste every inch of her, licking and sucking. I reach up to her breast, rolling her nipple between my fingers as she moans again.

"Don't stop, Blake, feels so... good." Her hands are in my hair as she pulls me closer into her, screaming out my name. "Blake, fuck, Blake, yes." I feel her body contracting around my fingers as she rides through her orgasm. Her body shakes as I pull her up into my arms, wrapping herself around me as I pick her up and walk down the hall to my bedroom. Her eyes are closed, and she completely relaxes into me. I can feel how ragged her breathing is as she tries to come down from her orgasm.

I lay her down on my bed and she pulls the covers back. The room is dark, only lit by the shining streetlight coming through the half-open blinds. Her silhouette on my bed is fucking perfection. I climb into bed with her, and she wraps her body around mine as I cradle her face. She looks up at me through her long lashes, her eyes fiery with need. I draw her in, kissing her with force. I'm desperate for more of her. I want her to feel every part of me as I fuck her. I want her lips bruised, to still feel me on them tomorrow.

She runs her hands over my back, digging her nails in slightly, and I run mine down her body. Her soft, silky skin feels so good on mine. Our bodies press into one another as we kiss aggressively, desperate for more of each other.

She pulls back. "More, Blake. I want you to fuck me, make me forget." We're tangled in the sheets, my hard length pushing up against her. I'm just as desperate for more as she is. The temperature in the room is set to burning.

"So greedy," I tease, as I reach over and fumble through my drawer for protection. Rolling the condom over my throbbing cock, I position myself between her legs, spreading them wider as I dive straight in.

She cries out, "Fuck! You're huge," but her look is joy, not fear at my size. She fucking loves it.

I pull out, then slam in again, harder this time. "You're just little."

She lets out a breathless moan like I have knocked the wind out of her with my deep thrust. "Yes, I am. You going to go easy on me?"

"Fuck no, I can see how much you love my big cock in your tight little pussy. I'm going to stretch you so you can handle me, pump you over and over again till the burn turns to overwhelming pleasure and you scream out for more." I move inside of her, slower this time, circling my hips a little, pulling almost all the way back out then pushing back in. Her body responds so well to my slow movements, her hips raising off the bed slightly higher each time I grind into her.

She reaches her hands around me, clinging to my back, her nails lightly scraping my skin. "Stop this slow torture and fuck me, Blake."

I push straight in again, harder this time as I pick up the speed and really start to give it to her. She claws at my back, and it's hard to tell if her moans are of pleasure or pain. "Is that what you wanted, baby?"

"Yes, fuck me hard. I need it." Her voice is barely recognisable. That's what I needed to hear.

Who is this girl? She can keep up with me and begs for more. I pick up the pace, slamming into her as she cries out in pleasure. The headboard is smashing against the wall with each hard thrust, *bang, bang, bang*. I'll be lucky if there's not a hole there to patch up tomorrow. I keep going, completely losing control, as I feel her body contracting around my dick. I let go myself, filling her up.

I roll off her and pull her into my chest, stroking her hair away from her eyes. I kiss her shoulder. My heart is hammering in my chest and I can feel hers is as well. That was insane. Fast, hard, and hot as fucking hell. Just the way I like it.

"Fuck, Blake. What was that? I'm lightheaded," she says, her body relaxing into me, still gasping for breath.

"You're fucking crazy, Violet," I murmur into her hair.

"Me? That was all you," she giggles, "and your jackhammer dick."

I laugh. "Jackhammer dick? I haven't heard that before."

She runs her hands through my hair, pulling me closer into her, and I place small kisses down her neck. "When can we go again?" she asks. "I don't want to sleep tonight. I just want that on repeat, all night."

"If you think you can handle it," I tease. She wiggles her arse at my crotch, signalling she's ready when I am. "I'm already hard again, baby."

The sunlight filters through my room, waking me from the deepest sleep I've had in forever. It's so bright. Why didn't I close the blinds last night? I cover my eyes to block it out. Then I remember last night. How could I forget? It was fucking incredible. I kept the blinds open so I could see her while I fucked that perfect body of hers.

With that thought, I wonder if the sexy Violet is up for another round this morning, because I'm hard and ready to go. I roll over, reaching my hand out, but the bed is empty. I get that sinking feeling, knowing she's probably not in the bathroom. She's gone.

Damn. Why did she just take off? I know last night was supposed to be a drunken hook-up, a distraction to help me get over Lexi, and for her to get over her ex. But it ended up being so much more than that. We didn't fall asleep until the early hours. She was determined to fuck all night.

In between the hottest sex of my life, we talked and laughed. She's honest and funny and says whatever she's thinking, no filter. There's something about her, something special. She's so intriguing. I want to know more. But that's not going to happen now. I didn't even get her number or last name, and I know little else about her. She's going to be nearly impossible to track down in a town I hardly know.

CHAPTER ONE

BLAKE: SIX MONTHS LATER

The gym is empty, eerily quiet, the only sound my beating heart and the panting breaths I take as I push myself to run harder. It's still early Sunday morning, and most normal people are home in bed, sleeping off their poor choices from the night before. But not me. My feet pound the treadmill at a fast pace to warm up.

My head throbs with memories of last night, lack of sleep, and way too many shots with Elly. That girl is a bad influence. The pain I feel is all self-inflicted, of course, so I'm going to suck it up and run through the persistent thump at my temples. Last night was the first night I have had out with a girl in a long time, and it wasn't really a date, I couldn't let it be. I'm still hung up on Violet. Vivacious Violet. We had one night of unbelievably hot passion six months ago, and I have thought of no one else since. After that night, though, she vanished into thin air, and I've had no luck in finding her again. I know it's time to move on. Can't keep pining over a one-night stand for forever, even if it was the most thrilling night of my life.

My night out with Elena Walker—or Elly—was nothing

short of entertaining. I met her at her parents' house last week when I was there to do a building inspection on the new holiday villas her father is having our company build. We got to talking, and she said she's an interior stylist looking for work around here so she can build a business of her own. I loved her spirit, and I'm all for supporting anyone who is willing to put themselves out there and build a business. She would be a perfect addition to our team, so I talked her into coming in this week to meet with our architect, Fraser. I hope he likes her as much as I do.

She's such a sweet girl, down on her luck of late, and it looked like she could use a friend and a fun night out, truth be told. So could I, so I asked her out—as friends, nothing more. Italian food, pool, shots, cocktails, and drinking games didn't disappoint. It was nice to let loose, and Elly's a cool chick, funky fashion sense, blue hair and all, but there was no spark, no fire when we looked at each other. The desire that buzzed between me and Violet was electric, and I want that feeling again.

I glance down at my watch, 7.30am already? Good. I've been here for 30 minutes, and I'd like to get in another half-hour before I need to head home to get ready for breakfast with Elly. I promised I'd take her out to eat, help soak up all that alcohol from last night. When I run, it calms the thoughts that take over my mind. I have been using exercise as a coping mechanism since I was 18 and... the accident that happened. This morning I really needed to run. I woke up before the sun to the nightmare that frequents my mind, my body covered in a hot sweat, wishing I could change the past and what happened that day.

I shake off the thought from my past. I don't want to think about that now. I pick up the pace to a sprint, needing to rid myself of those memories, just focus on one foot in front of the other. The rest will fade away. Not today, though. Apparently, memories of the accident lead me to think about my fucked-up family, yet another thing I can't outrun.

I didn't have a standard upbringing like a normal kid from suburban Sydney. My family didn't fit the normal mould at all. My dad owns a string of high-end strip clubs, restaurants, and night clubs across Sydney. These clubs have been in our family for generations, and the oldest son always takes over the family business when the boss dies or steps down. Sounds simple, and not so bad, but this family business is so much more than just a few establishments. My dad controls the underworld of Sydney. I guess you could say he's the king pin, the one everyone looks to for advice, and the one who makes all the big decisions.

Growing up in this world exposed me to all sorts of things a kid shouldn't see or even know about. But, to my family, this seedy scene was all normal. They were training me up to take over when the time was right.

I don't think my dad is a bad person, he's just doing his job keeping things in order. At least that's what he says. I can't stand the whole scene and wish more than anything I was born into another family. A normal family with normal parents. Ones that cared about my wellbeing more than the dollar in their pocket.

My mum supports my dad because she loves the money and notoriety. She isn't one of those kind, caring mothers. She's hard and mean, only ever cares about herself. That was why I knew I had to get out of there before I ended up like them. I'm not like them, and the accident—if it even was an accident—was the final straw for me. I moved away to Newcastle and started my building traineeship, and that was when I met Fraser.

My dad isn't happy but he's giving me space to experience life the way I want to, before I come back and take over when I'm needed. As much as I don't want anything to do with it all, Dad keeps me in the loop and calls on me whenever he needs help with various projects up this way. I've seen things and done things I'm not proud of. But, when you're born into a family like this, the only way out is death, and I have too much to live for.

I've inherited some traits from my dad. I'm highly ambitious and spend all my free time building my company, The Green Door, the one I started with a couple of mates. Fraser, he's our architect, and Ash runs the developments. I'm in charge of our team of builders and project managements. After just six short months, we're already one of the most successful companies in Byron.

Some people say I'm cocky, but I'm not. We're good at what we do. We're fucking hard working and successful because of it.

My phone buzzes, breaking me out of my thoughts. It's in the holder in front of me, on the treadmill. I glance down to see who it is. Lexi again. I slow the speed to a walk and lower the incline. I'm not in the mood to talk to her this morning. I have no idea why she keeps calling. This is the third time this week.

It's been six months since we broke up, just before Fraser and I moved to Byron to start our business. I got over her months ago, but she keeps calling and begging to try again, to do things differently this time. It's never going to work. She wants something I can't give her. I mean, I have tried my fair share of kinky shit, but a polygamous relationship, sharing her with my best friend and business partner, is just not something I'm ever going to be up for. Well, not again, anyway. I have never regretted a drunken night so much.

We were all drunk, very drunk, and it started with a harmless game of truth or dare, then somehow ended up with Lexi talking us into playing out her ultimate fantasy. It was a big mistake, huge! That night caused a downhill spiral to the demise of our once-happy relationship. I was lucky to save my relationship with Fraser.

Now when I look back, I'm at peace with it. Lexi and I were never going to last anyway, so it was better it was over before we wasted any more time.

My phone rings again. Lexi's name lights up the screen. I sigh. I know if I don't answer it, she's not going to leave me alone until I do. She's very persistent. I stop the treadmill, wiping the sweat from my brow, and answer the call. "What do you want, Lexi?" I sigh.

"Hey, babe, I miss you. Just want to talk. I was thinking, I'm free this weekend. I want to come and visit you guys, see if we can work something out." I don't know why but her voice sounds hopeful, like I would actually let her. You think she would know better after the number of times I've said no already.

"You know that's not going to happen. It's over. We're done." I step off the treadmill, wipe my forehead with my towel, and walk over to the locker area.

"See, Blake, I don't believe you. I have been watching your social media posts and you haven't moved on from me. You know you won't find anyone who will compare. Just let me come and see you. I'll come and stay for the weekend with you guys. I'm sure, by the end, you won't want me to leave."

Lexi is actually starting to scare me. She's giving off a

crazy stalker vibe with all the calls; she won't take no for an answer. Thank God she's six hours away.

"And there it is, the reason this will never work. You need to give up trying and move on." She wants to see *us*. Not just me, but Fraser as well.

"What reason?"

"You want to stay the weekend with us both," I huff.

"I didn't say that."

"Yeah, but you implied it, and I know it's what you actually mean. Goodbye, Lexi. Please stop calling."

There's a pause like she's considering what I just said. "Not until I know you've moved on and I can see there's no hope."

For fuck's sake. What else do I need to say to convince her? "I am moving on! For your information, last night I had a date, and this morning I'm taking her for breakfast."

I'm lying, it wasn't a date, more like drinks with a friend. But I did go out with a nice girl last night. It could have been something, but she just wasn't a certain little brunette. I just can't seem to forget. Elly doesn't seem like she's up for anything more than just friendship anyway. But as promised last night, I'm taking her for breakfast.

"What? I don't believe you." She's like a dog with a bone, she just won't give up.

"Bye, Lexi." This time I don't wait for a reply. I've had enough of this conversation, so I terminate the call.

I grab my stuff from the locker, feeling better after the run, but wishing I had never answered my phone to listen to Lexi's crap. I need to get home for a quick shower before I pick Elly up for a late breakfast like I promised her drunk arse I would this morning. Knowing how much she had to drink, the girl's going to need a big breakfast and lots of coffee to get through today.

. . .

Elly and I walk over to the café on the corner just up from her place, taking a seat at one of the outdoor tables out the front. This place is funky; it has a beach-shack kind of vibe in an old house that has been refreshed with rustic timber floors and mix-and-match chairs and tables and smells like fresh coffee and bacon. Yum, that's exactly what I feel like, a greasy breakfast to soak up some of the alcohol from last night.

Elly smiles, her face coming back to life. She didn't look so good when I picked her up. "It smells so good. I'm starving," she says.

"It smells amazing! Now I know it's here, I'll be here all the time. We're living just around the corner. Until we get ourselves better set up here, so it's close. I'll go order the coffee. Do you want anything to eat as well?"

She glances over the menu. "I'll just have the sourdough with avo, thanks."

I walk into the café. There is a line-up to order; looks like they have heaps of staff on, but they're overrun. I make it to the counter and place our order. As I go to tap my credit card, I notice the chick on the coffee machine. She looks vaguely familiar. My heart starts to beat a little faster. Have I finally found her?

"Another two lattes, Indie," calls the lady on the register.

Indie, that's interesting. Indie, not Violet. Definitely looks like her, just without all the makeup. She's in a pair of skinny black jeans and T-shirt with the company logo on it. While I wait, I'm willing her to turn around so I can get a proper look at her. But she is churning out coffees and doesn't look around at all. My eyes continually scan her body, looking for clues. It was just one night, and I had had a couple of drinks, but I'd say that's her arse, looking fine in those tight jeans. My bet is it's her and she gave me a fake name that night. Very sneaky.

The lady on the front counter hands me the coffees, and I make my way back out to the table. I look back again, just to make sure she hasn't turned around. Nope, still working hard. Damn.

"They'll bring our food out in a bit. They're super busy," I say to Elly, sitting back down at our table.

"Thank you," she says. "How good is the smell of coffee. I hope this makes me feel better. What on earth did we drink last night other than wine and shots of tequila? I can't even remember when I felt this badly."

I laugh at her. She was so pissed last night and gave me a very interesting insight into her past.

"It's not funny. How are you okay?" She pouts.

"I'm twice your size. You were determined to drink everything in sight." I sip my coffee, wondering how I can get another look at the barista to see if it's her. But I don't have to wonder long; she arrives at our table with our food, and I know it's her. I have finally found her.

Indie

"Another two skinny lattes," calls Rachel, my boss and owner of Hill Top Café, from the front counter. I nod, too busy trying to remember all the orders to speak.

I'm on the coffee machine, churning out the orders as quickly as I can. Whenever it's busy, I get stuck here because this fucker of a coffee machine is temperamental and only seems to work properly for me.

Our little café sits on the top of a hill just up the street from the beach, in the main part of town. It's buzzing today with all the local surfers and chicks in bikinis, who are probably trying to enjoy the last of the nice weather before the season turns. It's good for business, but we haven't stopped all morning. My feet are already killing me from standing in the same spot behind the coffee machine. These boots are cute, but they're not made for standing all day.

I started working here five years ago. It was a way to make a bit of money while I finished my art degree. I've always dreamed of being a full-time artist, with my next masterpiece really the only thing I think of these days. But at the moment, I gotta pay the bills. Especially now that I'm on my own after Hayden and I split six months ago. I need this job more than ever. I don't hate working here—my boss is lovely, and the work is easy—it's just not where I thought I would be at 25.

I catch sight of Lucy, one of the younger girls, as she walks through the front door to the café, ready to start her shift. I wave her over. "Hey, Lucy. Take over for me. I've fixed the machine again so you should be okay with it."

She smiles. "I'd better be. This thing hates me," she grumbles, taking over.

I need to go for a walk. I go clear some tables and run some of the orders, mounding up at the counter, out to the seated customers.

"Indie, can you take this order out to table five?" calls Rachel.

"I'm on it." I collect up the two plates, one with a bacon-and-egg roll and the other with avo on sourdough, and walk out the front to table five. As I approach the table, I see it's an old school friend of mine, Elly, and I'm guessing her fiancé. I can only see him from behind. I haven't seen her in so long. I wonder what she's doing home.

"Elly, I didn't know you were home. This must be your fiancé," I say, placing the orders in front of them. And when I look up, I realise my mistake. Fuck, I hope that's not her fiancé, because I know that face. He has frequented my dirty dreams many times over the last six months.

"Hey, Indie," she squeals, excitedly jumping up from her seat to hug me. "It's so nice to see you. This is Blake, a friend of mine, not my fiancé. He's the builder working on Mum and Dad's renovation," she babbles. She can't get the words out fast enough.

"Oh, that's lucky. Nice to meet you, Blake," I say awkwardly. I wonder if he even remembers me. I'm sure I was just another number on a very long list a guy like him would have. That night would have meant nothing to him.

"Ahh, yeah, hi. Indie, is it? Nice to meet you too." His gaze sweeps over me and a sideways smirk crosses his handsome face. He really is very nice to look at, and I keep my eyes on him a second longer than I should. From the hungry look he has, I can see he remembers me. I have no doubt about that.

I turn away from his gaze. I could easily get lost in his eyes, and that's a bad idea, especially since he's here with an old friend of mine. And not just any friend, either; she was my best friend for all of high school.

"What are you doing home, Elly? Having a holiday from your perfect life in Sydney?" I ask her, feeling even more deflated about my life.

Her eyes lower to her plate as she pushes some of her food around, her radiant smile losing its brightness. "Ah, not quite. I've moved back in with Mum and Dad for a bit. Things didn't work out with Jessie, and I need a break from Sydney. Just looking for some work so I can stay here a bit until I figure out what's next. How are things with you?"

She regains her composure, offering a smile even if it's a little forced when she is clearly sad about her move back home.

I feel bad her life has taken a turn, but it's nice to see her again. I've missed having her around. God, we used to get into some trouble together when we were younger.

"Yeah, same old stuff, commissioning some art, but need this gig just to tide me over." I gesture to the café. "If you need work, we've got a waitress job going, if you're interested? It could be like the good old days."

Even though I'm not looking at Blake, I can feel him watching me, and I feel my face turning bright red. I hate that my face gives me away whenever I'm embarrassed or nervous. Why did I have to run into him again here, in my daggy work uniform? I'm in a sage-green T-shirt and black skinny jeans with a denim apron over the top and black converse on my feet. I'm not wearing any makeup, except my red lip gloss, and I'm sure my short, wavy hair is a total mess after this morning's rush. Of course, he looks totally edible.

That night we had together was the hottest sex of my life, and I still haven't recovered. Not that I've hooked up with anyone else since, but I just know he has ruined me for any future partners.

"Really? Yeah, that would be great. Thanks," she says excitedly.

"Drop by tomorrow afternoon. I can show you the ropes and we can catch up properly when it's not so busy."

"Thanks, Indie. It's so good to see you." She smiles warmly.

"See you later, Blake," I say shyly. I need to get out of here before Elly notices the colour of my face.

"I'm sure I will, Indie." He offers me a sexy smile and a

wave. Why do I get the feeling this is not the last I will see of the sexy builder?

The rest of my shift is just as crazy busy, flying by. I can't believe Elly is back in town. It was such a surprise to see her this morning. I love that girl! It's going to be so much fun having her home.

Her having breakfast with Blake is interesting; I wonder what is going on between them. Oh well, not really for me to worry about, but seeing him again brings back the memory of that night.

A one-off, I will never do it again. But what a night, and at the time, it was just what I needed after the shock of Hayden unexpectedly breaking up with me. Hayden and I were high school sweethearts, and he was the only man I had ever been with. Him leaving me so suddenly, I was hurting big time. Being with one man for nine years, I thought he would be the one I would marry and have kids with. Then it was all taken away when he dumped me in search of something better. It was almost more than I could take.

When I ran into Blake that night, he offered a night of mindless fucking to help me forget that I wasn't worth staying with. Something to numb the pain I was feeling. And boy did Blake do that! That man is some kind of sex god, and as much as my body would enjoy that ride again, I'm in a much better place now. Random hook-ups with tall, sexy men just aren't my thing.

I finish wiping the last of the tables and hang up my apron. "Bye, Rach," I call to my boss.

"See you tomorrow, sunshine," she calls back from the kitchen.

I walk out the front and my eyes widen when I see who is

leaning up against one of the tables. Blake. He's so fucking hot. I thought it must have just been my beer goggles that night, but he's even better in the light of day. Broad, muscular chest and arms that look like they're made for heavy lifting. His hair is dark, almost black, and cut short with more length on top. He's in some relaxed-fit jeans and grey T-shirt. He looks up at me and smiles, so I walk over to where he stands, not sure what to expect, but he came back to see me, so I'd better be polite.

"So, it's Indie, is it? Not Violet?" he asks with a sideways smirk.

I offer a little laugh. "Ah, yeah, sorry about that. Violet's my middle name. I'm not in the business of giving out my name to complete strangers."

"But you'll go home with them and fuck their brains out all night." He raises a thick, bushy brow.

"Not normally," I say shyly. Geez, why did he have to say it like that? "Just you, in a moment of weakness." The air crackles between us, just like that night, making me feel extra self-conscious talking to him here in my ratty clothes. Why did he come back to the café today? To have a go at me for not giving him my real name?

"You're a hard woman to track down," he says bluntly, a little more serious.

"You tried to find me?" I mutter, genuinely surprised. I thought he wouldn't have given me a second thought after that night.

He takes a step towards me, closing the gap slightly. "I wasn't finished with you. I woke up and you were gone."

Wow! The feminist in me thinks I should be totally offended by what he just said. But, instead, my lady parts are tingling at the thought that he wanted more of little old me. I have no idea why. "I thought you would've been grateful I wasn't some stage-five clinger, expecting breakfast."

"I was planning on having you for breakfast. So no, I wasn't grateful you left before I could." His dark eyes hold mine and I can feel my face heat up under his stare.

Oh my God, did he just say that? I don't even know how to respond. "Sorry." I shrug.

"Sorry? Is that all you have to say for yourself? You owe me a do-over."

He's starting to piss me off now. I mean, I'm flattered and all, but really. "Is that right, Blake? Are you asking me out on a date or just for a dirty night of fucking?"

"Depends on how you classify a date. I'm not looking for a relationship, but I do want to see you again, and there will definitely be fucking."

Man, this guy is so confident. He just says exactly what he wants. He strikes me as the kind of guy who gets it too.

"I'm not looking to date either, but thanks for making me feel extra special," I say sarcastically. "Anyway, I feel like, now that I know we have Elly in common, another night isn't such a good idea. What's going on with you two anyway? Were you her rebound? Is that your thing, you go to bars looking for girls who are broken-hearted, so you can fuck them until their heart's fixed?"

He crosses his arms over his chest and his biceps almost pop out of his shirt. I don't think this little conversation is going down the way he was expecting it to. "We have only really just met, but we're just friends. I'm not her rebound! So, you and Elly went to school together?"

"Sure did, she was my best friend. We weren't in the popular crowd, but we had each other. I haven't seen her for a while. She moved to Sydney right after graduation and we kind of lost contact. I'm glad she's home. She's a lot of fun."

"Yeah. I bet the two of you got up to all sorts of trouble at school."

I shake my head, remembering. "You have no idea! It was all Elly's doing, of course. She's a bad influence." I laugh. God, we had so much fun together.

He takes another step towards me, cupping my face. His dark eyes holding mine, trying to read me. His handsome features are even better in this close proximity. With his dark hair short, I'm tempted to run my fingers through it, drawing him to me in a passionate kiss. Just like I've imagined so many times over the last six months. The stubble along his jaw scratching up against my face as he kisses me. I sigh.

"So, when are we having the redo then, Indie?" he almost whispers, his eyes now on my lips, making it very clear what he wants.

"You're not going to let this go, are you, Blake?" I whisper back. Tempted... I'm so tempted.

"Not a chance. If I want something, I keep going until I get it. And, right now, I want you on your back, legs spread wide open, wanting me."

I step back out of his embrace. Did he just say that? I can't believe how cocky this guy is. "Wow! You certainly have a vivid imagination. Lucky for you it will come in handy later tonight, when you're alone at home with your hand. This little chickee isn't into the whole random fucking thing. Sorry." I turn to leave. No matter how hot he is—and he is super-hot—I'm heading for my car that's parked on the street in front of us.

The memory of the night we had together plays through my head. It was an amazing night of sex, the best I've ever had. But I'm not interested in being someone's hook-up girl. No, thank you. I've got too much pride for that. And that's all this would be. I can feel it already. It would appear neither of us want a relationship at the moment, so that's that. I press the button on my key fob to unlock my car. The door opens and I go to hop in.

Blake, looking a little stressed, has caught up to me and grabs my arm. "Indie, I didn't mean it the way it came out. You're just so fucking hot." He runs his hands through his hair. "You mess with my head. I can't think straight when I'm around you."

I pull out of his hold and hop in my car. "Well, maybe stop thinking with your dick and use your brain. You might have more luck next time. Gotta go. Catch you around, Blake."

He stands back, looking a little wounded. But, seriously, who talks like that? Do girls really just do what he says because he's so hot? Not me. Well, not again anyway.

I close the car door. I smile back at him and drive off. I'm not a total bitch, I just know who I am, and that night we had together, I wasn't myself. I was hurt and angry with my ex. I needed something to take away the pain and distract myself from what I was going through. Sorry, Blake, as hot as you are, it was a one-off.

CHAPTER TWO

INDIE

The delicate peppercorn tree dances in the breeze. Its long weeping foliage dusts the grass as it moves. I stand gazing out the window. The room is warm with the mid-morning autumn sun streaming in through the window. We're on the second storey so no one can see in, but it's a nice view for the models to look out at. The class is quiet; the only sound I can hear is the scribble of the charcoal on the parchment paper as the artists sketch.

I should be warm with the temperature of the room, but my hands still shake a little, I'm not sure what from. Who am I kidding? I know exactly what from. I've been like this since the conversation I had with Blake on Sunday. Running into him again has shifted something for me. I know I turned him down in a spectacular fashion—*go me!* —but I've been off-kilter ever since. I wouldn't admit it to him, but the effect he has on me is overwhelming.

Get out of my head, Blake, so I can concentrate and do my job, I scream at myself internally. Nope, it doesn't work. He's still there with that cheeky smile and his jackhammer dick tempting me to do naughty things, things that I want to do so badly. That's what you get for six months with only your vibrator to keep you company at night.

Over the last two days, thoughts of him have filled my head more than I would like to admit. I'm taken back to that night and his strong, masculine body. The confident way he conducts himself. The dominant way he talks. This guy goes through life demanding what he wants, and he gets it too. I'd say at least 99 percent of the time, anyway.

The way he made me feel that night, I have never felt before. It was like time stood still and we were the only two people on the planet. He worshipped me. Treated me like I was the only girl he had ever been with. My body was everything he had been missing his entire life. He had me feeling things I had never even imagined I could. In the whole nine years I was with Hayden, I hadn't even felt like that. Let alone with a one-night stand. That's why I got out of there so quickly after he fell asleep. Who feels things like that with a random hook-up, on the night they've just had their heart broken by someone else? I put it down to girly hormones or the release of oxytocin. There is no way anything I felt that night was real. And Blake, he was just in it for the sex. That's the only reason he's looking for more. We had fun, and he wants a bit of that again.

A bell chimes through the studio. I change positions, adjusting the fine, white silk fabric over my shoulder so it falls down my back, pooling on the floor. I try to get comfy so I can stand like this for a bit, one leg slightly bent and most of my weight on the other.

My mind wanders again, but this time I think back to what I had with Hayden. Before Blake, he was the only guy I had ever slept with. We met in high school and I never let myself even think about anyone else. It's been six months since he left me, but it still stings that I wasn't enough for him to stay and plan a life with. We were together for nine years. It didn't feel like that long, time went so fast. I thought he was the one. Mama thought I was so lucky to have him by my side. A stable man who loved me and would care for me forever. She thought I must have finally broken the family curse.

All the other Martin women were cursed, so Nana used to say anyway. Destined to get knocked up young, by a man who would never commit to or love them. Destined to be alone, a single mum struggling through life. Every other woman in my family fell pregnant early to an arsehole who didn't stick around and support her.

I was raised by my mama. I never knew who my father was. She refused to talk about him. My nana was the same, and her mother as well. Mama thought I had broken the curse when I didn't get pregnant at 21, like the rest of them. That was never going to happen, though. Mama was on to it, taking me for the depo shot every three months from when I confided in her that Hayden and I were sexually active. She wasn't going to let me suffer the same fate as her.

But, instead, the man I thought would be my one and only left me for something more exciting. Apparently, he had been thinking for a while that he needed space to find himself. To see what else there is to life and what he's been missing out on because we were high school sweethearts. I mean, I can't say some of those thoughts hadn't crossed my mind at different times over the last few years, but I also couldn't imagine my life without him in it.

If he hadn't left, I wouldn't have had that night with Blake, feeling things I didn't even know I could. I get a strange tingle low in my body when I think of him, and I little goosebumps run up my naked body while I stand here. I'm not cold, it's just the thought of him. He does things to me. I wish I could just shake off this feeling and do my job properly. Standing still while the class sketches me isn't normally such a problem. But this morning my body is betraying me.

This is just one of my many jobs to pay the bills. As well as barista at a local café and artist, I pose as a life-drawing model a couple of days a week. It's easy work, you just have to get your kit off and pose without moving. That's the part I'm struggling with today. How do you stand still and focus when all you can think about is the hottest man on the planet?

Stop thinking about him, Indie. Focus.

I'm a busy girl, and until my art business takes off and I get a real name for myself, this is the way it has to be. As I said, I come from a long line of single mothers. There's never been a lot of money in our family. We work hard to get by and that's just the way it has to be. I never went without as a kid; it was just a simpler existence than some of the spoilt brats I went to school with.

Cindy, our drawing teacher, rings the bell again, and announces it's time to change models. I scoop up the silk fabric, wrapping it around my body, and leave the stage, heading through the door to our change room. One of the other models, Sara, sits on the bench in just her underwear, moisturising her legs. She's up after Elton, who has just taken the stage to pose.

"Hey, chickee." I smile as I walk over to where I left my bag and dress earlier.

"Hey, Indie, how was your weekend?" she asks excitedly.

"Just worked." I shrug, slipping into my dress.

"All you do is work, sweetie. You need a night out with me and Elton," she says, continuing to rub the lotion into her skin.

"Probably." I sigh, grabbing my bag to leave.

"You haven't forgotten we're going for lunch with Elton after we finish up here, have you?" she calls after me as I head for the door.

Bugger. I had totally forgotten about lunch today. "Ah no. I just have to do a few things first, so I'll meet you guys there." My mind is a scrambled mess. I need to stop thinking about Blake and get back to reality.

She shakes her head. "You totally forgot, didn't you? Where's your head at today? You're more spacey than usual."

"I don't know." I shrug. I don't need her to know about Blake. She won't let it go. She'll insist on all the gory details. Sara lives for gossip. The more details the better. She thrives on knowing the business of everyone in town. I love her to bits, but if there's something I don't want the entire town to know, I keep it close to my chest.

She looks me up and down and smirks. "What's that smile then? That looks like a guilty smile. I think your weekend was more fun than you're letting on."

"It definitely wasn't," I say, trying to get her off the trail.

"You can fill me in at lunch," she says, waving a dismissive hand in my direction.

"Whatever you reckon. I'll see you there."

"Don't be late."

"I won't. It's Mama's birthday. I was just thinking about where to get some pretty flowers for her, then paying her a visit. I won't be long."

She blows me a kiss. "Willow and Rose, they're only two streets over. See you soon then, sweetie."

"Thanks," I say, giving her a wave.

Brenda Martin 1977-2016
Loving mother
An angel visited the green earth and took a flower away.

I BRUSH AWAY THE OVERGROWN VINE FROM THE PLAQUE and place the blush-pink roses in the vintage crystal vase that sits behind the plaque. "Happy birthday, Mama," I say as I kneel by her grave. It's been four years since she passed away, and occasions like birthdays still aren't any easier. Cancer is a fucking bitch, and helplessly watching someone you love slowly fade away breaks your heart in a way from which you can never fully recover.

I miss you, Mama. Why did you have to leave me? I have no idea what I'm doing without you here, to talk things through and guide me.

Mama was the only family I had left. I was only six when my nana passed away, and from then on, it was just me and Mama. Since I never knew who my father was, and I didn't have any siblings, it was just the two of us. I didn't really mind. I never felt like I was missing out or anything, we were super close. Sometimes I would see another kid with their dad and wonder what it would've been like, but I felt lucky because I had my mama. She was the best mother, so supportive and loving.

The day she died left a massive hole in my life, and I miss her every day. What would she think about where I'm at in life? I'm sure she would be wondering when I'm going to get on with it and make something of myself. I tell people

I'm an artist, but really, I'm a barista and life-drawing model, who paints when I'm not too exhausted from my real jobs, the ones that actually pay the bills. I've sold a bit of my art over the years, and since I started doing the markets here once a month, I have regular customers who come back looking for something new—but really, it's a hobby at best.

And then there's the love life. Mama would be sad to know that Hayden and I split up. She loved him and was at peace leaving this world knowing he would be here to take care of me. But I guess that's the thing when people die, the rest of life keeps moving and changing, and no matter how hard it is at times, we have to move with it.

"Bye, Mama," I say as I kiss my fingers then place them on her plaque.

I HEAR SARA BEFORE I EVEN WALK THROUGH THE DOOR to our usual hangout, Daisy's Diner. She's killing herself laughing and would have to be the loudest person in the place. They're sitting at our usual table under the window that looks out over the street. Sara likes to people watch or, should I say, look for new things to gossip about, so she always picks this spot.

"Sorry I'm late, guys," I say with a weak smile, I'm not feeling it today. I just want to go home to bed.

"All good, sweetie. You okay?" She smiles softly. She knows how hard these days are for me. She's been my friend for years and was there with me when my mother was really sick.

"I've ordered your usual, babe," says Elton. He's a big sweetie. I have no idea how he is still single. He looks like a Greek god and has a heart of gold. He just has no luck and always picks the wrong type of girl.

"Thank you," I say, kissing him on the cheek as I slide in next to him.

At least once a month, after work, we come and have lunch here and catch up on what's happening with our lives.

"So, what's the goss, guys? Spill," says Sara, her eyes wide with excitement, waiting for her entertainment.

"I've got a date with a girl I met online," Elton smiles shyly.

"Oh, really?" I ask, excited for him.

Sara reaches across the table. "Show me her profile pic. I can tell just by her photo if it's going to work out or not."

He hands over his phone, and we both lean forward to have a look.

She's strawberry blonde with green eyes, very striking. Her smile radiates confidence. I say she would be perfect for our shy friend. "Oh, she looks lovely. I'm sure you'll have a nice time together," I say.

Sara takes his phone to inspect the image more closely.

"What's the verdict? Should I bother going?" he asks.

"She looks perfect, sweetie. You should definitely go. This one is marriage material." She smiles up at him, handing his phone back.

Our burgers and chips are delivered to our table by the waitress, and I go straight for a handful of chips.

"What about you, Indie? Anything exciting going on?" asks Elton.

"I'm actually going out Friday night with a friend I went to school with, Elly. She's just moved back to town. So you don't need to worry about me. My life isn't as sad as you think."

Sara claps, all excited. "Very exciting. I wasn't worried

about you, honey. I know you have all sorts of exciting things going on. It's written all over your face!"

"It is not, because I have nothing going on," I say, throwing a chip in her direction. What is she talking about?

She pulls a face at me. "I can read you like a book, sweetie. I know when you're hiding the good stuff from me."

I roll my eyes at her dramatically, and Elton laughs. He knows how bad she is, always in our business.

She taps me on the leg. "I have the perfect dress for you to wear as well." She pulls out her phone and starts scrolling, showing me a cute, short black dress.

I hand her phone back. "You sure? We're not really the same size. You're like a lot taller than me."

"You're being nice, sweetie. I know we're not the same size. You're teeny tiny and I'm like a gladiator compared to you. I've been sent some free samples from someone who wants me to advertise their clothes on my Insta page, and I'm pretty sure this dress is a six, it would be perfect for you."

"I've always thought of you more like an Aphrodite type; so tall, with amazing curves and that flowing, blonde hair. You're stunning." She has to know she is. She models bikinis for some surf brand as a second job.

"You crushing on me, Indie?" She laughs.

"Totally. You're hot." I laugh.

"Look at yourself, babe. You're a perfect, petite size six with flawless skin and dark, wavy hair I would die for. Don't even get me started on your eyes; that colour, wow, emerald green. They're gorgeous. Seriously, girl, every guy in the place is going to be looking at you Friday night, wishing he could take you home."

Elton clears his throat. "What is this? A 'compliment

your bestie' convention? Can you hear yourselves?" He laughs.

"Well, why not? Someone's got to," says Sara.

My eyes catch sight of a man walking through the door to the diner. I have to do a double take, thinking it must be my imagination running away with me, since he's been all I can think about. But when his eyes meet mine, a broad smile crosses his face, and I know he's real. Blake, the man in the flesh. What's he doing here? He stops at the counter to order.

"Earth to Indie. Where did you go?" asks Elton, clicking his fingers in front of my face, which is now probably the colour of the beetroot on his burger.

I whip my head back to him, realising they had continued to talk and I had tuned out. "Sorry, Elton, nowhere. I'm just tired, I guess."

"Likely story, sweetie. I can see what you're looking at, or should I say *who* you're looking at. Nice, Indie. Is this why your head's in the clouds today?" asks Sara.

Elton looks in the same direction as her, then back to me with a smirk. "You do have something going on that you're hiding from us."

"Don't look," I say, hitting him on the arm, "he'll see you." And, of course, at the same time, Blake looks back over to me. He has a cheeky grin on his perfect face when it's obvious we're talking about him. He collects his order and makes his way over to us.

"Now look what you've done. He's coming over," I say, giving my friends the evil eye for causing a scene.

"Oh, Indie, he's gorgeous. If you don't want him, I'll take him off your hands." Sara's eyes are wide as she dreamily watches him walk across the room. She's loving this. I won't hear the end of it now, till I tell her the full story. So much for keeping this little secret to myself. I give her another filthy look and she laughs.

"Behave yourself," I threaten, looking between the two of them.

BLAKE

How convenient. This diner was a good choice for lunch. I was hoping I would bump into Indie again this week. And here she is.

"Indie, how nice to run into you again," I say with a smile.

She looks up at me, her cheeks already giving away how she feels about me. "Blake," she says shyly. She looks lost for words. Good, I'm glad I have the same effect on her as she does on me.

"Since Indie is being rude, I'll introduce us. This is Elton and I'm Sara. We're Indie's friends from life-drawing class," says the blonde with a flick of her hair.

I hadn't really noticed her two friends until now, I was so focused on her. The blonde is staring up at me, eyes wide; she's a little full-on. The guy—Elton, I think her friend said—looks pretty uninterested and is eating his burger. Don't think I have anything to worry about there. "Oh, hi. Nice to meet you. So, you're both artists like Indie?" I ask to be polite, though all I really want to do is talk to her.

"No, silly, we model with Indie. You know, life drawing? In the nude." She raises her eyebrows to emphasise what she's saying. Here I am thinking she's the artist, but she models as well. What the fuck? And nude? Nice.

Indie covers her face, and her cheeks redden further.

She looks embarrassed by her friend's comment. Don't think she wanted me to know that little detail of her life.

"Very interesting. I'd like to see that sometime." I need to get her away from her very loud friend. "Indie, can I see you for a sec out the front?"

"Um, okay," she answers quietly.

"Nice to meet you both," I say, but my eyes are fixed on Indie. Is she going to come with me or sit here looking at me? She chews on her bottom lip, and her friend Sara gives her a nudge, so she grabs her bag and hops up and follows me. I can feel her eyes on me as we walk out the front of the diner.

I make my way to an empty table and lean up against it. She stops just out of my reach. Her eyes roam over me and she continues to nibble on her lip. "What's up, Blake the builder?" she says, finding her confidence again.

"What's up is I want to see you again. Even more now that I find out you're a nude model! You're full of surprises." I grin.

She groans, crossing her arms over her chest. "Bloody Sara and her big mouth! Actually, you should ask her out. She thinks you're hot and she's a nude model. You two would be perfect for each other."

I cock my head to the side, watching her and trying to work her out. She's a mystery. Most girls are happy to talk to me; most girls act like Sara, looking up at me, batting their eyelashes. But no, this one, she watches me from a distance, not giving me anything to go off. "I don't want to ask her out. I'm asking you out." I take a step closer to her, closing the gap. She looks up at me. Her expression serious.

"Blake, I told you the other day, I'm not the kind of girl for you."

"I think you're exactly the girl for me. You can't tell me

there's not something going on between us. That night we had was something else. You can deny the attraction all you want, but your body gives you away. Every time I'm near you, your cheeks are flushed."

"They're not," she whispers, touching her face.

I cup her face and run my thumb over her lips. "They are. I know you want me. Why are you playing hard to get?"

"I'm not! I just don't want a quick fuck or a relationship, so what's the point?"

Our faces are close now, really close, our lips almost touching, the chemistry buzzing between us. I could just kiss her and show her what she's missing out on by denying me. But I won't. I release her face and take a step back. "You're not going to make this easy for me, are you, Indie? Just know, I won't give up. This will happen again," I say as I walk off.

I don't look back. I'm not going to keep begging, but I'm not giving up, either.

The drive back to the office is quick, and just as I pull into our car park, my phone rings. I can see from the screen on my dashboard that it's my dad. It's been a while since I've heard from him. It's never a conversation I really want to have. He only calls when he needs help with something.

"Sir," I answer the phone.

"Blake, hope life as a builder is treating you well."

"Everything's going well. How's Mum?" I park the car and make my way into the office.

"Your mother is well. She sends her best. She wants you home, she misses you."

Somehow, I doubt that; that woman has only ever thought of herself. She couldn't care less about me. "What do you need?"

"So blunt, Son. Can't a man just call his son to catch up?"

"Yeah, he can, but we both know that's not the type of relationship we have. You call when you need me to do something for you. What is it?"

"Need you to keep an eye out for someone that's rumoured to be living in your area. I'll send through a photo. If you see her, let us know."

"Who is she?"

"Vinnie's girl. Her name is Cassie. She's done a runner on him, and he wants her back."

Poor girl. Vinnie is one of Dad's heavies. He does some security, collects money, jobs like that. He's a total pig. It's no surprise she's done a runner. There's no way I'll be helping to track her down for them, but to keep the peace and appear to be doing the right thing, I say what I have to. "I'll keep an eye out. If I see her, I'll let you know."

"Yeah, well, make sure you do. And, Son, I hope you're getting whatever it is out of your system, 'cause we need you back sooner rather than later. There's a shift up here and a lot's changing. It doesn't look good, you not being here."

I can feel my heartbeat kick up. I hate talking about going back. Whenever I do, I can feel all the muscles in my body tense. "I'm not coming back. You know that. Not after what happened. Start training up someone else to take over. What about Morgan? He wants the job. It's never going to be me." I have never actually said that to him before, but he has to know I'm not coming back. I have set up a new life for myself, one without the family and the shit that comes with being associated with them.

"It has to be you! Stop acting like a petulant schoolboy. You're my only son. You will not disgrace our family name by not keeping up the family business. I won't allow it," he spits aggressively.

"So, I get no choice at how my life turns out?" My voice rises to meet his. I'm a little surprised at myself for sticking up for what I want.

"You think I did when I was your age? Not a fucking chance, Son. We were born to run this business, and we will die to protect what my father started. That's your birthright." He's yelling down the phone now, fuming mad.

I need to defuse this call. We will never see eye to eye on this topic. I've had this same conversation with him on repeat since the accident when Bella was killed. I ran that day and have been running from it all ever since. I thought he would have tracked me down at the time, and dragged me back to Sydney kicking and screaming, but he didn't. He knew that, after what happened to Bella, it hurt too much. I think, deep down, he never wanted this life and wished he had done the same as me. That's why he let me go to start my own life.

He holds the threat over my head that I will have to go back, but I'm not sure if he will ever really make me. So, for now, I defuse and agree. "I understand, and when the time is right, I will come back and take over, if that's what you still want. But it can't hurt to train up someone else as well, and I know Morgan wants the job. Just so you have options. What if something happens to me?"

"Nothing will happen to you, and you need to get prepared. We will need you soon." His voice is a little calmer now.

"Okay. I've got to go. Send me the picture of the girl and I'll let you know."

"Done. Talk soon."

My phone gives a buzz of an incoming text, and I glance

down and see a photo of a pretty girl, wearing way too much makeup with long bleach-blonde hair. She's young, way too young to be with Vinnie. She couldn't be any older than early 20s. You have to wonder how she got messed up with a creep like him. Maybe she was born into a messed-up family like mine and had no choice.

What I wouldn't give for a normal life, like Fraser or Ash, and not have the fear of having to leave everything I've built for myself, to go back to a life I despise.

CHAPTER THREE

BLAKE

Last night, I went for drinks with Fraser and one of his best mates from school, Drew. He's back on a holiday, so it was supposed to be a catch-up. Drew is also Elly's twin brother, and since Elly was the one organising the night out, she invited Indie. It would have been a good opportunity to see her again and maybe get to know her better, but jealous Fraser stuffed up any chance of that when he lost his shit over Elly dancing with some guy. Can't say I was happy about the dicks the girls chose to dance with, but he could have handled it better than getting into a fist fight and having the four of us kicked out before the night had even really begun.

Hopefully, tonight will be different. It's Elly and Drew's birthday party, and Fraser and I have just arrived at the Walker house. This place is nice, the perfect family home. When I first visited this house for the building inspection, I was so impressed at how beautifully they had renovated. It looks modern but has still kept its quaint Queenslander charm. Mostly Elly's doing, from what I can see. That girl has such a good eye for design.

I wasn't sure about coming tonight. I haven't really known either of the twins for that long, but Elly texted earlier today to make sure I was coming. It will be nice to have a distraction from reality. Since Dad called, that phone conversion has been playing on me. And now I've made up my mind: I'm not going back to Sydney to end up like him. No fucking way. I just have no idea how to get out of it, either. But tonight, I'm going to drink my troubles away and have a good time.

Drew greets us at the front door. Sounds like the party is in full swing. Music pumps from the backyard, and the noise of chatter and laughter, as people try to compete with the music, travels through the house. They must have invited half the town. I hear Elly before I see her. She comes running through the house excitedly and, I would say, slightly tipsy.

"You guys made it," she says excitedly, kissing Fraser on the cheek then me. She looks back to Fraser and his eyes roam over her, landing on her gaze. They share a moment, and you can see the history between them. They may both be trying to deny it right now, but they're crazy for each other.

I remember why we're here. "Happy birthday Elly," Fraser and I say in unison.

She smiles sweetly. "Thank you. I'm so glad you boys are here. After last night I thought you might not show." She looks back to Fraser, obviously not impressed by his jealous outburst last night.

Then she grabs my hand, dragging me through the house to the party out the back. "You need to meet my friend Indie."

The yard is decorated with fairy lights in the trees. There are little tables and cushions to sit on, allowing people to gather in little groupings around the enormous backyard.

"You have to meet my friend, Indie. I was going to introduce you last night, but it all got so crazy." She's talking fast and beams with excitement.

"You trying to set us up, Elly?" I question with a sideways smirk.

"No." She smiles cheekily.

"I think you might be." I nudge her as we walk.

I don't think Indie has shared our little secret and told her friend we know each other intimately. I want more time with Indie, and this is the perfect opportunity, so I play along with Elly's matchmaking game.

"Blake, this is my friend, Indie. You kind of met at the café that day when we were having breakfast."

Indie smiles up at me, her eyes sparkling in the twinkling fairy lights. She looks stunning in a striped off-the-shoulder top. The flawless skin of her shoulders with that flower tattoo gives me flashbacks to that night, her perfect lips in the same red. They do things to me. But I can't think of that again. I need to try to control myself tonight, so that she gives me a second chance.

"Oh yes, I remember Indie. How could I forget? So nice to see you again." I put my hand out for her to shake to be polite, but mostly just because I want to touch her again. Touch her and watch her squirm, like I am every time I'm near her.

"Blake," she says shyly, her cheeks blushing as she takes my hand.

"Oh, you two are just too cute. Take a seat, Blakie. I'm going to get some drinks for us." Elly thinks she's playing matchmaker. I can tell how much she's enjoying this. Not sure I like her calling me *Blakie*. That's a bit too cutesy for me, but I'll put up with it because I like her.

I pull up a seat next to Indie. "Do you get the feeling Elly is trying to set us up?" I smile.

"She thinks she's queen of the matchmakers. If only she knew the truth." Indie giggles.

"So, it looks like we're going to be bumping into each other a bit, with friends in common. I know you don't want anything from me, but how about I promise to stop hitting on you and we settle for being friends?" I hold out my hand for her to shake.

"I think I can handle that." She places her hand in mine and we shake on it. She smiles back at me, dropping her shoulders and relaxing a little.

Elly comes back with a tray that has cut lime, a saltshaker, three shot glasses, and a bottle of tequila. "Look what I've got! Are we celebrating or what?"

"Looks like we're celebrating," says Indie, looking scared. "Geez, Elly, I haven't done tequila shots since we were 18."

"You've been missing out, babe." She places the tray down in front of us and we watch as she prepares the shots, pouring the liquid, licking her hand, then shaking on the salt. She grins, passing me the salt. I do the same as she throws back the shot, slamming the empty glass on the table in front of us, grabbing the lime and sucking. She stomps her feet on the ground as she sucks it. Indie and I follow her cue and do the same.

Tonight's going to get messy. Things always get messy when you drink tequila.

Four rounds of shots later and the girls are definitely tipsy, laughing at everything they say.

"I think we should play a game," announces Elly.

I shake my head. "We're not playing the two truths and

a lie game again. Don't you remember what happened last time?"

"Yes, and that's why I want to play. It gave me some very interesting insight into you, and that's how we became friends," she says, poking me in the arm. "So, it's definitely a good idea."

Indie turns to look at her friend. "Oh, really? What did you find out, Elly?"

My eyes shoot to her. "Elly, don't you say a thing," I demand.

She laughs. "I won't give your secrets away. All I'm going to say is that Blake is less vanilla than I originally thought." She holds up three fingers, trying to signal to Indie, and I shoot her another look. Indie knows a bit about my ex, I told her a little on the first night. Just how we broke up because she wanted a polygamist relationship with my best friend, but she has no idea it was because I had a threesome with Lexi and Fraser. I only let that slip with Elly because I was intoxicated. I will tell Indie that story of my ex when I'm ready. Indie's eyes widen and I know she's already putting that question away for later.

"And Elly is vanilla all over," I grumble under my breath.

"Well, I knew that already," Indie teases. "She can't even say sex without blushing."

"I'm not that bad. I can say it," she whines, throwing one of the cushions at Indie, and Indie falls backwards, giggling.

"You so are, Elly!" She laughs, sitting back up, and turns her attention to me. " I want the story, Blake. Fill me in."

"Another time, maybe," I say, giving Elly a look for bringing it up. But she might be right, this could be a good opportunity to find out some more about Indie, without looking like I'm fishing.

"Okay, it is Elly's birthday, let's play a little game if that's what she wants to do. How about 'Never have I ever'?" I suggest. "We each take a turn making a statement, 'Never have I ever...' then, if the others have at some point in their life done this thing, they have to drink."

Elly claps and Indie rolls her eyes. "What are we? In high school?" she whines.

"Come on, Indie. It will be fun. Please. I need a distraction from you-know-who." She looks over to Fraser, who is sitting with her brother Drew on the back deck.

Indie softens, feeling her friend's pain. "Okay. Only because it's your birthday."

"Yay, all right, I'm going first... Never have I ever had a one-night stand?" Elly looks pleased with herself, like she's onto us, but I don't know how she could be. I doubt Indie would have told her.

Indie gives me a sideways glance. Does it classify as a one-night stand if we're now kind of friends? I guess it was at the time. She takes a drink and I follow.

"I'm so surprised, Indie. I know you were with Hayden since high school, so this has happened recently. I want details," Elly teases.

"It was just some guy. I needed to blow off some steam when Hayden dumped me. Wasn't a big deal." She drops her eyes, avoiding eye contact.

I know she's just trying to not give too much away, but that stung a little. It certainly wasn't nothing to me. I couldn't stop thinking about her after that night. That's why I'm here now.

"Your turn, Blake," says Elly, clapping her hands excitedly. God, this girl has a few drinks and turns into an excited little kid.

"Ah, okay, never have I ever... experimented with my

sexual orientation?" Both girls look at each other, then drink. Very interesting. "I think I need more information, girls."

Indie shakes her head.

"No, that's our secret," says Elly, and Indie thumps her on the arm.

I point to the two of them. "You two?"

"Elly!" Indie yells at her, annoyed.

Elly shrugs. "What? It happened. It was just a kiss when we were 16, not a big deal. I'm sure lots of best friends do it. We did it, but it wasn't for us, and we moved on to men."

"Nice," I say.

"Don't be a creep, Blake, stop imagining it," Indie warns with a death stare.

"How can I not? I'm a red-blooded male, and the picture you painted is kind of hot." Elly laughs at me; she's having fun causing trouble for Indie. "Okay, fine, I'll forget I ever heard that story. It's your turn, Indie." I smile over to her. What's she going to come up with?

Her face softens. "All right, um, I don't know." She pauses for a second. "Never have I ever cheated on a partner?" Indie asks, looking satisfied with her question. Her eyes are on me, and I know this is directed at me.

We all look at each other, but no one drinks. Indie gives me a small smile. She's happy with that answer.

"None of us are cheating bastards like my ex. Good! My turn. Never have I ever gotten busy in a public place?" says Elly. Indie and I both drink. "Eww, gross. Are you guys serious? I could never. Where? Oh my God, your lives are so much more exciting than mine."

"Lots of places. It's not a big deal, Elly," I say.

"What about you, Indie? I can't believe you would have."

"What? Haven't you ever been caught up in the moment

and just got carried away so much that it didn't matter where you were?"

"No, never. I haven't even done it out of the bedroom," murmurs Elly, a little more quietly now.

We both lose it and break into laughter, then realise she's serious. Shit, this girl is a 26-year-old nun.

"Stop laughing at me. Sorry I'm not gross like you guys." She pouts.

"Okay, my turn," I say. "Never have I ever been caught masturbating?"

"Are all the questions going to be sex-related?" whines Elly. I think she's starting to feel left out.

"Probably," I say, taking a scull, and so does Indie. This game is not helping me try to only think of her as a friend. Now I'm imagining her alone in her apartment. The lighting is low, she's lit only by a bedside lamp. Her breasts are on full display, her nipples hard from the cold air and her arousal, as she circles her clit with a finger. I walk in and catch her in the act, and instead of being annoyed by me, she smiles wickedly and asks me to join in.

I have to adjust myself so I can comfortably sit with the hard-on that is pushing against my jeans. We need to change the subject. My imagination is running wild. "Indie's turn."

"All right, last one, though, then I'm getting food. My head is spinning, I can't keep up with you two alcos."

"Never have I ever paid for sex?" Indie asks. She watches my face as she asks the question. This is also a one just for me. And this one I don't want to answer.

I hesitate. I'm not sure if I should drink or not. Hmmm, do I drink, then they both know more about me than I want to share? I can't lie, though. Lying only comes back to bite you later. So, I drink. And just as I expected, their eyes widen.

"Something you want to share with us, Blake?" Indie asks.

"No, not really. It's not something I'm proud of." Their eyes are locked on me, and I know they're not going to let this go now until I tell the story. "Fine, I didn't grow up in a nice beachside town with a normal family like you two. My family is kind of screwed up. I grew up in Sydney, in the city, and I was exposed to all sorts of things because my family's business is kind of seedy."

"Go on. How can this lead to you paying for sex?" questions Indie.

"When I was 16, my dad, being disappointed that I was still a virgin, booked me two high-class hookers to take care of it, and that was that."

They're both covering their mouths with their hands, in shock, looking between each other in a silent conversation. "Oh my God! That was not what I was expecting. I was thinking you got drunk on a buck's night or something," says Indie.

"Nope."

"Your dad doesn't sound like a very nice man," says Elly. I know she's now feeling sorry for me, and that's why I don't talk about shit from my past. The pity in their eyes. I don't need it.

Indie has gone quiet, like she's trying to process what I've just told her.

"He's not. Like I said, didn't have the best upbringing. But life goes on." I try and shrug it off like it's not a big deal.

INDIE

Elly's mum announces it's time for cake, and it couldn't have come at a better time for a distraction. Plus, I'm starving. We all go sing Happy Birthday to the twins. I stand with Blake. I'm not feeling the urge to run from him like I have the last couple of times I've seen him. Knowing he's happy just being friends is helping, and I guess getting a little insight into his past kind of helps to make sense of him a bit.

"Wait here. I'll be back in a sec," he whispers.

Blake sneaks his way through the crowd that's gathered for cake and brings back two slices. I follow him back to where we were sitting earlier. I'm not sure where Elly has got to, so the two of us sit and eat our cake in silence. Blake has gone all quiet since he shared a little from his past. Maybe we shouldn't have played that game.

I finish my cake, wiping the cream off my hand with the napkin. "Blake, we all have shit in our past we would rather forget about, but it's what has shaped us. You know, maybe your childhood wasn't the best, but look how awesome you turned out."

He looks up from his cake with a little smile. "Is that a compliment?"

"Nah, just saying, you're not as bad as I originally thought," I offer with a smile.

"You have no idea just how unusual it was, Indie. My family is pretty fucked up."

"My childhood wasn't all picture perfect like Elly's either. My mother was a single mum. I've never met my dad. We struggled to get by at times, but I was lucky because she was the best mother, and we had each other."

"You still close with her?" he asks, looking over to me, happy I'm opening up to him.

"Up until the day she died, I was, yeah." I blink to stop the tears that are forming. Ahh, I can normally handle talking about Mama; the alcohol must be making me emotional.

"I'm sorry, Indie." He must be able to feel my hurt. He reaches for my hand and we sit in silence for a bit, both lost in our own thoughts.

"It is what it is. I think I've had too much to drink. It's making me a sooky lala. I need more food."

"Yeah, me too. I'm starving. We got here too late for dinner. You want to go for a walk, get a kebab or something in town?"

I go to stand, pulling his hand up with me. "Come with me. I'll get us some food." We sneak into the kitchen. There's no one around. The party has died down a bit, but whoever is still here is out the back dancing to the music.

I open the fridge and it's stocked with all the leftovers from earlier. "Bingo. Pass me a plate from over there." I grab two of the crusty bread rolls and rip them open and go back to the fridge and load them up with the leftover cold meat and salad, squirting on some mayo.

"I was wondering where you guys got to. Raiding the fridge." I look around the fridge door to see Elly, a little worse for wear.

"We're hungry, sorry," I say.

"Take as much as you want. Mum made so much. We're going to be eating leftovers all week. I'm going to head to bed," she says sadly.

"Okay, chickee. You all right?"

"Yeah, just had too much to drink. You kids have fun now." She blows me a kiss and disappears down the hall to her room.

"Here," I say, handing Blake one of the rolls. "You want

to walk me home while we eat? I'm not far from here." I know it's dangerous to have him walk me home, but I'm not ready to say goodnight just yet, and it's unsafe for a girl to be out this late walking the streets by herself. I'm just being careful.

"Walk you home, hey?" He raises his brow.

"Not code for anything. Don't go getting any ideas. You're a big tough guy, you can make sure I don't get mugged on my way home."

"Whatever story you have to tell yourself, Pix. I'll be your big strong protector if that's what you need."

"Pix?"

"Yeah, short for pixie, cause you're cute and little."

"Yeah, I remember now, from the first night. That was what you said you were going to call me until I gave you my real name."

"Yeah, except you didn't, did you? You gave me your middle name instead. So, I have decided as punishment, your nickname will forever be Pix."

"Whatever." I laugh at him.

We walk for a bit and eat our rolls. The night air is fresh, and I can feel the goosebumps scattering up my arms. Luckily, I'm not far from here. I finish my roll. "Best idea I've had all night. It's making me feel so much better, soaking up the tequila. Not Elly's finest brainwave."

"You know, Indie, you're not a sooky lala. Anyone would be sad if they had gone through what you have. If you ever need anyone to talk to, I'm a good listener."

"Thanks." Blake is definitely different to how I first thought, after that night we spent together, when he came across so cocky and conceited. I mean, the sex that night was amazing. That was the only reason I went home with him, nothing to do with his personality.

I can see now that there's so much more to him. You can tell he's seen things. Maybe even done things. Lived a different life to the rest of us. He's wounded. He hides it well, with his perfect smile and overconfident personality. You would have no idea to look at him. But it's there, behind that smile; I could see it tonight when he was telling us that story. His eyes give away the pain. I can't help but be a little intrigued by his past. As an artist, you're trained to look for what makes people tick, paint what's behind the mask they put on for the rest of the world—their pain.

"This is it. My place." We stand in front of a three-storey, red-brick apartment building, probably built in the 1950's. My place is nothing special, but the rent is not ridiculous like a lot of places around here, so it will do until I find something better. "Thanks for walking me home."

Blake gives me a sideways glance, like he is starting to work me out, then smiles. "I better come in, make sure you don't get mugged in the hallway or something. You never know who's hanging around this time of night."

"No, you don't. I guess we better be extra safe." He smiles like he's won.

I fumble for the keys in my bag, finding them, then opening the front door of my apartment building. I hold it open for him and he follows me in. We take the three flights of stairs, and I can feel his eyes burning a hole in the back of me as I walk. I'm a little wobbly on my feet, on account of the alcohol, and him watching my every move is making it worse.

"Don't worry, I'll catch you if you fall," he offers.

"I have no doubt." We make it to the landing, and I head for my door at the end of the hall. I turn and lean up against it. I'm intrigued to see how far he's going to push this. "This is me. Thank you for making sure I got home safely." I smile up at him. Fuck, he's good-looking. Why is he so hot?

"I think I need to come in, to make sure your apartment is safe and someone didn't break in while you were away. Plus, I think it's just polite to offer your big strong protector a hot drink before he walks home to his lonely, cold bed."

"Oh, you're pulling the sympathy card. Making me feel sorry for you, are you? I guess you can come in for a bit." I push open the door, and he follows me in.

He looks around, though there's not much to look at. A tiny kitchen and living room, with a bedroom and en suite, that's it. It's not much bigger than a bedsit, but it's all I need. "Nice place," he says.

"It's nothing much. It's a total mess tonight. I wasn't expecting company."

"It's really funky." He walks over to where I have my finished canvasses stacked, leaning against the wall, and he flicks through. "I love this." He holds up a portrait I did of Sara a few years back.

"It's Sara, you met her the other day."

"Oh, yeah, I can see that. I like the way you use colour and layer it, different from anything else I've seen. You're really talented."

"Thanks. You want that drink?" I ask, dumping my bag on the breakfast table and heading into the kitchen.

"Please. Just a coffee, if you have it."

"Sure do. Can't believe you can drink coffee at this time of night. I'd be up all night if I did." I make a coffee for him and peppermint tea for myself. I place the hot drinks on the coffee table and take a seat on the lounge.

Blake's still flicking through my canvasses when a text pings on his phone. He takes his phone out of his pocket and looks at it. He scowls when he sees the message.

My curiosity gets the better of me and I have to ask, "Who's texting you at this hour?"

"My ex. She's relentless." He tucks his phone back into his pocket and makes his way over to where I'm sitting, taking a seat next to me.

"Oh, is it a recent break-up?" I sip my tea, trying not to look as interested as I am. I'm being super nosy, but I can't help it. I want to know if he is emotionally invested with someone or not.

"No, this is the chick I broke up with before that night. It's been over six months. She won't leave me alone."

"Oh! That's a bit much."

He sips his coffee and thinks for a minute. "She said she won't stop calling until she knows I've really moved on. I tried telling her I was seeing someone else, but she doesn't believe me. She said she's been watching my social media and I'm definitely still single."

"Oh wow, she sounds kinda like a crazy stalker. Just stop answering her texts. She'll give up eventually, won't she?"

"I don't think so. I've tried that, but she just keeps calling." He shakes his head. I don't think this is a show for my benefit. He does look really frustrated by her.

"Hmm, I have an idea, but don't read anything into this."

He raises his eyes from his coffee to look at me, his interest piqued. "What's this idea?"

"Send her a text telling her you can't talk or message; you're on a date."

He pulls out his phone and texts her. "Yeah, now what? She's going to come back with 'you're just saying that' or something to that effect." She's quick. Within seconds of his text, she sends one back. He holds up his phone to show me. "See? Now you know what I'm dealing with." The text says: *Haha, good one. Call me, I'm bored and I want to talk to you.*

"Okay, she's persistent. Well, let's send her a photo for proof," I suggest. I know I'm digging myself into a hole here, but I kinda feel sorry for him.

"Might work. What kind of photo do you have in mind? It's going to have to look believable for her to leave me alone." He smirks.

"Let me think. Why don't you sit next to me on the lounge, like we're all cosy, and we can take a selfie?"

"That sounds like a good start." He comes over to sit next to me, wrapping one arm around my shoulder and holding his phone out with the other hand. I know we're just pretending, but it feels so nice to have his arm wrapped around me. It feels strangely too familiar. "Smile." He snaps the photo and looks at his phone to see how it turned out.

"Not too bad. That looks believable," I say.

"We just look like two friends hanging out," he complains.

"I wonder why," I say sarcastically.

"It needs to look believable. Where's your bedroom?"

I roll my eyes. "Nice try."

"Just for a quick photo, no funny business, I promise." He crosses over his heart as if to prove he's not up to anything.

"Hmm, okay. Just stay here for a second and I'll tell you when you can come in."

"Is it that messy?"

"Yes. I don't normally bring strange men home when I go to friends' birthday parties, so the state of my room before I go out isn't normally an issue," I call back to him as I walk into my room and flick on the light. It's as bad as I thought, clothes strewn everywhere, my bed a total mess. I pull up the covers, straightening them out, then throw the pillows and decorative cushions on. I scoop up all the clothes from the floor and throw them in the wardrobe, shoving the door closed, hoping it stays that way and doesn't reveal how much of a pig I actually am. I turn to inspect the room and see Blake smirking at me from the door.

"You done now? It wasn't that bad." He kicks off his shoes and jumps on the bed.

"I guess. You were supposed to wait for me," I sulk, a little embarrassed. He strikes me as the type of person who would be very organised with everything tidied up and in its place before bed at night.

"If we're going to be friends, you should probably know that I do what I want." He pats the bed next to him. "Come on, let's get this photo."

I sit up on the bed as he puts his arm around me, like when we were on the lounge, and right before he takes the photo, he kisses my cheek playfully, then snaps it.

I glare over at him. "You said no funny business."

"I'm just making sure we look the part." He smiles.

"You're very cheeky. Is the photo okay to send?" He brings his phone down for us to look at the image, his arm still around me.

"Cute. All right, here goes, let's see what reaction we get."

I watch as he types the message so I can see what he's writing.

This proof enough for you? This is my girlfriend, Violet. He hits send.

I look over to him with a smile at the use of the name I gave him on the first night we met. "Your girlfriend, Violet, hey."

"Yeah, I figure she's the one who's into me as more than just a friend."

I look up at him, and with his arm around me, I can feel

the warmth of his body, smell his aftershave, and God, I'm tempted to go there again. One more time couldn't hurt, could it? A text pings on his phone, snapping me out of the thought. I look down at his phone to see what she's said.

Fine, have fun, I'll ring you tomorrow x

He shakes his head. "See? Doesn't matter what picture I send her, she won't give up."

"She's batshit crazy, Blake. You need to block her before she gets out of hand."

"Yeah, I think you're right, hey. I thought that might've worked. We could send her a photo of more."

"Nice try. A kiss on the cheek is where I draw the line. What kind of girl do you think I am?"

"I was just thinking maybe Violet could make a reappearance. That girl was a lot of fun."

My head is facing him, and our eyes are locked. The pain from before is gone from his eyes, and I see desire. He knew what coming into my bedroom, getting all cosy with me, would do. "Was she fun? It could be the tequila talking, but I think I agree with you, Violet is a lot of fun. Maybe she should make a reappearance tonight, just for a one-off."

As if that was the permission he was waiting for, his hand curls around the back of my head and his lips smash with mine, kissing me with such intensity. My heart is racing. I didn't mean to end up here with him like this tonight. In fact, it was my aim not to. But there's something about him, he's so tempting.

As we kiss, I melt into him, my body weak in his arms. He rolls on top of me, so his legs are between mine, my wrists above my head held in his hands. He radiates dominance, and man, do I want to be dominated by his muscular body. He pulls back with me pinned beneath him. I can feel his hard length pressing into me. He's ready for action.

"I only said 'maybe' she should make a reappearance. I didn't say she would."

"That's not what I heard, Violet." He smiles sexily and kisses me again.

I pull back. "We can't do this, Blake. You know we can't. It's going to get weird."

"We're both adults. I'm sure we can handle whatever this is. I know you want me, baby, your body's giving you away."

"I do, but this is a really bad idea." I wiggle my body, trying to break free from his grip. I feel like I can't breathe under him. It's hard to concentrate, and if I stay like this for too long, I'm going to give in.

He lets go and rolls off me, lying beside me. "Okay, Indie, if that's what you want." He stands, looking back at me. "I'll go home to my hand, like you said."

I start to laugh. That was the last thing I expected him to say, and it was perfect timing to break the uncomfortable tension that's building between us. "Thanks, right, you go home to your hand and I'll get out my vibrator."

He shakes his head at me. "You don't play fair. You know what you're doing to me?"

"I'm sorry, but it's for the best, you know it is."

"Night, Indie."

"Night, Blake. Thanks for being my big strong protector and walking me home."

He offers me a small smile and walks towards the door. I hear him leave, closing the door behind him, and I regret my decision as soon as he goes. Why do I keep turning him down when I want him just as badly as he wants me? I close my eyes to sleep, but my head is still a bit spiny from the alcohol—or Blake, I don't know.

Argh, he's under my skin. This is so very inconvenient.

CHAPTER FOUR

BLAKE

"Hey, Blakie," Elly calls from her place on the coffee machine as soon as I walk through the door to the Hill Top Café. I have seen her a lot over the last few weeks. Now she's landed the job as our freelance stylist and we're becoming quite good friends, even if she insists on calling me Blakie. Indie looks up from her spot at the till and smiles. She looks different today, her hair pulled back in a short ponytail. She's wearing a T-shirt with the company logo on it and a short denim skirt. She's quite the chameleon, looking completely different every time I see her.

She may want to pretend that we can start up a friendship, and that there is nothing else going on here, but we both know there is more. I can see it in the way her eyes light up when she sees me, how her cheeks heat with colour, and the way she nervously fiddles with her hoop earrings when she talks to me. She might be trying to trick herself, but she's not fooling me.

"Hey, Elly, Indie. How are you lovely ladies this morning?"

"So good. There is so much going on, and we have the most exciting news. We're going to be moving in together in a couple of weeks," says Elly enthusiastically.

"Is that right?" I say, looking to Indie.

"Yeah, Indie found us this cute place in Broken Point where she can have an art studio as well. We're so excited."

"Now that Elly has told you our exciting news, what can we get you?" says Indie, pushing her overly excited friend out of the way so she can enter my order into the computer system. Elly walks back to the coffee machine. "Don't think you came in here to chat about our living arrangements."

"Happy to chat about anything with you, anytime. But I would like a coffee, just an espresso. Thank you, Indie."

"You right with that, Elly?" Indie calls back to her friend on the coffee machine.

"Of course. Just got one more to make for that group that ordered online, then I'm on to it." She gets to work frothing milk for the other order she has lined up in front of her.

Indie looks at me as if lost for words.

"How was—" Something seems to malfunction with the coffee machine, and frothed milk starts flying everywhere, causing Elly to knock over the line-up of coffees she's just made. Elly screams. Indie turns to help her get the rogue machine under control, but something stops her. She hesitates, then falls forward, straight to her knees, in spectacular fashion.

Elly breaks into hysterics at the sight of her friend, the machine still going crazy. There's spilt coffee and milk everywhere.

"Shit, Indie, are you okay?" I run around behind the counter to help her up. She's now on her arse, trying to work out how she fell. I hold out my hand to help her up.

"Elly, hit the power button," Indie yells.

"What happened? How did you fall?" I ask.

She looks down at her boots, to see that the lace from one boot is tangled around the hooked eyelets of the other. I can't help myself and I start to laugh. "How on earth did that happen?"

"Some friends you two are. I have blood running down my leg, and you just laugh your heads off at me." She unlaces the tangled boots and storms off to a back room, returning moments later with a first-aid kit.

"I'm so sorry, Indie, but you have to understand how it looked. It was fucking funny." Elly is nearly crying, pulling a scrunched-up face to try to stop herself from laughing.

"I'm sorry, Indie, it looked pretty funny. Here, let me help you fix up your knee," I say, trying to contain my laughter and help her with the first-aid kit.

"Nope, don't need help from you. I can look after myself." She pulls the kit back, heading for one of the empty tables and taking a seat.

"Come on, don't be stubborn. I feel bad for laughing, let me help you." She hands me the kit, and I search through it for a band-aid. She cleans her knee with a tissue, and I place the band-aid over the cut. "There, all better." I want to kiss it better for her, but Elly is watching us, and Indie is already pissed at me for laughing at her, so I know it would only make it worse.

Indie looks at me for an extended period, taking me in, then she sighs. "Thanks." She smiles weakly as she gets up, a bit wobbly. It must have really hurt. This floor is concrete and would've been bloody hard. She hobbles her way over to the coffee machine where Elly is madly cleaning up the milky mess that drips over the counter and down the cupboards. She's trying her hardest to control herself and not laugh.

"You're lucky this place isn't packed with customers this morning and no one else was around to see," Elly says.

Indie glares at her. "You're lucky! You caused this scene by doing whatever it is you do to this machine to make it go nuts."

"I don't do anything, it just hates me." Elly pouts, while she watches Indie fix the machine and make my coffee, placing it on the counter in front of me.

"Here you go, sorry about the hold-up. Hope we haven't made you late for work." She offers a little smile. Her cheeks are flushed, and I'm not sure if it's from embarrassment or because she can read my mind and was thinking the same thing as me. I should have just kissed her. Even if she was mad at me, it would have been worth it.

"Not at all. You've given me a bit of entertainment for the day."

Elly giggles again, and Indie's face breaks into a little smile. "I guess it would have looked a bit funny from where you were standing."

"Just a little," I say. "Are you okay now?"

"I'll be fine. See you later, Blake, thanks for caring." She smiles back at me.

"Bye, ladies, hopefully the rest of your day will be less dramatic." I look at the coffee as I walk out the door and realise Indie has written a note for me, with her phone number and signed with a V and two Xs. Hmm, that's interesting. Is this a booty call number? If she's signed with the initial V, it has to be, right? She was very specific the other night, though. Just friends, nothing more. I don't know what to make of it.

I'm looking forward to finding out, though. I have a little surprise for her this week, so I'll wait until after that and see what this is all about.

INDIE

Not long after Blake left this morning, the café got busy, and we haven't stopped since. I've already stayed an hour after my shift finished, and I'm hoping to get out of here soon. I have a long list of things I need to get done this afternoon. First on the list, go through my paintings and work out what will tie in with the mood board Elly gave me.

Elly's an interior stylist just starting out with her own business after years of working on a TV show fixing up homes. She has just landed a gig with Blake and Fraser's company, The Green Door.

She and Fraser have some sort of thing going on, they have since back in high school, and now it seems to be heating up again since she is home. So, he has hired her as a freelance stylist to help out with some of their new developments that need styling for sale. Which has worked out perfectly for me, because she has asked me to provide the artwork for some of the rooms.

In my normally last-minute style, I'm not as organised as I should be, and I have to work out which paintings I want and get them bubble-wrapped and ready to take over to the townhouses in Broken Point for our first project. It doesn't mean I've sold them, just that they will hire them from me for a couple of months while they're showing people through, and until the townhouses sell at the auction. Elly said that, in the past, the artists she uses often end up selling their work to the new homeowners because they've seen the paintings up on the walls and love the vibe they give off. Hopefully this will happen, at least for some of them. Even if not, it's still exciting to be showing them off.

"Elly, when do you need those paintings delivered by?" I

ask as I clean over the coffee machine for the gazillionth time today.

She looks up from the table she's clearing. "Friday. I'm doing the set-up if you want to deliver while I'm there?"

"Friday's perfect. I have the early shift here, so I'll be done by 10am. I can give you a hand with the set-up if you like?" Gives me a couple more days to get them all sorted, but I would still like to get out of here soon so I can make a start on it.

"That would be great. Your paintings are going to be amazing in these houses, Indie. You have no idea just how perfectly they suit the style I'm going for. I reckon you're going to get so many sales out of this, hey."

"I hope so, Elly. I'd really like to be able to make a career out of my passion, like you have. I can't work in the café for Rach forever."

"I haven't made a career out of it yet, but it's going to happen for you too, Indie. I keep telling you, this is our year. Big things are going to happen for us, baby." Elly's beaming with that showstopper smile of hers, she's so excited for us.

Elly is the kind of girl that girls hate and all the boys gravitate to. She's stunning, like drop-dead-gorgeous, radiating charisma. She could have been a model or a famous actress if she wanted. But she's never had any idea just how beautiful she is. She used to get picked on at school because the other girls were so jealous of her, and the boys would throw themselves at her, but Fraser was always around to make sure the boys didn't have a chance.

We became friends on the last day term one, year seven. I will never forget that day because it changed my life. I couldn't be bothered with the bitches in our year and figured out early that if I told our art teacher I was working on a project, he would let me stay in the room during lunch.

So that's how I avoided them. I had the most amazing art teacher, Mr London. He was like a mentor, or maybe the father figure I longed for.

When I arrived this particular day, for my lunchtime art session, I found Elly in the back of the room crying. She'd been targeted, yet again, by the head of the bitches, Angela Cook. I can only think that they were jealous of her looks, because she is the kindest person I have ever met. She's always thinking about other people before herself. Before that moment, we had barely said two words to each other. From that day on, we were inseparable, and spent every lunch in the art room creating our masterpieces together. Elly would draw and I would paint or sculpt. It was our sanctuary and got us through high school. It would be amazing if, all these years later, we could both make our careers out of what we started doing back then.

"You look stressed, Indie."

She breaks me out of my thoughts, and I realise I've been cleaning the same spot on the counter the whole time. "Nah, I'm all good. You know me, Elly, I don't get stressed. Just got a lot to do this afternoon."

"Why don't you take off now? It's starting to slow down, I've got this."

"You sure? That machine might go nuts again."

"If it does, I'll work it out. Go home." She hugs me.

"Okay, I'll see you later." I hang up my apron and grab my bag for the walk home. That's going to be one thing I'll miss when we move, not being able to walk to work. But hopefully we won't be here for much longer anyway. Once the art gallery is open, I'll need to put time in there over the weekend, so I'll have to cut my weekend shift at the café. I'm hoping it won't be long before I can finish up here completely.

I think Elly is right, this is going to be our year, but I need to stop daydreaming and make it happen. If only I could stop thinking about a certain tall, muscular builder so I can focus. He did look really hot this morning in his building get-up. How could a pair of work boots get me going? I'm truly screwed when it comes to him.

CHAPTER FIVE

INDIE

I'M GETTING READY FOR WORK AT THE ART STUDIO, AND my mind keeps going back to my moment of stupidity yesterday. I have no idea what possessed me to give Blake my number and sign with a V when he came into the café. I must have taken a knock to the head when I fell.

More likely I'm just lying to myself, and I know exactly what possessed me to give him my number—I'm a dirty slut who wants more of what he has to offer, no strings attached. You just can't admit it to yourself because it's exactly what you don't want to be, and for good reason, too.

As much as I love my mama and nana, I don't want to end up like them; a single mother after a fleeting love affair, dumped when the worthless daddy-to-be found out they'd knocked them up. What arseholes. The beautiful female influences I grew up with were both in this position once upon a time, so blinded by love they couldn't see the future in front of them. I'm supposed to be smarter than that. That's what mama always said, anyway. But I'm not a nun. I love sex, and sex with Blake is fucking heaven, and I want more. I'm being careful. I'm on the pill, and I take it religiously. I've never forgotten. And both times we had sex, we used condoms, so there was nothing to worry about.

Why can't two people with a mutual attraction take pleasure in each other's bodies?

"Different group of artists tonight. I think you're going to get a kick out of who's front and centre," calls Sara as she comes off the stage, snapping me out of my train of thought. Probably a good thing, I could feel myself derailing quickly.

"What are you talking about? Ooh, is it someone famous?"

"You'll see. Better get out there, sweetie. Don't keep 'em waiting."

I drop my robe and grab the silk fabric, making my way to the stage. As soon as I step foot on the stage, my eyes meet his... Blake. I can feel the heat rise through my body. My face is instantly so hot it feels like it's on fire. Great, I'm going to look like I'm sunburnt or something.

He smiles. It's that cheeky overconfident smile. He knows that him being here is going to affect me, and he's loving every bit of it. What's he doing here?

I position myself with my back to him, head angled down so I can try and get myself under control before I have to face him. He might have a massive effect on me, but I don't want him to know how much. I've got the silk fabric over my shoulder, draping down my back and pooling on the floor. I gaze down so I'm not looking anywhere near him, otherwise there is no way I'm going to be able to stand still if I catch sight of his expression. I feel so exposed. Standing naked in front of an audience of artists has never bothered me before, and he's seen me naked, but this is so different. I have no idea how I'm going to last my session, but if my body doesn't overheat and explode, I'm going to kill him when I'm done.

I change position to face the audience, this time looking out the window, still avoiding making eye contact with him. I can feel his eyes on me. I don't need to look at him to know he's eating me up; I can feel it. My skin is still hot, and I feel almost faint. I need to get off this stage.

When the teacher rings the bell, I scoop up the fabric and almost run off the stage. I can't get off there fast enough. Sara is sitting in her usual seat, fully dressed, with a massive smile on her face. I know what's coming. She wants details. Oh, why did I have to be modelling with her the night he came in? I've been able to avoid this conversation, after lunch the other day, because she had to rush off for a photo shoot.

"Oh, thanks for the heads-up, Sara! Some friend you are. I almost died when I saw Blake sitting there."

She laughs. "Oh, the look on your face would have been priceless. Wish I was out there to see it."

"It's not funny!" I cry as I throw my dress over my head and sit to lace up my boots.

"Yeah, it's hilarious. So, who is he, Indie? And don't say no one; it's so obvious he *is* someone." She walks round to where I'm sitting.

"He's none of your business," I say, glaring at her.

"No worries. If you won't give me the goss, I'll go and talk to him after class. What was his name again? That's right, Blake." Her eyes light up. She's serious, oh God. "I'll go ask him how you two know each other and see what he has to say."

"You wouldn't." I give her a death stare.

"You know I will." She smirks.

"Fine," I huff. "Sit down, I'll tell you. Stop being all intimidating, standing over me."

She pulls up a seat next to me. "So, who is this gorgeous

man named Blake?"

"He's just a friend of a friend, but before I knew that, he was the one-night stand I had the night Hayden broke up with me. And now we keep bumping into each other because we know the same people."

"You've slept with him? Oh man, he would be a god in bed. How did I miss that you had a sexy one-night stand after your break-up?"

"It nearly happened again, after Elly's party on the weekend too. We agreed to be just friends but, I don't know, we drank too much and were mucking around on my bed. We were sending photos to his ex so she would know it's over between them. It sounds awful. It's a long story, but he overwhelmed me. It took everything I had to resist," I say, burying my head in my hands.

"You lucky bitch. Why would you want to resist that? If a guy that hot was throwing himself at me, I wouldn't be complaining. I'd be fucking him like crazy seven days a week."

"I'm not complaining." I glare at her. She doesn't understand my dilemma. "I just don't know what to do about it."

"Indie, he made the effort to come and see you tonight; he obviously likes you. Go talk to him."

"And say what, 'Hey, thanks for coming to perve on me while I'm working'?"

"I don't know, Indie, but go say something. He's here for you." Sara throws her bag over her shoulder and heads to the door. "See you next week. I want to hear all about it then."

I wave goodbye, lost in my thoughts about what to do with this situation.

The last model for the evening has just come off the stage, so I need to make a decision. All the artists will be packing up now.

All right, here goes nothing.

I grab my bag and walk out to the hall to wait for the class to leave for the night. I lean against the wall and flick through my phone while I wait. A few students walk past with their drawings, chatting as they go. No Blake yet. Maybe he left early. I pop my head around the door to see if anyone's left, and there he is, still packing up. He looks up and smiles when he sees me.

"I can't believe you came to my class."

"I wanted to check out what it was all about. Think I did all right?" He holds up one of the drawings.

I walk closer to inspect his work. I flick through. There are about ten drawings, all in charcoal.

"Have you done a class like this before?"

"No, never had the chance."

"They're fantastic, Blake. Are you sure you didn't just steal these off one of our regulars?" They're fantastic for a first-time life drawer. Some are close up and some are full body. The contrast and definition are quite amazing. He would give me a run for my money, and I've been doing this since I was 18.

"They're all mine." He smiles proudly, looking over his work again.

"You're quite the artist. I'm impressed."

His eyes scan my body, finishing by looking me straight in the eye. His gaze is filled with so much heat, I can practically see the desire dripping off him. "Thank you. I might make this a regular thing. I could get used to drawing your exquisite body."

Exquisite body, is he serious? He's trying to distract me with flattery, but it's not going to work. There is no way I'm letting him come and do this again. "You will not! This was a one-time thing, and I barely survived this time."

"Why can't I? It's so easy when you're drawing someone so beautiful." His hand reaches out for mine, and I let him intertwine our fingers, and the contact, even though so small, is thrilling, setting my body alight for him.

"Sara is beautiful," I mumble out.

"I'm not talking about Sara and you know it." His eyes are so intense I feel like I'm melting into a pool right in front of him, my ability to talk stolen and replaced with a throb of desire.

Why does he have to say nice things to me, things that set my lady parts alive? My cheeks are hot, he must be able to see how he is affecting me. His eyes stay fixed on mine as I try to say something, anything.

"Why have you gone all shy again?"

"I'm... I don't know?" I lift my shoulders in a slight shrug, unable to form a coherent sentence.

"You have no idea how gorgeous you really are, do you?" He holds his thumb up to my lips, dragging them down. This conversation is deeply intimate. He is making me want him more than I have any other time before, and I don't know how he is doing it, but I can't resist him. I see the promise in his eyes, and I want it all. But I'm scared of what I'm getting myself into by wanting him. Is this just desire to please a sexual craving? Or do I want more from him?

I need to change the subject and get him to stop looking at me like that or it's going to lead to so much more. I turn away from the strong hold he has me under with those alluring eyes, and look back to his drawings, picking one up and studying it closer.

"So, what are you going to do with your artworks?" When I hear my own voice, I realise how much trouble I'm really in. It's all breathy and slow.

He takes the picture from me and studies it. "Hmm, I

don't know. I think I'm going to have them framed and hung over my bed so you're the last thing I see before I close my eyes to go to sleep at night."

"Won't that be weird when other girls stay over?"

He shakes his head, then runs a hand through his hair. "There are no other girls, Indie. That's what I keep trying to tell you. I'm not the player you think I am. I haven't slept with anyone else since that night we had together six months ago. No one compares to you."

My lady parts do a little happy dance. "Really? Little old me? I'm nothing special. I'm sure a man like you could have any girl he wants."

"Well, you are special to me, and you're the only one I want. You feel whatever this is between us as well; that's why you gave me your number at the café. Even if you hid it by saying it was from your alter ego, V."

"My alter ego." I laugh. He's right, though. Violet has the confidence I don't. "Maybe V is just a little braver than me. She knows what she wants."

"And what is it that V wants?" His eyes roam over me, then stop on my face, staring into my eyes. He's so intense, and I'm back under his spell again.

I stare back, not wanting to break the connection. "You," is all I can say. He wraps his arms around me and pulls me into him, kissing me lightly on the lips. He smells amazing, and my body instantly melts into his. I kiss him back, his tongue sweeping through my open lips as our bodies press together. I pull back, remembering where we are.

He nods as if he has made a decision. "Are we going to hang at the art studio all night or can I take you out for dessert?" His hands slide down my arms, holding my hands in his.

"Blake," I say quietly, not really wanting to have this

conversation now but needing to. He waits for me to go on. "I'm not ready for a relationship or anything. I can't do the whole dating thing. I was with Hayden for so long, and he kind of broke me when he left. I'm not ready."

"Okay, I get it. What about friends then? Friends can get ice cream, right?"

"We both know we can't be just friends. We tried that the other night and didn't even last the night without both of us wanting more."

"What do you want, Indie? Tell me what you're comfortable with, and we can play this however you want."

I look down, trying to come up with the best way to say what I want. "I don't know. Maybe friends who fuck occasionally. No strings attached, no one gets hurt," I suggest, and I don't even know where that came from. Who am I around him? *Friends who fuck*, seriously?

His lip turns at the side. "What about other people? Will you be seeing anyone else at the same time?" he asks, eyebrow raised.

"You said you're not interested in anyone else anyway, Blake."

He squeezes my hands. "What about you?" His look has changed to one of concern, waiting for my response.

I shake my head. "I'm not either."

"So, you want *friends with benefits*, no commitment, but no seeing anyone else either. Is that right, Indie?"

"Ah, yeah. I guess."

"Okay, I can handle that." A huge smile crosses his face, and I realise I've played straight into his hands. This is what he wanted all along. Damn, he's good. He pulls me in for another kiss to seal the deal. "So, dessert?"

"Yeah, then we can get some ice cream after." I giggle.

"There she is. V is one naughty girl, with sex on the brain."

I bury my head in my hands. I need to stop talking around him. "It's true, she is," I admit.

"I'll just grab all my drawings, and we can head back to my place, if you like?" He gathers his things.

"Will Fraser, be there?" I ask. I don't want to complicate things further by anyone else knowing what's going on here.

He raises his eyes up to look at me. "Possibly. Is that a problem?"

I chew on my lip as I think of how to deal with this. "Why don't you come to my place? That way we don't have Elly and Fraser asking questions."

"Okay, I'll meet you there." He smiles.

BLAKE

Indie buzzes me into her apartment building, and when I get to the top of the three flights of stairs, her door is already open. Indie stands in the doorway. She's changed from what she was wearing at the art studio. She's in a black, silky dress with a lace V-neckline; her lips are red, and she's sexy as hell.

"You took your time," she says, smiling sexily as I make my way past her. She closes the door.

"I stopped to get dessert, for after, like you suggested," I say, heading into the kitchen, and she follows me in, taking a seat up on the kitchen bench.

"Ooh, what did you get me?"

I unpack the bag of goodies onto her bench. "I wasn't sure which flavour you'd like so I got some options. Plain old chocolate because you can't go wrong, cookies and coconut because it's my favourite, and hazelnut. With little waffle bowls that the chick at the ice cream place chucked in. Please tell me you like one of these?"

"What? No vanilla," she says, faking a pout.

"You're anything but vanilla, baby. That wouldn't have worked," I say, placing a little kiss on her lips.

"I love all three. You've chosen well."

"Good. I'll put them in the freezer for later. Right now, I want you."

"Did you want a drink or something?" she asks. "I have wine or beer."

"Just you," I say, running my eyes over her.

I place the ice cream in her freezer and turn round to see her completely naked, her dress pooled in a pile on the floor below her. Fuck, she's perfect. She's been waiting for me in nothing more than a slip of a dress. I stalk over to her, removing my T-shirt as I do.

"You don't like clothes much, do you?" I ask.

She shrugs. "They're overrated, and besides, I've waited six months for this. I can't wait another second."

I wrap my arms around her, cupping her bare arse and picking her up. Her legs wrap around my waist like they're supposed to be there, like we have done this same thing a thousand times before. Her perky breasts press into my bare chest. I can feel her heart racing just as fast as mine.

This moment feels perfect, with our bodies skin to skin. Her arms are around my neck, our lips meet, and we kiss with such intensity. This isn't just some throwaway kiss, it's the kiss of intense desire; the desperation to taste one another, melting six months of tension that's been building since that day we ran into each other at the café.

I can feel how much she wants me. She's all in. There's no hesitation like after Elly's party. This is the Indie I met that first night, needy and ready for anything. She clings to me as I walk us into her bedroom.

The lighting is low, with just a bedside lamp on. I softly place her on the bed, then stand back and admire her perfect body, laid out for me on her bed. "God, you're perfect." She smiles at my compliment. I know that look she gets, I've seen it before, the naughty one that leads to a dirty night of fun.

She sits up on the edge of the bed and pulls me to her, her hands making fast work unbuckling my jeans, which fall to the floor. She rubs her hands over my abdomen, then back down over my happy trail, teasing me. She tugs at my boxer briefs as she pulls them off my body. My cock jumps free, ready for whatever she has in store for him.

It's been weeks of torture, being close to her and not being able to give into the cravings my body has, and now I finally can. She palms my cock, running her hand up my length. The look in her eyes is pure delicious sin. The silky-smooth skin of her delicate hands feels amazing. My body is so sensitive to her touch; even the smallest movements could send me over the edge.

My gaze drifts down her body. She sits, legs wide open, her pussy on full display on the edge of the bed. And I can't wait another second to be in her. Watching her touch me like this is sweet torture. I need to be in her, fucking her hard and fast. Fuck this feeling out of my system. And, as if she reads my mind, she raises her gaze to meet mine. "I need you in me now."

"Fuck, yes!" I growl.

She crawls back up the bed and I follow her. I position myself between her legs, kissing her again. She reaches to her bedside table and fumbles around, grabbing a condom. "Safety first," she says with an over-exaggerated smile.

"Of course." I pull back so she can roll it down my length. She watches me as if entranced by my actions. "Like what you see, Pixie?"

"Yes, I like everything I see," she says breathlessly.

My hands dust her delicate skin as I make my way to her breasts, massaging them. They're perfect handfuls made just for me. I lower my mouth to suck her nipple, then release it with a pop. I follow the same with the other side, and the buds of her nipples harden under my attention. My hand slips down between her legs to the feel of pure heaven under my touch. I circle my finger through her wet folds as she rocks her hips to meet me. She's just as greedy as I am. This is what I remember from that first night; our sexual chemistry is undeniable.

My lips are on her neck, kissing her and nipping on her soft skin. Then back up to her mouth as our tongues battle desperately for more of each other.

She reaches down between us and wraps her hand around my cock again, guiding me to her entrance. "Fuck, Blake, I want you in me now. I can't wait any longer."

I tease her, rocking back and forth at her entrance, and don't push straight in like I know she wants. "This isn't going to be slow and easy, baby, you might want me to warm you up first."

She shakes her head. "I don't care, I want you in me now. Fuck me as hard as you want, I'm ready."

With one smooth thrust, I push straight in. She's so tight, and fuck, it feels so good.

"Fuck, Blake!"

"Are you all right?"

"Yes, keep going," she growls, her voice almost unrecognisable.

I thrust into her again and she lets out a delicious moan.

I pull back, then slide in again. I reach down to kiss her, lacing my hands through her hair and pulling her lips to mine. "You ready, Pix?"

"Yes, God, yes. Fuck me, Blake."

I reposition her, pulling her legs up to my chest, and slam in deep. She cries out, and I continue to pump her hard and fast. She cries out for more. I love it like this, so fucking deep.

Her hands go to her breasts, and she twists her nipples as I continue to slam into her. "You look so fucking hot like that, playing with yourself."

"So good... so fucking good," she cries, and I can tell she's getting close. "Don't stop... fuck." I can feel her body tighten as the orgasm rips through her, and I let go, filling her up. My body collapses onto her, our breathing ragged, as we both try to catch our breath.

I draw her to me and roll onto my side, placing kisses down her neck. "You're amazing, Indie. I'm going to worship this beautiful body of yours all night."

"Hmm," she says sleepily as I pull her into me, my body wrapped around hers.

We lie together for a while, neither of us wanting to move. Indie might even be asleep. Her breathing has finally settled down. But then I feel her stir.

"I could do with some of that ice cream now. You keen?" she asks.

"Sounds good, baby."

She hops up and walks to the kitchen, totally nude, her hips swaying as she goes. I love how completely comfortable she is in her own skin. And why wouldn't she be, she's a fucking goddess.

Indie

This man blows my mind in so many ways. I thought that first night was amazing because of my emotional state and the number of cocktails I'd consumed, but this just proves it was so much more. It's so cliché, but that was fucking mind-blowing, earth-shattering. I can't even process what that was. I feel like my entire body has shifted somehow.

I open the freezer door, my hands still shaking, and grab the ice cream, scooping it into the little waffle cones Blake brought with him. A scoop of each flavour. It looks delicious and I think it's the perfect choice; a cold dessert after some very hot sex.

I walk back to my bedroom and Blake is sitting up in bed. I could get used to this. A hot man in my bed, eating ice cream, after mind-blowing sex. For some stupid reason, I let myself imagine what it would be like to have him in my life. But that's not what this is. I can't get used to this, it's not permanent. It's just friends that fuck. He's probably just hanging with me until someone better comes along. But what do I care? I don't want anything permanent either, so why not have some fun for a bit?

"Here you go." I hand him the ice cream.

"Wow, I could get used to this." He smiles, then realises what he just said. "You know what I mean."

"Yeah, I do." I hop into bed next to him and pull the sheet over my lap, slowly eating my ice cream. It really is as good as he said. "This cookies and coconut is amazing."

"It's so good, hey?"

As I scoop the next bit of ice cream out with my spoon, the waffle bowl crumbles, and the cold ice cream falls down over my bare chest. "Argh, I was enjoying that."

He laughs at me. "How did you manage that?"

"The cone broke," I complain.

"Here, you can have mine." Blake offers me his cone.

"What will you do?"

"Eat yours, baby," he says with a wink as he moves between my legs, licking the sticky mess off my stomach. "Even better this way." He makes his way up to my breasts, licking as he goes, taking a large bite of the ice cream into his mouth then sucking my nipple. It's so cold it sends a shiver of goosebumps over my skin, but the sensation of the cold on my hot skin feels so good. "You're not eating," he says.

"How can I eat when I'm watching you eat off me? It's too much."

He takes another bite, then sucks hard on my other nipple. This is doing as much for him as it is me; I can feel the size of his erection on my leg. I have no idea how he's ready to go again, but he is. Who would've thought, innocently eating ice cream could be so much fun?

His lips come up to meet mine, and he swipes his cold tongue through my open mouth, pulling back as he bites my bottom lip. My sticky hands go to his hair, pulling him back down to kiss me again. There's a constant battle between us for who's the dominant one. He wants complete control in the bedroom, and I'm sure that's what he's got in the past, but I like to have my turn, and it makes for a fiery, fast dynamic.

We wriggle down in the bed as we kiss, and I can feel his cock at my opening. It's so tempting to just let him push in. But I can't take that risk. I pull back. "Condom... safety first."

He lets me out from under him so I can grab one from the bedside drawer. He's on his back and I crawl back over him, rolling it on. I slowly lower myself onto him. "You going to let me fuck you this time?"

"Not a chance, baby." His hands move over my arse, resting on my hips, his fingers digging in as he moves my body to meet his rhythm.

"You have control issues."

"Do not. I know who's in charge here, there's no issue," he says as he lifts me by the waist, like I weigh nothing, and places me on the bed under him.

"You don't play fair," I cry as he pumps into me again.

"Just proving a point, baby. You wanted big strong Blake to take care of you, so I am."

My hips rise to meet his fast thrusts, and I dig my nails into his back. "Fuck, Blake."

He pulls out and I miss the sensation immediately. "Roll over."

I roll over and he pulls me back to him. My hands dig into the mattress to get a grip as he slams into me. The sound of our bodies slapping together rings through the room as he pumps into me, his massive cock filling me up completely. My body is so sensitive, it's almost too much, but not enough.

I'm close to the edge, and my body shakes. It feels like I'm having an out-of-body experience as the ripples of pleasure take over and my body convulses around him. He slams into me again as our bodies collapse onto the mattress below.

The remainder of the ice cream has run down my front and we're both covered in a sticky mess.

"Right, shower time. You're a sticky mess," he says, slapping me on the arse.

"You're a sticky mess," I tease as we head for the shower.

CHAPTER SIX

BLAKE

Chloe has just come to pick up Ash, leaving me with grumpy Fraser. I don't know what is up his arse this time. We normally meet at the pub for a drink and a bit of a staff meeting on a Friday afternoon. It's a good way to end the week.

Fraser turns to me, frowning. "I heard you on the phone to your dad earlier today. You sounded pretty wound up. What's going on? Thought you weren't getting involved in the family business anymore."

That explains his mood, that fucking conversation with my dad today. I was trying to forget about it. "I don't really have a choice; you can't walk away from this type of family business, even if you want to."

He crosses one arm over the other. I can see he's not happy with me, but what does he want from me? This is out of my control. "So, what, you just give in and do as you're told? I thought you were stronger than that, man."

My shoulders slump, and I stare into my beer, knowing he's right, but it won't change anything. "There is nothing I can do. This is the job I was born to do. When he says it's time, I have to cooperate. You don't say no to Max Donovan. I might be strong, but I'm not stupid. I will leave in the next few months."

"What does that mean for our business, the one we built? We're supposed to be in this together, man."

"Don't you worry about that, my side of the business is my responsibility, I'll work it out."

"This is seriously fucked up. You know that, right?" He drains the remaining Coke from his glass. "You want another drink? I'm thinking about a scotch."

I turn to him, raising a brow. "You think that's a good idea?"

"Don't go getting all preachy on me. I'm a big boy, I can have a drink if I want."

"Yeah, and I have heard that shit before. Right before I dragged your drunk arse out of a gutter."

"I have it under control." But he doesn't look his confident self. Elly has him all wound up. I have seen the changes since he ran into her in my office.

"You want to talk about her?"

"Nope," he shouts me down, and I know not to push with him. He'll come and talk when he's ready.

"Okay." I throw back the remainder of my drink. We need to get out of here.

"Fine," he huffs. "She drives me fucking crazy, it's like she thinks she's too good for me or something."

This was what I was worried about when I heard who Elly was to him. Last time they went their separate ways was right before I first met him, and he was a mess, drowning his sorrows every night of the week. It took a lot for him to get back on his feet, and I don't want him to slip back there. Especially not now when he is going to need to keep things going back here for me while I work out what to do about my dad and the family business situation.

"I don't think that's what she thinks. She seems to really like you, you two just need to learn how to communicate with each other."

"Yeah, well, she won't tell her family about us, just wants to keep sneaking round."

"Aren't you taking her on a date or something tomorrow?"

"Yeah, but out of town so no one sees us."

"Maybe after that she will feel confident enough to tell them. She's really close to her brother and doesn't want to do anything to hurt him. I think that's all this is."

"I know how close they are, that has always been the problem. Maybe you're right, though."

"I always am, you know that."

"Fuck off, you're not."

I laugh at him, he's in such a mood. "We should go home, before you do something you will regret later."

He gives me a filthy look but pushes his bar stool back and stands to leave anyway. Elly must really be someone special to him. He never gets this crazy over girls. Normally it's them going crazy over him.

INDIE

All weekend I was tempted to call him and suggest we see each other again, but I'm not some needy chick, so I controlled myself, as much as it killed me. I kept thinking I could be having so much more fun if I was with Blake, my body wrapped around his.

I had organised the weekend off from the café to paint,

but I wasn't getting a lot done. I was too busy daydreaming, so by the time Elly called to say she was bored, I had given up on achieving anything, and we vegged out watching Pretty Woman, a classic top-five of mine, and eating popcorn then pizza then ice cream. I love having my bestie home. There is no one else I can hang out in sweats with, eating pizza and watching chick flicks.

By Monday I was kinda hoping I might have heard from Blake. I mean, I know we weren't dating or anything, but that night we had was awesome, wasn't it? Didn't he want to do it again? Maybe now that I had finally given in, he wasn't so keen anymore, the thrill of the chase over. He did pop into the café briefly for his coffee, but it was all business.

Tuesday, Wednesday, and Thursday were much the same, me working at the café, Blake would come in, flirt a little, grab his coffee, then leave, and I wouldn't hear from him again until the next day. I half hoped he would turn up at my class again, but he didn't. Only adding to my certainty that his curiosity had been satisfied and he was over me already.

On Friday I did the early shift at the café so I could go and meet Elly in Broken Point, with my car jampacked full of the paintings we picked out for the townhouses she's styling. By the time I got there she was in full swing doing her best to arrange the furniture by herself. I stayed with her a bit to help get all the larger items into place and the beds set up and made. Everything she had picked suited the spaces perfectly, and I have to admit my artwork looked really nice displayed on the walls. It was nice to see them being used, not just sitting in my apartment.

Elly and I make a great team, and working together, it didn't take us long to get it all sorted. And seeing her work so hard on her business makes me want to try something new and put myself out there as well. I have always been too scared to really take the leap. I'm so glad I have taken up the offer for the new apartment space and gallery. It's time to make a change, and I need to move out of the apartment that holds too many memories from my past with Hayden. I feel quite good that at least I have something working in my favour at the moment.

Blake

This week has been crazy, with the other boys leaving me the job of hiring our new office manager, and the site checks on the Broken Point townhouses. It's Saturday, but I've been in the office catching up on paperwork; this office manager can't start soon enough.

I've only seen Indie in passing this week, when I've intentionally stopped off at the café on my way to work every day. She's always her usual bubbly self, putting me in an excellent mood for the day. It makes me think of what it would be like to wake up next to her every day. The vibe of the house would be happy and fun.

I missed her this morning, she wasn't working today. I have been thinking about her ever since, and I need my Indie fix today. I'm hoping she might be free for a movie night tonight and some dessert, but I'm not one hundred percent sure where we stand with our little arrangement. I haven't pushed it this week, trying to give her space to see if she would come to me. But it doesn't look like it, so I guess I will have to chase her again, because I have had about enough waiting.

Me: What are your plans for tonight?

A text pops back almost immediately.

Indie: Why? What are you thinking?

Me: Fraser has some big first date planned for Elly. I want to make myself scarce. Was thinking we could have a movie night or something.

Indie: Sounds good to me. I'll be finished painting around four. You want to come round about five? We can order takeout.

Me: Perfect. See you then.

Nice, just how I wanted that to go. Things have definitely changed between us since I turned up at her life-drawing class. She's stopped pushing me away and is ready to give whatever this is a go. She's still not admitting anything to Elly, but it's kind of more fun this way, sneaking around, so I don't really care.

Fraser took Elly out on their first official date this afternoon, and there's no way I want to be in the house when they get back tonight. They'll either be fighting or mauling each other. There's no in between with those two. So, hanging out with Indie is the perfect option for tonight.

I arrive at Indie's place right at five, ready for a movie night. With a bottle of wine in one hand, I knock with the other. When she opens the door, that same feeling hits me that I get every time I see her. She's in a pair of loose-fitting, navy overalls, with just a bra underneath. Her hair is half up, half down in a messy bun and she has minimal makeup on. It's one of the things I like about her so much. Except for the red lipstick she likes to wear, she doesn't cover up her beautiful face with cosmetics. She's a natural beauty.

I wrap my arms around her, pulling her in for a kiss. I've waited all week, and I'm not waiting a second longer. As I run my hands down her body, I feel something hanging out of her pocket. I pull it out; it's a paint brush.

"Normally keep these in your pocket, do you?"

"Just when I'm painting," she says, like it's normal. When I walk into the room and look around, it's pretty obvious she has something different in mind other than the simple movie night I suggested. She's smiling smugly like she's about to laugh, waiting for my reaction.

"What's all this?" The room is set up with an easel and a small table, with different colours already filling the paint pallet. Her red velvet lounge is positioned in the middle of the room. There's music playing softly, something classical.

I wrap my arms around her again, pulling her in, kissing her, inhaling her scent. Her hair smells like spring with some sort of flower like jasmine. She smiles up at me.

"So?" I ask.

"You got to draw me, so it's my turn. I want to paint you."

"Is that right?" I kiss her again. I've missed her lips this week.

"Sure is. I've been looking forward to this since you messaged today." She laughs.

"Okay, but I'm not going to be able to sit still for long. You better be quick."

"I'll be quick, then we can order something for dinner." Her eyes roam over my body and she bites her lip. "Get your kit off."

"Wow, you don't muck around do you, no chit chat."

"Not when it comes to you getting your clothes off." She raises a brow.

I guess this is a little bit of payback for me just showing up at her class last week. But really, how could I resist? Once I found out she models for a life-drawing class, I had to see it for myself. And I'm glad I did.

INDIE

Blake strips off quickly and folds his clothes, placing them on the coffee table. I have to cover my mouth to stop myself from laughing at his awkwardness over this situation, but I'm going to take pleasure in it. He had to know I wouldn't just let that slide and not get him back. At least for him it's just the two of us.

He smiles over to me, that cocky confidence not affected at all by his state of undress; if anything, he's more confident. He's very comfortable in his own skin. And how could he not be, he's insanely hot.

"Okay, where do you want me? I'm not used to this like you."

I'm sitting behind my easel, paintbrush in my mouth, mixing my paints. "On the lounge," I mumble around the brush.

He lies down, and I can't take my eyes off his package. He smirks, knowing all too well this is going to be harder on me than I thought, and he couldn't care less. I think he's loving this. I get to work, first sketching out his shape, then filling in the muscles.

"Can I talk while you paint, or will it be too distracting?" he asks.

I continue to sketch out his figure. "Yes, please, anything that will kill the silence, the music's not working."

"You thought this was payback, didn't you? But it's harder than you thought."

"How did you know?"

"Just a hunch. Okay, I'll keep you busy talking to make it easier. How's your week been?"

"Busy. One of the girls at the café has been sick, so I've been doing her shifts as well. What about you?"

"Yeah, busy. We keep taking on more work than we can handle. I need to get more guys. We hired a new office manager, so that should help, a bit less admin." He thinks for a minute. "Okay, new topic of conversation, where do you see yourself in five years?" he asks.

"Wow, that's a bit much, isn't it?"

"It's just a question, Indie. I'm a planner. I like to write lists and plan out how I want my future to look. What do you want? To travel, to have kids, to make a million dollars when some rich investor finds out how amazing your art is and buys it all?" He winks.

"That's a lot of ideas. I don't really know. I'm not a planner, not at all. I kinda just like to go with the flow, see what life throws at me. That way I can't be disappointed when what I want doesn't happen." I shrug. I really haven't put a lot of thought into it. I know I probably should, as I'm getting older, but up until now, things have kinda just happened for me.

"Yeah, I get it, but if you plan then you have a goal to work towards. There must be something that you see for your future. A big house on the water? Something?"

I look around the side of my canvas so I can see him better. "You're not going to give up on this, are you?"

"Nope, I want to know what makes you get out of bed in the morning. There must be something you dream of."

"Well, mostly my dreams at the moment are just dirty ones of you." And that's the truth, my dreams have been filthy since the day I ran into him at the café. This man does all sorts of bad things to my imagination.

He smiles. "Being cute won't get you out of answering the question."

"Fine." I roll my eyes, knowing I need to give him something to shut him up. "Ultimate goal, you know, when I'm all grown up and stuff. I kinda want to have a big family, not any time soon or anything, but one day, if I find the right man, someone who loves me and who I know will stay by my side, no matter what. I don't really care for material things. As long as I know I'm loved, and have a big family around me, I'll be happy."

I didn't really mean to say all that, it just spilled out when I opened my mouth. But, if I let myself dream, that is what I want. And I guess it doesn't matter if I say it to Blake. After all, this is just a *friends with benefits* type of arrangement, so he knows I'm not asking him to get married and have kids with me.

"That's a beautiful dream." He smiles and looks over to me. I can't make eye contact with him. This conversation feels too personal for whatever this is we're doing. This is supposed to be fun, that's all, not planning for the future.

"Well, it's just, my mama never had that and neither did my nana; they were always alone. And I never had any siblings. I always imagined what it would be like to have a big family, with brothers and sisters around to play and fight with, people that looked out for you." Oh my God, I need to shut up now. Why am I telling him all this? I think it's because I'm hiding behind the canvas. I don't have to look at him while I'm saying it.

"Yeah, I always wondered what it would be like to grow up in a family like that as well. Like Elly. Her parents are so supportive and loving towards those three. They're so lucky."

I sigh. "Yeah, they are."

"It's funny, I've had this same conversation with Fraser. Were you guys friends in high school? He was kind of like you, he just had his dad and you just had your mum."

"Yeah, we were close. He spent a lot of time with Drew, and I was with Elly. The Walker house was always full of people. I don't know how Anne and Jim dealt with all those teenagers hanging around there, but they never seemed to mind."

I start applying the paint to the sketch, layering it on in quick brushstrokes. All my work is a little messy. I don't like neat and even; I like texture, mixed colours, depth. It makes it more interesting.

"It must have been nice growing up here near the water."

"It was. I love the water; I swim nearly every day. I haven't really left this area. I've never travelled except some small car trips up to Queensland and down to Sydney, but that's it. I've never been on a plane or anything."

"Are you serious? Never been on a plane. Where would you go if you could go anywhere?"

"Hmm, I don't know, I've never really thought. Maybe somewhere totally different from Australia, somewhere with some history, old buildings and art museums, or somewhere tropical. I've seen these luxury huts that sit out on the water, they even have glass bottoms so you can see all the underwater creatures swimming around. That would be amazing."

"That really does sound amazing. I haven't travelled much either. I've been to all the states in Australia but never overseas. I would like to one day, if I had the right person to go with."

I look back at my painting, studying it. "I'm done for now. It's not quite finished, but I can do the rest without you having to lie there for me."

"That was quick." He hops up from the lounge, coming round behind me to see my work, without a care in the world, that he is totally nude. As he looks over my shoulder, I'm acutely aware of his very naked body so close to me.

"Wow, Indie, it's amazing. I can't believe you can paint so quickly."

I shrug. "It's my one special talent. Pity I can't make enough from them to make a decent living."

"You will, you just have to keep on working at it. I can help you with some industry contacts if you like?"

I smile up at him. "That would be amazing. Thank you."

"Anything you need, Indie, baby, I'm here to help. And, just so you know, you have many special talents." He smirks cheekily.

"Is that right? What would you say they are?" I think I know where this is going, but I have to ask anyway.

He bends, taking his hand to the back of my head and drawing my lips to his, kissing me slowly. "This is one," he mumbles into my mouth, kissing me again. "You're very good at this."

"What else?" I murmur, pulling back, a little breathless already. My hand reaches down for his cock, and I stroke his hard length. "Maybe this?"

He groans. "Very good at that." He pushes the straps of my overalls down off my shoulders, so I'm left in my lace bra. His hands cup my breasts, rubbing his thumbs over the thin fabric, teasing my nipples, as I continue to stroke my hand up and down his shaft.

"And this?" I lick the tip of his cock, running my tongue down his long, hard cock. He hisses in appreciation. I part my lips and take him in my mouth, sucking. Then I pull back. My eyes look up to him, waiting for his answer.

"Yes, you're very skilled with your mouth. Keep going,

baby. Don't tease me." His hands go to the back of my head and lace through my hair, pulling me back onto his cock.

I open my mouth, happy with his answer and the need I see on his face. I love this, how I can make a man like him come undone with just my mouth. It drives me just as crazy as it does him. I keep sliding my mouth back and forth. I don't take my eyes off him, watching his face. He helps to guide the pace.

"Fuck, Indie, don't stop. That feels fucking amazing."

I continue sucking back and forth, picking up the pace. He grips my hair harder, fucking my mouth. I run my hand up his lower back, digging my nails in so I can hold on. His body is taut and tight, the muscles all flexing as he keeps thrusting into my mouth.

"I'm going to come." He jerks forward, and with one last thrust into my mouth, he releases.

I continue sucking, drawing out his orgasm, swallowing it down. I pull back, smiling up at him.

"Fuck, baby, you're very talented at that." He pulls me up to standing by my hands, wrapping his arms around me and kissing me on the forehead.

"You want something to eat?" I ask.

"Sure do, but I think you're overdressed; let's fix that." He pulls me towards the bedroom, and I know food is the last thing on his mind tonight.

CHAPTER SEVEN

INDIE

Blake has his arms wrapped around me, one hand on my thigh and the other cupping my breast. His lips are on my neck kissing, sucking, biting. I'm sure there's going to be a mark when we're finished. It's the early hours on Sunday morning and we've hardly slept. Our bodies have been intertwined all night. We can't get enough of each other. And this is how he wakes me up; slowly fucking me from behind as we lie on our sides. Walking is going to be a challenge today, but I'm not complaining. I'm riding high on the endorphin boost of an amazing night together.

"Can we stay like this all day?" I murmur sleepily.

"If that's what you want, baby, I'm not going anywhere." His hand digs into my hip as he really gives it to me.

There's the sound of a door opening and a loud thump of something being dropped to the ground. We both freeze.

"What the fuck?" I whisper. I locked the door last night, didn't I? The only other person who has the key is...

"Indie, you up?" The sound of Hayden's voice rings through the apartment. What the fuck is he doing here?

Blake looks at me, and I have no words.

"Who the fuck is that, Indie?" His voice is deep, his tone serious.

"It's my ex," I whisper, covering my eyes.

He pulls out of me, sitting up in a rush. "The one who took off to travel the world?"

"Yes. I have no idea what he's doing here."

Before I even have time to think, Blake is up, throwing on his clothes. "Well, I'll leave you to find out." He rushes out of the room.

"Wait. You don't have to go," I call after him, but it's too late.

"Who are you?" I hear Hayden demand.

"No one you need to worry about." With that, the door slams and he's gone.

Fuck! Worst timing ever. I throw on my dressing gown and head out to the living room to see what Hayden's doing here so early in the morning. The nerve of him to just let himself in, after all this time, like he still lives here. What was he thinking?

There he is, the man who broke my heart. He hasn't changed much. His hair's a bit longer and he's unshaven, which isn't like him, but he's still very much the same Hayden who walked out on me. "Hayden, what are you doing here?"

"Who was that, Indie?" he demands, ignoring my question completely.

Two can play at that game. "What are you doing here?"

"I'm finished travelling. I've come home to you." His eyes are hopeful.

Now I'm really pissed off. "What? And you thought I would just be here, waiting to take you back with open arms?" I huff. Is this guy for real?

"Who's the guy, Indie?" He looks pissed, but he has no right. He was the one who left me.

"None of your business. You can't dump me and take off to travel the world, then just rock up here and expect everything to be just the way you left it. Things have changed. I've moved on."

"Yeah, appears you have." He inspects the apartment, and I know what he's thinking. This place is a mess. After I painted Blake last night, we messed up the bedroom, then headed out here and ordered in takeaway and watched soppy movies. Who would have thought, big strong Blake is all romantic and likes chick flicks? The empty containers from our dinner are still on the kitchen bench, dishes in the sink. The easel and paint stuff are still where I left them. And the blanket we had covering us is half on the lounge, half on the floor. The place probably smells like a brothel. I don't even know how many times we had sex.

"What did you expect, for me to wait for you? You're lucky I hadn't moved into my new place yet or you would have been walking in on someone else. Did you not think to call or something, before using your old key to let yourself in?" I say, picking up the painting and placing it against the wall with the other canvasses so he can't see who it's of.

"I wanted to surprise you. I wasn't expecting you to be with some guy, in our apartment." He pauses. "Wait. You're moving?"

I whip my head back to glare at him. Is he serious? "It's not our apartment, it's *my* apartment. It stopped being yours the night you left and stopped paying rent. And yes, with Elly."

He looks down to the floor. "You're right, I'm sorry, I just kind of expected things to be the same when I got back. Elly from high school?" He looks confused.

"Yeah, good old dependable Indie, just waiting here for you to return, and yes, Elly, from high school. She's back in town." I storm into the kitchen and grab my phone to message Blake. I feel so bad about Hayden showing up. It must have looked really bad, him still having a key.

Me: I'm sorry. Hayden had no right to show up like that. I have no idea what he was thinking.

Blake: Don't worry about it. Not like this is something anyway, we're just friends.

Wow, okay, that hurt more than it probably should've. I know he's annoyed, but he didn't have to be a dick about it. I had no idea Hayden would just show up out of the blue. What was I supposed to do? And Blake got out of here so quickly, I didn't even get to explain who Hayden was or anything.

Hayden snaps me out of my thoughts. He's followed me into the kitchen. He puts his hands on my shoulders, and I turn around to look at him. "I'm sorry, Indie. I wasn't thinking. Would it be okay if I stay till I find somewhere else?"

I look up from my phone and sigh. Not like Blake is going to care, anyway. "Yeah, I guess, but you're on the couch. I move out of this place in a week. You could probably have the place back if you want, I don't think they've found anyone else yet."

"Yeah, okay, that would be good. Thanks. Will it put you in an awkward position with the guy, your boyfriend?"

"Not my boyfriend. He's just a friend." I sigh, frustrated.

"Oh, okay." I can tell he wants to know more, but he knows he's pushed me enough this morning, and if he wants somewhere to sleep for the next couple of weeks, he better keep his mouth shut.

"Where should I put my bags?"

"Just dump them in the bedroom, you know where it is."

He puts his bags in the bedroom, then takes a seat on the lounge.

"Coffee?" I ask.

"Please. It was a long flight."

"So, how was the world anyway? Everything you thought it would be?"

He smiles the warm, friendly Hayden smile, the one that used to feel like coming home to me, and just like that, it's like old times as he tells me the stories of his travels.

Blake

I feel a little bad about how quickly I took off, but what the fuck was that? Her ex rocking up, letting himself in. He still has a key! Were they even properly broken up or was he just travelling, expecting to come back to her? I don't know. I guess it's not my problem now that he's back. She's probably going to get back with him and move on with her life. Just when things were getting good. She was finally opening up to me. I was starting to think there might be something there, something more than just friendship, but I guess the chances of that are slim now. She texted me to explain, but what was I supposed to say?

I walk in the door at home. Elly and Fraser are sitting at the kitchen table having breakfast.

"Big night out, hey, man?" asks Fraser, looking up from his food.

"Must have been. He's still in the same clothes as last night. Walk of shame. What did you get up to, Blakie?"

They look very cosy. I think I like it better when they're not getting on, instead of ganging up on me about where I've been.

"Nothing, just drank too much and crashed at a friend's place. Thought I was being nice giving you two some space. Won't bother next time if I'm going to get one hundred questions when I get home," I hiss back to them.

"I'm not convinced. You look like you've been up to no good to me!"

"You can think whatever you want, Elly, I'm going to take a shower."

I can hear them still talking about me, but I don't care. Elly really can think whatever she wants. I just want a shower to clear my head. Then I'm messaging Ash; hopefully he's up for a boxing session at the gym.

Half an hour later I'm in the gym with Ash, beating the shit out of the pads he holds. I boxed a bit in high school. My dad got me into it because he didn't want me to be a pussy. I got to talking to Ash about a month after moving here and found out he was into boxing as well. Neither of us had done it much since, so we started coming to the gym together to get back into it. Ash likes to talk himself up, but he's all talk. If we actually got in the ring together, I'd kick his arse, for sure.

"Thanks for meeting me, man. I needed to get out of the house. Fraser and his new girl are a little too much to be in the same room as."

"Glad to get out of the house myself. Chloe's mum is staying with us until after the wedding. I'm sick of hearing about the wedding already. I'm not going to get through the next few months."

"Sounds like fun," I say, hitting him again.

"What have you guys got planned for my buck's party? Fraser won't let me in on the secret."

"He's organised the whole thing. I probably know about as much as you. Dinner then the Pink Flamingo." I hit him hard again.

His forehead is creased, and I can see he's having to try his best to hold me off. "Shit, Blake, what's got into you?"

"Nothing, just need to let off some steam."

"I'm regretting saying yes to this, now that I know what mood you're in. Has your dad called again?"

I thump the pad again, and he stumbles back. "No, it's not Dad this time."

"Right, that's it, we're switching. It's my turn to hit the shit out of you."

"Bring it on, going to be funny watching you try."

We switch gloves for pads, and I take my stance. I'm starting to feel better; this is exactly what I needed.

He swings at me, hitting the pad, but I don't budge. I smile at him to piss him off. He swings again.

"That's all you got?" He hits against the pads again. "Seriously, man, is that it?"

His forehead creases, and he narrows his eyes, throwing a punch with all he has, and I still don't budge.

"You're like a fucking brick wall." He throws down the gloves. I'm done, I'm going to lift weights."

I laugh at his pain. "Good idea, you need it, man, if you're going to beat me," I call after him.

I pack up the gloves and pads and head over to do some pull-ups. Okay, maybe what happened this morning isn't as bad as I originally thought. I don't really know the entire situation with Indie's ex. I'll give her some space to sort out what's going on with him. Give us both some time to cool off. It's probably for the best anyway. I can't really afford to get too close to anyone at the moment, not with Dad on my case about coming home to help him and the other boys out.

CHAPTER EIGHT

BLAKE

Tonight is Ash's buck's party, and we're at the only strip club in town, the Pink Flamingo. I can think of many other places I would rather be tonight, but Ash has become a good mate since we started the business together, and I'm here for him. Also, there was no way Fraser would have let me miss it. He organised the whole thing and has been pumped about it for weeks. We're in a private area roped off from the rest of the club. He mostly invited other guys from work and some friends from high school, and Drew, Elly's brother.

We walk through to the back room, and I have to admit, for a seedy strip club, this one is actually pretty cool. The room is set up like a circus tent with a yellow-and-red-striped ceiling. There's a stage in the centre of the room where two girls are doing all sorts of interesting things: hanging from silks that twirl around, and swings hanging from the ceiling. These girls are gorgeous and toned with flashy sequined costumes that barely cover their bodies. They're more like gymnasts than strippers.

I wish I could just relax and have a good time like the other fellas. I need something to take my mind off what Indie might be doing right now with her ex. All week I've had thoughts of her and what she's doing with him. But these places give me the creeps. Too close to home.

"You want a drink, man?" I ask Fraser.

"Yeah, a Coke, thanks." I go to the bar. A drink will help. Fraser finds us a table to sit at, and I make my way over with the drinks. We've lost Drew already. He's wandered off to watch the girls, distracted by something shiny and pretty. Ash is off his head, drunk already, and has disappeared into one of the rooms off to the side. I don't even want to know what he's doing. I know his fiancée and I like her. The fewer details I know, the better.

I sit with Fraser and watch the show. It's now changed, and there are two girls on the pole, while the ones that were on the silks walk the room, offering private dances.

"You okay, man? You're quiet," Fraser asks.

I shrug. "Yeah, just don't like these places, you know."

"Drew's having a good time, though. Look at him, he's been with that girl for a while."

I look over to where he sits. A girl is giving him a lap dance, and he chats to her while she dances around him.

Wait a second—that girl over there dancing for Drew... where do I know her from? She looks vaguely familiar. Yeah, I know where from. I pull out my phone and check the text my dad sent through with the picture. Yep, that's her. The young girl he's looking for, Vinnie's girlfriend. She's not trying very hard to hide from him, working in a place like this. He would have connections with this club, for sure. I need to get a chance to warn her they're looking for her.

I bump arms with Fraser. "That girl dancing for Drew, this is her, hey?" I show him the photo on my phone.

He nods. "Looks like it to me. You stalking a pretty stripper, man? That's kinda creepy."

"Not stalking strippers. Dad's looking for her. She's apparently the girlfriend of someone who works for him, and she did a runner. He called me a couple of weeks ago to see if I'd seen her around and said they had heard she was up this way. He wanted me to keep an eye out and let him know if I spotted her."

"Shit. Is she in some kind of trouble or something?"

"I don't know, but I need to talk to her, tell her they know she's living in Byron. If we don't, they will find her for sure, and I don't want to know what Vinnie will do to her once he does."

"Let's go have a drink with Drew. See if you can talk to her, find out what the go is."

The girl, Cassie, and the other stripper with Drew move over to one of the other guys, so we take this opportunity to walk over and sit with him.

"Hey, man, you having a good night?"

"Yeah, this place is fucking awesome."

"This place or the chick that's been dancing for you the last hour?" asks Fraser.

"She's leaving with me tonight, man. Bet you a hundred bucks she leaves on my arm."

"You're on! Easy money." They shake on it.

"Like I said, she's leaving with me. I've been chatting with her. She's only working here because she's desperate for the money. She only just moved here and doesn't know anyone. She needs a friend who can help her," says Drew. He's completely smitten with her. Has this guy even been in a strip club before?

"And that's you?" I say.

"Sure is," he replies.

"Sounds like you got the whole life story. No wonder you were spending so much time with her. You know they make up that shit just so you feel sorry for them and give them more money. Most of the strippers I know do this because they love it. They find it empowering and get shit loads of cash out of suckers like you," says Fraser.

I shoot him a look because we know the story she's told him is true, and he's not helping me to talk to her and warn her.

"I mean, not this girl, though, she looks honest," he backtracks.

"No, this is really her story. She was telling me her stripper name is Bambi because she's an orphan. She won't tell me her real name, says it's against club policy. It's so sad, not everyone gets to grow up like we did."

We're all looking in her direction when she glances over to Drew. Her expression changes from the smile she was wearing earlier to worry as her eyes dart between us.

"You okay, man? How much have you had to drink?" I ask.

"Not that much. I just feel really bad for her," he says sadly. "Look at her, she doesn't want to be here."

"Can you call her over, Drew? I need to talk to her for a sec," I say.

Drew seems confused, but Fraser nods, agreeing.

Drew smiles over to her, where she's still watching us. "Bambi," he gestures for her to come over, "come meet my friends."

She whispers something to the other girl, then walks toward us, swaying her hips as she goes. She has a short pink wig on, and she twirls a strand of hair in her fingers playfully as she eyes us off. She's tall with long legs and has big brown eyes, surrounded by a layer of thick, fake lashes. I can see how she got the stripper name Bambi.

Drew introduces us. "This is Fraser and Blake. They're here for the buck's party as well; it's one of their business partners that's getting married."

"Nice to meet you boys," she says, batting her long lashes.

"Drew tells us you're new to the area."

She appears nervous, playing with the fringing on her costume. "Yeah, just been here a few weeks."

"You on the run from your boyfriend or something?" I ask to see the reaction I get.

Her eyes widen, then she darts her gaze back over to Drew, fear clear in her eyes.

"Ah, why would you ask that?" she says shakily.

"Because my dad is Max Donovan, and he sent me to find you."

She takes a step back and bumps into Drew. "W... why? I'm not who you think I am, sorry. I have no idea who that is, you must have the wrong girl."

"What are you talking about, Blake? Who's your dad?" asks Drew, appearing utterly confused by the entire situation.

I ignore Drew. She needs to know how much trouble she's in and quickly. "Why do you seem like you're about to run then?"

"Blake, stop it, you're scaring her."

Her eyes are glassy, and they dart between me and Drew. "I'm just confused. I don't know who you're talking about."

"Bambi, I'm not going to tell them where you are. I don't work for my dad. I'm nothing like him. But I just wanted you to know, they're searching the town for you. You're not safe working somewhere like this. They'll find you here. It's only a matter of time, my dad knows everyone in this line of business."

A tear escapes down her cheek; she wipes it away, leaving a trail of smudged mascara. "You don't understand. I don't have any choice. I have to. I need the money. No one else is hiring, and this is all I know. What am I supposed to do?"

"We can help you find you something different. You can't work here."

"You can't let him find me. I don't want to go back to him. He's not a good person. I... I saw things. I can't go back. Please don't tell him where I am."

"I won't, we won't, you can trust us," I say.

"How do I know that? I don't know you."

"Man." Fraser knocks me on the arm, tilting his head towards the door. "Is that your dad?" he whispers.

I follow his line of sight. "You have to be fucking kidding me," I choke. "Drew, your jacket, get it on her now. Cover her up and get her out of here."

"I can't go with him. I don't know any of you, I'm not going anywhere," she protests.

"We have to get you out of here. Seriously, if you don't want him to find you tonight, you need to get out of here now." She looks really scared. I wonder what she knows. What she saw, I can only imagine.

Drew wraps his jacket around her and grabs her hands. She looks up at him. "Come with me. You can come back to my place. My dad and brother are both cops in this town. I promise you can trust me. I will keep you safe. You can't stay here," Drew pleads.

She looks between us and over to the door, where Dad

and Vinnie are talking to the bouncer on the door, and I can see the recognition in her features. She knows it's a risk to go with Drew, but it's a bigger one to stay and have them find her.

"Okay, Drew, I trust you." He takes her by the hand.

"Is there a back door?" I ask. She nods. "Take her home, Drew. I'll go deal with Dad and his thug." I head through the club towards him. It's been a while since I have seen him face to face, but he's the same dad I grew up with. Black suit, stern expression, chest puffed out, so everyone knows who runs this underworld of his. His presence is strong and overpowering to most, but not me. I see through him, and I stopped being scared of him a long time ago.

His eyes meet mine, and the scowl he had for the bouncer turns into the fake smile he saves for family. "Son, what are you doing here?"

"Buck's night for my business partner. What are you doing here? This isn't your normal turf."

"Looking for Vinnie's girlfriend. We got a tipoff that she's working here. You haven't seen her around, have you? According to the bouncer, she's working tonight."

"I've been drinking pretty heavily with the lads, and these girls all start looking the same, but if I spot her, I'll be sure to call and let you know."

"Hmm. This isn't just a case of her running, Son. Vinnie thinks she might have seen something. She walked in on him at one of the clubs when he was dealing with a situation. If she talks, we could all be in trouble." His tone is clipped, expression serious. This man means business, and no one should mess with him.

"Yeah, that's a really shit situation. What did she see?"

"I'm not sure, but Vinnie is worried so it must have been bad."

"Not like you to be travelling all this way if you don't even have the details. How do you know she didn't just get sick of his ugly face and dump him?"

"Because unlike you, Vinnie has been around lately, and I trust his word when he tells me a situation happened. I'm going to back him up."

"I'd be careful if I were you blindly following a thug like Vinnie. This girl could be totally innocent, and he's just a revengeful ex and you're helping him. Don't you have bigger fish to fry?"

I've pissed him off now. His scowl is back, and there is an intensity to his stare that I don't like. "Son, I know you have been drinking, so I'm going to let this slide, but you are edging very close to overstepping the mark here. You need to stop asking questions and just do as you're told. You may not be actively participating in the family business at the moment, but you're still a part of the family, and I expect you to respect me and whatever decisions I make regarding the business." His voice is low and harsh; he means business.

"Just trying to look out for you. I will definitely keep an eye out for her, but I haven't seen anything tonight."

He glares at me for an extended period. "All right, we better keep moving then." He goes to walk off then turns back. "Your sister's wedding's coming up. You haven't let your mother know if you're coming."

He's here to look for a girl, who saw some guy get killed, and he wants to talk about Amy's wedding! My fucked-up family. "Yeah, I'll let her know."

"Good. Be in touch soon." Off he goes into the crowd. No emotion, cold, hard. Off to fix the next problem before he gets himself killed or locked up. Why would anyone want that life?

I return to Fraser who has been watching from our original table.

"What did he say? He looked pretty mad."

"I pissed him off, told him he can't trust Vinnie, and he's just following him blindly. It wasn't what he wanted to hear, but it's what he *needed* to hear. Vinnie's a piece of shit that leaches off him for protection, but I haven't trusted him for a long time. Dad needs to be careful."

"Heavy shit."

"Isn't it always with my family? Hopefully, I got him off the scent of her, for tonight at least, but they won't stop looking until they find her."

I finish up my drink then say my goodbyes, leaving Fraser with a very trashed Ash, but that place has been just giving me the creeps, and even more so now after the events of the night.

On the walk home, I can't help but wonder what Indie is doing tonight. Is she back with her ex all happy again because he came home? Or did she kick his arse to the curb like she should have. I'm tempted to call her and see, but I won't.

INDIE

It's closing time at the café, and I wipe the counter more aggressively than I probably should be. I have been in a pretty shitty mood all week. For one, I'm pissed at Blake for just leaving and not even bothering to hear me out, and second, I'm pissed at Hayden for just showing up and expecting to stay. I have had about enough of it, and I know I need to have the chat with him about moving on. I don't know how to go about any of it, though. I need to talk to someone about it all, it's messing with my head.

"Elly, I have no idea what I'm doing," I cry dramatically.

"Wiping down the counter, that's what it looks like to me anyway." She laughs, the smart-arse.

"I mean with my life, with the men in my life anyway. I've heard nothing from Blake all week, and after the text from him on the morning Hayden arrived home. I haven't bothered to try contacting him again. Blake made it pretty obvious what this is. S.E.X. Was I the only one who thought it was something more?"

Elly's packing away all the leftover slices and muffins into little Tupperware containers from the fridge. She looks up at me sympathetically. "Oh, honey, I know it sucks, but I don't think you can totally blame him, can you? I think anyone would get out of there pretty quickly if the ex showed up. It would have been awkward as fuck." She packs the tubs into the fridge for storage overnight.

I turn away from her and start to clean the coffee machine. "Thanks, you're supposed to be on my side."

"I am, don't worry about Blake, though. He likes you, and when you get the chance to explain it all to him, I'm sure he will understand, and everything will go back to normal, and you will be friends again." She wraps her arms around me, hugging me.

"What am I supposed to do about Hayden?"

"Just be honest with him. He left, you moved on. It's simple, hun."

"Yeah, I guess." It doesn't feel simple, though. I don't want to hurt him, he was a big part of my life for a long time, but he left, and I moved on. Even if Blake's not that keen on me anymore, there was something between us, something I didn't feel when I was with Hayden. Something that felt more than just friends that fuck. Maybe it was just in my head. I'm romanticising something that should have been simple.

Elly and I finish packing up and go our separate ways.

Having Hayden home has been kinda nice. I didn't realise how much I missed his friendship. He was the closest thing to family I had after Mama died, and you don't have someone in your life for that long and not miss them. But having him back has cemented in my mind how over it really is between us. It's just friendship now, nothing more.

I'm so tired I can barely pick my feet up off the ground as I walk myself home. I can't wait to have a shower, something easy for dinner, then head straight to bed. I open the door and immediately want to cry. Oh my God, what is going on here?

The room is filled with lit candles. There are rose petals scattered around, and the smell coming from the kitchen is divine. Hayden has cooked my favourite dinner; I can tell by the aroma.

"W... what's all this?" I get out, a little more wobbly than I wanted.

Hayden looks up from where he's standing in the kitchen preparing dinner. His smile is hopeful, and I instantly feel sick to my stomach. Does he want to get back together? The scene is very romantic, and after nine years together, I know him. He doesn't have a romantic bone in his body. His idea of romance is cleaning the house for me on my birthday. Whatever this set-up is, it's unusual for him.

"I thought we could have a nice dinner. I wanted to say thank you for being so understanding and letting me stay this week."

"Oh, that's nice." It definitely seems like so much more, though. I'm getting an uneasy, sinking feeling.

"I'm nearly finished with dinner. Go have a shower, you must be tired after a long day at work."

"Thanks." I head for the shower. I'm too tired to process the scene out there. What do I say to him if he asks me to try again?

I turn the shower on and the steam fills the room. I jump in, feeling the hot water hit my back. It feels so good on my tired muscles. I just want to stay here. I don't want to get out and face him. I know I'm going to have to disappoint him, and I hate disappointing people. But us getting back together is not going to happen. Come on, Indie, pull yourself together and go face the music. I shut off the shower and hop out. I throw on my faded, comfy jeans and my favourite cream knitted sweater. The weather has started to turn cold this week, and tonight is especially chilly. I towel-dry my hair, letting it dry naturally, and it curls up at the ends.

There's a knock on the bathroom door. "Dinner's ready," Hayden calls.

"Okay." Here goes. Get your shit together, Indie, and just tell him how it is. He left you. You moved on with your life while he was off travelling. It's simple. Okay, I can do this.

When I walk through to the living room, the table is set with dinner all ready to go. There are salmon steaks, little chat potatoes, green beans, and cherry tomatoes. It all looks so amazing. It's been a while since someone has cooked me dinner. It's normally just me and a salad, on the couch watching TV, unless I splash out and get pizza.

"Wow, this looks amazing. Thank you. You didn't have to go to all this trouble for me."

"I wanted to show you how much I appreciate you." His eyes meet mine, trying to hold my gaze. I can tell he's looking for so much more, and I just can't do it.

"Thanks." I smile weakly.

We start to eat our dinner, and Hayden chats about his plans for the future. He's so chatty, but I'm finding it hard to focus on what he's saying. My mind is racing. What is he expecting from me?

He's smiling at me like he's just asked me a question, but I didn't hear what he said.

"Sorry. What did you say?"

"I was just asking you, 'What are your plans, Indie?' How do you see the next few years playing out?"

Why does everyone keep asking me that? Do I look like a planner? I don't think so. I push my food around my plate trying to think how to answer. "Well, my five-year plan went out the door when you left, and since then, I have been just going week to week. You know I'm not much of a planner," I say with a shrug. And that's the truth, I don't have a five-year plan or anything. There are things I want for the future, but how exactly do I say that it doesn't include him?

"I know I messed up our future plans when I left. That's one thing I wanted to talk to you about tonight. Are you finished with your dinner?"

"Yes, thanks. It was beautiful."

He collects the plates and takes them to the kitchen. He returns with little cups of chocolate mousse and raspberries, placing them on the table in front of me.

"Before we have dessert, there's something I want to talk to you about."

"Okay. What is it?" My heart is thumping in my chest. I don't even want to hear the words. I just want to cover my ears like a little kid and block it all out.

"Indie, I know we've had a few months apart. I don't know about you, but it gave me time to think, put things into perspective, and I know what I want from life now. I'm ready to settle down and start a family... I want that with you."

I knew this was coming when I walked in the door tonight and found the room like this, but I'm lost for words. I literally can't get them out of my mouth. How do I tell him I don't feel the same anymore? I hate disappointing people. But he broke my heart when he left me, and now it's too late.

"Indie, talk to me." His hand is on my leg, and I look down to watch him slowly stroking it. Why can't I find the words to tell him?

"I don't know what to say. I'm surprised. You left me. I thought that was the end."

"Yeah, but I came back for you." He pulls a small red velvet box from his pocket and my heart is pounding. I think I might pass out. What is he doing? I want to scream, but I'm frozen in shock. I didn't see this coming.

"Indie, I came back for you because I want to spend the rest of my life with you. Will you marry me?" He looks so hopeful. It would be easy just to say yes. I know him, and I loved him once, but this isn't the life I want, being slotted into his life when he's ready. I'm worth more than that. If I was supposed to be the one, he wouldn't have left, or we would have gone travelling together. But we didn't.

"Hay, I'm sorry, but when you left you broke my heart. It took a while, but I'm finally in a good place again. You were right when you broke it off. We had been together a long time and we were comfortable. You were my first love, and you will always hold a special place in my heart because of everything we shared. But I can't marry you. I'm sorry."

His sad eyes hold mine. "I'm too late, aren't I? It's that guy who was here on Sunday."

A tear escapes down my cheek. This is so hard. I know I'm hurting him and that's the last thing I want to do, but I can't just go along with what he wants to keep him happy. "No, it's not. It's me. I'm different now. What we had was beautiful, and you will always be my first love, but it's over."

He puts the little box back in his pocket and drops his head. "For the rest of my life, I will always regret leaving you. That was the stupidest decision I could have made."

I grab for his hand. "It wasn't. You needed to do that for you, and now you'll be ready when the right girl comes along."

His sad eyes rise to look at me. "You're the right girl for me, Indie."

"I'm sorry, Hay. I'm not."

"Yeah, I'm sorry too, but I get it. I destroyed what we had when I left." He pulls his hand away and pushes his chair back and stands. "I'll go stay with a friend. I can't stay here if this isn't going to happen. It's too hard."

"Okay." Another tear escapes and I swipe it away. I never cry, but this is too much.

He disappears into the bedroom. I can hear him packing, and I just sit here. I feel heavy, like the weight of the world is on my shoulders. If this is the right decision, why is it so hard to do? I hate hurting someone I care about, even after what he did to me.

He returns shortly after with his bags. "See you, Indie."

"Bye, Hayden."

He closes the front door slowly, looking back to me as he does, and I know that's it, I won't see him again unless in passing around town. But it won't be the same. This man was such a big part of my life for so long. And now it's over.

I'm so tired, I just need to sleep. I know this is the right decision. Tomorrow is a new day, and I'm sure I will feel better about all this after a good night's sleep. I curl up in bed, hugging my pillow, and cry myself to sleep.

CHAPTER NINE

BLAKE

AFTER EVERYTHING THAT HAPPENED LAST NIGHT, I'm on my way over to the Walkers' to check on Cassie, the girl from last night. She needs to know just how dangerous Vinnie is and how close she came to being found by him.

I knock on the yellow front door and Anne, the twins' mum, opens it. She looks surprised to see me but offers a warm, friendly smile and signals for me to come into the house.

I make my way into the lounge room with her. "Blake, how lovely to see you. Are you looking for Elly?"

"No, just here to see Drew about something. Is he around?"

"He's out the back with the friend he brought home last night. I'll leave you kids to it then." She points to the deck, where the two of them sit deep in conversation.

"Anne, is Jim around? We might actually need both of your help. That girl Drew's with, she's in trouble, and Fraser says I can trust you and Jim." She frowns, and we hear Jim's beaming voice enter from behind us.

"What kind of trouble is she in, son?" His voice is deep

and commanding; you can tell he was in a position of authority on the force.

"It's a long story. I don't know what Drew's told you about last night and what happened."

His eyes hold mine, and I can tell he's trying to work me out. "Not a lot, just that she needed somewhere to stay, and we knew she wasn't like the girls he normally brings home. She slept in the spare room," he says with a laugh. "Not like Drew at all."

"Good. He needs to hear this as well."

We walk out the back to the deck where Drew's sitting with the girl. They each have a bowl of cereal and half-finished coffee in front of them.

Drew looks up when he sees me, his smile less confident than normal. "Hey, man, you remember Jenna from last night."

Her eyes rise to meet mine, but she doesn't smile. "Hi... Jenna, is it? How are you this morning?" She looks scared shitless to see me again, and I would too, if I knew who my dad was. She probably thinks I'm here to turn her in to him. Interesting that Drew called her Jenna. I wonder who she really is, because Dad and Vinnie know her as Cassie. "Drew, we need to talk."

Her eyes dart to Drew, and he smiles at her reassuringly. "I might just go have a shower, if that's okay, Mrs Walker?" asks Jenna in a small voice.

"Of course, love. I put some of Drew's sister's clothes on the end of his bed. You're probably about the same size, and you can't keep wearing Drew's oversized T-shirt.

"Thank you." Jenna offers a small smile before she walks inside. She can't get away from me quick enough. I hate it. Not that I need her to like me or anything, but I don't want her scared of me, either. I'm here to help her.

"We need to talk, Drew," I say again, taking a seat across from him. His parents sit down as well.

"Yeah, we do. This situation is fucked up, man. I can't believe you're the son of some thug." His brow is creased, and the look of concern is written all over his face. He's not his carefree self today. This has shaken him.

"He's not a thug," I say. I have no idea why I feel the need to defend him, but I don't want the Walker family thinking this is any sort of reflection on me.

"Yeah, well, whatever he is."

"It doesn't make me the same as him, Drew. You can't help the family you're born into." I don't know why I care so much what this family thinks, but I do, and I don't want to be painted with the same brush as my dad. I'm not him or the business.

"Totally, I can see you're not like that. You were there to save her last night."

"Do one of you want to fill us in on what's going on here?" says Jim, looking confused.

"Dad, Jenna's ex-boyfriend is the kind of man who makes your blood curdle. And he's looking for her. I'm not sure how much trouble she's in if he finds her, and I don't want to find out, either," says Drew.

"What do you know about all this, Blake? Who is your dad?" Jim's steely gaze is on me, and I feel like I'm in his interrogation room now. He's turned serious. The smile from before is gone, now that he realises the severity of the situation.

I sigh. "Jim, do you know who Max Donovan is?"

"Yeah, I've heard the name thrown round the office. He's a big deal in Sydney. Owns some strip clubs, amongst other things."

"Yeah, well, he's my dad." Anne looks confused, but Jim knows who I'm talking about straight away.

"Your dad?" Jim's eyes widen in shock. I'm sure he's wondering how he ever let me take his daughter out or how I'll be the one building the villas on his property. God, he probably won't let me near this house after today.

"I'm not like him, Jim. That's why I left when I was 18. I wanted nothing to do with what he's about."

His eyes soften a bit. "All right, son. I can see you're a good person. What's this situation here then?"

"His mate is Vinnie Carver. He's the girl's boyfriend. I'm sure you have heard of him as well. Does that paint the picture?"

He nods. "Yeah, I'm with you, son. How can I help?"

"I don't know, but we ran into her at the club last night, when we were on the buck's night for Ash. Max and Vinnie were there looking for her. Drew got her out of there just in time, but she can't go back to work. It's not safe. They will find her. They think she may have seen something she shouldn't have."

Drew's eyes go wide. I can see he's somehow already attached to this girl, and he's scared for her. He has no idea how bad this could really be. He's lived a sheltered life, protected by his loving parents, but I know Jim gets it. Having been on the force for such a long time, he would have seen all sorts of things.

Drew says, "We need to make her see it's not a good idea to go back there. Find her a new job, somewhere she'll be safe. Do you know of anything, Mum?"

"I'll have a think. What work has she done in the past?" Anne asks.

"I'm glad you're all talking about my situation while I'm out of the room," Jenna says, stepping onto the deck. "I don't need your help. I'm fine on my own." She looks pissed off. I can tell she's a tough cookie, but that won't help her if Vinnie gets hold of her.

Drew jumps up and goes straight to her. He takes her hand. "We just want to help. Blake says you're in real trouble if they find you, Jenna. Please, let us help you."

"What kind of work have you done in the past, love?" Anne asks kindly, patting the seat next to her for Jenna to come and join us. She looks over at us, unsure what to do.

"It's embarrassing, but I have only stripped. I'm good at dancing. It's all I've ever done. I didn't even finish high school. I needed the money, so I had to work."

"I see. That's okay, we don't have to be defined by our past. You have us to help you now. Let's reinvent you. What are you into, love? What have you dreamed of doing if you could do anything?" asks Anne.

"Don't think I could do the job of my dreams. I know that's not possible for a high school dropout," says Jenna, looking deflated.

"Yeah, but if you could, what would it be?" asks Drew.

"I love reading and how you can escape into a completely different world from your own. I never had any money to buy books when I was growing up, so I would spend all my time in the library of whatever town I was in. Books were my escape."

"A librarian, hey, that I might actually be able to do," Anne says. "Leave it with me, I'll make some calls." She leaves the room.

"You can't go back to the club, Jenna, do you understand? If you need money, I can give you money to get by until we find you a job. Max and Vinnie talked to the owner last night, and she knows they're looking for you. Do they have your address at the club?" I ask.

"No, I never gave them any details of who I am. Vinnie doesn't even know my real name. I knew he was into some shady stuff, so I gave him a fake name. He knows me as Cassie."

"Good, that will help now. Has the place where you're living got good security?"

She shrugs. "Yeah, I guess, it's an apartment. You have to have a key or be buzzed in to get in there."

"Okay, that's good."

Anne walks back onto the deck. "Okay, good news, love. Luckily for you, the town library is looking for someone for the front counter. It's more of a reception type job to start with, but there's a chance for you to do some study and complete a degree in information, to become a full librarian. If you're interested, I've set you up with an interview for Monday."

"How on earth did you pull that, Mum?" asks Drew.

"I know everyone in this town. Just made a few calls." Anne smiles, proud of herself.

"Thank you, Anne, that sounds amazing. But I don't even have a resume or any skills, I can't even really use a computer."

"They're happy to train you up, love, don't worry about all of that. They just want to meet you, that's all."

"Good, that sounds much better," I say, feeling hopeful we might be able to turn this girl's life around.

"Jim, can you let Theo know Vinnie's hanging around town?" I ask. "See if they can keep an eye out." Theo is Elly and Drew's older brother and one of the cops in this town. He's probably the best person to talk to about this situation and to keep an eye out, but I don't know him all that well, so it's probably best coming from his dad.

"No worries, son. I'll talk to him today."

"I've got to go, but Jenna, if you need me for anything, or if Vinnie turns up, call this number." I hand her my business card. "You might want to think of a new look as well, something that will fit in more with the locals."

"Yeah, I was thinking that. Thank you, Blake. I'm not sure why you're helping me, but thank you." She offers a small smile.

"See you later, Blake, thanks," says Drew. He looks completely overwhelmed with the situation. I guess most people would be, but I grew up on edge, waiting for the next problem to happen.

I go to leave then turn back around. "Drew, maybe don't mention any of this to your sister."

"You don't want Indie to find out?" he asks with a smirk.

"Is it that obvious?"

"Don't worry, I won't say anything to either of them," he says.

Indie and I might not be on speaking terms after what happened last Sunday morning, but on the off chance she isn't back with her ex, I don't want her finding out about my past through some second-hand story from one of the twins.

Indie

Just like I thought, today I feel so much better after a good night's sleep. I've been for an early morning swim at the beach, and the heaviness of last night is gone. I'm surprisingly okay with the thought that it's completely over with Hayden. That phase of my life, it's done. Now I can move on properly with the closure I need.

Elly and I move in together tomorrow, and I have so much to do before then. I have the day off from the café to pack, and in typical Indie fashion, I've left everything to the last minute. I haven't even started. Elly dropped some boxes off to me earlier this week. She's probably already got it all sorted, knowing how organised she is.

I look around my room. I don't know where to start. I have a lot of stuff. I've been living here for nearly five years. It's amazing what you accumulate in that time. Luckily, most of my art is being displayed in the townhouses already, so I don't have to move all of that as well. I'll start with my clothes, then the kitchen.

THE BOXES ARE LINED UP THROUGH THE LIVING ROOM, and three hours of packing later, there's just my knick-knacks to go. As I go to grab one of the ceramic vases from my dressing table, I knock over the photo of Mama that was sitting behind the vase, and it falls to the floor, smashing. Damn it! I loved that frame. It was one she gave me the week that she passed away. It's a photo of her when I was five. I'm sitting on her lap and she's laughing. We're at a party with Mama's best friend and her husband. They're both in the picture as well. Everyone is happy.

We spent a lot of time with Auntie Susan and her husband. She wasn't my real aunt, just Mama's best friend, and I'm not sure of his name. I always just called him Dr Lennox because he was our family doctor as well when I was growing up. They always threw these big, elaborate parties, inviting half the adults in town. They didn't have any kids of their own, so I would mostly sit with the adults, listening to their conversations while I pretended to play with my dolls. I was fascinated by the adults, their beautiful clothes and jewellery, but mostly how complicated they were. Auntie Susan always knew what was going on around town, she loved to gossip. I guess that's what you get being married to the town doctor.

I pick up the broken frame. It's bent out of shape and all the glass has fallen out, so I go to the kitchen for the dustpan to sweep up the glass. I pull the photo out of the frame. I want to keep this as a memory of a special time when things were so much simpler than they are now.

My mama was so beautiful, with her long, dark, wavy hair and green eyes. People used to say I looked exactly like her. I guess I can see the resemblance, but she was different from me. She radiated this happiness and could brighten up any room just by being there. I wish she were here. I need her today. I touch the image of her face, trying to remember what it was like to have her here, and as I do, I feel there's something written on the back. I turn the photo over and there's a note scribbled in Mama's handwriting. *Indie 5 with Auntie Sus, Mum & Dad.*

I read it again, trying to make sense of what it says. That's a bit confusing. She must have written it wrong. Why would it say mum and dad? Dr Lennox is Susan's husband, not my dad who knocked Mama up and didn't want anything to do with us. I don't get it.

My heart starts to beat a little faster as I scramble for the box with the other frames she gave me that same week. My hands are shaking as I lay them on my bed. I open them one by one and look on the back. They all have handwritten notes. Dr Lennox is in quite a few. I knew they were good friends, but until this moment, I didn't even realise how many photos I had with him and Mama together. The first one says: "Indie's first birthday with Mum and Dad." The next: "Indie 2 at the zoo with Mum, Dad, and Auntie Sus". What the actual fuck? I don't understand. Why has she labelled Dr Lennox as my dad?

I sit on the edge of my bed and look at the photo of us again. If he is my dad, why would she hide it from me my whole life and... does he know? Does Auntie Susan know? Why didn't she tell me? What if I never looked at the back of these photos? Could Dr Lennox be my dad? I have so many questions. Maybe I don't even want to know. If he is, I've gone my whole life not knowing, what difference would it make? I don't need a dad now, I needed one when I was a little kid. And if he knew, how could he just stand by and watch and not want to be a part of my life?

My hands are still trembling, and I shake them to stop it, but it's no good. I check my watch. I have half an hour before I need to meet Elly at her place, to walk to Fraser's rugby game.

I put all the photos and frames back in the box and tape it up. I want to unsee what I've seen. Why did that photo frame have to smash today? I don't want to have this shit playing through my mind. There are too many questions, and the one person I want to get the answers from is dead.

I grab my jacket and purse and slip into my ballet flats. I run out of the apartment as fast as I can, a shiver running down my spine at the thought of what all this means.

CHAPTER TEN

INDIE

Elly and I were having fun playing pool with some guys we met at our local pub. We actually kind of already knew the guys from the coffee shop, since they come in all the time. We *were* having fun... but that was until Fraser got jealous and made another scene—he has a habit of doing that—and dragged Elly out the front to talk. Now the two guys, Tristan and Luca, just look uncomfortable, and Blake looks kind of pissed off too, though I don't know why. Well, maybe I do.

"Thanks for the game. It was fun till Elly's macho boyfriend ruined it. See you at the coffee shop on Monday, Indie."

"See you, boys. Sorry about Fraser." They leave via the front door to the pub, and I turn, pool cue still in my hand, back to Blake, who is glaring at me.

"What?" I ask him, trying not to turn this into a big deal like Fraser has.

"Nothing," he says, his face softening a bit. It's obvious he is pissed we were playing pool with the guys from the coffee shop, but he has no leg to stand on. He hasn't made contact since Hayden rocked up to my place last week, and the only communication we have had was today at Fraser's rugby game Elly dragged me along to, and it wasn't more than a few words. It is awkward as fuck between us, and I'm not quite sure how to fix it.

He looks me over, studying me. I do the same, my eyes not leaving him for a second. He might stand a foot taller than me, but I'm not intimidated by him, and two can play at this game. He wants to fuck me with his eyes, then game on, baby.

"Don't like rugby much, Pix? You looked bored as hell during the game this afternoon."

We spent the afternoon watching Fraser's rugby match, and Elly caught Fraser flirting with some trashy girl on the sidelines, which was why Elly was trying to make him jealous with Tristan, a customer from the café. I played along with it, quite happy to make Blake a little jealous as well. "Nope, I'm not into sports, I could have done with the extra time to pack up my place."

"That's right, you're moving tomorrow."

"Yeah, and surprise, surprise, I'm not ready." I sigh at the thought of having to return to my apartment tonight after what I found out this afternoon.

"Pool?" he asks, lining up the balls as if he already knows the answer.

"Sure, why not," I say, offering a small smile. I have no idea what to say to him. Flirting with our eyes is easier than actual words when it comes to Blake.

He breaks, sinking two of the solids. "Looks like you're stripes, babe."

I glare at him for using his annoying nick name for me. I take my cue and step up to take my shot. I'm terrible at pool, but it's helping to ease the tension, so here goes nothing. I somehow sink a ball. "Woohoo." I'm not a total unco in front of him. I take my next shot but miss. "Well, at least I got one. Might be the only one. It's probably not going to be a very good game for you, sorry."

He smiles and takes his next shot, sinking three more balls in a row.

"Whoa, you're really good. I should just give up now," I moan.

"It's just practise, spent a lot of time playing when I was younger. We used to have a table in the restaurant I worked in. You don't have to give up. I can help you, if you want?" he offers, with that sexy-as-fuck smile. Considering I haven't seen or heard from him all week, he is very flirty tonight. And after the serious, future-changing night I had with Hayden last night, and the photos I found today, it's a wonderful and well-needed distraction.

Blake always offers a pleasant distraction. This man is as hot as hell and so much fun. A thrill of excitement runs through me. I have never had such an attraction to another person, and the electricity buzzing between us feels so powerful, I'm sure the rest of the place must be able to see it.

"Okay, what should I do now?" I say, batting my eyelashes, playing along, all hopeless.

"For starters, you're holding it wrong."

I look down at my hand, confused. This is how I've always held the cue. Maybe that's why I'm not very good. He walks up behind me, wrapping his large muscular arms around mine. He takes the cue and places his hand over mine, slowly moving my hand just slightly, so I'm holding it correctly.

Being this close to him like this does things to me. His smell consumes me. He brushes my hair behind my ear so he can see over my shoulder better. The contact with him has my body alive, standing to attention and tingling all over for him.

"Now what? Which one should I aim for?" I whisper. His face is so close to mine.

"Okay, we're aiming for the green ball over there. I'll help you. Get down a little lower to the table." I move lower, and he helps me line it up, his arms still wrapped around me. "There, that should be perfect." He steps back from me, letting me take the shot.

I shoot, and the green ball sinks into the pocket. "Yes!" I jump back and can't help but do a little happy dance. "What should I go for now?"

"Hmm, let's try the red."

Just as we're about to take the shot, Elly and Fraser walk back in through the pub, his arms wrapped protectively around her. We quickly pull apart from each other. "Looks like the love birds have made up," I whisper to him.

"For now." He laughs.

With the four of us, we start up a new game, and this time, it's a bit more competitive. Loser has to do a nudie swim down at the beach. In summer this wouldn't be a big deal, but it's winter and it's pretty cold in there. I should know, I swim most mornings. I'm not worried, though. My pool skills might be less than impressive, but with Blake as my partner, he well and truly makes up for what I lack. As I suspect, Elly and Fraser lose in spectacular fashion, after three games, with Elly missing the final shot, tripping over herself and falling to the floor.

So, now, they are currently in the freezing water having a little swim while Blake and I sit on the sand. I'm dying to talk to him now, tell him how much I missed seeing him this week, tell him what happened with Hayden. Where do I even begin?

"Blake, I'm sorry about what happened the other morning. That was weird how Hayden just showed up. I had no idea he was even in the country. I hadn't seen or spoken to him since the night he left." I glance over to him. I want to see his reaction. He looks back to me, frowning.

"Yeah, it was weird. Bet that conversation was uncomfortable. What's going on with you and him, anyway? Are you guys back together?"

"Would I be sitting here on the beach with you if we were?" I say with a crooked smile. He has to know I wasn't going to get back with Hayden. Can't he see how into him I am?

"I don't know. That's why I'm checking. I thought that might have been why he was back, to get back together," he says, looking down. He normally has so much confidence, but this has him rattled. He's worried I would go back to my ex over pursuing something with him.

"It was... he proposed last night!" I watch Blake's face, waiting to see his reaction.

He slowly lifts his head. His eyes go wide. He wasn't expecting me to say that. "What did you say?"

"Do you see a ring?" I hold up my hand, showing my empty finger.

"I guess not. Are you okay?"

I shrug. "Didn't think you cared, since we're not anything anyway." I raise my eyebrow. I'm kind of being a smart-arse, but he did say it, and it stung. Now I want to know where I stand.

"I'm sorry, that was harsh. I was pissed the other morning. I shouldn't have said that. You know that's not how I really feel."

"How do you really feel then?" Now it's my turn to avoid his gaze. I'm drawing circles in the sand with my finger, trying not to look at him. This feels a little too intense, and he's so fucking hot tonight in that white shirt. If I make eye contact with him, I'm probably going to launch myself at him—right here on the beach—but we need to have this conversation first. I need to know where I stand before I get any further invested in him.

His finger comes to my chin, raising my face so I'm looking at him. "Like I want to spend more time with you, see where this goes. I like you, Indie. We always have fun together."

He's so handsome, and this close up, it's hard to concentrate. "Yeah, we do." I'm lost in his big brown eyes, willing him to kiss me. I want to feel his lips on mine, but I'm not making the first move.

"Why did you turn him down? Your ex. I thought he was the love of your life." He looks confused.

"So did I, when he was all I knew. But he wasn't. I know that now. He kept asking me what I want to do with my life, what my plans for the future are, and honestly, I couldn't see myself spending the rest of my life with him. So much has changed since he left. I've changed."

I take a deep breath. How do I tell him how I feel without sounding too clingy or over the top? "I just kept thinking about... you," I whisper, looking back at him. Why did I just say that? The way he's looking at me now, this is too intense. I can't stand it. I don't know what to do. If he would just kiss me, the tension will disappear, but he keeps gazing into my eyes like he is trying to see into my soul. I pull away from him and hop up quickly, not thinking, just knowing I can't stay here with him staring at me like that. I strip off my clothes.

"What are you doing? We won. We don't have to do the

swim." He looks at me, puzzled by my behaviour, but it's unexplainable. I don't even know what I'm doing.

"I feel like a swim." I shrug, then turn to run for the water. Water, please numb my brain so I don't say anything else stupid.

"Great, now I'm going to have to come in or look like a complete pussy," Blake calls as I run off.

"Probably." I giggle as I run through the water. It's fucking freezing but also kind of refreshing. I love the ocean. It's my calm place. From a young age, my mother and I would come for an early morning swim. It's the best way to start the day.

Blake has followed my lead and stripped off. Fuck, he's so hot, his ripped body on full display in the moonlight. He must do a crazy amount of exercise to look that good. I kick up my foot, splashing him as he tentatively walks through the water to where I stand. "Quit it, it's freezing!" he yells, unimpressed to be here.

"You don't have to come in if it's too cold for you," I tease him, splashing him again.

"What? And never hear the end of it from Fraser." He scoops me up in his arms. His body feels warm and strong and, God, I want him.

"Come on, you're cold. Let's go do something warm," he pleads. He's right, my body is covered in goosebumps.

"You're cold, pussy," I tease.

"Yeah, I'm fucking freezing. You're crazy."

"You've finally worked me out."

I look up at his handsome face, my free hand playing with his hair. I can't wait another second. If he's not going to kiss me, I'll kiss him. I reach up and place my lips on his, kissing his delicious mouth. He pulls me into him closer, kissing me back with force, his tongue swiping through my open mouth.

"Come on, I'm taking you home for a hot shower," he says with a glint in his eye.

"Okay, as long as I can get a kebab on the way home; drinking makes me hungry."

"Deal."

He puts me down when we reach the sand. We practically run back up the beach to where we left our clothes. I scoop mine up, dressing as fast as I can to get out of the chill of the cool night air. I'm glad I brought my jacket tonight; I chuck it on over the top and am instantly much more comfortable. Blake is dressed just as quickly, and we walk to Elly and Fraser, huddled together already dressed. Fraser has his arms wrapped around a freezing Elly whose teeth are chattering like crazy.

"We're going to get a kebab on the walk home. You guys in?" I ask.

Fraser looks down to Elly and shakes his head. "I'm going to take Elly home. She's freezing. We'll see you guys in the morning."

"Okay, see you then." We wave them off.

"Looks like it's just the two of us then," I say, bumping arms with Blake.

"Just the way I like it, baby." He smiles, pulling me into his body again.

WE STROLL BACK TOWARDS THE MAIN PART OF TOWN, picking up a kebab on our way back to my place. It's not a long walk, but I'm glad I'm wearing my jacket now. Luckily the night air isn't freezing like it could be for this time of year.

"Kebabs were a good decision," says Blake, unwrapping his food and taking a massive bite.

"Definitely," I mumble around a mouthful. We walk in silence for a bit. I'm looking forward to a warm shower and getting into some dry clothes, but it was so worth it. "I feel like all I do around you is get naked and pig out on junk food." I laugh.

His face breaks into a broad smile. "What's the problem with that? Two of my favourite things: naked Indie and junk food."

I roll my eyes at him and take another bite of the greasy wrap, the sauce running down my chin.

"There's no way you eat junk food on the regular with a body like yours. It's ridiculous," I say.

He shrugs. "I do, but I have a fast metabolism. I just work it off. I like to exercise. It's the way I unwind."

"Fair enough. I swim. What do you need to unwind from anyway? You have a pretty awesome life. I can't imagine building would be all that stressful."

"Sometimes things aren't as simple as they seem, Indie. And my body's not ridiculous," he whines. *Aren't as simple as they seem*. I wonder what he's talking about.

"It kind of is. I've never seen anybody with a body like yours. Not up close, anyway." He rolls his eyes at me, and I laugh at his dramatics. We arrive at my apartment building and stop out the front, both of us a little unsure of what to do next. "If you're going to stay tonight, you can't keep me up all night with your sexy shenanigans. We're moving tomorrow, remember?"

He tries to laugh but chokes on his food.

"Sorry, you okay?" I laugh back.

"Yes, I just haven't heard someone say *sexy shenanigans* before. Where do you come up with this stuff?"

I open the door and let us in. We start the walk up the stairs.

"I don't know. You know what I mean, though," I say, bumping his arm. "Besides, we don't have time, I still haven't finished packing."

He looks over at me, unimpressed. Think I just destroyed his plans for tonight. "What! Are you serious? You're as bad as Fraser, you're both so bloody unorganised. I have to babysit him on the regular, just to make sure things get done."

"I'm lucky big, strong babysitter, Blake, is here to help me then," I scoff.

"Hmm. What would you lot do without me? Didn't they teach any life skills at Byron Bay High?" he grumbles. He definitely had other plans for tonight. Whoops, sorry, Blakie boy.

"Well, I did try and be organised. I had today off work, but as I was packing, I found something kind of shocking. And I had to get out of the apartment; it was all too much. So, I didn't get it all done. I'm definitely not as bad as Fraser," I snap back at him. Comparing me to Fraser! I'm not *that* bad.

He looks over at me, concerned. "What did you find that was so shocking?"

"I think I found out who my dad is!"

"What? How do you find that out while you're packing your apartment up?" His eyes go wide, and I can see the concern on his face.

I put the key in the lock and let us into my apartment.

"I'll show you. You tell me what you think." I walk through the apartment to my bedroom where the box is. I almost expect to open the box and find it was just my mind playing tricks on me, the words not really there, purely a figment of my imagination. But I open the box and take out the photos, lining them up on my bed, back sides up, and they all very clearly say "Indie, Mum, and Dad" in some form. "See?"

BLAKE

Wow, Indie's right. I turn one of the photos over to see who he is. "Who is this guy, Indie? Do you remember?" Her head is down, studying the photos placed on the bed in front of her.

"Dr Lennox. He was one of my mother's friends. I used to call his wife Auntie Susan because she and Mama were best friends. They were super close and had been for years before I was born. We spent most weekends at their place when I was younger. I don't get it, hey?"

"And your mum never said anything about him being your dad?"

She shakes her head. "No. Never even hinted at it. I can't even think of his first name. I always just called him Dr Lennox. He was my doctor as a kid, and Mum worked for him for years as his receptionist."

"Sounds like she might have been more than his receptionist."

"Well, clearly!" she snaps at me. "She always said my dad was a one-night stand, and when she told him she was pregnant, he didn't want anything to do with her or the baby. But, if this is true, and he is my dad, I grew up knowing him, so why didn't he want me?" She throws the photo pack onto her bed. This is a lot for her to take in.

"Oh, Indie, baby." I wrap my arms around her, kissing her hair. "I'm sure it's not that he didn't want you. It sounds like this was a very complicated love triangle or something. Can you see the way they're looking at each other? If you didn't know better, you'd say they were in love."

"What sucks the most is, I can't talk to her about any of this. Why didn't she tell me while she was alive so I could ask her? So she could've explained. It's not fair," she cries, her words crackling out as a tear runs down her face.

"Don't worry, baby, I'm here. We'll work this out together." I pull her in closer, hoping this will help to take away her pain slightly. I wish I knew how to help her, but this situation is fucked up. We sit in silence for a bit.

"Thank you," she whispers, looking up at me. I cup her face in my hands and bring her in for a kiss, her lips salty from her tears.

"What was she like, Indie? I'll never get to meet her. Tell me about your mum?"

We sit on the side of the bed, and Indie looks down at one of the photos of her mum and her, then hands it to me with a small smile.

"Most people say I look just like her. She was so much more beautiful than me, though. She wore her hair long, all the way down her back. She was warm and a kinda free spirit, a hippie type. She was creative like me, but she never really got to explore her creative side. She needed to pay the bills, so she had to work in a job that she didn't really love. That's why she made sure I went to uni and studied whatever I wanted. She wanted me to have a better life, have options she didn't. She would've loved the opportunity to do something like that, but it was never to be for her; Nana just couldn't afford it. I always wondered how Mama managed it. But I guess, knowing my dad is Dr Lennox, he might have had a hand in that. I miss her so much. This world just isn't the same without her in it."

"She sounds like an amazing woman, just like someone else I know." I take her hand and pull her towards me, kissing her lips, softly and sweetly. Then pull her up to standing. "We better pack now before we get distracted." I pat her on the arse.

"Oh, it was just getting good," she complains.

"Well, if you had been a good girl and got all your work done today, we could've played now. But you didn't, so looks like you'll just have to wait. Let's get you in a warm shower then pack this place up."

CHAPTER ELEVEN

BLAKE

Indie's organising some breakfast for us, and I'm having a quick shower, before we start loading my ute with some of the smaller items. We'll then head over to Elly's and meet up with the others. We finished packing sometime after 3am and collapsed together on the lounge. Not the most comfortable place to sleep when you're a man of my size, but we just didn't make it to the bedroom.

We woke as the sun was rising, surrounded by a fort of boxes. I tried to take away Indie's pain as we slowly fucked, holding her close as the sun came up and the room filled with light. It was so different to every other time we've been together. This felt like more than fuck-buddy sex; this was deep with emotion. When I looked into her beautiful, green eyes, I felt lost in her. Sad for her. I felt like I was looking into her soul. I have never felt this connected with another human being. I didn't want it to end; I wanted to stay buried deep inside her, connected this way forever.

She's sad and confused this morning, which is understandable. I've never seen her like this, she's normally so bouncy and full of life. As we packed last night, we talked about what she's going to do with the information about her father. It must be such a hard thing to discover. I can't imagine what it would be like, not knowing your dad your whole life, then suddenly working out he was a family friend. She said she might approach him about it one day, but for now, she's not ready. I get it, this guy stood by and watched her grow up. How could he not say anything if he knew, especially when her mother died and she was left all alone? It's so sad, she has no family at all.

I hop out of the shower and dry myself off. I know I'm falling for Indie. When she told me her ex was out of the picture, I couldn't have been happier. This isn't going to be easy to walk away from, when the time comes. And it will. This life is just temporary, while Dad lets me get away with it. But I know it won't last forever, and he's been calling a lot lately. He wants me back in the city with him and the other boys; it's only a matter of time. So, I guess as selfish as it is, I'll make the most of a normal life while I can. Even if it means it's going to break me when I have to walk away.

What's that saying? *It's better to have loved and lost than never to have loved at all*. Something like that, anyway.

"Something smells delicious," I say, walking out of the bedroom in just my jeans.

"Bacon and egg roll from the café. I know you like these." Indie smiles softly, looking me up and down. "But first, shirt. You can't come eat breakfast with me like that."

"Why not?" I protest.

"Because we don't have time for you and your shenanigans this morning, and that's where this is going if you don't cover up your ridiculous chest."

"Fine," I say, grabbing my shirt from last night. "We're going to need to stop off at my place and grab a change of clothes before we get to Elly's."

"No worries. Thanks to your awesome babysitting, everything is organised here for when the truck arrives."

"This is so good," I mumble around my mouthful. "You guys make the best food."

"It's just a bacon and egg roll, pretty standard."

"What's your boss doing without you this weekend?"

"She's hired a new girl for the weekends. She knows I can't work there as much anymore. I need to concentrate on the gallery. Think it's time to grow up a bit, make Mama proud of me."

I grab for her hand and rub my thumb back and forth over it. "I'm sure your mum would be proud of you, no matter what you do, Indie."

"You know what I mean. I know I'm unorganised and kind of just go with the flow, but I do want to make something of myself, and it's kinda inspiring watching you, Fraser, and Ash making a success of the business you've created. I want that. I'm just not as driven as you guys."

"I can help you, if you've made up your mind that you really want to make this work. It's possible, Indie, and I can help with whatever you need."

"Thank you." She smiles sweetly, kissing me on the forehead. She then pulls out of my hold and marches over to the pile of boxes at the front door, picking one up.

"Come on, Blake. We better get going."

"What do you want in the ute?" I ask, shoving the last bite of my breakfast in my mouth.

"Just what's over there." She points to the pile closest to the door, and we get to work loading my truck.

A FEW HOURS LATER, I HAVE HELPED INDIE AND ELLY move everything to the new place in Broken Point, with the help of Fraser and Drew. The boys were starving after all their hard work, so we are going for lunch at the local sushi place to regain the energy needed to unpack this afternoon. Elly and Fraser have stayed behind to unpack—or whatever else it was they just had to do that was more important than food.

I really like this town. It's not crazy busy with tourists like Byron, and it's still set on the beach, with a main street of cafés and shops. And there's a long boardwalk-type path along the shoreline. It has a nice vibe about it. I've spent a lot of time here over the last few months, working on the townhouses we built, and I could see myself settling down in a place like this one day. That would be the dream, anyway, if I didn't already have my life mapped out for me by my father.

We order and take our seats at a table by the window which looks out over the main street and across to the beach. I'm hoping to catch Drew for a few minutes to find out how Jenna is going.

"You okay, Pix?" Poor Indie looks exhausted. It's been a massive day, on top of everything she figured out yesterday about her dad.

"Yeah, just really tired. I can't wait till we're done so I can cuddle up in bed and sleep."

"I'll stick around and help you get it done," I offer. "It won't take too much longer."

"I bet you will," says Drew with his normal cheeky smirk.

"Always one thing on the mind with you, isn't it, Drew," Indie teases.

"What? I know I'm right about you two. It's so bloody obvious." He looks between us. Indie smirks, trying not to be noticeable, but she is totally giving it away.

"Don't know what you're talking about. I'm going to the ladies' while we wait for our food to arrive," she says, poking her tongue out at him, and he smirks back at her. At first, I thought there was something between the two of them, but I can see now that they have this playful brother-and-sister kind of friendship. I guess that comes from growing up so close with someone. This whole group is like that. I wish I'd had the same kind of friendships growing up. They don't know how lucky they all are that they have each other.

I turn to Drew. "Have you heard from Jenna since yesterday?" I ask. "I noticed you left the pub with her last night and she'd had a makeover."

"Yeah, she's stayed the last couple of nights. I think Mum sees her as a little project. She took Jenna shopping for some new clothes for her meeting at the library. And they got her hair done, no fake blonde anymore. She said her natural hair colour is a chestnut-brown colour, so she's gone back to that. God, you should see her in a pencil skirt, fuck, man."

"Drew, you're supposed to be helping her get back on her feet, not trying to get into her skirt. She's has a thug after her, remember? Not the type of one-night stand you want to take home."

"That's what I'm doing, I'm helping her. Plus, Jenna is no one-night stand. I can see why Vinnie was so crazy about finding her. She's sweet and caring and beautiful. She's the kind of girl you settle down with. Besides, there's no harm in looking, and she looks good as a librarian. That's all I'm saying, not that I'm going to do anything about it. Don't think she'll have any trouble getting the job."

"Don't go there, man. Sounds like you're already in love," I joke.

"I know, I know! I won't," he assures me as Indie returns, and we need to get off this subject before she catches on.

INDIE

I make my way back from the bathroom and stop to watch the boys. What are they talking about so seriously? I didn't even think they knew each other that well. Now they're all chummy. Very intriguing.

"You won't what?" I ask, butting into their conversation.

"He won't be a sleazy perve," Blake replies, giving Drew a look.

"Yeah, right, Drew. But don't worry, we wouldn't have you any other way. The stories you have from your—let's call them *overseas adventures*—are our entertainment." I laugh.

"Thanks, I guess," says Drew, looking a bit hurt. But I doubt he is. He loves the playboy life.

Our sushi cones arrive, and we dig in. I love these little cones, what a cute idea. The boys have gone all quiet, and I know it's not just because food has arrived. They were having some *deep and meaningful chat,* and they don't want me to know what it was about. Think again, boys. I will find out what's going on. I'm a master detective. I bet Drew got up to no good on Friday night at Ash's buck's party and is now in some sort of trouble and doesn't want Elly or Theo to find out. That would be just like him.

"So, how was Ash's buck's party? You boys get into any trouble?" I look at their faces, waiting for some sort of reaction.

Blake is as cool as a cucumber. "No, just a standard night out with the boys. Ash got hammered, ended up on a bus somehow heading to the Gold Coast, and called poor Chloe in the middle of her hen's party to come and save him. He was in deep shit."

"Oh, poor Chloe, that sucks. What a way to wreck her night. Ash sounds like hard work." I turn my attention to Drew. He can't keep a secret. I'm sure his face will give away anything they might be hiding. "What about you, Drew? What was that story you were telling last night about some bet?"

"Ahh, yeah, just picked up some chick. Fraser bet me a hundred bucks I couldn't get her to leave with me by the end of the night. Said she was out of my league. As if, bro. It was so easy." He laughs. "Every girl wants a bit of the big surf star." He winks at me.

"Oh yes, Drew, all the girls fall at your feet." I roll my eyes. Well, if they're lying, their poker faces are bloody good ones.

"Come on. We better get back up there and set up our apartment before I fall asleep," I say, and I'm serious. I'm so tired I can barely keep my eyes open.

We head back up to the apartment. Theo has arrived to help and is setting up the lounge room.

I head straight for my room as Drew and Theo get into some heated discussion about Drew being irresponsible. There is definitely something fishy going on with the boys in this group, and I intend to find out what.

I thought Blake would have followed me into my room, but he must have stayed to help the boys. Or sort out the argument.

AN HOUR LATER, I'VE SET UP MY BED, MADE IT, AND decorated my room. This place is feeling like home already. I love the light that comes in through the large window, and as the breeze comes in, the white chiffon curtains float around gracefully. Not much of a view from my room, but from the balcony, you can almost see the beach. It's the nicest place I have ever lived in. Elly is in love with it because it's *totally vintage*—her words—but she's right. It's got so much character with the dark timber floorboards.

I've hung one of my large artworks of navy-blue above my bed. The room is overfilled with different textures and colours. It's an eclectic mix of deep burgundy, pale pink, mustard, and blues in silks, velvets, and linens. Just the way I like it. I got the big room so there is even enough room for my burgundy velvet daybed. This place has such a good feeling about it, and I'm so ready for the change. My old place held too many memories. This is the fresh start I need.

I'm so tempted to just curl up in my bed and sleep, but I better not with all the helpers still here. So, I wander out into the living room to see how the boys are going. It's almost all done. These boys have worked hard. All the electronics are set up. Elly has clearly told them where to put everything, because the place looks like it's been styled by a... well, a stylist.

"Wow, guys, this place looks awesome," I say, a little surprised they got it all done.

"Yeah, we've done a good job! We're gonna head off now, though, Indie," says Drew.

"Sunday night family dinner," adds Theo.

"No worries. Thanks for all your help, guys, we owe you," says Elly.

"Yeah, thanks, guys. Next night out is on us."

Elly's brothers leave, and it's just the four of us. I feel like this is going to be a regular thing, and I could totally get used to it; the four of us hanging out in our awesome place by the beach.

Fraser and Blake have gone to get us pizza for dinner. I've been dying to talk to Elly about my big idea all day, and now's the time, while I'm too tired to overthink it.

"Hey, Elly."

"Yeah, Indie," she says, curled up on the lounge half asleep.

I go stand right in front of her. "Open your eyes. I've got an idea."

She reluctantly opens her eyes and sits up. "This sounds dangerous! What's the big idea?"

"Hear me out. You know how you've been trying to start up your own business and now we have this massive space, well, it's too big for just an art gallery, and there's an underground storage space too."

Elly smiles. I can see her brain ticking over.

"I'm thinking, why don't we join forces somehow, my art, your styling? We could start collecting some of our own special furnishings and styling pieces, which we can store downstairs, to go with what you can get from that hire place you use. If we join our experience and money together, it will be a lot easier to get it off the ground. You know, kind of like how the boys have. We can start small, with the jobs we can get from The Green Door boys, then we can set up a website so people can find us, and if we do it together, we will always have someone to bounce ideas off."

"Are you serious about this? You won't get sick of me? You know I'm a pain in the bum, and you're already living with me," she says, sitting up now, more awake.

"Yeah, of course I'm serious, otherwise I wouldn't be

saying it. We'll organise it so we have our roles and we're not on top of each other."

"Sounds like you've already given this a lot of thought. Why not, hey? This is a fantastic idea. I've been too scared to leap by myself, but if we do it together, we have each other." We jump up, hugging each other, as the boys walk back into the apartment with the pizza.

Blake puts the pizza boxes down on the dining room table. "What's going on? You two were half dead when we left, now you're jumping around smiling."

"We're starting a business together," we both say excitedly.

Fraser looks over to Blake with one eyebrow raised. "How long were we gone for?"

Elly grabs glasses from our kitchen and pours the wine. We toast to our exciting new home and workspace and the opportunity it brings. This is *our* year.

CHAPTER TWELVE

INDIE

I HANG THE LAST PAINTING, AND THE ART GALLERY IS finally all set up. This space is unbelievable. It's just how I always dreamed it would be. The walls are not as full as I would like them to be just yet, with a lot of my work displayed at the townhouses until the auction. But a friend of mine is an amazing potter, and we've set up some of her pieces down the centre of the room, on white pedestals, to help fill the space. Her work is so beautiful; collections of fat little jugs in bright colours, mustards, blues, and greens with geometric designs etched into the surfaces.

Some of Elton's black-and-white photos hang along the back wall in rustic timber frames. He was here yesterday, with his new girlfriend Mave, helping me set up. He's quite the photographer. Even though he has never been trained, he just has an eye for it. Mave is so lovely and really smart. She works in marketing. While she was here yesterday, she had so many ideas for us and what direction we should take the gallery and interior styling business.

We all decided an auction would be a good idea to get our name out into the community as the place to come for modern art and interior styling. Maybe it will be something we can do seasonally, four times a year or something, just to keep things moving and show off our new collections.

"Indie, I love these, they're so cute," says Elly, picking up one of the little jugs. "Do you think we can get your friend to custom make some for me? They would be perfect in the new show home project the boys have just given us."

"Totally. What colours do you think? I'll chat to her and see what she can do."

"I think this kind of pale blue and white. What do you think?"

"Yeah, that would be perfect." For now, I'm organising inventory, so we have enough to style all of the jobs we're taking on, and Elly is planning the designs, finding new clients, and telling me what we need more of. Then we both go and set up the spaces. It would be almost impossible to do alone. We've been lucky that Blake and Fraser have been able to help with the heavy lifting on some of the bigger jobs. It won't be this way forever, just while we get started, then we can hire someone to do our heavy lifting, and a junior stylist to help out.

The hardest part of a start-up is that funds are limited. We have big dreams for our designs, but for now we have to make do with what we can. So, for the larger items like lounges and stuff, we still have to go through a hire company. The one we're working with seems to be great so far. Blake and Fraser have offered to lend us money, to get it all happening faster, but that's not what we're about. We're two fiercely independent women, and we want to do this on our own. Even if only to prove to ourselves that we can.

Elly puts the little jug down and turns to look at the wall of black-and-white photos. "So, you're all good for organising the spring auction we talked about yesterday?" she asks.

"Yes, I think so. I'm so excited but also so scared. If it turns to shit, it's all on me." I give her my best scared face, and she giggles.

"It won't, babe, you're going to make this amazing. Your work speaks for itself, look at these paintings. I don't even know how you come up with the colour combinations, but they all look so perfect together. You're a true artist, Indie, and it's time the world gets to see your exquisite paintings."

"Thank you, Elly. I couldn't do this without your support." I smile over to my friend, so glad we ran into each other at the café that day. Otherwise we may never have reconnected, and I would still be doing the same old stuff.

"You could, but I'm glad we're doing this together. It's more fun this way. I feel like we're back in high school, hiding out in the art room, talking about our big dreams for the future. But this time, it's real."

"I know what you mean. It feels like my dreams are all coming true. This stuff just doesn't happen to me!"

"What dream is that?" Blake says from the doorway to the art gallery, hot as ever. "The one where the best-looking guy in town takes you out for the night?"

"So modest, Blake!" Elly teases. "What are you doing here in the middle of the afternoon? Shouldn't you be building something?" She excitedly goes to him and gives him a hug. They have become such good friends.

"Can't I just drop in and surprise you girls?" he says, wandering over to me.

"Well, I guess." He is looking over at me, his eyes hungry, and I know why he's here. It's been a few days since we've seen each other. We've been texting back and forth, and by the time I went to bed last night, the texts had escalated to X-rated. Blake is a very dirty man. I bet it took all he had not to come and see me earlier today. I know it took me a hell of a lot of restraint not to turn up at his place in the middle of the night. He's been trying to give me some space to get set up, and I've really missed him.

He stands in front of me, pushing some hair behind my ear, and kisses my cheek. My skin tingles where his lips touch me. I'm so turned on by this man; my entire body's on high alert when he's around.

"Oh, you two are just so cute. I knew you would be a perfect match for each other. Elly does it again." She smiles proudly over at us and high-fives herself.

I lose it laughing at her. "Did you just high-five yourself?"

"Yeah, it's called a self-five." She pulls a face at me.

"You're such a nerd, chickee."

"I'm not, all the cool kids are doing it," she whines.

Blake and I both laugh at her. Only Elly.

"Don't go getting yourself all excited, though, we're just friends."

She gives me a look. "Yeah, friends that go at it like crazy. These walls are paper thin. How dumb do you think I am?"

"Friends can have all sorts of relationships, Elly," Blake offers in my defence. We haven't said we're anything other than that, so having this conversation in front of her now isn't going to happen.

I shrug, giving her the same look back that she gave me, then I turn my attention back to Blake. "I'm actually here for two reasons," he says. "I've a little surprise for you both. A little something I whipped up in my spare time this week." He gets out his laptop and places it on the countertop. Opening up a tab, he types in a website: *brokenpointstylingandgallery*. That's our business name. What has he been up to? He hits enter and a beautifully designed webpage comes onto the screen.

"Blake, this is stunning," gasps Elly.

It looks like he's built us a website, and it's amazing. "Wow, you did all of this for us? Thank you. This is amazing. How did you do all of this without me knowing?" The site is in two parts. The first is the styling, outlining the options we provide, and the second is an online gallery of my art and everything that's currently in the real gallery. "When did you take all these photos?" I ask.

"I have my ways, girls. I wanted to surprise you. I know you didn't want to accept any money to get started, but this is my way of helping. I know this business is going to go really well for you girls, and now people have a place they can come to find you."

Elly squeals and hugs Blake. "You're the best, Blakie. What would we do without you?"

I turn to hug him as well. "Thank you. This is totally amazing." He wraps his arms around me and places a kiss on my lips, pulling me in tight to him. This is the first time we've kissed in front of someone else, and I know it's just Elly and she figured out already there's something going on, but it still feels like we're taking a big step.

"Oh my God, you guys get a room already," Elly complains, still flicking through the webpage. She's got a little smirk on her face, loving this. She thinks she's been the perfect little matchmaker.

"What's the second reason?" I whisper to him.

"What second reason?" he asks, a cheeky grin on his face.

"You said you had two reasons you came here today."

And I'm pretty sure I know what the second reason is, but I need to hear him say it.

"You." He picks me up and throws me over his shoulder, stalking out of the gallery and down the hall towards my room. I laugh and try and struggle down.

"What are you doing?" I laugh again.

"Sorry, Elly, this just can't wait," he calls over his shoulder to her.

"Too much information," she yells back. She mumbles something else under her breath, but I can't hear it.

Blake

"What are you doing? Put me down, Blake." Indie laughs and hits me playfully on the back.

I throw her down on her bed. It's very convenient, her art gallery being so close to her bedroom. She's so fucking cute in skinny jeans and tan knee-high boots with a baggy, cream knitted sweater that hangs loose across her shoulders, her lacy bra peeking out the top. But these clothes aren't going to last long, not with the way she got me all worked up last night. She's lucky I didn't turn up here in the middle of the night. I only didn't because I knew how tired she was. This week's been huge for her, working out who her dad was, moving, and setting up a business. And if I'd been here, we wouldn't have gotten any sleep.

I kiss her aggressively, swiping my tongue through her mouth. Her hands are in my hair and mine in hers. I can't get close enough to her. I've missed her, and this week my desire for her has just gotten stronger.

"So, last night you said you wanted me to fuck you from behind, hard, so you could really feel it. Feel my big, hard dick deep inside you. Were you just saying that to drive me nuts, Indie? Or is that what you want from me?" Her texts last night were so dirty and had me distracted all day with images popping into my head of what I was going to do to her.

Her eyes are extra intense today as she smiles up at me. "That's what I want. I want you to fuck me so hard, I cry out your name. In pleasure and pain."

"That was what I was hoping you would say. I haven't been able to stop picturing your naked arse in the palm of my hand, you hanging onto that blue velvet headboard, just like you described. It's been very hard to work today."

"Well, we need to fix this. Can't have you unable to work, can we?" She has a little smirk on her face as she slowly bites into her lip. Those delicious red lips drive me fucking crazy. It's only been a few days since I last saw her, but my body craves her when we're not together.

I reach down and unzip her boots, one by one, throwing them to the floor. I then crawl over her and undo the buckle on her jeans, sliding them down her legs, revealing a tiny, black lace G-string. I leave it on. Her new closet has a large mirrored sliding door, and I want her to watch this, so I lift her legs and reposition her body so she can see what I'm about to do to her. "Open your eyes, baby. Watch me in the mirror."

She looks at me and smiles playfully. She likes the sound of that just as much as me. And her eyes go to the mirror as I spread her legs, running my hands back up her thighs to the spot I'm craving. I bite her thigh, not hard, just enough for her to feel it. I follow it up with a kiss, then I bite the other thigh a bit further up this time, and do the same, following it up with a soft kiss. I pull her closer to the edge of the bed, and I run my finger over her pussy. She's so wet already. I circle my finger over her clit through the fabric of her panties. I continue to circle, building up the pace as I bite her again, this time closer up.

Her eyes roll back. "Keep watching," I demand. I pull the thin lace fabric to the side and run my tongue through her folds, tasting her sweet nectar. I lick and suck her, tasting her, teasing her, and she arches her back off the bed. But she keeps watching, her eyes wide, her cheeks flushed. She's fucking perfect like this, coming apart in my hands.

"That feels so good, don't stop." Her eyes close in pleasure as she tips her head back, enjoying everything I have for her.

"Keep watching, baby."

I reach under her sweater to her breast. She pulls the sweater over her head, revealing just a black lace bra. I cup her perfect breast in my hand. Her nipple is hard, and I rub my thumb back and forth over it as I continue devouring her. I circle my tongue around her clit, sucking then biting, just slightly. Her hands are in my hair. I continue at the same pace, my hands digging into her hips as she lifts her body to meet me. I continue to lick, suck, and nip at her, circling her clit and sucking hard.

She tugs at my hair. "Blake, fuck, don't stop, I'm going to..."

I feel her body contracting around me, and I eat her up, every last drop.

Her face is flushed, and she smiles shyly down at me. I shake my head up at her. "That was so hot, Indie, you have no idea."

"I think I do. You made me watch, remember?" she says, covering her eyes as if now embarrassed by what we just shared. I climb up the bed over her, removing her hands from her eyes and holding them over her head. She looks up at me.

"Do you even know how fucking perfect you are, Indie?" She shakes her head. "You're unbelievable. I can't believe how good this is with you."

"You have too many clothes on," she whispers. I let her escape my grip so she can reach for my shirt, tugging it over my head as I unbuckle my pants and slide them off. She unhooks her bra and goes to wiggle out of her G-string.

"Leave it on," I say.

"Okay." She looks up at me, confused.

"Bend over, hands on the headboard, like you said last night." She does as I say, and the sight is fucking amazing, her arse firm and toned and hot as ever in that lace G-string. She turns back to look at me, her eyes filled with desire.

I slap her on the arse.

"Ouch."

"You said you want it hot and hard, baby. Is that still true?"

"Yes, fuck, yes," she pants.

And I slap her again. "You look so fucking hot like this. Watch in the mirror again." She turns her head to the side to watch.

I pull her G-string to the side, dipping my finger into her wet pussy. I need her really ready for me. I'm not going to go easy on her today, and as much as she says she wants to be screaming my name in pleasure and pain, I don't want to hurt her. She moans as I push my fingers in and out, getting her ready.

"Condom in the side drawer." She can barely talk but she gets that out.

"You're so safety conscious. I'm not sleeping with anyone else, and I'm sure you're on the pill."

Her reflection glares back at me. "No fucking way, Blake. Condom now, or we're done!"

"Okay, okay." I go to the side table and pull out a condom, rolling it on. Then I'm back behind her, palming her arse and reaching up, cupping her breasts. I run my cock up and down her glistening pussy, teasing her. "Hold on, baby." I position my cock in place and push into her.

She grips the headboard, and I thrust into her again and again, harder and faster as the momentum builds. She pushes back, wanting more, and I give her everything she wants, over and over again. I have one hand on her hip and the other cupping her breast, rolling her nipple in my fingers. As I slam into her, I watch her in the mirror, and she watches me, our eyes connected.

"Fuck, so good. Harder, Blake," she cries.

"Are you sure?"

"Yes."

I move one hand to her waist, and with my other hand I grab a handful of her hair, as I ride her with fast, deep thrusts. I groan. This is so fucking hot. She is wild, and I can't get enough of her.

"Blake," she moans. Her cries of my name are driving me crazy.

She throws her head back, screaming my name, as her body constricts around me once again. "That's it, baby, make that tight pussy come all over my cock."

And, as she lets go, so do I, slamming into her hard one final time, before filling her up.

Our breathing is ragged as we try and calm down from the high. My heart is racing frantically. I move slowly, still inside her, not quite ready for our bodies to be separated. Then I hug her body to mine and lower to the bed, spooning her from behind.

I brush the hair away from her face and kiss down her neck. I don't think I could ever get enough of her.

"That wasn't the only reason I wanted to see you. I wanted to make sure you're okay after the week you've had," I whisper, still out of breath.

"Is that right?"

"Yeah, I mean, I've been thinking about this since your dirty texts last night, but I want to know you're okay too."

She lies still for a minute. "I'm all right. It's weird knowing who my dad is after all this time, but it's not like it changes anything really. I'm still the same person. It is what it is, I guess."

"That's true, but if you want to talk about it, I'm here, and if you ever decide you want to go and see him, I'll come with you to support you."

"Thank you. I might take you up on that offer. I don't think I could face him on my own. I don't even know what I'll say."

"You don't have to rush. Think about it for a while, and you'll know when you're ready."

She sits up, pulling on her clothes. "You want something to eat? I can order in."

"I think we should go out tonight. I want to take you to dinner."

"With Elly and Fraser?" She looks a bit confused, and I realise we've never been out with just the two of us. We either go out in a group or eat in.

"No. Just us," I say, grabbing her hand and lacing my fingers through hers. She looks me over, her eyes bright with excitement.

"Okay. That sounds nice."

"Where do you want to go?" I ask, kissing her again.

CHAPTER THIRTEEN

INDIE

It's Wednesday afternoon, and I arrive at the office space of The Green Door boys, to collect Fraser for our shopping expedition. It's a little favour he's asked of me because he wants to surprise Elly with the perfect dress, for the awards night this weekend. I haven't been to their office before. This place is nice, all dark timber and leather, just like their house.

I wonder if Blake is in his office today or on site? I didn't tell him I was coming here, but I'm hoping I might bump into him. Fraser and Blake have invited Elly and me to join them at the awards ceremony that's on this weekend. Fraser's promising a weekend away, all expenses paid, so why not? I could do with a weekend away, and this place we'll be staying looks fancy. I'm mostly excited for the opportunity to meet someone who could aid my business, and Blake assures me that there will be plenty of people I should rub shoulders with.

I walk through the big, double mahogany doors to a large foyer. The floor is a shiny timber, and I walk carefully so as not to slip. Knowing my luck, I will, and Blake will be there to witness it again. Strange, there is a reception desk but no receptionist. On the other side of the foyer there's a brown leather lounge and a couple of large plants. I decide to take a seat and message Fraser that I'm here. I don't want to go snooping around the office looking for him. I send the message and wait. A text bounces back from Fraser, telling me he'll be five minutes. I sit on my phone, scrolling while I wait.

The front doors push open, and there he is, Blake. My heart almost skips a beat at the sight of him in his work boots. I have no idea why, but it does things to me. Who would have thought I have a builder fetish?

"This is a pleasant surprise. What are you doing here, Indie?"

I stand up awkwardly, not knowing how to greet him in his workplace. He walks straight to me, wrapping his arms around me, and pulling me in for a kiss. "I'm just waiting for Fraser. I'm taking him shopping for a dress for Elly."

Blake looks a bit disappointed that I'm not here to see him. "Oh, that's a bit cute, Fraser dress shopping. You should definitely take some photos. I doubt that guy has ever stepped foot in a dress shop before."

"What, unlike you, hanging around in dress shops all the time?" says Fraser, walking into the foyer.

"Haha, yeah, I hang out in dress shops." Blake turns his attention to me. "You picking out something for yourself for this weekend? Maybe I should come and help." As he says it, he runs his fingers up and down my arm, and it sends a scattering of goosebumps in their trail.

"We don't need your help, Blake," I say. "We only have this afternoon to get this done, and you would be distracting. Plus, don't you have some work to do? I'll come round and see you tonight."

"I could be very helpful." He brushes some hair away from my face, cupping my chin.

"You're already distracting."

"Come on, Indie," calls Fraser, making his way to the door. "We need to go, times a wasting, and I'm not standing around watching you two flirt all day."

"Coming," I call back, my eyes still on Blake. He's not happy about me leaving here with Fraser. I can tell. His eyes are still on mine, pleading with me silently.

"Fine, I'll see you later, baby. Behave, Fraser," Blake calls to him, then pulls me back in, kissing me possessively. Kinda feels like he's making it clear to Fraser that I'm with him, even though there's nothing official. I catch up with Fraser, and we walk through the front doors. I turn back to wave. Blake's still standing there, watching us.

He knows he has nothing to worry about. Fraser and Elly are crazy about each other, and he knows I'm into him. I don't see Fraser that way, I never have.

"You have Blake wrapped around your little finger," says Fraser as we hop into his expensive-looking car.

"I do not, don't be silly."

Fraser looks over to me. "I have never seen him like this, Indie."

"Not even with his ex, Lexi?"

He shakes his head. "No way. They had some weird fucked-up relationship. He's really into you. He'll be in his office now, sulking because you wouldn't let him come."

"Really, I think you see a completely different side to him than what I see. He seems so put together when he's with me."

Fraser takes off in the car, screaming round the corner,

and I have to hang on so I don't go flying. "Probably, we have known each other for a while now. I know him pretty well."

"Tell me something, Fraser. What happened on that buck's night?" He glances over to me, then glues his eyes back on the road as he takes the next corner way faster than he should. "What do you mean?"

"I know something happened. You boys have been all secretive about it, and Blake and Drew are all chummy now. What's the go?"

"No idea. You should ask Blake if you're worried." He keeps his eyes on the road, not giving anything away. Damn, something totally happened that night. I wonder what it was.

"Hmm, you boys all stick together. I know something's going on, and I will get to the bottom of it."

We pull up to the boutique in some sort of record time. Fraser drives like a hoon. I'm lucky to still be alive. This is the only dress shop in town, and I'm praying we can find what we're looking for here for this weekend's awards ceremony. We make our way into the boutique. It's not a massive store, but unless we want to go to Sydney or the Gold Coast, this is the best we are going to get here. There are dresses in all sorts of fabrics in every shade you can imagine. Fraser looks instantly overwhelmed. It's a pretty funny sight, a guy like him in a dress shop.

"What style are you thinking?" I ask.

"I dunno. Something sexy."

I roll my eyes at him dramatically. "You want me to pick out something sexy for my friend?"

"You know what I mean, Indie. I think something in a deep red, you know, like that lipstick she wears sometimes." I look at Fraser. I'm surprised he pays that much attention.

"Okay, red." I get to work looking through the racks,

holding up dresses to show him as he walks around, looking confused. "What about this one?"

He shakes his head. "I'll know it when I see it."

I pull out a few more, and he scrunches up his nose. This is going to be harder than I thought. As I search through the rack of long gowns, I come across a stunning black lace number, and it's in a six, my size. It will probably be miles too long for me because I'm such a short-arse, but I'll try it before I leave, just in case. The shop assistant finally spots us and makes her way over to where we're standing flicking through the racks.

"Can I help you with anything?" She smiles. She's a well-dressed lady, probably in her 50s. She's wearing a cream blouse and navy, fitted skirt with her hair up in a French twist. She looks a little stuck-up and unimpressed that we're in her shop disturbing her. You'd think she would be happy to have the business, but maybe we're not her usual type of customer.

"Yes, please. I want to try this on, and we're looking for something in a deep red for my friend. It's for this weekend so we don't have a lot of time."

Fraser has given up and sits on the lounge looking bored. She looks over to where he sits, studying him. "Don't think I have anything in his size, love."

"Not him." I laugh. "It's for his girlfriend. She's an eight. I'm thinking long. It's for a fancy awards ceremony."

"Hmm, you know what? I think I have just the gown. We had a new shipment today so it's still out the back. Wait here, I'll be back in a sec." She rushes off, returning quickly with a red gown draped over her arm.

She holds it up and the silk fabric drops to the floor. It's slinky and in a wine-red colour, with a plunging neckline. "That's the one. Thanks."

"It's very expensive," she says.

"That's okay. He's paying for it; he can afford it. Fraser, we have the dress," I call out to him.

He makes his way over and a smile crosses his face. "That's perfect."

"Yeah, it is. Fix up the payment while I try on my dress."

I head into the fitting room. I hate trying on clothes. It's so hard to find a good fit when you're my size. Most things are too long, and I have to get them taken up. This dress is amazing, it's so glamorous. It will be a miracle if it actually fits me.

I pull the dress off the hanger and slip it on. I can't do the zipper up by myself, so I leave it undone and stand back. Wow, this is next-level, and the length actually fits me perfectly.

"Do you need a hand in there, with the zipper?" asks the shop assistant.

"Yes, please," I reply through the curtain.

She pushes the curtain aside and zips up the dress. "Come out and have a look in the big mirror."

"Oh no. That's okay. I can see here."

"Come on, Indie," Fraser calls, "I want to see. It'll give me something to tease Blake with."

I walk out into the open room and stand back, looking in the mirror. I look stunning. The fabric hugs tight in all the right places, pushing my small but perky boobs up a bit higher. The split runs up my left leg, almost too high. It's the perfect combination between classy and sexy. This dress will drive Blake nuts. It's perfect.

"Wow, Indie, you look amazing. You should definitely get that one. Blake's going to jizz in his pants when he sees you."

The shop assistant gives him a filthy look, and I can't

help but let out a little giggle. "Fraser," I say, embarrassed. He's right, though, Blake will love it. I don't even look at the price. "I'll take it, thank you," I say to the lady.

The shop assistant wraps up the dresses, and we pay. I'm so excited for this weekend.

CHAPTER FOURTEEN

INDIE

Today has been incredible. We all arrived together at our hotel, the Palazzo Versace, on the Gold Coast. The boys took off shortly after, to watch some game or something, and I've spent the afternoon with Elly, being pampered at the day spa. We've had a massage and our hair and nails done. The boys planned it for us and have paid for it as part of our weekend away. It's a little bit sweet that they've thought this all through so much. Apparently, they have big plans for us tomorrow as well. I can't wait. It's been a long time since I've had any time away.

I now sit on a table with Ash, his fiancée Chloe, Fraser, Elly, and Blake. I'm enjoying the most decadent food I have ever consumed, drinking the most expensive champagne out of the finest crystal, in the fanciest ballroom I have ever set foot in. Who am I kidding? I have never even been in a ballroom before, and this room is amazing. I'm sure it must be the fanciest around. Massive chandeliers hang from the ceiling, and the tables are dressed with an abundance of flowers, together with candles in purples and burgundies. It's so over the top.

I've been feeling slightly awkward and out of place since we walked in. I'm just not like these other fancy people. But I'm here to support the boys and, hopefully, meet some of the right people to help our little business along. At the start of the night, Blake introduced us to some of the art connoisseurs he knows, and we exchanged cards. I guess only time will tell if something comes of it or not.

We have listened to all sorts of building-related awards tonight. The boys' category has just been announced. I can see how nervous the three of them are. They all have that tough exterior, but when it comes to their business, they have given it their all, and they really want this.

There are four other nominees in the same category, and each of their designs flash up on the screen. I have to admit, the library the boys designed is unbelievable, and I love that they focussed on sustainable design.

The MC announces the winner, and the name *The Green Door* is called out. We all clap excitedly for them. Elly's eyes are huge like she can't believe it. She's so proud of Fraser, and I feel the same for Blake. It's such an impressive achievement as their business hasn't been around for long at all.

Blake returns from the stage and takes his place at the table next to me, his hand straight to my thigh, and I lean over and kiss his cheek. "Congratulations." He looks so handsome in his charcoal suit. He's freshly shaven, which is unusual for him, and he looks good enough to eat. I can't decide what I like better, him in a suit or his work boots. Both are sexy as hell.

"You can help me celebrate later." His eyes are eating me up, and it sends my body crazy. How is it that just the way he looks at me has me ready to beg him to take me to bed? Must be some kind of magical power.

I run my hand up his leg; two can play this game. "Is that right?" I tease.

"Sure is." He kisses me, and then we reluctantly turn our attention back to the ceremony. I continue to run my hand up his leg.

We listen to the last few awards, then Elly and Fraser announce they are heading to bed, which isn't surprising since they've been all over each other all night. They should get a room. Party poopers. The rest of us want to party on, so we make our way onto the dance floor. I'm not much into dancing, but I'll accept any excuse to have Blake put his hands on me.

The music starts out fun and fast. Ash tries out some flashy dance moves, dramatically twirling Chloe across the dance floor. She giggles at him. After a few songs, the music changes to a slower pace, and Blake wraps his arms around me, our bodies slowly swaying to the music.

"You look so beautiful tonight. This is the perfect dress," he whispers, running his hand over the fabric and my arse.

"Thanks. Fraser thought you might like it. His exact words were *Blake will jizz in his pants when he sees you in this dress*. The shop assistant was not impressed."

He laughs. "He didn't say that in front of her."

I nod.

"Well, he wasn't far wrong. I nearly did!"

"Good, that was the effect I was going for," I say, wiggling my hips for a little extra effect.

"It was hard watching you walk away to go dress shopping with him the other day." He turns serious now.

"Why? What were you worried about?"

"I don't know. It's just, you know, my ex, the one who wouldn't leave me alone, we broke up because she was into Fraser as well. Kinda worried history might repeat."

Fuck, I didn't even think of that. "You have nothing to worry about. I'm not into that, and besides I see him as more the annoying little brother. He's not the type of guy I would ever go for. You're the one I'm into, Blake. And I'm really into you." I hope I'm not saying too much by telling him that, but it slips out before I can think about it. And it's the truth. This is becoming so much more than *friends with benefits*.

"Good, because I'm really into you too." He cradles my face, pulling me in and kissing me softly.

"We're heading to the casino for a bit, if you two want to join us?" asks Ash.

We look at each other, and I shrug. "I'm happy to keep partying, if you are?" I say.

"We're in," Blake tells Ash, and we make our way out the front of the hotel.

We catch a cab over to the casino. The four of us walk in, and this place is abuzz. There are large card tables set up around the room, with a massive bar in the middle, and pokies rooms off to the side. I feel way too overdressed in this gown as I walk through the front door.

"What's wrong, baby?"

"I feel a little fancy for this place in my dress."

"You look stunning, stop fussing. Let's get you another drink so you can relax and have fun." The boys head over to the bar, and Chloe and I wait for them. Chloe is stunning with a short, blonde bob which she wears super straight and longer in the front than the back. She's in an elegant, blush-coloured jumpsuit with a lace overlay on the bodice. She's tall, and with her long legs, she would easily be the best-looking chick in the place.

I like Chloe. She doesn't put up with any of Ash's shit—and I'm sure there is a lot to deal with, he's a very cocky guy.

The banter between them is hilarious. You can see how they make a good match, with him keeping her on her toes and her putting him in his place.

The boys return with our drinks, and Blake has a familiar-looking pink cocktail.

He hands it to me with a smirk. "Try not to spill this one down my shirt, baby."

I can't believe he remembers what I was drinking the night we met. I guess he did end up wearing it. "I'll do my best. I'm sure I'll be okay as long as you don't bump into me, not looking where you're going."

"Lucky I did, otherwise I wouldn't have met you," he says, pulling me in for a kiss, and I nearly do spill my drink.

Blake

What a night this has already been, winning the award, and the most beautiful girl in the place on my arm as we party the night away. The drinks are going down very easily, and the four of us are all having fun. The girls haven't met before tonight, but they're getting on so well, and Ash is his usual entertaining self. It's my turn to get the next round, so I'm at the bar waiting for my drinks to be made.

"Mr Donovan, long time no see. How the bloody hell are you, mate?" I turn to see an old friend from back home, Matty. I haven't seen him since I left, but we were good mates at school. Very strange for him to call me Mr Donovan, though.

"Hey, Matty. Mr Donovan's my dad, you know that."

"Yeah. But word on the street is you're about to take over, and we all can't wait for that."

"Nope. Where did you get that idea from?"

"The strip. It's been circulating for a while. We need you back, man. Things are starting to get out of hand and your dad's getting on a bit; trusting the wrong type of people."

"I'll be back in a couple of weeks for Amy's wedding. I'll talk to Dad then. But I'm sure he's got it under control. You still getting yourself into trouble with the police?"

"Nah, not for a while now. I'm totally clean. I want to come and work for you lads, when you take over."

I feel an arm wrap around my waist, and I jump, not expecting it. I hadn't realised how tense I was. But talking to anyone from where I grew up will cause that. Especially when Indie's around. I don't trust any of the guys from back home, not even an old mate. You never know who they're working for.

"I was wondering where you got to. Ash wants to play a poker tournament, you keen?" says Indie, nuzzling into my chest.

Matty looks her over, and then turns back to me with a knowing smile on his face. I need to wrap this up. I take our drinks off the bar. "Anyway, man, got to go. I'll catch you later."

"Yeah, man, real soon," he says, eyeing Indie again. I wrap my arm around her and usher her away from him and his creepy glare. I don't like the way other men look at her. Especially men like him.

"Who was that?" asks Indie.

"Just some guy from back home. No one important. Let's go kick Ash's arse in the tournament," We take our drinks back over to where the others are sitting and start the game.

Four hours later, we have just finished the tournament. Ash lost early on. Chloe took him home before he could start a new game at another table. One by one we knocked the other players out, and the last round came down to Indie and me. I thought I had it for sure, but the girl has skills when it comes to poker and took the game.

She's beaming with excitement after her win. I think she can hardly believe it herself. She checks her phone in her purse. "Blake, it's five am. We need to head back to the hotel."

I had no idea what the time was. We've been having so much fun, time has flown by tonight. "Okay, baby, let's cash in your chips and get going."

We hail a cab out the front of the casino.

"To the Palazzo Versace, please," I say to the driver as we hop in. He nods, not giving us much attention at all.

I pull Indie's legs over mine and she snuggles into my neck. It's been a massive night, but I've still got plans for her, especially after that performance in the casino. As she relaxes into me, I slowly slide my hand up her exposed leg where the split is.

"Blake, what are you doing?" she murmurs, her eyes still closed.

"Nothing, baby, just relax, you're tired," I mumble into her hair, kissing her.

She smiles softly, and I go back to what I was doing, slipping my hand up a bit further under the lace fabric of her dress. Running my finger over the silky fabric of her panties, I hook my thumb under the top of them. She wiggles up a little, giving me access to drag them down her legs and over her heels. I place the panties in my pocket and return my hand to her awaiting pussy.

"You're a very naughty boy, Mr Donovan," she whispers, and I stiffen a little at the use of that name.

She looks up to me. "You okay?"

"Yeah, all good." I shake it off. She doesn't know what she's saying.

I continue circling my finger round her sensitive nub as she moans into my neck. She might be tired, but her body is still responsive to my every move. With my other hand, I pull her in for a kiss, swiping my tongue through her open mouth. She tastes extra sweet from all the cocktails. As we kiss, I bury my fingers into her, and she moans into my mouth. We feel the car pull to a stop, and I quickly pull my fingers out, before the driver of the cab turns around.

"Enjoy the rest of your evening or, I guess, morning, sir," he says.

I hand him the money for the fare, and we hop out of the car. "Thank you, I intend to."

Indie loses it as the car pulls away. "You nearly got us caught then." She laughs, hitting me on the arm. We make our way through the deserted hotel foyer to the lift. I guess not many people are around at this hour on a Sunday morning.

"So what if I did? Didn't hear you complaining when I was doing it."

"You're such a bad influence on me."

"You love it, baby."

She smirks at me. She might have been tired when we got in the car, but right now she's ready to go. I push the up button on the elevator. She hasn't taken her eyes off me. I grab her, and she wraps her free leg around me as I push her up against the wall, our mouths smashing together again.

Desperate for more, the elevator can't come fast enough. It arrives with a ping, and I drag her in, still connected to me at the waist, my lips on hers. We're making out like two horny teens at the end of a school dance. When the elevator arrives at our floor, we straighten ourselves out and walk down the hall to our room. Indie is still giggling. I think she's so tired, she's delirious. I open the door and slam it closed behind us, lacing my hands through her hair once again. I pull her into me, kissing her. "Turn around, baby."

She does as I say, and I kiss down her neck to where the zipper of her dress starts. Her skin is soft and smooth, her golden tan still perfect, even for this time of year. I slowly unzip her gown and watch as it falls to the floor. She steps out of it, just in her fancy suspender belt and bra.

"I like this even better than that amazing dress. You can leave all this on while I fuck you, looking out the window over the city."

I throw my jacket off, and she gets to work on my shirt buttons. Her fingers work quickly, and she slides my shirt down my arms, kissing my chest down to where my pants sit. She unzips my fly, my suit pants falling to the floor. She runs her pretty manicured nails over my lower stomach, and it gives me shivers. A quick tug at my boxer briefs and they're off, my cock springing free. Her hands wrap around me, massaging my hard cock. As she strokes up and down my shaft, she bites her bottom lip and lowers to her knees in front of me.

Right as she's about to place her mouth over my throbbing cock, there's a knock at the door. She quickly jumps up. "What the fuck! Who's knocking at this hour?"

I pull my pants up, trying to contain my massive boner, as Indie runs to grab a robe. I open the door. "Fraser, what's wrong?"

Fraser is in our doorway, dressed in only a T-shirt and his boxers. He looks a mess.

"Haven't you been to bed yet?" he grumbles.

"Ah, no! We got carried away with a poker tournament at the casino. What's wrong, man?" I ask, unsettled by his tone. Indie comes to join me at the door, wrapping her arms around me.

"Elly's dad has had a fall while on his morning run. We need to head home now!"

"Oh my God. Is he okay?" Indie says as she starts to panic.

"We don't know much, except that he's on his way to the hospital as we speak. Elly is freaking out. I need to get back to her."

"Okay. I'll pack up. We'll be out the front in five," I say.

"Thanks, guys," says Fraser, rushing back off to his room.

"Oh my God, poor Elly. Quick, pack," Indie says, throwing stuff in a bag, her voice wobbly.

A COUPLE OF HOURS LATER WE ARRIVE HOME, AFTER dropping Elly and Fraser straight to the hospital to check on her dad. I'm worried for him, but there's not a lot we can do from here, and right now, the two of us need sleep. I wrap my arms around Indie, who is really upset about Elly's dad, and we crash out.

We wake at 2pm to a text from Fraser saying Elly's dad is out of surgery after having suffered a heart attack and a bleed on the brain when he fell. He has now been transferred to recovery. They believe, at this stage, he will make a full recovery, thank God. A massive scare for the Walker family. Hopefully, he will be okay and recover quickly.

Their family is all so close, and you can see how much they all rely on Jim, especially Elly. I have only known him a short time, but I can see what an amazing man he is, the kind I would like to be one day. A father with a loving family, a beautiful wife, doting over our cheeky kids. He's the kind of man that makes you want to be a better person.

Unlike my dad who could care less what kind of a person I am, as long as I keep the business running smoothly, growing at a steady pace, and keep our family name on anyone's mind who thinks they know better. That world is all about having the best of everything and staying at the top, no matter how you have to do it.

I peek over at Indie. She has drifted back off to sleep, the slow rise and fall of her chest as she breathes peacefully, her full lips parted just slightly, her dark hair falling around her face. She's so beautiful, so innocent to the kind of world I know.

She's not the kind of girl I could bring back with me. I feel guilt wash over me because I know what I'm doing here with her is so wrong. Someone is going to get hurt. I can't keep her, she will never truly be mine, but I'm a selfish prick and I want to pretend if only for a little while that this life with her could belong to me.

CHAPTER FIFTEEN

BLAKE

I arrive home from work when there is a knock at the door, and I wonder who it could be. I open it to find Indie, and she looks pissed. "Hey what's going on?" I ask.

She storms past me into the living room where she stands, hands on hips. "Why don't you tell me? Is Fraser here? I'd like to kick his arse for what he did to my friend."

I close the front door and take a seat. "No, lucky for him he's not. You're scary when you're angry."

"You should remember that." She glares at me, but I don't know what she wants me to do or say. Whatever is going on with Fraser isn't my story to tell. I don't agree with the way he handled the thing, and the fact he hurt Elly in the process—well, I could kick his arse for that too, but he's hurting, and he just needs time to work out his life. Then I'm sure he will fix the mess he's made.

"What do you want from me, Pix? You know I can't tell you what's going on with him. Just tell Elly to hang in there. I'm sure when he's ready, he'll talk to her himself." I pat the seat next to me. She needs to sit down and stop looking at me like that.

"She's devastated, Blake." She takes a seat next to me, sighing loudly. "She's your friend as well, you should want to help her. The dick dumped her with no real reason why, just some shit about him not being good enough for her."

"I do want to help her, I don't like seeing her hurt, but what he's going through is some heavy shit, and he needs time to process." Fraser's bitch of a mum has just recently come back into his life to drop the bomb that the man that brought him up and who he thought was his dad his entire life, isn't. He did the paternity test, and she wasn't bullshitting there. They're not related.

"What could be so bad he couldn't share it with her? She is the kindest person ever, she will help him through whatever it is." Indie nudges my leg. "Tell me so I can help her understand." Her eyes plead with me.

I run my hands through my hair. I'm just as frustrated by Fraser's behaviour as the girls. He's spiralling out of control, and it's taking all I have not to lose my shit with him, but he needs my support now. Ash and I are the only ones that know what he's going through, and he doesn't want anyone else to know. For some stupid reason, he thinks blocking out Elly is easier than telling her and letting her help him. Since the night he dumped her, he has been drinking again, hardly coming into the office. He's a fucking mess, and it's affecting my relationship with the girls as well.

"Indie, I really can't, I'm sorry. He will tell her when he's ready."

"Is it some other chick? Is that what it is? And you guys all stick together to protect each other."

"It's not another girl. Stop letting your imagination run wild. He's just going through some family stuff, okay? Just tell her that."

"All right." She pauses for a moment, thinking something over in her head. "Is everything okay with us? I haven't seen you much this week."

I reach out for her, taking her hand in mine, and she turns to me. "Yeah, I just have a lot going on at work and with Fraser. There's just a lot going on. I'll come over later tonight if you like."

She looks worried, nibbling on that plump bottom lip of hers, and I wish I could reassure her better, but the truth is, Fraser dumping Elly and the four of us not hanging out together so much has given me a bit of space to distance myself. It's not that I want to be away from her, she is really all I think about. I'm fucking crazy about her, and that's the problem. I can't be falling for her like I am, I just can't. I'm going to hurt her and there is no way out of it.

"Okay, I have class this afternoon anyway."

"Is Elly's dad okay?" I ask.

"Yeah, he's recovering well. Elly's so sad, though. I don't know what to do for her."

"All you can do is be there for her and hope they work this all out."

"Yeah, I guess you're right." She stands to leave. "I've got to go, I'll see you later tonight."

I follow her to the door, pulling her in for a long kiss. "See you tonight. Make sure you come as V. I have been missing that naughty girl this week."

She gives a half smile. "Ha, yeah, she's been missing you as well." She turns to walk down the driveway.

I'm so screwed when it comes to her, and instead of telling her all that I should be, I let her believe everything is okay. Because that's what I want to think as well.

INDIE

I pull up at the studio for tonight's life-drawing class. My head is scrambled after that conversation with Blake. The last month has gone by in a blur of working my various jobs, in my happy, loved-up bubble of Blake. The awards ceremony was a turning point for us, and I can feel how fast I'm falling for him. It scares me, but I can't stop the way I feel, either. We can't get enough of each other. And I wouldn't want it any other way. It's funny how things work out. When Hayden left me to go overseas, I thought it was the end of the world, but something so much better was waiting just around the corner, and now I couldn't be happier.

That was how I felt, anyway, until this week when Fraser broke things off with Elly, and Blake... well, I don't know what's going on with Blake. Today, when I walked away from his house, I felt a little apprehension slip in. Even though things have been amazing with us, this is still just a *friends with benefits* kind of arrangement. Nothing more has been discussed between us, no talk of the future or anything more serious, and I'm starting to feel... I don't know, kind of uneasy, I guess. Does he feel the same way I do? I have fallen for him and I want more out of this than what we originally discussed. I want him to be mine, and for me to be his, but how do I bring it up? He already seems a bit off whenever I bring up my real feelings. I might just scare him off completely.

I enter the studio where Sara and Elton are getting ready in our dressing room. "So, what's happening with you and the guy with the muscles and work boots?" asks Elton before I even have time to dump my bag in my locker.

"Um, I don't know. I think we're kind of seeing each other. We haven't made it official or anything, but there hasn't been a day we haven't been with each other this past month. It's been really nice. I think I really like him. He is so different to Hayden."

Elton looks at me, lines forming on his forehead. "You think you really like him?"

"I really like him," I smile. Who am I kidding? "I really, really like him, Elton, he's just so..."

Sara interrupts us. "Well, good. That dick was never good enough for you anyway. And Blake is very scrummy. Did she tell you he turned up to life-drawing class and drew pictures of her? How romantic is that?"

"I thought it was a bit more pervy than romantic." I laugh. I guess you could say it was romantic. It was more romantic when I drew him, but I'm not telling them about that.

She puts her arms on either side of mine and grips hard. "This guy is seriously one of the good guys, Indie. I can just tell. You need to lock him down."

I roll my eyes at her. She's so serious, but what does *lock him down* even mean at this point? Up until this week, I would have said the same thing, but I feel a little strange about it all now. "Oh yeah, and how would I go about doing that? We kinda have an agreement that this is just a *friends with benefits* kind of arrangement."

She still holds my arms and I prepare for the Sara lecture that's coming. Elton rolls his eyes at her, knowing where she's going before she even opens her mouth. "Just have a chat with him and tell him things have changed for you. You want more now. It sounds like he probably feels the same. He might just be waiting for you to say it first."

I shrug her off and turn my attention to Elton. "What do you think? You're a guy, you know the way they think."

He mulls that over for a second. "If things have changed

from your original agreement, you do need to talk to him, Indie, make sure you're on the same page."

"Yeah, you guys are probably right. I've just been putting it off. It will ruin what we have if he doesn't feel the same." I shove my bag into my locker. Is it all getting too real for him, is that what it is? I like what's going on between me and Blake now. It's fun and light-hearted and sexy as fuck. Do I really want to wreck that by getting feelings involved, especially if he doesn't feel the same way?

Sara grabs my arm, trying to bring the attention back to her. "Yeah, but if he does, it will be amazing."

"And if not, you want to know now, before you're more invested," Elton says, with a nod of the head.

What they're saying makes sense. I do need to talk to him, but it's too late to save my heart if he's not as into this as me. If we have to end things, I'll be devastated.

CHAPTER SIXTEEN

BLAKE

Dad has been ringing today, but I'm avoiding his calls. It will be about my sister's wedding on Saturday; I haven't RSVPed. I look over the invite in my hands, white with gold lettering. This wedding will be a fancy affair. The family will have invited anyone who is anyone in Sydney. I know I should be there to support Amy, she's my only sibling, but I haven't decided if I'm going yet.

Going back home is not a pleasant experience for me. It brings up all the memories of Bella. The reminder that she's gone. She was so young. I should have got her out of that fire faster. It's all my fault she's gone. It hardly seems fair that I get to go on living my life and she doesn't. It was my dad they were trying to get at. She had no part in the feud that has been going on for generations. She was just in the wrong place at the wrong time, and it cost her life. It was my responsibility to keep her safe, and I didn't.

On top of the guilt, I will have to deal with Dad and the others. They will want to know when I'm coming back, but I'm not ready to answer those questions.

The last month with Indie has been so much more than

I ever thought it would be. At first, I thought it was just the amazing sex, but it's become something else. There is undeniable chemistry even out of the bedroom. We have a strange connection I can't explain. She's beautiful and funny and so talented, but most of all, it's the way I feel when I'm with her; like I'm complete. She's all I need to be happy. I don't like to admit it, but I'm in love with her. I know I am. Which scares me. I can't afford to fall in love with her, or anyone. The last girl I loved died because of me and my fucked-up family.

Claudia, our new office assistant, buzzes through the intercom. "Blake, there's a man here to see you. He doesn't have an appointment, but he says you know him. A Mr Carver."

"Send him through, Claudia, thanks."

Hmm, Vinnie Carver, not someone I want in my place of work. But knowing he's been in town, I've been expecting him to show up for some time.

He walks through the door, shoulders back, hands in his pockets. All the confidence in the world. He's in a black suit with an open shirt. Thick gold chains hang from his neck. Vinnie is in his early 40s. His longish hair is slightly thinning on top and slicked back. His oversized muscles bulge through the fabric of his suit; seriously, this guy is built. I could see why Jenna would fear him. Even when he smiles, there's a hardness to him. Not the kind of guy you want as an enemy. Probably why Dad has kept him so close for all these years. I can't understand how he talked Jenna into being with him.

"Blake, son, nice to see you." He holds out his hand for me to shake. His smile is fake. There is no way he's happy to see me.

"Vinnie." I shake his hand firmly, his eyes not leaving

mine. With guys like this, so much is said without words, and he's not happy to see me. This is not going to be a friendly chat. I motion to the seat across from me, and we sit down. "What brings you into my office, Vinnie?"

He looks around the room and nods. "Nice place you have here, Blake. You're doing all right for yourself, aren't you?"

"Yeah, I guess." I shrug. What am I supposed to say to that?

"Hmm, well, I know your dad has been in touch about Cassie, my girl. We're still looking for her, and I have reason to believe you know more than you're saying." He straightens in his chair, his dark eyes piercing through me, waiting for answers. But he's going to be waiting for a very long time.

I sit upright in my seat and stare back. This piece of shit doesn't intimidate me. Yeah, he used to when I was a kid, but not now. I'm a head taller than him, and my boxing in the gym isn't just for fun. I could take him with my bare hands, no problem at all. "Don't know what you're talking about. Why would I know anything about your missing girlfriend?"

He runs his hands through his greasy hair. He's getting pissed now; the veins on his neck are more prominent, a dead giveaway, as he tries to keep his cool. "She hasn't been back to the strip club where she was working since that night we ran into you there. Did you get to her first, tell her I was looking for her, so she ran again?"

I smile. He really has no fucking idea, if he thinks he can just walk in here and I'll be intimidated by him and hand her over. She's safe from him for now, and I intend to keep it that way. "I didn't see her that night, sorry. We were on the piss and spent most of the night in a private area with the girls the groom had handpicked. I was concentrating on the beautiful ladies dancing for me, not thinking about the whereabouts of your girlfriend. Sorry I can't be of more help, Vinnie."

He smiles. Not a nice smile, a sickening one. "You ever been in love, Blake?"

I shrug. Where is he going with this? "How is that relevant?"

"Because then you would know how I feel and why I want her back. Cassie is a very special lady and the love of my life. We're supposed to be getting married this summer. She's just running because she's scared, but there is nothing to be scared of. I would never hurt her."

"Really? I doubt someone like you could love anyone." My words are filled with more venom now, thinking of poor Jenna. She's so young. She must have been in a desperately bad place to ever date such a pig like him. It makes me so mad, the kind of power these guys have and the way they can throw it around and get what they want.

"You need to watch your mouth, son. I know your daddy protects you, but there is more of a target on your back than you or he knows."

"Who would bother targeting me? I want nothing to do with that scene."

"Yeah, but we all know your dad wants you back there, running the show."

"He doesn't get everything he wants."

"It would make me happy if you didn't come back too, son. Then the position would go to someone who actually deserves it. But we both know daddy will make sure it's you taking over. I'm watching you, Blake. You better be careful. If I find out you had anything to do with Cassie taking off again, I might have to deal with that cute little brunette you've been seeing."

I keep my face unemotional. I don't want him to know Indie is someone special or she'll become a target. "Don't know what you're talking about. I'm not seeing anyone."

"I have eyes, son, and this town ain't that big. Wouldn't want any unfortunate accidents to happen, just like the last time, now would we?"

"What the fuck are you talking about?"

His face is smug, and he knows he has me by the balls. "You know what I'm talking about. Such a shame how these accidents can happen. She was such a sweet girl too, so pretty, and she was just in the wrong place at the wrong time. Or was she? Guess we will never know."

Something inside me snaps. This guy is such a sleazy arsehole. He thinks he can come into my business and bring up shit from the past. Is he trying to threaten me and Indie? Shit. And he's obviously been watching us and seen her with me.

I push my seat back and launch at him, pulling him up by the shirt. "I've had enough of this conversation. Get the fuck out! You don't get to talk about Bella and what happened that night, and if I ever find out you had anything to do with what happened to her, your life won't be worth living."

"Hey, hey, settle down, son, you don't need to go getting all up in my face. It's just a friendly chat between two old mates."

I pull back from him, shoving him as I do. "We are not old mates."

"I think your father would see it differently." He pats down his suit, straightening it out.

I have lost my patience for him. He needs to go before I kick his fucking head in. "It's time for you to leave, Vinnie."

"You just remember what I said. We all look after each other. It's what Mr Donovan's boys do. But if you're not looking after us, we don't look after you. Choose where your allegiances lie, son."

He leaves my office, and I pick up a stapler and throw it across the room. It hits the wall, smashing into pieces. Fuck, why is this happening now, just when things are getting good with Indie? My fucking past has to come back to haunt me again. I know one thing for sure: fucking Vinnie isn't getting anywhere near Indie. And as much as it's going to kill me, I know what I need to do to keep her safe.

CHAPTER SEVENTEEN

INDIE

I'M IN A RUSH TO GET TO LIFE-DRAWING CLASS. I'm next up on the schedule. But first, I need to quickly drop off one more painting to the townhouses for Elly. I pull up out the front and go to the boot of my car, pulling the canvas out and shoving it under my arm, then running up the driveway. She said she would be in the first townhouse, I think, so I knock at its door, hoping that's where she is. I'm tapping my foot impatiently as I wait. *Come on, Elly, hurry up, I'm going to be late.* She abruptly opens the door.

"Thank you so much for dropping this over. Hope I didn't make you late?" She smiles sadly. Poor Elly has had her heart absolutely ripped to shreds by Fraser. She has been devastated ever since he left her. It came from out of nowhere too, he just walked out, no explanation. The way I see it, she's better off without him. But she's worried about him. She thinks there is more to the story. She's got a bigger heart than me. I want to kick his arse for what he did to her, and I will if I run into him again.

"It's okay. Just got to get to work. I'll see you tonight." I turn back to look at her, I can't just rush off and leave her like this. "Elly, you want me to stay for a bit and help?"

"No, you need to get to your art class. Go, I'll be fine."

I pull out my phone and quickly type a message to Sara to tell her to go on for me. I still have half an hour anyway, I'm sure it will be fine. I'll be there soon. "I'll come in for a sec."

"Sorry, Indie. It's just hard to be in these places. How am I supposed to keep working with him?"

"Have you seen him? Did something else happen?"

"No, nothing. I have heard nothing at all. Has Blake said anything?"

"Not really, just that he is working through some family stuff. He's pissed at him for what he did to you as well."

She shakes her head, her hands covering her face. "I just don't get it," she mumbles through more tears.

"I'm sorry, hun, I don't either. Hopefully he will work out his shit and come round." I wrap my arms around her and pull her in for a hug, patting her on the arm. "I really have to go. I'll see you at home tonight." I let her go and walk towards the door. "The house looks amazing."

"Thanks." She offers a small smile.

I blow her a kiss and run back down the driveway and jump in my car. As I turn on the engine, I see what looks like Blake's ute pulling up the driveway and parking out the front of the second townhouse. He gets out of the car then goes around to the passenger side to let his passenger out, a very young-looking leggy brunette.

She smiles up at him, looking shy. She's stunning with long, dark hair and tanned skin. Her legs go on for days, making her a much better height for him than me. This is an interesting development. What is going on here?

I'm in a massive rush, but I don't care. I want to know

what's going on with them. They look too familiar with each other to me.

Is this why he's pulled back from me? I've hardly seen him lately, and if I have it's been late, like booty-call late, then he's gone before I wake up. It wasn't making any sense to me, but maybe he's started seeing someone else—a very young someone else. God, she could still be a teenager, she looks so young.

They make their way into the second townhouse. I hop out of the car and run back across the driveway to the house. I peer in through the side window. I can see them walking through, looking at the kitchen, then they disappear out of sight. I run to the next window to see if I can see them. But I can't. I run back to the front and hide behind a small shrub, to wait till they come back into view. He's probably just showing her through the house. She's probably just a client wanting to buy it. But wouldn't the real estate agent show her through then? I keep a lookout for them out the front. I don't want him to catch me doing this. How would it look? He would think I was a total stalking psycho.

They come back into view. She's laughing, and he smiles at her. She says something to him and then she hugs him. My phone starts to ring, and they turn to look in my direction. Shit. I duck behind the wall. Sara's name lights up the screen and I hit decline. Shit, shit, shit. I've got to get out of here before he sees me. I look through the side window and they seem to have forgotten the distraction out the front. They are at the kitchen bench, looking over papers. I quickly make my way down the driveway and out of there. I start my car in a panic and take off.

What was that? She has to be just a client, right? They were looking through papers. But what was the hug then? I'm going to make myself crazy over this until I see him next.

Whenever that will be. I'm not messaging him. He's acting so strange at the moment. He can contact me if he wants to see me again, and then he better have some answers for me. I'm nobody's booty call.

BLAKE

I show Jenna through number two of the Broken Point townhouses. Drew and I are hoping we might be able to help her buy one before it goes to auction. Drew has done more of his share in the organising. He is convinced this is the best place for her and has gone out of his way to make it happen. Ash tells me, if I can save him on agent's fees for it, he'll drop the price. He acts all tough, but really, he's a big softy and wants to help her out. These places are going to have the highest of security and she would be safe here. It would be the perfect place for a fresh start for her. There is no telling how long it will take Vinnie to give up on finding her, or if he even will. We have tried to talk her into going away with Drew for a while, but she said she doesn't want to. She wants to start a new life here, so we're going to do our best to help her.

"This place is perfect, Blake, but do you think I can afford it on my salary?" She looks up at me, her big brown eyes filled with hope. She's so fragile. You can see by just looking at her that she's about to break down at any time, but she's trying to keep it together.

"Don't worry about that. We've saved all the agent's fees by selling privately, and Drew has worked out all the stuff with the bank, the loan amount has been agreed to. You'll be fine."

She smiles warmly, relaxing a little. "Thank you so

much for everything. You and Drew have been amazing. I can't believe how lucky I was to run into you that night. You have changed my life." She throws her arms around me, and I hug her back.

"I'm just glad you're safe and not back with Vinnie, or at that club." We hear a phone ring in the distance somewhere and turn to see where the noise is coming from, but there's no sign of anything weird. Must have been from the other house. Elly is there today styling. "Here are the papers I need you to sign for Ash. I'll get them all sorted straight away, and as soon as these places are registered with council, you'll be able to move in."

I watch as she signs the papers and hands them back to me. "I can't believe how much my life has changed in such a short period of time. Thank you again."

"Now we just have to make sure Vinnie doesn't find you. You're still being really careful, aren't you?"

"Yes, of course. I only go to the library and then home, and I shop once a week. Not anywhere he would find me. He has probably lost interest now anyway and is back in Sydney after someone new."

"I don't want to scare you, but he hasn't. He's been to see me this week. He's still here in town; you need to be careful. Ring me or Theo if you see him, okay? It's not too late to take Drew up on his offer of travelling with him."

"No, I can't do that," she says a little shakily, "I don't want to drag him into my problems, and he doesn't need me following him around." She looks at me like she has made up her mind. "No, this is for the best. I knew he wouldn't give up that easily, I just hoped he would. I will be careful."

"Okay, if you're sure. Come on, I'll get you back to work." We lock up and hop in the car. "How are you liking working at the library, anyway?"

"I love it. It's like a dream come true. Another reason I don't want to leave, this is the first time in my life I have had a job I love, a chance to make something of myself. My manager is so lovely, and I've started my uni degree. Mrs Walker has been checking in on me as well. I think Drew has been sending her in. They're such a nice family. I wish I grew up in a family like that." She looks down, fiddling with the strap of her bag.

"Don't we all. I'm glad you're happy there. It's a great opportunity for you."

"Yeah, it really is. I'm still so embarrassed how we met."

"Don't be. You know how my family are. I grew up around strip clubs. It's the norm for me."

"Yeah, but I don't want you or Drew to think of me like that. I want a fresh start. You know, Jenna, the librarian."

"That is how I think of you. That night is forgotten."

She smiles. "Thank you."

We pull up in front of the library, and she opens her door. "You really have no idea what all this means to me, Blake."

"I think I do, Jenna. Everyone deserves a fresh start, a chance to make something of their lives, especially those of us who didn't have the best start through no fault of our own."

"Maybe you do. See you later."

"I'll be in touch when the paperwork goes through."

"Thanks." She walks back up the stairs to work.

I look at my steering wheel, like it might be able to give me all the answers I need. We do all deserve a fresh start, but this isn't my time yet. Unfortunately, I'm still living with too many ghosts of the past, and what I have to do now is going to break my heart more than it is Indie's. But for her own safety, it has to be done.

I'm in love with her, that much I know for sure, and I can't have what happened to Bella happen to my Indie. She doesn't deserve to be dragged into this world, and the less she knows about the realities of it all, the better. This way she can get on with her life; find a nice man who can take care of her the way she deserves.

I won't go around to her place till later tonight. Since Vinnie paid a visit to my office last week, I've been really careful to only visit her late and to leave before it's light. I don't want her messed up in this, and I heard Vinnie's threat loud and clear. Even if Dad thinks we can trust him, I know we can't. Theo has been in contact with the Sydney police, and they've been doing a thorough analysis into his past offences. He's hard to convict because he knows too many of the right people, but there's a list as long as my arm of offences they can't convict him on, and sure enough, he's been a person of interest in the fire that killed Bella.

I head back to the office to finish up for the day. I need to get this paperwork to Ash so he can get it all happening for Jenna. I knock on his door, but surprise, surprise, he's not in. So, I leave it on his desk with a sticky note attached to the front. I check my watch and it's only 4pm, but I've been working since 7am, so I'm going to head to the gym to get in a workout. Maybe that will help me get through what I have to do tonight, but somehow, I doubt it.

I ARRIVE HOME JUST AFTER 7PM. I WAS HOPING THE gym would ease the tension I'm feeling, but it was no use. I feel like shit. How do you break it off with someone you have such strong feelings for? I push open my bedroom door, and on my bed sits the most beautiful person I know, my Indie. She's not going to make this easy. She looks amazing in that fucking outfit with those boots she knows I love.

"What are you doing here, baby?"

"I think we need to talk. Fraser let me in." She means business tonight. Her arms are crossed over her chest. By her body language, I can tell she's pissed off.

"Yeah, I know. I was going to come over later tonight and see you." I drop my gym bag down and walk over to her. She watches me, flicking her legs over the end of the bed, like she's ready to run at any time.

"You're making a habit of coming over late. I'm starting to think you just want me for a booty call."

I sit down beside her on the bed. "You know that's not what this is, baby. You could never be anyone's booty call."

"And I won't be." She looks up at me. Damn her eyes, they kill me every time, I just want to get lost in them. I don't want to tell her this is the end. I want to lay her down in my bed and love her.

"Good, you should never have to settle, Indie." I sit next to her, lacing my hand through hers, looking into those big, emerald-green eyes. God, I can't do this. I need to be close to her.

She's still looking over my face, trying to read me. I've noticed this is something she does, taking everything in while we talk. "Are you seeing someone else, Blake? Is that what this is?"

"Why would you say that?" I stroke my thumb over her hand, I think to calm myself, and just to touch her. This is the hardest thing I have ever had to do. It would be easy to let her believe it's over because I'm seeing someone else, that way she will hate me and won't ask any more questions. But I don't want her to hate me, I'm too selfish. I have to tell her enough that she knows we can't see each other like this anymore, but not so much that she never wants to see me again.

"Because you're pulling away from me. I can feel it. You only come over late at night, and you leave early."

"I'm not seeing someone else. That's not why. It's complicated."

She cuts me off. "Who was the girl you showed through the townhouse today then?"

She was there? I knew I heard a phone. "Why were you there? Have you been spying on me?" I pull back from her, a bit affronted by her question.

She stands up. She's really pissed now. "Wow, way to get all defensive. She is someone then!"

I grab her arm to stop her from leaving. "She's no one but a potential client, there to buy a house. Ash couldn't walk her through, so I did. Why were you there, Indie?" I don't like lying to her about Jenna, but I also don't want her to know who she is. This is so much more complicated than she could possibly understand.

"Dropping off art to Elly. She was finishing off the first house and was one painting short. I saw you arrive with her, and the two of you looked too cosy for her to be just a client."

"We weren't cosy at all. She's just a client, nothing like that."

She stands in front of me, and I hold her hands in mine. "What is it then? Why are you pulling away? I mean, I know this was never supposed to be something serious, but I kinda thought things might have changed."

"It's so complicated, Pix. I can't really tell you all the details, but I'm worried for your safety if I keep seeing you. That's why I haven't been coming until after it's dark and leaving early. I didn't want him to see where I was going, and work out that you're someone special, and where you live."

She straightens up, looking worried. "Are you in some kind of trouble, Blake?"

"You don't need to worry about me, I can look after myself. It's you I'm worried about. I'm so sorry, Indie. I just think it's for the best if we go back to friends and I keep my distance for a while, till all this blows over."

"For a while, or for good? Is this it, Blake? Just tell me if it is. You don't have to go saving my feelings. I'm tough. I can handle the truth."

"Indie, I can't give you the future you deserve. The big, happy house with a husband you love and kids. That's not in my future. Sometime in the next six months, I'm going to have to go back to Sydney and help my dad. I don't get to choose my future. But you do. And I want for you to be happy and have everything you dream of. You can't have that with me."

"I don't understand. Why did you start something with me if you were just going to end it when it started to get good?"

"I'm sorry, I'm selfish, and I couldn't help myself. I thought we would be able to just fool around and walk away, but this ended up being so much more than that. Indie..." I look up at her beautiful face. I can't leave without saying this, even if it hurts to say it, knowing I have to leave. "I'm in love with you... but I can't be."

She takes a step back from me, pulling out of my hands. "Don't, don't you do that. Take it back. You can't say that to me knowing you're about to end this. Take it back." She glares at me. She's fuming mad; I knew she would be, but what else can I do?

"I'm sorry, Indie, I can't. I do love you."

"No! You don't get to be sorry." She turns and marches over to the door, turning back to me. "It's okay. This is what we said it was, just an arrangement between friends. *Friends that fuck*. We had our fun. It's not love. Let's not pretend it was ever anything else. I'm a big girl, I get it."

I go to her side, cradling her face. "You don't get it, Indie. It's not like that at all. It's so complicated."

"Don't worry about it. I don't need you to explain. All good. We're back to friends. I'll see you round."

"Indie." I try to wrap my arms around her, but she pulls away and strides towards the door quickly. I follow her. There's nothing else I can do. I can't explain this to her. Especially not when she's this pissed off.

"See you around, *friend*," she says as she slams the door shut. She is pissed, and I expected nothing more from her. I would be too.

But this hurts like a fucking bitch. This isn't the way it's supposed to go when you're in love with someone. We should be starting our lives together, not ending something so good because of some arsehole crook, never knowing what it could have grown into. Judging by her face when she walked away, she feels it too, I know she does. This was a once-in-a-lifetime kind of connection. But I'm not risking her life so we can be happy for the short-term.

CHAPTER EIGHTEEN

INDIE

Fucking arsehole! He wants to see someone else or something, and just doesn't have the balls to tell me the truth. *He loves me?* Fucking bullshit! You don't love someone and break up with them. I stomp off to my car, slamming the door shut. I'm so angry. I'm glad I came here tonight and got the answers I needed. No more booty calls while he sees the brunette on the side. I will not be my mama. This little chick is a strong, independent woman. I don't need some arsehole dictating my life round his schedule with the person he really loves. I'm so angry. I hate men; all of them. They're all the same.

I pull out from the curb and scream up the street, my tyres squealing as I round the first corner. Oops. I need to calm down and not drive like a crazy person, so I slow down to normal speed and try to take some deep breaths. The headlights of the car behind me shine through my mirror, almost blinding me, and snap me out of my angry rage. It's dark and I can't see the car behind me, but it's travelling way too close. Probably because I just braked too hard.

I flick on my blinker to pull into a side street, off the

main road, to get back to my place. That's a bit strange, they do the same. Is it just a coincidence or is someone following me? My thoughts go back to what Blake said, something about me *getting hurt* if we stayed together. What was he talking about? Maybe I should have stuck around and found out.

I turn down another side street, and the other car does the same. My heart beats a little faster. Now I'm getting freaked out. The likelihood that another person would be going home the same way as me is pretty slim, especially at this time of night. I press the car phone monitor and look for Theo's number, hitting call before I can even think about it.

He answers quickly. "Indie, is everything okay?"

"I—I don't know. I think I'm being followed by someone," I whisper.

"Where are you?" his deep voice beams through the phone.

"On Mongolia Lane, heading south. I was just at Blake's. I'm driving home. I only noticed them because they were driving really close. They've backed off now, but every turn I take, they do the same. It's probably nothing, but how do I know?"

"Don't drive home. I'm on duty. Drive straight to the police station. I'll stay on the line with you while you do."

"Okay." I pull over to the side of the road and turn back the way I came. Watching in the rear-view mirror, I can see the other car has done the same. Shit, they are following me!

"Are they still following you?"

I'm starting to shake now. I know I'm probably just scaring myself over nothing. I'm just worked up because of what just happened with Blake. "Yes, it's freaking me out, Theo."

"It's okay, Indie. Calm down and drive carefully. You'll be here soon."

A couple of minutes later, I pull up out the front of the police station and the car following me takes off, their wheels screeching as they do. Theo is standing out the front, and I hope he got their plates.

He runs over to the car and helps me out.

"Indie, you're okay now." He wraps his arms around me, pulling me into his body. "You're shaking."

"Scared the shit out of me," I mumble into his chest.

"It's all right, they're gone, I've got you. Nothing to worry about."

I pull back to look at him. "Yeah, but why were they following me?"

"I don't know, but we got their plates. Come inside with me for a sec so I can get the boys to run them, then I'll drive you home."

I follow him inside the police station and Fi, Theo's fiancée and partner, is on the front desk. It's nice to see a friendly face. "You all right, sweetie? I'll get you a warm drink." She comes around the desk and wraps her arms around me, her pregnant belly getting in the way.

"Yeah, thanks, that would be nice. I feel a bit silly making all this fuss, but they kept following me. It just spooked me."

"Indie, don't ever feel silly asking for help when you think you're in trouble. That's why we're here, to help."

Theo disappears down the back of the station while Fiona and I sit in the break room and have a hot tea.

"Aren't you supposed to be on maternity leave?"

Theo re-enters the room. "She is, but we can't keep her away from the place."

They look at each other, and she smiles. "I'm on mat

leave, they made me take it early. I'm already bored out of my brains at home, and I still have months to go. Plus, I just had to check on something quickly before I picked up Theo. It's date night. We're supposed to be catching a movie."

"Oh, I'm so sorry. You should get to your movie."

"Don't be silly, we'll get you home. We can stop in and see Elly as well. I'm worried about that girl."

"Yeah, me too."

"We ran the plates, but no luck. The vehicle was reported stolen earlier in the week. The boys sent out a car and tried to follow. We'll see how they go. Sorry, Indie, wish we could have been more help," says Theo.

"Great, day keeps getting better," I say into my drink, taking a sip, still trying to calm my nerves.

Fi looks over to me. "Why? What else happened?"

"I was just at Blake's. He's been acting weird lately, so I went round there to see what was going on. He broke it off. Said he was worried about my safety if we kept seeing each other. I had no idea what he was talking about, but after tonight, maybe I do need to be worried. You don't know what he would be talking about, do you, Theo?"

He looks to Fi and then back to me. He knows I can read him like a fucking book. I've known Theo long enough to know when he's withholding information from me. "Not exactly, Indie, but I'll talk to him, try and work it out. Don't worry yourself, we're onto this now. I'm sure this won't happen again."

I give him a look to let him know I'm not as dumb as he thinks. But I'll let it slide for tonight, until I know the right questions to ask him. "Hmm, okay. Thanks, Theo."

"Indie, for what it's worth, Blake was right to let you go. You don't want to get mixed up with him. I would say he's trying to do the right thing and protect you."

Fiona whips her head over to Theo. She has no idea what he's talking about either, but there's definitely so much more to this. "What do you mean, Theo?" says Fiona. Her voice is harsh, and it looks like she's pissed that he is keeping something from her.

"I'm sure Blake will tell you when he's ready."

I look over to Fi, and she shrugs. Fucking guys, all sticking together.

Theo drives me home in my car, and Fiona follows us. They both stay for a drink to catch up with Elly. I excuse myself, saying I'm tired, but really, I want info, and it seems all the men in my life are keeping it from me for some reason. So, I'm going to do a little investigating of my own.

An hour later, Elly knocks on my door. "Can I come in?"

"Yeah." I sit up in the bed, and she comes to sit next to me.

"What happened?" she says softly.

"Who knows, Elly, he broke off whatever it was we were doing, said it was all too complicated and he needed to protect me. I don't even know who he is."

"Yeah, Theo said you got followed by some car tonight leaving Blake's. Are you all right?"

I sigh. "I'm okay now. I was a bit shaken when it happened, but now I'm kinda just pissed off. All the boys seem to know what's going on, but we can't know because they want to protect us. It's fucked. Theo hasn't even told Fi."

Her eyes go wide. "Really? That surprises me, they're so close."

"Yeah, well, apparently whatever this is, us women can't handle it. Makes me so mad. If he would just talk to me, let me be the judge of what I can handle." She nods in agreement. "Why did he get involved with me in the first place?

He was the one that pushed me, I was happy doing my own thing. But he couldn't help himself, and now look what happened. I'm back where I was when Hayden left, feeling like shit because of some fucking guy. I wanted to be stronger than that this time, you know, not need some guy for my happiness."

"Yeah, I know exactly what you're talking about. We're as bad as each other. Fucking men!"

"Fucking men!" I almost scream. I'm getting madder about this situation by the second. How did I let him get so far under my skin that I can't stand the thought of life without him already? We never even made it official. I should have fucking known this meant nothing to him. Or if the truth is, he doesn't want me to be in danger because he cares so much, then why put me in danger in the first place, when he didn't need to? He could have just left me alone, not come back to the café that day. The whole thing is fucking with my mind.

Elly's hand squeezes my leg, bringing me back from my angry thoughts. "Now what?"

"Now I work out who the fuck he actually is and what's going on."

She wraps her arm around me in a hug. "Good luck, babe. I'm going to head to bed. I'll let you work on all of that, I'm too exhausted."

"Night, hun." I grab my laptop and open Google. Come on, internet, give me some answers.

I WAKE ON TOP OF MY BED COVERS, MY BODY CURLED around my laptop. I have no idea what time I fell asleep, but it was late. Ahh, my body hurts. What a shitty night. Once I started down the rabbit hole of who Blake Donovan actually is, I just couldn't stop. I thought I was falling in love with this man, but I don't think I even knew him at all.

I'm so hurt and annoyed that he didn't share this side of his life with me. I mean, he touched on it at times but never gave too much away. I could have handled all this. Families are complicated, I get it. Although I couldn't find much on Blake himself, most of what I found was news reports from the Eastern Suburbs Newspaper about his dad. He's the owner of a few strip clubs, restaurants, and night clubs across Sydney.

Blake's family is loaded. I mean, *ridiculously* loaded. From what I've been able to piece together from the articles of shootings or fires, or articles on his establishments, his dad is some kind of underworld king pin or something, who is respected and feared across Sydney. Theo must know more than he was saying last night, to give me the warning he did. He has to, right?

One of the articles got my interest; there was a fire in a restaurant where a young girl was killed. I can see a very young Blake in the background of the photo. He looks devastated. I wonder what happened there.

I guess that's why he was trying to warn me about his family and his life in Sydney, and why he has to go back to the family business. I get now why he broke it off, I really do. I wish he could have just been more open with me. I could've handled it. He knows all the secrets from my past. Why couldn't he talk to me about his?

Now I know how poor Elly has been feeling since Fraser broke it off with her. We will just be two lonely, old spinsters. I have no motivation to go anywhere or do anything today. My body aches, and I'm so tired I feel like I can barely move. But life goes on, even if I can't see the point at this moment. I'll just lock my heart up in a little box so no one else can hurt it. This year has thrown enough shit at me already.

I start my shift at the café, setting up all the cakes in the front display cabinet.

"You all right, sunshine?" asks Rachel, my boss. She's been out the back in the kitchen preparing food for the day.

"Yep, just peachy." I don't even bother looking up from what I'm doing to offer a smile. I just keep arranging the cakes like it's the most important job in the world. That's what kind of mood I'm in today.

"That good, hey?" She makes two coffees, setting one down in front of me.

I rub my eyes. I'm so tired from last night, I can barely keep them open. This coffee is much needed. I take a sip and sigh. "Men, pfft, I'm over them! I'm thinking of changing teams." I bend down to grab some more takeaway cups from under the counter, preparing for the rush. Rachel seems very relaxed today, standing by the counter sipping her coffee. The rush hasn't hit yet, but it will, and we need to be ready. I want to get out of here on time today, and not have to play catch-up later because we didn't get everything sorted now.

"Yeah, right, Indie! You love men. Just wait, when the next cute thing walks through the door, you'll change your mind." She smiles down at me as if knowing something I don't.

I continue to place extra napkins and cutlery on the counter so we can top everything up. "Will not. This little chickee is officially off the market, for good," I add, making my way to standing again.

And, like the universe is watching over me and laughing, at the counter stands Luca and Tristan, ready for their morning coffees. These guys are regulars every morning, and since Elly and I played pool with them at the bar that night, what seems like ages ago, we have kind of made friends. Rach must have been able to see them coming; she's such a stirrer.

"Morning, boys. Be careful with this one today. She's a little delicate," Rachel says.

I throw her an evil look for her comment, then plaster on my best fake smile. "What can I get you boys this morning?"

"Had a rough night, Indie? You do look tired today." Tristan is such a smart-arse and thinks he's funny drawing more attention to my tired state.

"Thanks, Tristan. Just what I needed to hear."

Luca thumps him in the arm and gives him a look. "Ignore my friend. He's not wearing his glasses. You look beautiful as always."

"Thank you, Luca. Just the usual today, boys?" Luca is sweet and the kind of guy you imagine would be a lot of fun. I always have time for him. His mate, Tristan, I'm not so sure about. I think they must work together. They always come in at the same time every morning, in their suits.

"Yes, thanks," says Luca.

"Where's Elly?" asks Tristan. The boy's got it bad for her, that's been obvious for a while. He hangs off her every word, and whenever she's not here, he wants to know where she is.

"She's not in till later today."

He frowns. "Oh, guess I'll have to come back later then."

"Yeah, if you want to see her, you will."

I get to work on their coffees. Rachel has disappeared back to the kitchen.

Luca leans up against the counter, watching me as I work the coffee machine. "Are you okay, Indie?" He looks genuinely concerned, and it's nice to know someone cares.

I sigh. "Yeah, I'll be fine, just a bad night. Learnt some good life lessons."

He raises a brow in question. "What were they?"

"Trust no one, and things aren't always what they seem."

"Sound like you're better off without him then, anyway. You should come out with me this weekend. We would have fun together." He winks. And I'm sure we would. He looks like a lot of fun. But my broken heart can't handle that. I'm still kind of in shock from what happened last night. Just when I thought my life was falling into place. How did it all turn to shit so quickly?

"Yeah, you could bring Elly as well," adds Tristan over his shoulder.

"I guess I could check with her if she's keen, but I don't like your chances, sorry, Tristan," I offer him. What else do you say? The girl's hooked on her ex.

"Well, just you then?" Ahh, this guy is very cute and charming. But I'm not in the right head space to go out with someone else. My head's all scrambled with Blake and all his stuff, even though I know he called it all off. *What do I even say to him? Sorry, I'm in love with some guy, who has this whole other side to his life he kept from me, and it has my head all fucked up now, so I'm ruined for anyone else. Probably forever.*

"I can't this weekend, sorry, Luca. Maybe some other time." I place the coffees on the counter in front of them and offer as much of a smile as I can manage today.

"I can live with that. You should definitely think about it. I think we would have a lot of fun together."

"Have a nice day, boys."

"See you tomorrow," he says with a cheeky smile, and I can't help but actually smile back. His smile is infectious.

They take their coffees and make their way out of the café. I go back to preparing for the rush in a slightly better mood than I was in earlier. Blake might not want me anymore, because of whatever fucked-up situation he has going on, but I can still get hit on when I look this tired. It's not all bad. Maybe I won't end up a lonely spinster after all.

CHAPTER NINETEEN

BLAKE

This week went as well as I thought it would. Theo rang not long after Indie left my place last night, when I broke it off with her, to say she had been followed. Luckily, she was smart enough to go straight to Theo at work. Unfortunately, they couldn't trace the car because it was a stolen vehicle, but we both know who was following her, and I need to do something about it.

On top of all of that, Fraser is out of control. After breaking it off with Elly, he completely fell apart and back into old bad habits, drowning his sorrows with drinking. I have seen him like this before, and last time, it took a big reality check to snap him out of it. He has hardly been at work all week, and when he turns up, he's not really there.

Poor Elly is a shell of the girl I met earlier this year. After her father's heart attack and now dealing with Fraser dumping her, she's not coping well. He needs to get his shit together or he will lose her for good this time. He's a total mess, and his shit is the last thing I need to deal with at the moment. I'm not sure I should have even come away tonight and left him alone, but there are things I need to deal with.

I've just arrived in Sydney for my sister Amy's wedding this afternoon. The timing is probably good. Not that I ever enjoy these trips to Sydney, but I need to talk to Dad about what Vinnie said the other day. I know my dad trusts him with his life, but he's a total creep, and I get a bad feeling about him. I don't think he's the trusted friend my dad really thinks he is.

I keep thinking back to last night. What would have happened if he'd worked out where Indie lived? We're lucky he didn't. A shiver runs down my spine. As much as I don't want to admit it, I think I need Dad's help to keep her safe. But how do I tell him his trusted mate is a crook, playing for both sides? I have no proof. I'm just going off a hunch from what Vinnie said that day in my office.

My cab pulls up in front of the Donovan family home. This place isn't really a home; it's a massive mansion that sits on the top of a rock face, looking over the water. There are security fences surrounding the property and a guard that sits at the front gate 24 hours a day. They have definitely upped the security since I was here last. Dad said that, a couple of months back, there were some threats against him and Mum, and you can't be too careful, so I guess that's why. The family is all meeting at my parents' house then going over to the church for the wedding together.

My dad is waiting for me at the door when I pull up.

"Son." My dad smacks me on the back in a hug.

"Sir."

"Oh, darling, you're home." My mother swans through the house, her long gown swaying as she walks, glass of champagne already in her hand, even though its only 1pm and the wedding hasn't started yet. She kisses me on both cheeks.

"Mother." I sigh, already regretting my decision to come.

She takes my hand and drags me through the house. "Don't just stand there, come through to the kitchen. There's someone here you'll be excited to see." She smiles, one of the fake smiles she's practiced so well over the years.

There, standing in the kitchen, is a familiar face; one I would prefer not to see again. Her long blonde hair curled and hanging down her back. Her curvy body fitting snugly in a red, full-length dress a bit over the top for a wedding guest, her tits on full display.

"You remember Lexi, don't you, darling?" My mother goes to her, taking her hand, and they smile at each other. What the fuck is Lexi doing here? She met my family a few times when we were together, but that's it. Why would she be at a family wedding? I feel like I'm being set up. Because I am. My manipulative mother and ex-girlfriend have joined forces.

"Yes, Mother. She was my girlfriend for four years," I say, a little exasperated with her.

Lexi comes over to me, wrapping her arms around me and kissing me on the cheek. "What are you doing here?" I whisper so only she can hear.

She pulls back, smiling at me. "Your wonderful mother thought it might be time for you to come home, Blake, for good. They thought I might help sweeten the deal." She bats her eyelashes at me, trying to be cute.

"Why on earth would she think that?" I throw my mother a look over my shoulder.

Lexi smiles up at me and grabs my tie, playing with it. "Because I told her how you feel about me, silly. We're so good together. Your mum can see that."

My mother and Lexi smile at each other. They clearly

have been planning this for a while. I'm not even sure what to say. So, I'm going to pretend this isn't happening.

Frustrated, I run my hands through my hair. I have been here all of five minutes, and already I'm regretting the decision to come. "Sir, can I talk to you in the study for a minute?" I say to my father.

My dad nods, and we make our way to the study. I can see the disappointed look in Lexi's eyes, but what on earth did she expect to happen? The last time I talked to her was to tell her to stop calling. I want nothing to do with her.

"What's on your mind, Son?"

I take a seat, and he pours me a whiskey. Probably a little early in the day for it, but if I'm going to get through this wedding, I'm going to need something.

He hands me the drink and sits across from me. He has aged a lot over the last few years. His hair is more grey than black, and he was never a small man, but he has gained quite a bit of weight. The wrinkles on his face are very obvious now. I can see how much this lifestyle has taken a toll. "Vinnie came to see me this week. Are you sure you can trust him?" I ask, watching his face as I do.

"With my life. I have never doubted that for a second." He takes a swig of his drink then places it on the desk in front of him. He watches me like he's trying to read my mind. His eyes narrow.

"Hmm, okay. We had an interesting conversation. I got the impression he was threatening me, so I would be convinced to help him find his girlfriend. He implied my girl would end up like Bella. To me that sounds like he had something to do with what happened to her. And we never did find out why the Barrett brothers targeted the restaurant that night. Did we?"

"There's no way he did. We all loved Bella, and besides,

she was the daughter of his best mate. Why would he have had anything to do with it. It was the Barrett brothers; they had a vendetta with us over territories."

"Yeah, I know all this, but at the time you never worked out what happened, or why. Maybe there was more to it. I just think you should be careful, that's all. You don't really know you can trust him. Maybe there is more to all of this than you know."

"So, now you want to get involved in the business?" He smiles at me smugly.

I take another sip. "No, I'm just saying be careful with him. I don't think you can trust him as well as you think. I have heard you say that there's someone feeding the brothers information. It's why they're always one step ahead of us."

"You have a point. I will make some calls, have a look into it." He picks up his phone, then looks back to me. "You were born to do this job, Blake. That's why you can't help but get yourself involved."

"You got me involved when you called for my help with his girlfriend—or was that your plan all along?"

"It's time, Blake. We've received some intel that the Barrett boys are trying to move in on our territory again. And they play dirty, Blake. Shot up the house of one of my men last week. Lucky no one was hurt. But there is a war coming. I can feel it. We need to be ready."

"I'll do what I can from Byron, but I need to be there at the moment. The boys need me with the business."

He thinks for a bit then nods. "Okay, for now."

"So, what is Mum doing inviting my ex to the wedding?"

"Who would know? Some game to keep her amused, I'm sure. You still got your heart set on the little brunette, Indie?"

He knows everything, with his spies everywhere, but I'm still surprised to hear him say her name. "How do you know about her?"

He grins. "If you're not going to tell me what's going on in your life, I will find out."

I really don't want my father thinking she is anyone important, or anyone else round here for that matter. "Well, we have broken up anyway, so you don't need to worry about her."

He nods. "Go keep your mother company while I make this call. Then we can go celebrate your sister's wedding."

HALF AN HOUR LATER WE ARRIVE AT THE CHURCH. My mother sits Lexi next to me, and I try my best to ignore her flirtations. I need to get through the ceremony... then we will be having a little chat. This shit is not going to continue. I don't care what my mother wants.

My sister, Amy, looks stunning in her massive gown. The train is so long she has four little flower girls holding it up and running along behind her. She is radiating happiness as she walks down the aisle to her husband-to-be, Morgan. I don't think I have ever seen her like this. It's not like we're close, so I really have no idea how content she is with her life normally, but it's nice to see her so happy.

Her fiancé is one of Dad's men. I'm not surprised; always keeping it in the family. The church would fit about 400 people seated, and we have the doors open so people can stand down the back to fit all the extra onlookers in.

My family are very well-known, and this wedding is big news. The man she is marrying is Morgan Redman. He's ambitious and cocky, and has been in this world his whole life, just like Amy and me. His dad worked with our dad, until two years ago, when he was shot while on a routine home collection job. The fucker they were collecting from couldn't pay his gambling debts. They got into a fight and Morgan's dad came off second-best. Dad took Morgan under his watch, and he's been shadowing Dad ever since. He would be a much better option to run the business than me. And he wants the job. To me it's a no-brainer. But Dad's mind is set.

The minister announces Amy and Morgan as husband and wife. The crowd cheers wildly. I watch as the happy couple make their way out of the church.

Lexi runs her hand up my leg, leaving a cold shiver in its place. "This is where I want to get married. This church; it's so beautiful. Don't you think this is just the most perfect wedding, Blake?"

"Yeah, it's something," I say, removing her hand. She looks up at me, disappointed. I need to get her alone to tell her that whatever this little game is she and Mum have going on, it's not going to happen.

The other guests make their way out the front of the church, and now's the time. I grab her arm and pull her out the side door. "Lexi, we need to talk. What on earth are you doing here?" I say a little louder and angrier than I intend, but I'm so sick of whatever this is with her. It's bordering on stalking.

She looks up at me, stunned by my outburst. "I'm here for you," she mutters, barely above a whisper. "Your mum and I both think it's time you stop mucking around with that girl and we make this official."

I run my hands through my hair, frustrated at the conversation I need to keep having with her on repeat. I don't want to hurt her, but I don't want to do this again. "What are you talking about? We're done. We broke up months ago. There is nothing between us. I don't understand why you're here."

She looks down, fiddling with her purse, then looks back up to me, her eyes hopeful. "Because I know you still have feelings for me."

I shake my head and take a step back from her. How do I explain this so that she gets it this time? "No, I don't. I'm sorry, but I don't. This will never happen again. Please, for the final time, leave me alone, and don't go getting involved with my family."

I have no idea why, but she looks shocked, and her eyes start to water. Oh God, don't cry. I can't stand it when girls cry. I want to be able to fix what's wrong, but I can't fix this. She broke it, and it's now way too late. The tears start to trickle down her face, and she reaches for my hand. "Can I at least stay with you tonight; one last night together?" she gets out through her sobs.

I take her hand. "No, Lexi, I'm sorry, this was over long ago. Please, you have to understand. I don't want to hurt you, but we're done. I've moved on, and I want you to be able to do the same."

She takes a step back. She looks so hurt, and I feel terrible. "Okay, I'm sorry, I shouldn't have come today. I just wanted to try one more time. I'm done embarrassing myself now, Blake. Don't worry, you won't hear from me again."

She walks away, and I know that's the last time I'll see her. I'm sad; not for me, but just because once upon a time I thought we had something special, and I don't like to be the one to hurt someone, especially someone I once cared about.

I feel heavy hands on my shoulders. "Son, you handled that well. This brunette must really be something to let a stunner like that go."

I turn to look at him. "She might be stunning, but it's for the best."

"I'm sure it is, Son. You're coming with us over to the reception."

I turn to look at my dad. His expression is serious. "Ah, I was going to wish Amy all the best then head home. Got lots of work to do."

"It wasn't a question. You're coming over with us to the reception. I'm not finished talking to you."

"I have a flight to catch."

"Cancel it. You can take the jet later." He stares at me, his eyes narrowed, and I know I'm not getting out of this. Looks like I'm going to the reception after all.

We're driven over to the reception in one of Dad's many cars, along with my mother. She chats about who was at the ceremony. I can barely listen to her carry on. We pull up in the car park. This place is insane. It almost looks like a palace or something. It's a bit much for a reception venue.

"You go inside, dear, I need to have a little chat with Blake. We'll meet you in there."

He kisses her on the cheek, and she makes her way inside.

We walk through a door to the side of the main building. It's an office space with a couple of chairs and a table. I look around the room and out the window at the view. This place is grand. It must be on some massive acreage. There are horses in the paddocks and an enormous stable off to the side.

"Have a seat, Son. I'll get you a drink." He makes a call. Moments later, a young woman in a fitted black dress and a high ponytail enters the room carrying a tray with a bottle of whiskey and two glasses on it. She fills our glasses then leaves without a word.

I take a seat, picking up my drink. "You really do have people everywhere."

He nods. "I just bought this place. It's good to have an event venue on your property portfolio."

"Yeah, I guess it would be." Of course he had to add a venue to his long list of properties, he is so extravagant in his need to grow the family name and show how much power he has. I'm so different from my family, and it just highlights it for me now more than ever when I come home and see the way they're living. I don't want any part of this. I just want a simple life with the woman I love, a nice house but nothing over the top. I don't understand why anyone needs all these things. I immediately take a swig.

He sips his scotch. His eyes are darker and more intense than before. Something has happened since our conversation this afternoon, I can tell. "These are the things you need to learn. For when you come back."

"We have talked about this."

"Blake. This life is in your blood. You can't run from it. I looked into what you were telling me earlier about Vinnie. I reckon you're onto something there. I've trusted him for so long, I didn't see it. But I had a guy, a copper mate, do some looking around, and what we found isn't good. He's playing me for a fool, Son! He's working with the Barrett brothers and he has for some time. The accident with Bella, that was no accident, it was a set-up. We're pretty certain he was after you."

My heart starts to beat faster. It's all my fault that she's dead, he was after me. My heart breaks for her and her family all over again. "What? Are you fucking kidding me? I knew he was fucking bent. Bella died because of him. When her dad finds out, he'll have his head." I run my hands through my hair, trying to calm myself down. I'm so fucking mad, knowing that a man on our side did this to her. "We need to deal with him. You need to tell his dad, he'll sort this out."

My dad's loud voice echoes around the room, breaking me out of my anger. "Take a seat, Son, you need to learn to control your temper or you'll get yourself killed. This is all about who is the smartest, not the toughest. Marcus won't find out about this, Son. We'll deal with this ourselves. Vinnie has run out of chances now, and I will deal with him."

I reluctantly sit. I really feel like her dad should know about what happened. He was the one that had to grieve for his little girl, he should be the one to deal with him. I just want to get back to Byron before Vinnie has the chance to hurt anyone else. But I know my dad has been doing this a lot longer than me, and when it comes to Vinnie, we don't really know what we're up against yet. "Why would we not tell Marcus? He's her dad. I saw him at the ceremony today. He has never recovered from what happened to her. He needs justice."

"And justice he will get, but you get a man worked up over the murder of his only daughter and things are going to get messy. My guys at the Byron police are aware of the situation with Vinnie. I have been in contact with them tonight. I will deal with this. But I need your help."

What? He has friends in the Byron police station as well? I need to ask Theo about that. "What do you need from me?"

"I need you to come back and help me get things under control. With Morgan and you working together, we have a chance against Vinnie. He has many friends on his side, and there is going to be trouble."

"If I'm helping you, I want protection for my girl back in Byron. He's already threatened her. What's next?"

"Indie? I thought you said you split up?" he says with a frown.

"We did, but Vinnie knows about her. And last night he had her followed. I'm worried he's going to hurt her."

"Okay, Son, we have a deal. I will get protection for your girl, but you're back here when I say the word."

I nod.

I leave the fancy function centre my family has just acquired, in one of the family cars with Dad's driver. We head straight for the airport. I'm not staying here tonight; I need to be back at home. I want to be close to Indie, even if I can't be with her.

Dad has organised an undercover guard, Anthony Ryker, to watch over Indie until we get all of this under control. He's an ex-army reserve commando and is built like a tank. He leaves on the same private plane as me and will be in Byron from tonight. Dad has set him up in an apartment in the same building as the girls. I have no idea how he sorted this all so quickly, but it's amazing what you can organise when you have his kind of money and influence. I will feel better once we land, knowing someone with be there to watch over her.

Our flight was pretty quick, and I walk in the door just after 1am, totally exhausted. After running Anthony through Indie's schedule on the flight, he is set up and ready to go. She would kill me if she knew I was doing this, but I'm not taking any chances.

I have a shower and hop into bed. I'm so tired, but I'm not sure that sleep will come easily tonight. I have so many thoughts going through my head. I feel like I've made a deal with the devil. But what choice did I have? I couldn't forgive myself if anything happened to Indie because of me. And now I know she will be safe. I close my eyes and try to sleep.

There's a loud bang at the front door and then something is knocked over inside. What the fuck? I jump up and run to the front of the house. It's just fucking Fraser. He is drunk as a skunk and has brought Shea, our real estate agent, home. What the fuck is he doing now? Trying to completely self-destruct any chance for a future with Elly. I won't let him do this to himself or her.

He's out of control and has picked the wrong night to push me over the edge. We have all put up with this shit for long enough. Tonight, I'm putting my foot down. This will be the end of this drinking whether he likes it or not.

CHAPTER TWENTY

INDIE

It feels like there is a dark cloud hanging over Broken Point at the moment. Elly and I keep saying *this is our year,* but as soon as we get one thing sorted, the rest of our life turns to shit!

We have finally sorted out our new business and the art gallery. The website is amazing. We're making money and booking jobs like crazy. Our living arrangements are working out really well. I love living with my friend. It's so much easier to live with a girl than a messy boy. Elly is amazing! She likes things tidy so is constantly keeping the place in order. I take care of the cooking. We're a great little team.

It's just the love life that's fucked up.

The last couple weeks have been hard. I've missed Blake's company. Even though it wasn't supposed to be something serious with him, my heart didn't know that, and I'm still really hurt that he didn't trust me enough to talk to me about everything properly. After what I read, I know I'm better off not being with him, but I still want him.

I'm not moping around anymore, thinking about him

and what could have been between us, so I finally took Luca up on his offer of a double date with him and Tristan and Elly. I know she's not that keen, but I need this. I need the distraction; something to get me out of the funk I've been in since Blake took us back to *just friends*.

Friends, ha! I haven't even seen him at all. He is totally avoiding me, and I am him. Part of me wants news to get back to him that I'm on a date with someone else, just to make him jealous, show him what he's missing out on. But the other part just wants to forget about him and move on; have a little fun while I'm young and single. The pact with myself to give up men lasted all of two weeks. Rachel was right. I guess we will see what tonight brings.

I take a step back and look in the mirror. Just need my red lippy. I apply it and blot my lips with a tissue. They're perfect. "You look hot, chickee," I say to myself, trying to get the boost I need to actually go through with this date. "Now go out there and have a fun night." Blake has no hold over me. He broke it off with me. Tonight is about having fun. *Stop thinking about him.*

I do a little shake, trying to get rid of the constant thoughts of him, but it's no use, they're still there. Grr! Get the fuck out of my head, Blake.

I'm going to need alcohol and a lot of it.

Luckily, we started at a local bar, and now I'm happy to say I'm feeling the buzz and starting to relax and have a good time. We moved from the bar to the restaurant upstairs to have some dinner at the best seafood restaurant in Byron, Ocean View. This place is next-level nice. The tables are full of delicious seafood, and the restaurant is loud with the chatter of happy couples on dates and families celebrating special events.

Luca hasn't taken his eyes off me the whole night. He is different from the Luca that comes into the café, and I have to admit, he is seriously good-looking. His long, dirty-blond hair is worn in a man bun. He's unshaven just how I like, a little rough around the edges, and his tattooed arms are just yummy. I don't know what to make of Elly's date Tristan yet. I'm a little tipsy already from the drinks we had downstairs, and it's great I'm forgetting about *what's his name, the builder* or *underworld boss's son*—whoever he even is. Tonight, I'm having fun.

Luca orders another bottle of wine for the table and winks at me sexily. This boy is out to get drunk tonight, and I can get on board.

"Top-up, Indie?" Luca offers.

"Please." I smile.

"So, you're an artist. What kind of stuff do you paint?"

"Kinda like psychedelic pop art. Mostly people, but sometimes landscapes. You'll have to come to my gallery and have a look. It's all set up now." I giggle. I have no idea why that's even funny, but everything seems funny right now.

"I would like that. I need something new for the walls in my house. I've only just moved in so they're pretty bare."

"I'm sure I could help you out. If you don't see something you like, I could paint you something." I take another mouthful of my barramundi. It's so good. "The food here is amazing, hey." I feel like I'm scarfing my food down too quickly, but it's really good, and I just want to eat it all. "Am I talking really fast? I feel like I'm talking really fast."

"You are talking pretty fast. You might want to slow down on the wine; you're a lightweight."

I laugh. "Sorry, I know. I don't normally drink so much."

"Do I make you nervous, Indie?" he says sexily. His eyes roam over me with a look that's pure sin. I wasn't before, but now I'm nervous.

"A little," I reply, biting my lip. I know what game I'm playing, and I know it's dangerous, since my heart lies elsewhere. Only hurt can come from flirting with a guy like Luca, but I'm just drunk enough that I don't care about the consequences.

"You're sexy as hell, Indie. I can't wait to get you home to bed," he whispers into my neck, so the others don't hear.

I can feel my face heat. That escalated quickly. I give a little nervous laugh and scull some more of my wine, spilling half of it on the table when I put the glass back down.

Elly and Tristan head outside to the balcony. She looks extra sad tonight. Poor Elly. I thought this might help, but maybe I shouldn't have dragged her out.

"Good. I've finally got you all to myself," he whispers, placing his lips on my neck, kissing his way down to my shoulder. I close my eyes and imagine it's Blake. Fuck, I'm messed up.

I feel his hand on my leg and my body stiffens. What am I doing here with him? He rubs his thumb over the bare skin of my thigh, innocent really, but it feels like so much. His lips are on mine, distracting me, but not enough. I try to relax and be in the moment with him. He's a nice guy, good-looking, smart. I should be more into this.

But my mind is on Blake.

I wrap my arm around Luca as our kiss intensifies, and I try to drown out the thoughts. *Fuck off, Blake, you can't stop me from moving on. I bet you have.* Even if he hasn't, he did this to us, discarded me, so why do I feel so guilty doing this? I pull back from Luca, searching the table in front of me for my drink, grabbing for my glass of wine before drinking it down. I need more alcohol to drown out the constant chatter in my head.

"You know what we should do?" I squeak, my voice too high. "We should get new tattoos tonight. I feel like a change, and that would be fun. We should get Elly and Tristan to get one too." I know I'm babbling like a crazy person, but I need to change the subject before he takes this any further, right here in this expensive restaurant.

And, with fantastic timing, I'm so grateful to see Elly and Tristan come back inside. Thank God.

"Hey, they're back. We're going to get tattoos," I call out, a little relieved to break the tension and get me out of this situation.

Luca pulls his hand back, and I grab my purse so I can stand up. I get up a little too quickly and I wobble a little on my heels.

"Are you trashed, Indie girl?" says Elly. "Hey, why don't we pay for our dinner then go for a bit of a walk? You can work out what you're getting while we walk."

"Sounds good, chickee. Hey, I've got an awesome idea. You should get one too. It'll be so much fun. It'll make you feel better too, I promise," I say.

Luca is behind me, with his arm around me, trying to steady me. "Come on. I'll help you out of here." I stumble and nearly fall, cracking up laughing, and Luca loses it. "Indie, let me help you," he laughs.

"I'm sorry. Just a bit spinny."

"No more alcohol for you, missy."

"Good plan, mister." I laugh. Shit. I'm so drunk. Elly and Tristan have fixed up the bill, and we make our way out of the restaurant. "One step at a time. I've got you." Luca laughs at me.

"I don't think I trust you. You're as drunk as me. We're both going to end up on our arses."

We somehow make it to the bottom of the stairs without a stack and start the walk up the street. The others are behind us chatting away. But I'm on a mission straight to get a new tattoo. I love them. They're my go-to when life falls apart or I feel shitty. Something about them brings me back to life again. I got the flowers up my arm the day of Mama's funeral. I felt so out of control. So unbelievably sad. I didn't know what to do. So, I sat there for hours. The pain of the tattoo gun was good. It made me feel alive when I felt numb inside.

I walk fast with Luca's arm wrapped around me. What we must look like to Elly and Tristan. The long walk in the fresh night air is helping me feel slightly less intoxicated. We arrive at the tattoo studio and walk through the door. I go straight to the front counter. "Hey, Bill, I need some new art. Just something small. Where are your books?"

"Indie! I haven't seen you in months. How have you been?" he says, handing me the book of small designs.

"Good, Bill. What about you?"

His face breaks into a toothy smile. "Always good, Indie. Who's your friend?"

"This is Luca. We're on a date. He needs something too."

"All right, honey. Well, you let me know when you find something you want, and I'll get ready for you." He wanders off to help someone else who's just walked in.

I flick through the book and come across the perfect little tattoo for Elly and me. It's a coffee cup on a girl's wrist.

Elly and Tristan finally catch up to us and make their way into the shop.

Elly looks scared. I would say she has never been in tattoo studio before. "Elly, I've found the perfect one for us," I call to her, showing her the book. "It's perfect, right? Coffee besties, like us," I say, nudging her arm, trying to convince her.

She thinks for a minute, studying the image in the book, then raises her eyes to me with a big confident smile.

"Okay, Indie, I'll do it with you."

"Yesss," I squeal excitedly. Bill shoots me a look. "Are you serious?"

She nods. I grab her hands and scream excitedly again. I can't believe she's going to do this.

"I thought we were supposed to be the sensible ones, talking them out of it," says Tristan, bumping arms with Elly.

A look of determination spreads across her face. I know that look; all the Walker kids get it when they're set a challenge. They can't back down. "I know, right, but I'm sick of being the sensible one. Aren't you?"

He shrugs. "Yeah, I'm in too." I think he would agree to do anything Elly says. The guy is totally besotted with her. Luca shows him the design he's been looking at. The boys get theirs first, as Elly keeps giving me a look of fear, like she's about to run out of here. But she doesn't, and when they're done, we get the nod from Bill that it's our turn.

We take our seats and Bill and his mate get to work. I look over to Elly. They're only a few lines in, but she doesn't look so good. I squeeze her hand.

"I love you, Elly. I'm so glad you moved home," I say. I've missed her so much, and it's so nice to have her around again.

"I love you too, Indie." She smiles back at me.

It's so small it takes no time at all, and I'm sure the alcohol is numbing the pain because I barely feel it. "All done, girls," says Bill.

Suddenly, Elly looks as white as a ghost.

Shit, there she goes, fainting, as Tristan catches her before she falls too far from her chair. I would be more worried, but I have seen Elly do this on many occasions. She has a major fear of needles, and I'm surprised she got this far and actually had it done.

"You okay, Elly?" Tristan asks, fussing over her as she blinks back at him.

Luca and I crack up laughing, probably a little too loudly. "Now I've got a new Elly fainting story to tell."

Elly is still a bit shaky, but I think she's proud of herself for going through with it.

We all catch a cab back to Elly's and my apartment after deciding the boys had had way too much alcohol to drive. Elly is the only sober one. She could have driven, but she can't drive a manual, so a cab was the only option.

Luca has his arm wrapped around me again. He's very touchy feely, and I know exactly what he wants when we get home. I'm not exactly sure how to handle this because I don't know what I want, and in my inebriated state, I'm not in a good way to make a decision about it. I'm actually feeling really tired all of a sudden.

Elly lets us all into our apartment, and she and Tristan head to the kitchen for coffee. They have been chatting away all night. Good for her. She's made a friend.

"You want to go straight to bed?" Luca whispers to me.

"Yeah, I'm really sleepy."

"You're really drunk." He laughs.

"So are you." I laugh back. "Night, guys," I call over my

shoulder.

My head hits the pillow. There's nothing better than your own bed when you feel so tired, and my linen sheets feel so warm and comfy. Luca takes off his shirt and pants. He's got a great body, very impressive. I should keep watching the show, but I can't help it... my bed is so snuggly, and I'm so tired. My eyes flicker closed, and I drift off into a peaceful sleep.

When I wake up, my head is pounding. I feel terrible. I can't even remember getting home. Bloody Blake! This is all his fault. If he'd just left me alone in the first place. I told him I didn't want to get into anything. But no, he kept pushing until he got what he wanted. God, I'm stupid, letting a guy get to me like he has. Now look at me, nursing a broken heart. It's so bad that I got so insanely drunk. I can't remember half the night. Elly is going to kill me.

"Oh, God. How much did I drink last night?" I groan out loud to myself.

"A lot," comes the voice from beside me.

Shit. Luca is in my bed. I sit up in a rush and immediately regret it when my head spins so fast I have to close my eyes to stop the vertigo. I bury my head in my hands. "What did we do?" I mumble, so embarrassed. I'm still in my clothes from last night, so that's a good sign.

"Had a nice dinner, a few drinks. Not much once we got home; you passed out before we could."

"I'm so sorry, Luca. I don't normally drink like that. I don't know what got into me." I'm such a liar. I know exactly what got into me: fucking Blake. I hate him right now. I'm so embarrassed. I can't believe I passed out on the poor guy.

Kind of solved the problem of not knowing how to deal with him coming onto me, though.

"Some guy pissed you off, apparently."

I tilt my head to the side to look at him. "What?"

"Yeah, you said last night, as you were going off to sleep, you blamed it all on some guy. Blake, I think his name was."

"Did I? I'm so sorry. I'm kinda a mess."

"It's okay, Indie. We had a fun night. Don't worry about it. But if you want me to help you forget this Blake guy, I can finish what we started last night," he says with a cheeky smile.

"Umm, thanks for the offer. I don't think I'm up for it this morning. My head is killing me."

The smell of bacon and eggs wafts in from the kitchen. Oh, thank God, Elly must be making breakfast.

"You want breakfast? Smells like Elly's cooking," I say, trying to offer a distraction. He's so full-on.

"That would be nice."

We make our way out to the kitchen and Elly has music playing. She's humming along to some song as she fries the bacon and eggs. She seems happier than she has been. Maybe last night was a good idea for her after all.

"Morning, chick," I say.

"Morning. Thought you guys might want a greasy breakfast after the amount of alcohol you consumed last night."

"Thank you, my friend. You thought right. I feel terrible." I hug her from behind while she cooks.

"Serves you right. There's coffee ready for you, and this won't be long."

"Did Tristan stay?" Luca asks, taking a seat at the table.

"Yeah. He's in the shower," she says.

Elly gives me a look like she needs to talk about this all

later, and I offer the same look back. We've been friends for so long, we know what the other one is thinking with just our eye telepathy.

She places the delicious-smelling breakfast in front of us as Tristan arrives back from the shower.

"You two finally up? Must have been an extra big night for you to sleep in so late."

"Ha, yeah," I say, looking over to Elly, trying to read what's happening with her and Tristan. He loiters around her while she cleans up in the kitchen. My memory of last night is a bit hazy from all the wine, but I'm surprised he is even still here. She didn't seem keen on him, and by the looks of it, she's still not. There is something about him today, the way he looks at her or something. Has he always been this shifty looking?

"What do you girls have planned today?" asks Tristan. "We could head out for the day."

"I have to open the gallery at ten," I say. Which is true, I do, but it's going to be a mammoth task today with this hangover.

"Yeah, and I was going to help you today. Remember?" says Elly with the same telepathic eyes. She obviously wants to get rid of the guys.

"Yes, sorry. I do need your help today," I reply.

"Oh, another time then," says Tristan.

"Yeah, definitely," she says.

Luca is devouring his breakfast. I think he couldn't care less if he sees me again. He seems like the kind of guy who would just be happy to go with the flow. Doubt he ever has a steady girlfriend, more just ends up wherever the action is.

"Fun night, girls. We better get going. Don't want to overstay our welcome, do we, Tristan? See you lovely ladies around." He kisses me on the cheek and grabs his jacket.

Tristan looks back to Elly like he wants to say something more but decides not to.

"Bye, Elly."

"Bye, Tris."

The boys leave, closing the door behind them, and Elly lets out a massive sigh, like she had been holding her breath the whole time they were here.

"You okay, chick?"

"I don't know. That was weird last night, Indie. Maybe you can move on that quickly, but I just can't."

"Elly, we didn't do anything. I passed out before we could. And it didn't feel right when he touched me. I might not show it in the same way as you, but I am hurting. I really thought there was something there with Blake, and now I've found out he's like a different person to what I thought. I dunno. It's kinda messed with my brain."

She walks over to me and wraps her arms around me. "They suck. Both of them! Now I know why they're friends."

I hug her back. "Yeah, both as bad as each other. But we will get over them eventually. At least we have each other."

"Maybe I'll get over him, but you're right, at least we have each other," she says sadly.

"Either that or we'll end up crazy cat ladies." I laugh, trying to lighten the mood. She giggles at the thought.

"We better start collecting cats now."

I sip on my coffee while Elly cleans up the kitchen.

Blake

I've just arrived on the second work site for today, a house we're working on just outside of town. I run my hands through my hair and take a deep breath. I'm so on edge at the moment, and the boys don't need to know that. I need to get myself together before I enter the site.

I've had to take on so much extra work for Fraser. After he came home drunk with Shea, it was the last straw. I arranged for a therapist to meet him at the house, and he has agreed to take the necessary steps to get his drinking problem under control. He wants his life back, so he can fix everything with Elly.

The extra stress of the last few weeks has me almost at my tipping point. But he's my mate and he's going through some pretty heavy stuff, so Ash and I have given him some time off to get his shit sorted. Not ideal when I'm already stretched between this business and keeping up with the Vinnie situation, but we need Fraser back to his normal self, and fast. So hopefully a week off and some time to work through everything will do the trick.

Just as I'm about to enter the site, my phone buzzes in my pocket. It's Drew from God knows where in the world; the lucky bastard is back on the world surfing tour. It's funny how this shit situation has brought us closer together. He checks in with me most weeks to see how Jenna is. The guy has obviously got it bad for her. More than just looking out for her, but he won't admit it.

I lean up against a pallet of bricks out the front. "Drew, man, how are you going?"

"Yeah, not bad. Won another comp, so I'm on my way to where I want to be; the top. I wanted to check on how Jenna is going?" The concern for her is evident in his voice.

"Yeah, I have sorted out the house. The bank loan has been approved. The other townhouses go to auction in a couple of weeks. She can move in after that, so not long now."

"Perfect. The sooner the better. She doesn't know I funded the deposit, does she?"

"Nope. I just told her Ash gave us a discount. You should tell her, though, mate. You don't want her to find this out on her own. She's very independent and will be pissed if she ever finds out later. You know how these things go."

"Yeah, that's why I'm not telling her. She won't want to let me help her out and won't be able to afford it without the help. What she doesn't know won't hurt her."

"Why are you helping this girl, anyway? What's in it for you?" I ask. He's gone to an awful lot of effort to help out some random girl he met at a strip club.

"Nothing. I just know not everyone has it as good as me, and if I can do something to give her a better start, then I want to help. Like you can talk, anyway, man. You're doing the same thing, even to the detriment of your own relationship.

I see our site manager coming my way, and I hold up my finger to signal I'll be one minute. He turns and walks back into the house. Drew is right. I know getting involved in the Jenna situation and accepting my father's deal has probably destroyed anything that Indie and I could have ever had. But I couldn't, in good conscience, stand back and watch this unfold the way it was going to.

"Yeah, tell me about it! But I have to. She wouldn't be in this situation if it weren't for guys like Vinnie, and he works for my dad. So that's on me."

"Yeah, I get it, man, but I'm just saying, Indie is a top chick, and you're going to lose her if you don't talk to her about all of this."

"I will talk to her when I know this has all settled down, when Jenna is safe and Vinnie can't get to Indie."

"Hope it's not too late. Elly will kill me for saying

anything, but she and Indie went on a double-date last weekend."

That is not what I want to hear. Ryker had told me they had a night out, but he left out that detail. I can't say I blame Indie, the way I treated her. Why wouldn't she move on? "Did they now?"

"Elly said Indie was a total mess. Drank way too much. The guy was all over her. You're going to lose her, man, if you're not careful."

Fucker! Taking advantage of my girl when she's hurting. "Yeah, I know. But what can I offer her, anyway? It's only a matter of time until I end up back in Sydney, and I don't want to drag her into my family's mess. I can't offer her the future she deserves."

"Don't you think she should be the one to decide what she wants?"

"No. I'm not dragging her into this life. She's better off without me. It's just the way it has to be."

"Okay, man, your choice. Call me if there are any changes with the Jenna situation."

"No worries. Hey, call Fraser. He needs us at the moment. And good luck with your next comp."

"Thanks, man, talk soon."

I need to keep a closer eye on Indie. Up until this point, I've been trying to keep my distance. I don't want to hurt her more than I have, but I don't like that she was out with this guy with his hands all over her. I want to know why her bodyguard didn't tell me the full details. I try not to ask him too much because I know it's a creepy invasion of her privacy, and he really is only there to keep her safe, not fill me in. But details like this I need to know. This guy could be anyone, and even worse, work for anyone, including Vinnie.

CHAPTER TWENTY-ONE

BLAKE

Knowing Indie went out on a date is messing with my head. I've looked into the guy. From what I can see, he's no one to worry about. He works in environmental planning for the government and has no links at all to Vinnie or any of his guys. I should let her move on with her life like I told her I would, but I'm a selfish prick and I can't do that. Ryker texted me to say she's having lunch with some friends at her usual lunch hangout, Daisy's Diner. So, looks like Daisy's Diner, it is for lunch today.

As soon as I walk through the door, I see her. She's hot as ever in a leather jacket and funky red pants. I miss her. My body aches to touch her. I walk to the counter and order my lunch for takeaway. She's with Elly, her friend Sara, and two guys I don't recognise. Might be the guy Drew was talking about that she went on a date with. I'm the one that broke off our arrangement, and I should just let her move on and be happy, but I don't want her to move on. I want to talk to her, even though I know I shouldn't. So, I pull out my phone and send her a message.

Me: Enjoying your lunch? With your new boyfriend?

Probably too much. Oh well, I'm about to find out, and I'm sure I'm going to get a good reaction from her. She reaches for her phone, reads the message, then scans the room, her eyes settling on mine. She looks at me wide-eyed, surprised to see me, I guess. She offers a small smile then types into her phone.

Indie: It's okay. Are you stalking me?

Am I stalking her? Well, kind of, but she doesn't need to know that.

Me: Not stalking. It's a small town, we're bound to run into each other. Who's the dude?

I can see her typing into her phone then she looks up at me. I'm assuming looking for my reaction. I look down to see what she wrote.

Indie: Not that it's any of your business, but I'm on a date.

It's what I was expecting, but it still stings. I knew when we ended things someone would snatch her up quickly; she's a catch. I guess I just didn't expect it to hurt so much.

Me: Didn't take you long!

Indie: What's that supposed to mean? If I remember correctly, you dumped me!!

Me: Not because I wanted to.

She whispers something to Elly, then pushes her chair back and storms over to me. I got the reaction I wanted. She's now talking to me, not him. Even if it's because I pissed her off. I offer a small wave to Elly and she offers a half smile back.

"What are you talking about? You see me trying to move on, and you think you can get under my skin again, so I'll feel guilty or something. Well, you're wrong. I don't. You dumped me," she yells at me. She stands just out of my reach, her hands on her hips, glaring at me, waiting for my answer. Fuck, she's so hot when she's angry. Her low V-neck blouse with her lace bra peeking out tempts me. I want so badly to touch her. Have her in my arms again. It's been so long.

I take a step closer to her, closing the gap. "I'm sorry, you're right. I guess I just didn't expect to see you on a date. Drew told me you were seeing someone, but I didn't believe him."

She looks puzzled, and I probably shouldn't have said I've been talking to Drew.

"What did you expect? I would be at home crying into my pillow over you? I'm not that kind of girl, Blake. You tell me you don't want me, I move on."

"I do want you." I take her arm and drag her around the corner so the others can't see our conversation. I need some privacy with her.

She pulls out of my grip, still looking annoyed. "You can't say that to me," she whispers.

"You're all I can think about, Indie. You drive me crazy. I can't stand seeing you here on a date."

"You don't make any sense to me, Blake. What do you want from me?"

I lean in closer, our faces almost touching. "I don't want you dating."

"You lost the right to say that when you broke it off," she whispers.

I look down at her. I really am sorry. I wish things could have been different between us. In another lifetime, we would have been perfect together. "I'm sorry, Indie." I cup her face, running my thumb over her luscious lips. Her breath catches, a flush rising over her cheeks. I know the effect I have over her, and I know this is unfair. But I want her.

"It's not really a date. Sara is here as well, plus I'm feeling more like the third wheel—or more like fifth, I guess."

"Well, good. He's not the right guy for you. I'm sorry about our situation. I know this won't make any sense. I wish I could tell you, but the less you know the better." I drop my hand to hold hers, and she lets me. I run my thumb back and forth over her silky skin. It feels so good to touch her.

She looks up at me. "Why are you and Drew talking, anyway? He's back overseas now. What could you possibly have to talk about?"

"He was just looking out for me. We're mates." I shrug.

Her eyes narrow. "Hmm, how stupid do you think I am? I know there's stuff going on with you boys, and I know it all started that night you went on Ash's buck's night." That again. I know I need to shut her up before this conversation goes any further, so I grab her, pulling her to me, placing my lips on hers.

She pulls back in a half-hearted attempt to stop this from going further, but her hands are bunched in my shirt. "What are you doing? I'm on a date."

"Yeah, but I bet when he kisses you, it doesn't feel like this." I smash my lips with hers again, and she lets me, her body caving into mine. I run my hands through her soft, silky hair, and she digs her fingers into my back.

Our kiss is desperate and fiery, the heat between us insane. I run my hand down her body, cupping her arse. Her hand slips under my shirt, her fingers lightly running over my chest as we kiss like horny teenagers. Our breathing is ragged. We're desperate for each other, and if we weren't in a burger place, I would take everything I need from her and give her all she needs from me.

My lips are back on hers, and I swipe my tongue through her open mouth, claiming her. I want so badly for her to be mine, for this to be my reality, a simple life with the woman I love.

She pulls back to look at me. Her hair's a mess, her eyes ablaze with desire. "What do you want from me, Blake?"

I stroke her hair, holding her close to my chest. Breathing her in while I can. She smells amazing. "Everything," I say softly.

She pulls back a little further. "But you can't, and it's complicated." She sighs.

I close my eyes as I breathe her in again. I don't want to answer that; I want to hold her like this and never let go. "Yes," I whisper.

"Let me go then, Blake." She steps out of my grip and stands back to look at me. She's hurt, but she's strong. So much stronger than I am. She's right, I need to let her go. Her sad eyes hold mine. She squares her shoulders. "You need to let me go." She turns and walks away, and I watch her go. I love her, but I have to let her walk away. No matter how I feel, this isn't the right time for her to fall in love with me.

I walk back to the counter and collect my order. I don't look back over to the table. I can't. If I do, I will cave and carry her out of here over my shoulder, but that wouldn't be fair to her.

Indie

I rush back to the table, hoping I wasn't too missed. I'm

not even sure how long I was gone for. I lose time when I'm with him. It could have been ten minutes or an hour, I have no idea. My heart still hammers in my chest. My face is hot. I must look a mess. I feel a mess.

What is he doing to me? I'm strong. Independent. I don't need him. But, oh God, do I want him. I don't get it. Why is life torturing me with this man, tempting me, showing me everything I want, then taking it away? It's so unfair. But when has my life ever been fair? It's just the way it is. I'm not destined to have that, a person who's mine. Happiness is held just out of reach, and that's why I need to be strong for myself. Because I don't have anyone else.

"Is everything okay?" asks Luca. "You look strange." He gives me a knowing look.

Shit. Did he see me or something? I flatten down my hair and plaster on a fake smile. "Sorry, yeah, I'm fine. Just talking to an old friend I haven't seen in a while."

He watches me. "Okay, if that's what you say, Indie."

Elly gives my hand a squeeze under the table, she's had enough of being here with these guys, I can tell.

Sara whacks me on the arm, and I turn to look at her. "Ouch."

"Oh my God, Indie. Has Luca told you some of his camping stories? It sounds like so much fun." Sara is grinning from ear to ear, and she's giving Luca her full attention. She has since he walked in. I might as well not be here at all.

"Yeah, we should all go together sometime. Could be a lot of fun," suggests Luca, raising a brow in my direction. He has clearly seen me with Blake just now and could care less. Who is this guy? I'm pretty sure he's suggesting some sort of dirty weekend camping with me and my friend. It's so hard to tell with Luca. He's the type of guy who's up for anything, so I never know where the conversation or day will go when I'm with him.

"Yeah, Elly, we could go to have our own tent set up," says Tristan.

Elly gives me a look. She has already said she just wants to be friends, and he says he's okay with it but constantly tries for more. I think she has had about enough of it. "Oh, no thanks, I don't really camp. Plus I have work every weekend."

I'm trying to stay present in the conversation even though I'm anything but.

Luca nods and smiles his cheeky smile. "I think we should go this weekend, if you're interested, girls?"

"Yes, I'm in." Sara claps, all excited. She's giddy over him. This is insane to watch. I have known her for years, and I have never seen her like this before.

"Nice, you're going to love this little spot I've found, Sara. It's private, and the beach is close by." He turns his attention back to me. "Indie, what about you? You in? Might get your mind off the guy."

"Um, oh, I've got the gallery to run. I can't. Maybe some other time. But you guys should definitely go together, that would be fun."

"Are you sure?" asks Luca, looking a little disappointed.

Sara could care less if I come or not, her eyes still glued to him. I think I'm going to take that as my cue to leave and save Elly at the same time. We came in the same car so it's as good an excuse as any.

I smile over at him. "Yeah, you should definitely go. Hey, I just remembered, Elly and I have that meeting with a new client." She looks at me, confused at first, then clues in and smiles.

"Yeah, it's that time already, we should be going."

"We better run." I hop up and grab my bag, and Elly follows.

Tristan grabs her wrist. "When will I see you again?"

"Um, at the café, I guess."

"I'll message you."

"Okay, Tris," says Elly, taking a step out of his grip.

"Okay, babe," says Sara, still looking at Luca. "Have fun with your work thing. I can keep the boys company."

"Yeah, sorry. You guys are getting on so well. Don't stop on account of me. I'll catch up with you guys later." I blow air kisses to them and rush out of there as quickly as I can, without falling flat on my face, Elly close behind me.

I stop when I get out the front and bury my face in my hands, trying to get control of myself. I'm all shaky. What's wrong with me? I've just pushed a perfectly nice guy into the hands of my very good-looking and slightly slutty friend. But I don't care. I had to get out of there. My skin feels like it's on fire from what Blake and I did in the hall.

How does he have this effect on me? Even when I'm pissed at him, I want him. I was just moving on with my life, and he had to show up here today to mess with me again. Now I'm back to square one. I can still smell his aftershave on me, sense his hands running over my skin. I drop my hands, taking a deep breath, and try to shake off the feeling of him.

"Are you okay, Indie?" Elly asks, rubbing my back.

I look over to her, and I know she gets it. She knows what I'm going through because she is dealing with the same, her lingering feelings for Fraser. "Yeah, sorry, it's just Blake. He drives me fucking crazy. I try to move on from him because he dumps me, then he tells me he wants me. I'm so confused. Are you okay? Tristan is kinda intense with you."

She shrugs, then lets out a little sigh. "I know, right? I have told him so many times that I don't want anything more than friends, but he keeps pushing."

"You might have to be more firm with him. I don't know how to say this without sounding like a total bitch, but he kind of gives me the creeps, hey?"

"Does he? I'm starting to feel a little uneasy with him. He's really nice and everything, but he's just too full-on, and I can't be what he wants. I'm in love with someone else."

I squeeze her hand. "I know, chickee."

CHAPTER TWENTY-TWO

INDIE

Today was my last shift at the café. Elly and I have decided that, since our business is taking off and we've just landed a new client for the styling business, our time needs to be spent on that. It's a beautiful sunny afternoon and a few of us are out the back of the café, in our courtyard, for a quick farewell party. After years of working here, I can honestly say today was the only day I slacked off. I sat drinking chai lattes and chatting with my boss, Rachel, while the younger girls took over the workload.

I'm going to miss Rachel. She has become more than just a boss to me. She's seen me through so much: my mum getting sick and passing, my massive break-up with Hayden, and all the other shit life has thrown at me. She has always been the voice of reason.

Two familiar faces, Luca and Tristan, come round the corner. Rachel must have invited every customer we have. I haven't seen Luca since the awkward lunch the other day, when I left him with Sara. She messaged me after, saying how much she liked him, and if I wasn't going to do something with him soon, she was making a move on him. She acted like she was joking, but I know her, and I could see the way she was looking at him. I gave her the green light; they would be good together. Who am I to stand in their way?

"Hey, guys. Looks like all my favourite customers are here to say goodbye." I smile as I kiss them both on the cheek.

"Rachel mentioned she was throwing a little party and we should stop by. Sad to see you're going. This place won't be the same without you," says Luca.

"Oh, thanks, but it's well and truly time to move on."

"Is Elly around still?" asks Tristan. The poor boy is obsessed with her, and he's got zero chance. She's still hung up on Fraser. He looks on edge today, looking around the courtyard.

I point to where she sits. "Yeah, over by the old tree."

"Thanks, Indie." Tristan makes his way over to Elly, and I feel sorry for them both. No one is going to win there.

"So, you going camping this weekend with Sara? Sounds like you made quite the impression on her the other day. She hasn't stopped talking about you."

Luca leans up against the table, hands in his jeans' pockets. "Yeah, maybe. Is that okay?"

"Yeah. Why wouldn't it be? She's a cool chick. You two get on, you'll have fun." I shrug like I don't care. Truth is, I don't. Luca is hot and all, but he's not the man for me, and stopping my friend from dating him, just 'cause I saw him first, would be ridiculous. Who knows, he might just be the love of her life, and I was the one who introduced them.

"I'm leaving. You coming?" Tristan calls out as he storms past us, heading for the door.

"Shit. Sorry, Indie. Better go see what's wrong with the grumpy one. I'll see you round."

"I'll see you round. Good luck this weekend." I wrap my arms round him, giving him a quick hug. Then he takes off after Tristan.

That was easier than I thought it was going to be. How funny, he's into Sara as well. She might get her Prince Charming after all.

I really need to head home and get everything sorted for tomorrow's spring art auction. I say my goodbyes and leave Elly. She wants to check in on her dad, and I need to get back to the gallery. There's a lot to do before tomorrow.

Back at the gallery, I get to work checking over the starting prices we have listed for the auctioneer. We have works here from six different artist and potters, so I have to make sure the auctioneer knows our minimums. There is so much more organising that needs to go into an event like this than I thought. And for once in my life, I'm giving it everything I have. It's going to be perfect.

I finally feel like I'm where I need to be career-wise, and it feels so good. I feel like my mum would be looking down on me smiling, saying, *You're doing it, baby. Keep on going, keep pushing for your dream.* So, I am. And tomorrow will be awesome, I just know it.

A text notification beeps on my phone. It's Blake again. Since I bumped into him in the diner the other day, he's been sending me random messages, just checking in on me. I should be pissed off by it, but I'm not. It's nice to know he's thinking of me as much as I'm thinking of him. Even if we're not together, he's making an effort to be friends, and I like it. I really missed him when we didn't talk, so at least this is something.

Blake: How is my favourite artist going in preparation for her big auction tomorrow?

Me: Still a lot to do, but I'm getting there.

Blake: I'm bringing some people I know, and they have deep pockets, so you better be ready to make some money.

Me: Nice. Thanks!!

Blake: See you tomorrow.

Me: See you then.

There's a knock at the door, and I turn to see a large man, probably in his mid-40s, with longish dark hair. He smiles, and I go over to open the door.

"Sorry, we're closed, preparing for an auction tomorrow," I say, holding the door open.

"Oh, sorry, sweetheart, I thought it was today. I can't make it tomorrow." He looks disappointed, and I feel bad.

I motion for him to come in. "Oh, that's okay. You can have a look around today if you like?"

"Thank you." He holds out his hand for me to shake. "Sorry, I didn't catch your name?"

"Indie."

His handshake is firm. "Vinnie. Nice to meet you, Indie."

"Nice to meet you. Have a look around. Let me know if there's anything you're interested in."

"Thank you, Indie. I will." He walks around, taking in the displays. I get back to working, checking over the paperwork.

"Indie," he calls, "are these all yours?" He points to the wall in front of him.

I walk over to where he's looking. "Oh, no, only this wall over here. But there are some beautiful works from some of our other amazing local talent. I'm sure you'll find something that you like."

"I'm sure I will, but I have heard so much about your work, and I hear it's going to be very valuable one day soon. I want to get in and buy up big before the prices soar." He smiles the most over-the-top smile. This guy is like super cheesy or something. He's probably some big art collector I should know about and be making a fuss over, but I have no idea who he is. And even if he is some big deal, I'm not treating him different to anyone else, just because he thinks he deserves it.

I smile warmly at his compliment. "Oh, that's very nice of you, but I'm sure my prices aren't going anywhere anytime soon. Don't think you need to worry about that." What a strange thing for him to say. Most art wouldn't normally rise so much in price overnight unless the artist dies. I laugh to myself. I don't plan on doing that.

He points to a painting of a young brunette in a blue silk gown. "I want this one here." Then walks further along the wall, his eyes scanning the art in front of him. "I'll take these two over here as well." Two more of the same girl.

Is he serious? Just like that. He hasn't even asked for the price. "Okay. Are you sure?" I frown, a little confused. Normally it takes some time for people to pick what they want, especially if they haven't seen my work before.

He nods and walks over to the counter where I stand. "Yes. Will $10,000 cover it?" He pulls out a wad of cash, and I almost gasp at the sight of it. Who carries around that kind of cash with them?

This is strange! Don't overthink it, just take it, Indie. He can obviously afford it. The fancy suit he's wearing would cost that much alone. He must be one of the art dealers who Blake talked to. "Um. Yes, that will cover it." I smile politely, trying to keep my cool when I really want to do a happy dance.

He places the cash on the counter and heads for the door. "Perfect, then. I'll go grab a coffee while you wrap them up for me. I'll be back in half an hour."

"Okay, no problems. See you then." I can't believe my luck. This is amazing for our little business. My body is tingling with excitement. What a rush it is to finally be making some real money.

I start to wrap up the paintings and stack them against the wall, ready for him to take. He has chosen all paintings of a young woman with long dark hair. A friend of mine modelled for me a few years back. Maybe he has a thing for brunettes. Who knows?

Elly pops her head in. She's just got back from her parents' place. "Hey, I'm home."

"Hey, chickee, how's your dad doing today?"

"Getting better every day." She manages a small smile.

I'm biting my lip. I can barely contain my excitement. I have to tell her what just happened. "Fantastic. Hey, you're never going to believe this. I've sold three paintings already today. $10,000 worth!" I squeal.

Her eyes go wide with excitement. "W-what?" she stutters.

"I know, right. The dude just offered it to me. Didn't even ask how much I wanted for them. He's coming back soon to pick them up."

She squeals and races around behind the counter to hug me. We do a little happy dance. "That's insane! Blake must have told him about you?" She's beaming. This is the happiest I have seen her in ages.

"Yeah, that's my guess. Can you ask him next time you talk to him? His name is Vinnie."

"You should ask him. I see you two texting each other. I'm not blind." She smirks.

Vinnie appears back at the glass door, and Elly wanders over to open the door for him.

"This is my business partner, Elly," I say as she offers her hand.

He shakes her hand. "Vinnie. Nice to meet you, Elly."

"I have them all ready for you. Did you need a hand down to the car?" I offer.

He looks at the wrapped paintings, then back to me. "No. I think I can manage. Thank you, Indie. You've made me a very happy man today." He smiles that same over-the-top smile from before. It's kind of creepy.

"Well, tell your friends the auction is from two till four tomorrow," says Elly, still beaming with excitement. "They can drop by and have a look."

He picks up his paintings and places them under his arm. "I'll be sure to let them know. Goodbye, girls." He carries his paintings out and gives one last creepy smile.

As soon as he's out of earshot, Elly screams again. "Oh my God! This is insane. Tomorrow is going to be awesome. I can just feel it."

"Totally," I reply, still beaming. Nothing can wipe this smile off my face today.

Just minutes after he leaves, some random guy comes running through the door, puffing like he's out of breath.

"Hi. Can I help you?" Elly calls after him as he rushes past her.

"Hi, sorry, I'm Ryker, your new neighbour. Moved in a couple of weeks ago. That guy who was just in here, was he troubling you?" He gets the words out as fast as he can, still puffing, trying to catch his breath. Ryker is big, like bulky-muscle big. He wears a leather jacket and ripped jeans. He's the kind of guy you would cross the street to avoid.

He's staring at me, his eyes boring through me, waiting for my answer. "No, not at all. He just bought some of my paintings. Why? Is something wrong?" I ask, my heart already beating a little faster just from seeing his expression.

"Don't let him in here again. Here's my card. Call me if he comes anywhere near you," he demands, his voice loud and commanding. The way he says it scares the shit out of me. Elly looks to me, wide-eyed.

"Um, why? You're going to need to tell me more than that if you think I'm going to listen to you. He just spent a shitload of money with me. Why would I turn him away?" I get out, a little more quietly than I intended.

His face is cold and hard, his eyes almost void of any emotion. He stares through me. "You don't want his money, sweetie, trust me."

"I have no idea who you are. Why would we trust you? Maybe you're who we need to be looking out for," Elly pipes up, coming round the counter to my side. She grabs my hand, and I can feel she is shaking just as much as me.

"I'm with the police. Call me if he comes anywhere near you again." I look over his card. It just has his name Anthony Ryker and a phone number. Is he like a detective or something? It doesn't say he's with the police on here.

I look back at him, trying to work out who he could be. "I have a friend that's a cop in this town. I'll find out if you're lying," I say, trying to sound braver than I actual am.

"I'm not lying, sweetie. I know Theo, your cop friend, as well. You need to be more careful, Indie. You too, Elly. Don't let random guys in, unless they have an appointment and you've done a background search."

"I didn't tell you his name is Theo or that..." I swallow the lump in my throat. "How do you know who we are?"

He must realise he's scaring the shit out of us, and his face softens a little. "I told you, I'm with the police. I'm looking out for you girls. That guy who was in here, he probably told you he was some businessman from Sydney. He's a crook. Don't let him in here again. Do you understand?"

"Okay, we won't, will we, Indie," Elly says, peeking over to me. She looks like she's about to burst into tears.

I shake my head, lost for words. What's going on? There goes my high from making an awesome sale. Now we're back to this *someone is after you* shit. What the fuck is going on? I want answers.

"Good. I'll be downstairs if you need me." He leaves the gallery as fast as he arrived, pulling out his phone and making a call on his way.

"That was weird. I'm kinda freaked out now. I'm going to call Theo about it," says Elly.

"Yeah, good idea. I'm going to lock the door." My shaky hands turn the latch, and I listen to Elly as she talks to Theo on the phone.

"Theo, some guy just came into the gallery. Said he knows you. Ryker someone." Her voice breaks, and she starts to cry. I go to stand with her, taking the phone from her and putting it on speaker.

"Theo, it's Indie. What is going on? Do you know some guy, Anthony Ryker? Looks like he goes by his surname. He's living downstairs from us, behind the shop front."

He lets out a sigh. "Yeah, girls, I do. Are you okay? What happened? Why is Elly crying?"

"Because he just came in here and scared the shit out of us."

"Why did he do that?" His voice sounds panicked now.

"Some guy, Vinnie..."

"Vinnie was there at the gallery?" he shouts down the phone. And it scares me. Theo is always cool-headed. He deals with all sorts of shit on a daily basis. If he's worried, I'm really terrified.

"Yes," I say, my voice quivering.

"I'll be there in a minute." He hangs up the phone.

I turn to Elly and wrap my arms around her. She's a mess, but that's not that unusual for her at the moment. "I'm sure it's all going to be okay. Theo will be here soon to explain what's going on."

After the auction tomorrow, I'm sitting Blake down, and he's going to give me answers. No more of this pretending everything is all good, when it's not. It's not normal to get followed home by cars, or to have random, leather-jacket-wearing guys come and tell you to watch out for men in expensive suits. It takes a lot to piss me off, and I've put up with this situation for long enough. I want answers, and I'm going to fucking get them!

Blake

I'm trying to train up the new project manager who'll take my place here with The Green Door, until I can come back—if I ever can. He's one of my builders who's been here since we started, so I know I'll have no dramas with him, and he can still call me any time he needs to. I will still be in charge of all operations from Sydney, I just can't be on site to run the checks and oversee the construction. He will need to take care of that side of things.

It would be easier to train him if I wasn't interrupted with new dramas every five minutes, but I have been on the phone to both Morgan and Dad today. They are nervous about Vinnie. He's gone completely off the grid, and no one has heard from him in weeks. Not since we worked out that he's working for both sides. We're working closely with Theo and Talon, his new partner now that Fiona is on maternity leave. They're doing what they can to help track him down, but so far nothing.

My phone lights up. It's Ryker. What does he want? Better not be any trouble with Indie.

"Vinnie knows where your girl's gallery is. He's just left there, after spending a fortune on her art." What the fuck? Vinnie was there with her?

"Are you fucking kidding me? Why didn't you stop him? That's your whole job." I run my hands through my hair. Who has my dad assigned to protect her? This is unbelievable.

"He must have someone in the force working with him. I was stuck in my apartment, answering useless questions from some dick in a uniform. You need to talk to your mate, Theo. Anything could've gone down today."

"Fuck!" I yell into the phone. I feel like I'm starting to lose control. This can't be happening. Someone on the force is crooked and working with Vinnie. "I know there are plenty of crooked cops, but they're loyal to my dad. This has never been a problem before. What do we do now?"

"Look, I know you're not going to like this, but it's time the girls know what's going on. It's too dangerous for them not to know. I dropped in and met them just now."

"You did what?" I yell again. I'm losing my patience with this situation. It's getting out of hand, and we need to fix it.

"Calm down, Blake. I just introduced myself as their

new neighbour. Made it out that I was on the force myself, and if he came near them again, they're to call me."

"Well, that's something. But he has their address, and he's letting us know it, too, by going there in the middle of the day. He could go back at any time. We need to deal with him now."

"You know we can't until Mr Donovan gives us the okay."

"I'm not waiting until it's too late," I spit, frustrated. My dad isn't here. This isn't his girl who's being threatened.

"You need to talk to her, let her know what's going on, so she can look out for trouble. She's too trusting of everyone because she doesn't know not to be. You're not protecting her by keeping this from her."

"Yep. Got to go."

"Let me know what you need from me."

"Yep." I hang up the phone. I'm so fucking pissed off. Fucking Vinnie was there with her today. Anything could have happened. Why was he there? He's just making us look stupid, showing us he can do whatever the fuck he wants. He has too many friends willing to help him. I don't care what my dad says, if I run into Vinnie, I'll deal with him myself. I don't care about the consequences, as long as he doesn't get to her.

"Fuck!" I scream out loud. What do I do? I need to tell her, but I don't want to. If I do, I know that's the end of us. There is no coming back from this, not even if I ever get out of my responsibilities in Sydney. She won't want me back. But if I don't tell her, it could risk her life, and I can't take that chance. I won't take that chance. Not with her.

I send her a text, letting her know I'm coming over to chat.

Me: We need to talk. I'm coming over tonight.

Indie: Yeah, we do. Tomorrow.
Me: I will be there tonight. This can't wait.

I linger over my phone, waiting for the little bubbles that indicate she is going to text back to try and stop me, but there is no response. Well, she knows I'm coming.

I call Theo and he picks up straight away. "I'm with them now. They're okay, just scared."

"Okay. What the fuck happened? The nerve of him, Theo. I thought no one could track him down, and he turns up in the middle of the day. What the hell?"

"Yeah, I know, mate. I can't say too much at the moment with the girls here, but we're looking into it. We will track him down."

"Don't tell Indie, but I'll stay there until we do. The girls can't be there by themselves at night. We don't know when he's going to show up again."

"Yeah, good idea. I'll stay here for a bit until they've calmed down."

"You need to look into this guy who had Ryker held up in his apartment for questioning. He said he was in uniform."

"There's no way he's with us. No one would be helping Vinnie. He must have had a fake uniform."

"Maybe, but we need to work out who it was and fast. Before they turn up at one of the girls' places and they go missing."

"On it, Blake. You let us worry about this, okay?" His voice is demanding with authority, but I think he is forgetting who he is talking to.

"You know I can't do that, Theo. If I hear anything, I will let you know. I appreciate you doing the same." Like hell I'll leave it up to them. If Vinnie has a crooked cop helping him, then we don't know who we can trust.

"Talk soon, Blake." He disconnects the call.

I run a hand through my hair, more frustrated than I think I have ever been. How am I supposed to protect Indie, Elly, and Jenna? He will target anyone we care about until he gets what he wants. We need to get this situation under control.

CHAPTER TWENTY-THREE

INDIE

I open the door, and there he is. The man that haunts my fantasies—sexy as hell and just as fucking infuriating. I tell him we can talk tomorrow, and he turns up today. Why does he still have this effect on me? I should be over him already, but I'm not. He's on my mind constantly. It's already 8.30pm; late for just a chat.

"Looks like booty-call time to me, and an overnight bag. You really are getting ahead of yourself, aren't you?"

He looks at me, his expression serious. "Let's talk then. I'll let you decide if I should stay or not." Cocky bastard. What would make me want him to stay? Especially after today. I motion for him to come in.

He walks in, closing the front door behind him, checking the lock. He's on edge big time, and it's scaring me. I walk down the hall to my room, and he follows, throwing his bag on the floor. I sit on my bed, the same bed where we've slept together many times before. But it feels different now. His eyes graze over to me. They're more intense than normal. His face looks tired too, with dark circles under the eyes, like he hasn't been sleeping.

"You going to sit down or just keep staring at me like that? You're kind of freaking me out, and after the day I've had, I don't need anyone else worrying me."

"If I sit on your bed with you, I'm going to want more, and that's not exactly what I'm here for, Indie." He takes a seat on the day bed, looking very uncomfortable.

I fiddle with the heart locket around my neck, hoping my mother will give me the strength to deal with Blake and this situation he has us in. She gave me this locket ages ago, but I have started wearing it again since I found those photos, and everything got strange. I need to feel close to her. I wish I had her guidance now more than ever.

Where do I start? I want answers, and tonight he's going to give them to me. "What are you here for, Blake? You ready to give me some answers?"

His expression gives nothing away. "Answers to what?"

I can tell by the expression on his face he knows exactly what I'm talking about. Why is he being so vague? "Okay, let's start with why is some guy watching over me?"

He sits up a little straighter. I have him on that one. He probably assumed I would buy that ridiculous story about our new neighbour coincidentally working for the police. Oh, please. I wasn't born yesterday. "I don't know what you're talking about." He stands, walking over to the window, moving the curtain to peer out.

"See, I think you do. Goes by the name of Ryker. Seems normal enough, except for how he came running into the gallery after I made a big sale to some businessman from Sydney. He was out of breath and very distressed that I'd let that man in. Gave me a warning and said if he tried to come near me again, I was to call him straight away. He would watch out for us, me and Elly."

Blake turns back to look at me. "Why do you think I've

anything to do with him? Sounds like that's all some sort of police matter to me."

I'm getting agitated with him. He's being so elusive. I want answers, and he's giving me nothing. I need to calm down, so this doesn't escalate into a screaming match. I take a deep breath and try to settle my voice. "Blake, now's the time to tell me what's going on. And before you try and lie to me, to protect me, don't. I know you boys: Drew, Theo, Fraser. You're all hiding stuff from me. I've done some of my own research since no one would tell me anything."

A frown crosses his brow, but still, he gives nothing away. "What did you find out with your research?"

Ahh, so frustrating. Every question I give him, he throws it back to me with another question. "Your dad's like some underworld boss or something. Your family seems to attract lots of media attention—lots of newspaper articles—and has millions in properties and businesses."

He nods. "I told you my upbringing wasn't conventional. That's why I moved away. I was hoping to get away from it all."

"But you didn't tell me to what extent. This is like extreme stuff your family is involved in, right? And that's why you're nervous about me getting hurt, and you hired the guard to watch over me."

"You're quite the little investigator. This is what I wanted to talk to you about tonight. And why I broke it off with you before. That was what I was trying to tell you. It wasn't because I didn't want to be with you. It's because I knew he was watching me, and I didn't want him to get to you. But he's worked out you're someone special anyway, and he's the guy that was here buying your paintings today."

"You're worried about the guy who was here today? He didn't seem like anyone to worry about. Was nice enough and paid $10,000 for a couple of paintings. Best money I've made off my paintings yet."

His face is hard, creases forming on his forehead, his eyes narrowed. "Indie, trust me, he is dangerous." He looks so serious, and it's kind of frightening me. I knew this was extreme stuff, but seeing his face, I know this is bad. As I remember what Vinnie said today, my hands start to tremble a little, and I flick them to get them to stop.

"That's why he bought them. He's going to try and kill me, isn't he? He said the prices of my art are about to rise significantly. He meant because I'll be dead!"

Blake looks at me and his eyes are glassy. He's afraid that Vinnie is going to kill me. Fuck, this is insane. I stand up and start to pace. Oh my God, this is so much worse than I originally thought.

Blake quickly closes the gap between us, pulling me into him. "I'm so sorry you're caught up in all of this, Indie. This is what I was trying to avoid."

"How am I supposed to trust you when you don't tell me what's going on? If I'm in some sort of danger, don't you think I should know the details, so I can protect myself as well?" I say into his chest. I can't even look at him right now.

He pulls me closer to him. "You'll have a guard looking over you during the day, and I'll stay here at night, until we track him down and get this sorted."

I pull back to look at him. "You can't stay here, Blake."

"I am. Until we've got him. I'm not taking no for an answer. You need someone here with you *all* the time."

"Blake, if it's all as bad as you say, don't you think I should know the details? I can handle it. I'm not some delicate little Violet that needs to be protected." I plead with him with my eyes. I need to know what I'm up against. "Just tell me."

He brushes some stray hair behind my ear. "It's a long story."

"I have all night."

He looks at me as if he's going to change his mind and not tell me. Then he takes a deep breath. "This guy, Vinnie, he used to work for my dad as a guard of sorts, helped with debt collecting and keeping things in line. About six months ago, his girlfriend at the time, Cassie—or Jenna as we all know her—oversaw him dealing with someone who had run out of chances and couldn't pay up. She saw too much. She had no idea what he was capable of and was horrified, so she made a run for it. A few months ago, my dad rang, asking for my help to track her down. They had been given information leading them to believe she might be in the Byron area. So, they just wanted me to keep an eye out and tell them if I saw her. At Ash's buck's party..."

"She was there. I knew something happened that night. I kept asking everyone, but no one would tell me."

"Yes, she was there. She was working, and luckily, we found her before Dad and Vinnie did. They were both there looking for her that night as well."

"She's the brunette from the townhouses, isn't she?"

He nods.

"So, how does all this affect you and me? I don't get it."

"Drew took a liking to her and managed to talk her into leaving the club with him. She couldn't go back to her job there, so with the help of his mum, we found her a new job in the hope Vinnie wouldn't find her. But he turned up at my office a few weeks later. He threatened me, saying he knew I had something to do with his girlfriend disappearing from the club that night, and if I didn't help him get her back, he would do the same thing to you that he did to my first girlfriend."

"What happened to your first girlfriend?" I say with a gulp.

"There was an accident." His voice is low, strained.

"The fire at the restaurant, there was a young girl killed, and you were in the photo in the newspaper article. He killed your girlfriend?" I whisper.

"The fire was meant for me. He knew I was being trained to one day take over Dad's position, and he wanted it, so he was hoping to make it look like our rivals, the Barrett brothers, had done it. Turns out he was working with them all along. All of this has only recently come to light. My dad had no idea, and now he's looking for Vinnie too, but Vinne's on the run, and he's angry as hell with me."

"What happened that night? If they were after you, how did they get her?"

"We worked together in one of Dad's restaurants. I was behind the bar, and she waited tables. She was a waitress. Our families are old friends. Her dad had worked with my dad for years, so we grew up together. The night she died, we were closing up. I went out the back to take out the rubbish. While I was out there, I heard the front windows smashing, and by the time I got back inside, the restaurant was fully alight. I got to where Bella was and carried her out the front; she was hardly breathing. The fire trucks arrived while I was carrying her out and tried to help me... it was too late."

A tear rolls down my cheek. I'm so sad for that poor girl, her family, and for Blake. I wipe my face. This is heartbreaking. "I'm so sorry, Blake. That's terrible. You were both so young. You shouldn't have had to go through that." I take his hand, and he looks up at me. His eyes are so sad. I could see it before, but I didn't know why. Now that I know, it makes it so much worse. I want to take his pain away. But how do you take away pain that stays with you for a lifetime?

"Now, can you see why I had to break it off with you? I can't have someone else I care about getting hurt because of me. This guy, Indie, if he knows we're together, you're a way to get to me. These kinds of guys, they don't care who they hurt or how, they just do what they need to, to get what they want."

"Yes, I can see. I don't know why you couldn't just tell me all this in the beginning, but I get it. What do we do now he knows where we live? He was at the gallery. I'm scared, Blake."

He squeezes my hand. "I know, baby. That's why I'm here. I'll stay on the couch. He'll have to get through me to get to you, and that's not going to happen. During the day, you have to take Ryker with you at all times. Just until Dad gives us the go-ahead and we can deal with Vinnie."

"What does that mean?" My eyes plead with him to say anything other than what I think he means.

"You don't need to worry about that." His thumb strokes over the back of my hand to comfort me, but it's not helping.

"Blake, what are you going to do?"

"Whatever has to be done," he says, his voice harsh and determined.

"I don't like that. Can't we just get the police involved? They can help. Theo will help us," I say hopefully. This doesn't have to go down the road he's hinting at.

"They are involved, but the problem is, just like there are good cops like Theo, there are bad ones, and someone is working against us as well. That's how Vinnie got in here today. Someone in a uniform had Ryker distracted."

I throw my hands up in the air and stand. I start to pace.

This is too much. "Great! We don't even know who we can trust."

"That's right, baby. Now you're getting the hang of this. We know we can trust Theo and Ryker, so if you have any trouble, that's who you contact. Okay?"

"Okay."

"Dad is doing what he can from Sydney. He called Vinnie back there, but he's not listening and has stopped all communication with us. There is no knowing what he will do next, now he knows we're on to him."

"So, you're going to stay here every night on that little day bed until you sort this out?" There's no way he's going to be sleeping on the day bed, he barely fits on there. But I'm not asking him to stay in my bed after the shit he's put me through, so if he's not going to ask, then it's on him. "It's not very comfy, but if that's what you want."

"It's not what I want, but I need to make sure you're safe, and I don't want you thinking I'm here for a *booty call,* as you put it."

"Okay. I'll get you a blanket and pillow then."

I go to the linen cupboard and grab a pillow and blanket and place them on the end of my bed. "These are for you. I'm going to take a shower and get ready for bed. You can have a shower after if you want."

He nods, watching me as I cross the room. He is acting so strange tonight. This is a side to him I haven't seen. He's serious, calculated, and distant, like his mind is elsewhere, running a million miles an hour. And I guess that makes sense. If I knew I had other people's lives in my hands, I would be like that too.

BLAKE

She walks back into her room in nothing but an ice-blue silk-and-lace nightie. Her hair is out and a little wavy. Is she trying to make this even harder for me? My skin pricks with excitement, even though I know this is not the time.

"You can have a shower now if you like." She walks past me, barely making eye contact, but the silk of her nightie brushes my leg, making it impossible not to pay attention to her. I watch her as she climbs into bed, fiddling with the heart locket she's wearing around her neck. She reaches for the covers, pulling them back and patting them down. Still not looking my way, she grabs a book from her nightstand and starts to read.

I let out a sigh, not knowing what else to say at this point. I grab my towel and make my way to the shower. Tonight is going to be more difficult than I had anticipated. I can barely be in the same room as her and not lose complete control. Even after the craziness today, my dick is hard as a rock just at the sight of her. I'm like a horny teenager. How am I going to sleep in her room without touching her, when it's all I want to do? My body craves her; it has since that first night when she spilled her drink down my shirt, and I looked into those green eyes. I need to be with her. But more than that, I need to know she's safe. That's why I'm here, and I have to remember that.

I shower quickly and make my way back to her room in my boxers, ready for a long night of no sleep. She's still reading but looks over her book, taking me in as I walk back in the room.

"Do you have to walk around without your shirt on? It's very distracting." Her voice is low, almost breathless, and I know I have as much effect on her as she does me.

"Oh, and the sexy-as-fuck nightie you're wearing isn't distracting?" I say, laying the blanket out on the lounge.

"This old thing is what I wear every night. You're just going to have to get used to seeing me like this, if you plan on being my big, brave protector every night." Her lips turn up on one side as she lifts her book back up and starts to read again.

She's playing a game she can't win. Neither of us can.

"You're a tease, Indie," I say, slumping down on the day bed—my bed for who knows how long. I pull the covers up, trying to get comfortable.

"That's what you get for dumping me instead of trusting me and telling me what was going on in the first place."

That's it. I throw the covers back and stand quickly, removing the book from her hands, placing it on the bedside table.

"Stop hiding behind your book, making snippy comments at me. If you have something to say, say it! I did what I had to do to protect the woman I love, and if I had to walk away from you again to ensure your safety, I would."

Her body stiffens under my annoyed stare. "Oh, please, how can you even know you're in love with me? We barely know each other. The man I was getting to know is completely different to this man standing before me. The son of an underworld boss." Those words roll off her tongue so easily, like she's rehearsed this speech. It stings to hear her say it, but that's not who I really am. She has to know that.

"I fell in love with you the first time I saw you, and who I am doesn't change how I feel about you. It might change the way you feel about me, and I understand that. It's one of the reasons I didn't want to tell you at all. How could you feel the same about me, when you knew what kind of a man I really was?"

She reaches up to me, cupping my face in her hand. Her eyes are glassy, and I feel like for the first time since I met her, she is really vulnerable with me. This is her with no walls up to protect herself. "I fell in love with you the first time I saw you as well, but I knew there was something that scared me about you." She pulls her hand back and drops her head. "That's why I ran that first morning; I wasn't ready to feel that way. I'm not scared of where you came from or what you've done. I'm scared of the way I feel about you when we're together. How much of myself I give to you. If I give you my all, you're going to break my heart, I just know it."

I lift her head. Our eyes meet, and she blinks quickly, a stray tear escaping. "I'm not going to break your heart, Indie. I'm here to protect every part of you. You're my girl."

"We should just run away together, leave all this behind us and start again somewhere else, somewhere all this won't find us. Why can't we just do that?" Her eyes are filled with hope. And I wish it was all as easy as she makes it out to be.

"Indie, in another lifetime, I would spend the rest of my life with you, making you happy and giving you the family you've been dreaming about. I would give it all to you. But I can't run away. There are so many people relying on me. You have to understand, I can't let them down. If I ran from this, my dad would track me down. I have responsibilities, being a part of the Donovan family, it's just the way it is."

"Why can't it be simple? How did this all get so hard?" Her voice is soft and trembles as she struggles to get the words out. It's killing me to see what this is doing to her. What I have done to her.

I pull her into me, wrapping my arms around her,

wishing we could just do what she says and run away together. "My life has always been complicated, and this time I made a deal with my dad. His men are protecting you while this is all going on. But when it's over, I go back to Sydney and take over the business." I try and hold her close, but she pushes me back so she can look at me.

Her lips tremble. "You made a deal to keep me safe?"

I nod.

"I'll go with you then. I'm not scared, Blake. You sacrificed your life here for me. I will come with you." She has renewed purpose now, and I can see how determined she is to make this happen.

I shake my head, trying to find the right words to let her down easily. "I don't even want to go. I'm not dragging you along with me. You have your life here, and there is no way I would ask you to come with me and be a part of it all. That's too dangerous, and I'm not risking it."

"But that's not fair. Don't I get to decide what I do with my own life? I don't care what happens to me, I just want to be with you." Tears flow freely down her cheeks now. I cup her face and run my thumb over her lips.

"Not this time. I'm not losing someone else I love."

She pulls away from me, turning her head. "So, what then? I'm in love with you and you're in love with me, and we go on and live separate lives? You're happy to watch me go off and marry someone else, have their babies, knowing that what we have is real, just in case something might happen to me?" Her voice crackles as she tries to get the words out over her tears.

"I'm not happy about it, but I'm prepared to see you live a happy life with someone else, knowing you're safe." Even though it will be the hardest thing I have had to do, and it will break my heart to see her move on and have a happy life with someone more deserving. But it's the only option. I won't let her risk her life just to be with me.

"Fine, if that's the way it has to be." She flicks off the bedside light and rolls over, facing away from me. The warmth of her body is gone, and I feel the loss instantly. I go back to the day bed, lying down, pulling up the blankets. "I'm sorry, Indie," I whisper.

"Yeah, me too, Blake," she whispers back.

And just like that, I can feel her walls are back up again. But as much as it hurts, I know I've done the right thing. Haven't I?

CHAPTER TWENTY-FOUR

BLAKE

I'VE STAYED WITH INDIE FOR A WEEK NOW, AND EVERY day we follow the same routine. We go off to work, and Ryker stays with Indie all day. Wherever she is, he is. She wasn't happy about it at first, but I think my conversation with her about how serious this is has her scared enough to know she needs him.

At night, I arrive to stay on her couch. She is polite, but her walls are back up. Her eyes have lost their sparkle. She's not the girl I first met. That girl had just broken up with her long-term boyfriend, had her heart broken, but she was more alive than what she is now. I broke her, I can see it, and it fucking kills to know it was me that did this to her. More than hurt, it's misery. There is no talk of us. We're both just going through the motions to get through the day.

She and Elly had their first ever art auction last Sunday, and it was a massive success. Some of the contacts Indie met the night of the building awards were there with open wallets. She couldn't believe how well the paintings all sold. But I could. Her work is amazing, and she deserves the success. She just needed the right people to see it, and now that they have, she will be unstoppable. I couldn't be happier for her. She didn't celebrate; instead, she spent the night painting until all hours. Every night since I started staying here, she disappears to paint until late into the night. I can't tell if it's just to avoid me or if it's therapeutic.

It's a beautiful spring day, and even though I'm sure it's the last thing Indie wants to do, today we've decided to have a beach day with Theo, Fi, Elly, and Fraser, in the hope that the two of them can finally work their shit out. Fraser has been sober since our chat, and he started seeing his therapist. He has begged for Elly's forgiveness, and they've both been miserable without each other. Besides, we all know it's time; Elly is just being stubborn. So, this is Indie's way of playing cupid and trying to get her happy friend back again. I guess she figures at least someone can be happy.

I'm at the beach close to the girls' apartment with Fraser, Theo, and Fi. The girls are running late, and I'm sure Indie had a hard time persuading Elly to come. Ryker will be with them but keeping his distance.

I sit on the sand next to Theo. "What's the latest, Theo, have you worked out who the corrupt cop is?" I ask, turning my head to look at him.

"We're working on it, but nothing as yet. What's the latest from your dad?"

"They've lost track of Vinnie completely. He hasn't been seen by any of his men since that day he bought the paintings from Indie." Not that we can believe a thing any of them say anymore.

Theo's forehead creases, and I can see how much this is playing on his mind. He's the type of guy who likes to keep people safe and fix problems, and this one is worse because it involves people he cares about, and we still have no solution. We're all just walking on eggshells, waiting for Vinnie to rear his ugly head. "I don't reckon he has gone far, Blake. Don't get complacent with Indie or Jenna. I'd say he's just biding his time. He knows everyone's looking for him. He's going to show up when we least expect it."

Fraser has been fidgeting all morning. He's dying to make things right with Elly, and I hope they can sort it all out. "What's wrong with you?" I snap at him.

"Elly's not going to be happy about this. She hates surprises, and I don't think she's ready to see me yet."

"Stop stressing, she is, and the rest of us are ready for you two to sort your shit out as well."

"I guess we're about to find out," calls Fi from her spot on the sand.

We all turn to watch as the girls walk towards us, dragging an over-filled bag, what looks to be some sort of beach umbrella, and God knows what else. "Elly has seen us and she's smiling. I think you're going to be okay, man. You can stop stressing now." Fraser's face relaxes.

As they approach, we hop up to help them get everything set up.

"Hey, you guys are finally here," calls Fiona excitedly. Being quite pregnant, she hasn't moved from her spot on the sand, but she sits up and holds out her arms for a hug from Elly.

"Sorry, I couldn't get Elly out of bed," complains Indie.

"It's a Sunday. How are you lot so happy about being up early?" says Elly.

"Wow, you girls brought the whole set-up." I take the handfuls from Indie and try to work out the umbrella. Bloody thing is impossible; how do you get it to go up?

"It pays to be prepared, Blake. You'll thank me later

when you need something," explains Indie, snatching the uncooperative umbrella from me and setting it up herself, grinning at me when she's done. Smart-arse.

"You know you live around the corner and could go home at any time if you need something else, right?"

"Yes, but I would prefer not to," Indie snaps back, laying out her towel next to Fi. She seems happy to see everyone else, but I'm still getting the cold shoulder and snappy remarks.

I go back to lie on my towel, still watching Indie but trying not to be obvious about it. She's wearing a strapless, red-patterned bikini top that ties in the front, with black bottoms, and over-sized, white-framed sunglass. She looks amazing. How can I not watch her?

Fi rolls over to face Indie. The two of them are huddled together as they lie in the sun on their towels. "Think it's about time the two of you figure your shit out as well. Don't you?" she whispers to Indie, thinking she's being quiet. But I can hear every word they're saying.

Indie looks over to me, then turns back to her friend. "It's complicated, Fi," Indie whispers back.

"It couldn't be that complicated. You clearly both like each other. Life's too short to muck around when you know you found your person. You don't know what tomorrow will bring. So just go for it, and somehow you'll figure out the rest of the stuff."

"He has to leave, though, and he might not be back. Then what? I'm left with a broken heart."

"Then you will have had this time together to remember. Rather than spending the last few weeks or months together arguing with each other because the sexual tension is so insane."

Indie hits her on the arm. "Fi!"

"You have no outlet. You will be blissfully happy for now, at least. Just fuck already; you'll be happier for it."

Indie grins back at her. And I don't know what she's thinking, but I like the sound of Fi's advice. "Look at you getting all motherly with your advice. How did you get so smart?" she giggles.

Fi grins back at her. "Seen a few things in my time."

What Fi is saying makes sense. Why are we holding back from each other? We should be making the most of the time we have left.

Elly and Fraser come back up the beach hand-in-hand.

"Finally." Indie jumps up all excited and goes over to hug them. "Nice to see you two have worked things out."

"Calm down, Indie," Elly says, hugging her friend, but I know why she's so excited—for Indie, this is a win. Someone she loves gets their happily ever after. Even if it's not her.

"We're heading in for a swim. You two coming?" I call, making my way to the water. I need to clear my head and probably stop eavesdropping, and what better way?

We spend the afternoon swimming and eating the picnic lunch Indie prepared. Indie has been looking over to me all day. Her eyes have that little twinkle she gets. She looks different after her chat with Fi, and I'm hoping tonight will go differently from the last week.

INDIE

We make it back to the apartment in the late afternoon. Elly heads straight to her room. She's rattled from the chat with me and Fi and has barely spoken since. We're pretty sure we've worked out she is pregnant. It would explain a lot. I hope for her sake that's not the case. She and Fraser might be working things through, but a baby, that's scary stuff.

I head straight to my room as well, to dump all the stuff from the beach. Blake follows me in. Closing the door behind us slowly, he turns to me.

He says, "I can't stand the way you've been towards me this week."

Is he serious? What about him? Mr Fucking Serious. "What do you want from me, Blake?"

He runs his hands through his hair. "I don't know, but you're killing me, you're shutting me out."

He takes a couple of steps towards me, closing the gap. I look up at him, his handsome face. I want to touch him, take Fi's advice. I know we have been at each other's throats this week, but I'm so frustrated. This situation is insane, and it's totally out of my control. He has made all the decisions for us. I'm not even allowed a say in it.

"What would you prefer I do?" I snap. "Act like this is all normal? That none of this shit happened and you didn't rip my heart out? Well, I can't pretend. You're going to move away and leave me forever, and I'm supposed to be okay with it. Well, I'm not!"

He stares at me, quiet, his face soft and kind, the old Blake. He runs his hands down my arms, pulling my hands into his and lacing his fingers with mine. I look at him, not knowing what to do. "I can't do this. It's too hard," I cry, dropping my head. I can't look at him. The pull he has over me is too strong, and if I stand here like this with him, I'm going to cave. "And I can't get away from you. You're here in my space, and I want you but I can't have you. It's not fair." I push his hands away and go to escape my room to the bathroom, or anywhere but here with him. In this intense moment, I can't be this close to him. I reach for the door handle as he grabs me and turns me back to him.

Cupping my face, his calloused hands run over my skin, brushing my hair out of my eyes. His eyes roam over me, bright and glossy. "You want me?"

"Of course I fucking want you. All that doesn't go away because you say it has to."

He wraps his arms around me, picking me up and pinning me against the door. The wood is cold and hard, but his body is warm, his masculine scent intoxicating, and my legs instinctively wrap around his waist. And our lips meet.

All the thoughts of uncertainty melt away. This moment is perfection. His lips on mine, his hard muscular body wrapped around me. Need throbs through my body, and my heart swells with hope. We shouldn't be doing this, but the words Fi said earlier today are coming back to me, and I know we need this. Even if it's just for a little while before it's over forever, we need this time together.

Our kisses roam everywhere. It's desperate and hurried, both of us scared the other will change their mind and it will all be over again. But I'm not going to change my mind now, this is too good, it's everything I need. He is everything I need. And I kiss him hard to show him just how much.

He moves his lips down to my neck, kissing and sucking, and I run my hands through his hair and down his back, digging my nails in as I go. We don't play fair when we fuck. It's hard and fast, and my body tingles with anticipation of what's to come. I need him so badly, it feels like a lifetime ago since we touched like this.

I'm tangled in his web of desire, and I want it all. He has

me pinned to the wall. He unties my bikini top, tugging at the tie on the front, and it falls to the floor. He reaches down and draws one of my nipples into his mouth and sucks hard. Then the other. I moan in pleasure. It feels so good to have his mouth on me. He does it again, rolling his tongue over my hardened nipple. God, I'm going to come just from this.

He slips his hand under my arse, and his finger strokes over my pussy. I can feel his cock pressed hard up against me. He slips his finger further up, pushing in under my swimmer bottoms and into my wet waiting pussy. He circles his finger, stretching me, pushing in and out as he takes my nipple in his mouth again and sucks hard. I ride his hand, rubbing myself against him. He pushes in a second finger, then a third. It's too much but not enough at the same time. I continue to ride his hand, his lips now back on my mouth, our kiss so desperate.

"Fuck, Blake, so good. I'm going to..." And I do. My body clenches around his fingers as I ride out the orgasm, his fingers still pushing in and out of me. My body relaxes around him as he pulls me closer, hugging me into his chest.

My eyes close. "Oh God, Blake, that was..."

He cuts me off. "Fucking amazing."

"Yes." I rest my head on his shoulder, and he carries me over to my bed. Placing me down, he steps back, undoing his board shorts and dropping them to the floor. His massive cock springs free. And he climbs over me, his weight on me, and it feels so good to be so close to him.

"Condom, Blake."

He growls and gives me a pleading look. I give him an *are you fucking kidding, we have talked about this* look back. And he gives in, reaching for my bedside drawer, grabbing a condom and rolling it on. He spreads my legs out wide and grabs his massive erection, giving it a couple of pumps, then pushes in, and I cry out. "Fuck!" I forgot how big he is.

He looks down at me, concerned. "You okay?"

"Yes, don't stop." I move my hips up to meet him, to show him I'm okay and I want more.

He starts to move in me, and my body arches off the bed, moving with the pace he is providing. He bends to kiss me, and I cling to him, my hands running down his back, digging my nails in. As our tongues wrestle, he pulls me closer, lifting my legs over his thighs. So deep like this.

I close my eyes. I'm on cloud nine, floating into another dimension of overwhelming pleasure. The warm tingles of desire wash over me as I wrap my legs around his back, hooking my feet to hold on. He slams into me over and over again. So deep, so fucking good. The headboard bangs against the wall, *bang, bang, bang*.

My mind is blank, all I can feel is him, his amazing body on mine and the way he makes me feel as he takes what he needs from me. My body is shaking uncontrollably, and I can tell that I'm about to be tipped over the edge. He slams into me again and rips the orgasm from me. I scream out. He slams into me one last time with short, sharp thrusts as he empties himself deep in me.

Our breathing is ragged, and I can feel his heart beating fast next to mine. He lowers my legs and pulls me to him as we collapse on the mattress in a sweaty heap. "Fuck, Indie, you have no idea how much I've missed you."

"Couldn't be as much as I've missed you," I mumble, still in some sort of fuck induced trance.

We stay like this, our bodies connected, until our breathing returns to normal. He brushes the hair away from my face, pulling my lips to his, kissing me. I wrap my body around him again; I can't get close enough to him.

"If we can have nothing else after the craziness is all over, I want now with you, Indie."

That's what I want too. If I can only have him temporarily, I'll take whatever I can get.

CHAPTER TWENTY-FIVE

BLAKE

I sit across from Indie, eating my toast and sipping my coffee, like we do every morning. We have quite the little routine going now, after practically living together for the last few weeks. Since the day at the beach, I've been upgraded from the couch and have been allowed back into her bed. We've decided to make the most of the time we have together.

Elly has moved in with Fraser for a while, since he wants to be able to look after her. She had a terrible fall last week, and now that we all know she's pregnant, it's best for her to be as far away from here as possible.

Indie looks up from her breakfast. She's been quiet this morning, deep in thought. Now she nibbles on her lip nervously. I wonder what's going on with her. "Blake, I have something to ask you."

This sounds serious. I put down my coffee to give her my full attention. "What is it?"

Her eyes are wide, and her hand fiddles with one of her large hoop earrings, turning it round and round. "You know how I found those photos from my childhood, before I moved?"

I nod.

"Well, I'm ready to go talk to him. My dad—my maybe dad. This might be a bit stupid, but I need to know more. I booked a doctor's appointment with him today. Will you come with me just in case I need the moral support? I have no idea how this is going to go." She's back to biting her lip again. She's really nervous about this, and I can understand. This is a big decision to make. He might have had no idea all this time and welcome her with open arms, or he might have known all along and want nothing to do with her.

I reach for her hand across the table and give it a squeeze. "Of course, Pix. What time's the appointment? I'll move some things around so I can be there."

She smiles at me softly. "It's at five; last one of the day. At the surgery on Main Street."

I walk around the table and pull her into a hug. She nuzzles her head into my chest; she fits perfectly here like this. I kiss her forehead. "Easy, I will meet you there."

"Thank you. I don't think I could do this by myself, and I haven't told Elly about the photos; she's had enough going on."

"It's no problem, baby. I think it's time you got answers. And I'll be there for whatever you need." I check my watch. "Right now, though, I've got to go. We're working on the Walker place today, and if I'm not there to watch over the boys, who knows what will happen. I'll see you at five."

"Have a good day."

"You too. Try not to stress about it too much." I kiss her again, grab what I need for the day, and make my way out.

. . .

I've been on the worksite at the Walkers' all day, but I stop in quickly at the office to tie up a few loose ends. I'll head over to the doctor's surgery to meet Indie at five.

I start up my computer and start scrolling the long list of emails when Fraser knocks at my door. "Hey, man, I just want to chat with you. I brought coffee." He smiles, holding up the coffee cups.

I motion for him to take a seat. "Is everything okay? How is Elly?"

He sits, placing the two coffees on my desk. "Yeah, she's doing much better, thanks. I just feel like since all the craziness and with you staying with Indie all the time, I haven't caught up with you in a while. I just wanted to check in."

"How are you going to cope when I'm working from Sydney?"

"I have no idea. Do you really have to go?"

I sigh. "Unfortunately, yeah. You know what my dad is like, and I made a deal with him. I can't back out of it."

"Are you ever going to come back?"

"That's the plan, I'm just not sure how yet. But I'll work it out. There is too much here in this town for me. I don't belong in Sydney; in that scene."

He cracks his knuckles, a serious look on his face. "Anything you need, man, I'm here. I never really got to thank you for what you did for me, getting me straightened out. But I'm here for you. I mean *anything*, I'm here."

I nod. "Thanks, man, I appreciate it. Hopefully it won't come to that, but It means a lot to know you're with me if it does."

He hops up to leave. "Good chat."

INDIE

We make our way in and sit, waiting patiently at the doctor's surgery for my name to be called. This place hasn't changed much over the years: the same green carpet on the floor, same cream walls, same wall of brochures about every health condition you could possibly have. I watch the receptionist as she works. She's young and pretty with long dark hair. That was my mama's job. She worked here from when she was 19 until she was too sick to keep working.

It's so weird being back in this office. I've avoided it ever since she died. I didn't want to come in here and see someone new behind the desk. And now that I'm here, I wish I hadn't come. But I wasn't just going to rock up at his house. This was the only solution I could come up with.

My knee bounces on the spot. I can't stop it, it's so annoying. I try to calm myself down, but I can't. Sitting still waiting is driving me crazy. Maybe I should just leave, tell the receptionist I don't need the appointment anymore. Blake places his hand on my knee, giving it a squeeze.

"It's going to be okay, baby, we're just here for a little chat, get some of the answers that you need."

I nod. I'm too nervous for words.

Dr Lennox walks into the waiting room and calls my name from the file in front of him, not even looking up, then walks straight back to the room he came from. I guess it's too late to leave now. I look over to Blake. He stands and takes my hand, pulling me up to standing with him. "You can do this, Indie." He smiles.

I nod. I can do this. Just get some answers, find out what he knows. It's simple.

We walk into his office hand-in-hand. I'm so glad Blake is here with me. Dr Lennox still doesn't look up. He just gestures for us to take a seat. So, we do, waiting patiently for him to say something.

He looks up from his file. "What can I do for you today, Indie? Been a while since you've been in."

Time has been kind to him. He's hardly aged, his dark hair a bit more salt-and-pepper, and there are a few more lines on his face, but he's still the man I remember.

I look over to him, and his piercing blue eyes look back at me. They're sad and he looks tired, but I know just by looking at him... he knows who we are to each other.

I'm at a loss for words.

He looks at Blake. "Is everything okay, Indie? Who is this?"

I look to Blake. Who do I say he is? "This is my friend Blake."

"Nice to meet you, Blake." He shakes Blake's hand, and they both eye each other off.

Dr Lennox looks me up and down. "I hope you don't mind me saying this, but you're the spitting image of your mother at the same age, Indie. It's uncanny."

I nod and offer a little smile. "People have said we look alike."

"You really do, I almost can't believe how much." He looks at me and blinks, then reaches for his glasses, putting them on and sliding them up his face.

I want to know how much he is willing to give away, without me having to actually ask. I'll start with his wife. "How is Auntie Susan? I think about her a lot. It's been a while since I've seen her."

He smiles. "She's been really well. She misses your mum, we both do." His eyes are sad, and I can tell how genuine he is. He loved her; I can tell. That just makes all of this even worse. How do you fall in love with two people at the same time? Especially best friends.

"So do I," I say sadly, "every day. She was the only family I had."

Blake squeezes my hand, reminding me he's still there next to me. And thank God he is, it gives me the strength to handle this conversation.

"I know, love. It must have been very difficult when she passed away. I know Susan would love to see you again. You should come over for dinner sometime."

He's not going to give anything away. He has no fucking idea how difficult it was when Mama passed away, and I was left all by myself. He could have been there for me. But for whatever reason he wasn't. I want to know why. I straighten in my seat, trying to muster the strength to ask. I tilt my head to the side, looking him over again, trying to work him out. "Don't you think that would be kind of weird, if I came for dinner?"

His forehead creases, showing his age more than I noticed originally. "Why?"

"Because you're my dad." The words just spill out of my mouth before I can stop them.

He blinks. "Pardon?"

"I said *you're my dad*. Wouldn't that make it weird if I had dinner with you and your wife?" I say a little louder, with more confidence this time.

His eyes have gone wide. "Did Brenda tell you that?"

Something in the way he says my mama's name makes my chest tighten, my breathing short. He knew... and nothing. That hurts more than I thought it would. He knew all this time and didn't try and contact me, even when Mama died, and he knew I was all alone. "So, it's true, and you did know all along."

"Yes, I knew. Why do you think your mother and I spent so much time together while you were growing up?" he says, snapping. What the fuck has he got to be annoyed about?

"Does Auntie Susan know as well?"

He shakes his head. "And I hope she will never find out. It would kill her if she did. Your mum was her best friend for many, many years."

I stand up, feeling like the room is starting to cave in on me. My chest is so tight. Why do I feel like this? "I don't understand, how did this happen? Why haven't you come to tell me? Why didn't Mama tell me? Didn't you want to be a part of your own daughter's life?" A tear escapes, rolling down my cheek, and I swipe it away. Stupid tears. It's just all too much, looking him in the eye and knowing this is my dad, the man I longed for so much as a child, and he knew I was his and said nothing. It's heartbreaking. I feel like I can't breathe. A sob escapes, and I bite my lip to stop myself from completely falling apart right here in his office.

Dr Lennox grabs for his box of tissues and holds it in my direction. I ignore him, and he places the box at the edge of the table.

"She deserves some answers," demands Blake from next to me. I had almost forgotten he was there.

I'm trying to concentrate on my breathing so I can calm down. I need to get out of here, this was a bad idea.

"So many questions, Indie, but here where I work isn't the place. Someone could hear us. I'll come and see you. Where are you living now?"

I turn back to look at him. He sits almost unaffected by this conversation. How can he be so calm? I search through my purse. "Here." I hand him my new business card and turn for the door. Blake follows me.

I almost run through the reception area. I need to get

out of here and fast. I make it to the car park and gulp for air. Why do I feel like I can't breathe? Blake wraps his arms around me, and I bury my head into his chest and sob.

Knowing who my dad is feels different than how I thought it would. I hate him. Perfect Dr Lennox sitting on his fucking throne, all high and mighty, unaffected by his bastard child's outburst. How dare he not feel anything for me? I fucking hate him. I wish I had never found those photos.

BLAKE

That was so hard to watch the woman I love go through. She deserves so much better than him as her father. He clearly only cares about himself. What a fucking arsehole! She is the one always thinking about everyone else, but still life continues to throw her these situations where she is the one missing out. I can't fix the fucked-up situation with her dad, but I can fix our situation. And after witnessing that today, I know there is no way I'm going to leave her on her own again. I want to be the family she is so desperate for, and I will be. I just have to work out how I can do both. Stick to the deal I made with Dad... and keep Indie.

We pull up back at her apartment and I follow her in. She didn't say much in the car, just stared out the window. She opens the front door, letting us in. I close the door and turn to her, pulling her into me. "Hey, why don't you go run a bath and I'll organise dinner." I can feel her heavy sigh on my chest.

"Okay, thanks. I think I might." She smiles sadly and makes her way into her room.

I wish I knew what to do for her, I hate seeing her like

this. We both knew today wasn't going to be easy. I'm sure it was hard for her dad as well, not knowing she was coming to see him, but I don't get it. How could he have been so matter-of-fact about the whole situation? I could never be so cold to anyone, especially knowing they were my child and obviously in pain.

Tonight, I need to let her know what she means to me. She needs to know just how special she is, even if her fuckwit of a cheating dad couldn't see it. She won't go to bed tonight feeling alone in this world. She has me.

Indie is normally the one who prepares dinner, but I know a thing or two in the kitchen, and tonight I want to do something nice for her, try and put a smile on her face again. I get to work chopping the vegetables and pulling the other items out of the pantry as I heat the wok.

She comes out for the bathroom, her fluffy blue towel wrapped snugly around her. Her face is red and blotchy, and it's from more than the heat of the water. This woman is one of the strongest I have known, but everyone has their breaking point. I smile over to her, not really sure what to say.

"What smells so good? I'm a little surprised to see you in my kitchen cooking." She smiles at me, her brow raising in surprise. The smart-arse Indie is still in there, regardless of her sadness.

"I have many talents you don't know of yet, Pix. It's honey soy chicken, and it's nearly ready so you'd better get a move on, unless you're coming to dinner like that, and I can't say I would object."

Her face brightens a little. "That sounds amazing, thank you. I'll get dressed quickly."

"You don't have to,.." I suggest cheekily.

She rolls her eyes at me exaggeratedly and disappears

into her room. I continue to mix the sauce through the stir-fried vegetables and chicken.

I scoop the rice into two bowls, followed by the stir fry, and I feel her arms around me. I turn to face her and pull her into me, holding her close. She smells amazing, fresh and florally. She's dressed in a simple burgundy wrap-around dress. Her hair is a little wet, still messy with a curl through it. She is so beautiful. I'm so lucky she has let me into her life, even if the circumstances haven't been ideal, and now, I just need to not fuck it up so I can keep her in my life somehow.

I cup her face and draw her lips to mine, kissing her softly. "Are you feeling any better?"

"A little, the bath helped. And coming out to you cooking dinner was an instant mood booster just from the shock. I thought you would order in. You haven't cooked for me before."

"I know. But I wanted to do something for you tonight. My cooking skills aren't as good as yours, but a stir fry I can do," I say with a wink.

"Thank you. If it tastes as good as it smells, I'm sure you will have done all right."

"You want something to drink?"

"Sure, why not." She takes a seat at the table, and I take two glasses from the kitchen cupboard and pour us each a glass of Sauvignon Blanc. I pass one to her and place the other on the table. She takes a large sip, then another.

"You trying to get drunk, Pix?"

She shrugs. "Getting drunk tonight wouldn't be the worst thing."

I place her bowl in front of her and mine at my setting, then take a seat across from her. We devour our meals quickly. It's not as good as the meals I have become used to when she cooks, but it's edible, and I was hungry.

"That was delicious. You're the one doing the cooking from now on," she says, licking her lips clean.

I raise a questioning brow in her direction. It really wasn't all that great. "Really? I think you'll get sick of the same option every night pretty quickly, but for you, I would."

"Well, maybe once a week then."

"I can definitely do that." I'm going to have to learn how to make something more than that, though, or we're both going to get sick of my stir fry pretty quickly.

She looks better than she did when I first brought her home, but still not herself. "Are you okay?"

"Yeah, I guess I just wanted it to be some amazing reunion, you know, but I guess that was just the fantasy five-year-old Indie was holding onto. I know it's not reality."

I reach my hand across to hers, giving it a squeeze. "I'm sorry, Pix."

She offers me a small smile. I pull her up from her seat. "Let me make you feel better." I lead her down the hall to her bedroom, pushing her down to the bed. "How about I do the same deal as I did the first night we met and help you forget all the pain and disappointment."

She smiles up at me, that glint of naughty Indie in her eyes. "I think that sounds like a good idea."

I reach down, pulling the tie of her dress so the bow comes undone, and the dress falls open, revealing the cutest set of wine-coloured lace panties and bra. "I haven't seen this before."

She runs her hands down her body, up over the lace fabric of her bra and down her stomach to play with the little heart charm attached to the front of her tiny panties. "I ordered them online, do you like?"

"I love! You look good enough to eat, and that is exactly what I intend to do. Tonight, Indie baby, I'm going to worship you the way you deserve."

CHAPTER TWENTY-SIX

INDIE

It's been a month since Blake moved into my apartment to protect me from the crazy situation we've all found ourselves in. So far, nothing has happened. Every now and then I get a tingle up my spine like I'm being watched or something, but the boys are never too far away, and I have never actually seen anyone. I think I just have that creepy feeling because we're all so on edge. They've completely lost Vinnie, no one knows where he is. He's not bothering us, so that's all that matters. I'd say he has moved on and we're all going to be fine. Well, at least that's what I keep telling myself so I can sleep at night. And I secretly love that it's forced us to live together. Blake has finally started to relax a bit, and things are slowly getting back to normal.

The four of us—Fraser, Elly, Blake, and I—are spending a lot of time together, mainly at the beach 'cause I can't get enough of the place this time of year, and with us just being a short walk over to it.

Today is no exception; it's 30 degrees outside, and it's my 26th birthday. What better way to celebrate? A bunch of us went down to the beach for a swim, and I've just rushed home to grab some snacks and bottles of water. I check the fridge and start piling food into my big straw bag.

It's so weird. I pull out the punnet of strawberries and sitting on top is a white feather. How on earth did that get in the fridge? Okay, Mama, I hear you loud and clear. *Happy birthday, Indie.* Thank you. I finish packing up the bag of food for the others, when I hear a knock at the door. Who on earth...? It's 4pm on a Sunday afternoon! Shouldn't be anyone for the gallery.

I open the door and there stands Dr Lennox. He looks more casual than I remember, in a pair of jeans and polo shirt. I was wondering how long it would take him, if at all, to contact me and have that long-overdue chat. Not the best timing, but I'll take what I can get. I have calmed down slightly from our last conversation. I still hate him, but he's the only one who can give me the answers I so desperately want to hear. So, I guess I need to try and be nice, hear him out.

He smiles warmly. "Indie, can I come in? I need to talk to you."

"Ah, okay." My mind has gone blank, I don't know what to say. I wanted to be more prepared for this conversation, not dripping wet in my bikini. I show him through to the lounge, and he takes a seat. "I'm just going to chuck on some clothes, won't be a sec."

He nods, and I rush into my room and find a dress to throw on over the top of my swimsuit. Just breathe, Indie, it's okay. Whatever he says, you can handle it. You have gone this long without him in your life. If he doesn't want anything to do with you, you'll be fine. Just get answers about what happened with him and Mama, and then you can move on.

He looks more uncomfortable than at his surgery. "Would you like a drink or something? It's too hot for a coffee, but I can make an iced tea."

"No, I'm fine, thanks."

I pour myself a water, adding ice, and sit down, acutely aware of how cold the glass is on my skin.

He stares at his hands, rubbing them together, then lifts his gaze to me. "Indie, that day you came into my surgery, I couldn't really talk, and it's taken me awhile to think of what to say. I never thought I would have this conversation with you. Your mum promised me you would never find out."

"She didn't tell me, I worked it out."

"How?"

"She left me photos when she died. On the back there were handwritten notes from her. I guess she couldn't tell me, but she wanted me to find them someday and work it out."

"I see," he says, his lips forming a thin line. He can't really be annoyed at a dead woman for wanting her child to know who her father was, can he?

I place my glass on the table in front of me. If I don't put it down soon, I'm going to smash it in my hand I'm gripping it so tightly. I'm going to let him off the hook. "Look, it's pretty clear you don't want anything to do with me and you would prefer to keep this a secret, so why are you here?"

"It's all very complicated, Indie. It's not that I don't want anything to do with you. I tried to be as much a part of your life as I could when you were growing up. It's just that Susan can never know about this. About our relationship. What happened with your mother... it would break her heart. She loved your mother, and if she knew what we did, I don't even know what would happen."

"I don't understand how this happened. You were married."

"Your mother and Susan were best friends since high school, then when I met Susan, we fell in love and got married very quickly. We were young. A few years later, your mother was looking for a job and I was looking for a receptionist, so she started to work with me. At first it was just like any normal work relationship, but over time, we developed feelings for each other. I loved your mother very much. But neither of us wanted to hurt Susan, so we kept it to ourselves."

"So, you just fucked behind her back. Poor Auntie Susan. That's awful."

"Indie! We didn't *fuck* behind her back; we were in love." He raises his voice, unimpressed by my comment.

"You can paint it however you like but sounds like that's exactly what you were doing."

He looks down as if embarrassed and scrubs his hands over his face. "It wasn't. One day, when you're in love with someone, you'll know that it doesn't matter about the consequences. You can't help yourself." He looks back up to me. "In another life, if I had met your mother first, things would have been different."

"She worked for you until she died. Was this all still going on that whole time?"

He looks at me as if lost for words. "Yes," he says, shaking his head.

I stand. I think I've had enough of this conversation. I'm fucking mad for Mama, for Susan. How could he do this to them? "That's why Mama could never see anyone else. You selfish pig! You let her suffer alone, watching how happy you and Susan were, knowing she would never move on.

How could you do that to her—to both of them?" I almost yell.

"I know what I did was very selfish, but I couldn't let her go, I tried. After she told me she was pregnant with you, she asked me to leave Susan and be a family, but I couldn't do that either. I love Susan. She was unable to have children, so I knew this was my chance to have a family, but I couldn't do it to her. Your mother and I came up with an arrangement, so I could help her with everything and still be able to see you grow up."

"I can't believe the words you're saying. I just don't get it. How can you be in love with two people at the same time? I have gone my whole life thinking my dad was some one-night stand my mother had. What now? Where do we go from here? It sounds like it's pretty obvious you're not going to tell Susan."

"I'm not, Indie, I'm sorry. What would be the point in telling her now after all this time?"

That's what I thought. "Oh, I don't know, that you might actually get to know your only child, and I might have some family."

"I know it must be awful for you now your mother is gone, and I would have loved to have a relationship with you in some way, but I can never be your dad."

"Don't worry about it. That's what I thought you would say." I turn to leave for the kitchen or anywhere else but here listening to this shit.

"Indie, stop. I know you're angry but come and sit back down. There's something else I want to tell you, something I think you should know, because it might help." His eyes plead with me to come back.

"What could possibly help this situation?"

"A few months before I found out your mother was pregnant with you, there was someone else."

I whip my head back to look at him. "Are you fucking kidding?"

"I'm not proud of this moment. Just let me tell you what happened. I knew this woman well. She was a patient and had been trying to get pregnant with her husband for years with no luck. She was certain it was his fault. One night, we bumped into each other in a bar, and she talked me into helping her conceive."

What the fuck is he talking about? I close my eyes, trying to process what he's saying. "You what?"

"I know how bad this looks, but at the time, I was thinking, what the hell? It will be my only chance to father a child. She didn't want me to have anything to do with the child, and I was okay with that."

"What about Susan and Mama, who you were supposed to be in love with? How many illegitimate children do you have running around out there? Do I need to start asking for a blood test before I date to make sure we're not related?"

"Indie." His voice is loud and commanding again. He is getting irritated with me, but is he fucking kidding? "That was it. It never happened again." He pulls out his wallet, and hidden in the back, he pulls out a folded piece of paper and hands it to me. "I have his details. You should contact him. He's around your age, and he's your half-brother. Family."

I look back at him in disbelief, then down to the paper he handed me. Do I want to know who this is? I unfold the crumpled-up paper to see a photo of a boy in his school uniform. He would be about 14. He's had this photo awhile.

I gasp. I know this boy.

"Say something, Indie."

I shake my head. I don't know what to say. I go to open my mouth, but I can't. My brain is madly trying to connect the dots. I'm so confused. This is all too much. The apartment door swings open, and I can hear the loud chatter of the others. The others. Shit. I forgot I was supposed to be taking them food who knows how long ago.

"Hey, Indie. What took you so long? We're starving," calls Fraser. "These pregnant ladies couldn't wait another second."

"The food's in the bag, on the counter," I call, still frozen, my eyes on the photo of the boy.

I hear Elly and Fi go straight to the kitchen and riffle through the bag. "Thanks, Indie, this looks amazing," calls Elly.

"Pix, you okay?" asks Blake, coming to stand by me, his hands on my shoulders.

"Um, this is Dr Lennox, you met at the surgery that day," I say in a daze.

"Yeah, I remember. Is everything okay here?" Blake asks, looking between me and the doctor.

Dr Lennox's eyes flick from the others then back to me. His eyes widen, and I realise he's just worked out why I can't get the words out. I shakily hand the photo to Blake. "Dr—Dr Lennox has a son our age as well. It seems he was a very busy boy that year."

Blake glances at the photo, then back over to Fraser, then to me.

Elly seems totally confused, looking over to Fraser. "What? I don't get it?"

"Why is everyone staring at me?" asks Fraser, as he makes his way over to where we sit. "Why do you have my school picture, Blake?"

"I think Dr Lennox can explain that. I have no Idea

what's going on. I'll get the others out of here for a bit, okay, Pix?" Blake kisses my head, but I barely feel it. I'm numb. This is all too much. He ushers the others out onto the balcony with their bag of food. Elly throws me a worried expression, but she follows Blake, Fi, and Theo out onto the balcony.

Fraser sits beside me, looking over to Dr Lennox. "Who is this dude, Indie? What's going on?"

"Wow! You two already know each other; that make this easier."

"Fraser is with my best friend, Elly. They're having a baby," I say.

Fraser's eyes dart between us. "Is somebody going to tell me what's going on here?" asks Fraser again.

"Fraser, this is a friend of my mama. He so kindly donated the sperm needed to conceive me all those years ago. He was very generous that year, and it looks like he kindly did the same for your mother as well."

Fraser pushes out of the chair. "What the fuck are you talking about, Indie?"

"Ask him." I gesture towards Dr Lennox.

"Thanks, Indie. What she's saying is true, but it's a long story, and I wasn't expecting you to be here this afternoon. Fraser, I'm the man your mother came to when she couldn't get pregnant. I'm your biological father. I was telling Indie because I was hoping you two might be able to find each other and have some family."

Fraser is freaking out and looks like he's going to thump Dr Lennox.

I stand and start to walk over to the door. "Dr Lennox, I think it might be time for you to go and let me and Fraser process what you just told us." I open the door, waiting for him to catch up.

"Okay, Indie, if you want to talk again, either of you, this is the best number to contact me." He hands me a card with a mobile scribbled down on it.

"Yep," I say as I take the card. He walks out the door without another word.

Fraser turns to me. "You're my sister?"

"It would appear so." I offer a small smile. I have no idea what to do in this situation, and Fraser is not taking it well. He's a total hothead and could completely lose his shit over something like this.

"How long have you known he was your dad?" he snaps at me.

"I worked it out a few months back, but I had no idea he was your father as well."

Elly and Blake come back in from the balcony. "This is crazy, that guy is your father?" says Elly.

"I don't know. That's what he said. He had a photo of me. This is so strange. I need to call my dad." He gets up and leaves for Elly's room.

"Wow, Indie, this is crazy, are you okay?" says Elly.

"I'm okay," I say because I don't know what else to say, I'm still processing all of this.

Elly takes my hand, she looks worried. "I don't know how Fraser is going to deal with this new information, Indie. He has been through so much already this year, finding out the man who raised him wasn't his biological father. He thought he would never know who his real dad was, now this."

"Yeah, I'm still trying to wrap my head around it."

She studies me, her eyes roaming over my face. "You know, I can see it now. You and Fraser, you look alike," she says.

I don't know why but I run my hand over my face. "Do

we?" I don't know about that. Maybe we do. I need to find Fraser and make sure he's okay, this is all so unexpected.

I walk down the hall, and I can't hear him talking on the phone, so I knock at the door. "Fray, it's Indie, can we talk?"

He opens the door, then sits on the end of Elly's bed. I go to sit next to him.

"I'm sorry you found out like this. It's weird, hey?"

He looks up at me. "You're my half-sister."

"I guess, I mean, I'm not sure I believe anything that comes out of his mouth. This all feels pretty unreal, but that's what he's saying."

"And he's our dad."

I nod. "Looks like it."

"I mean, my mum used to take me to him as a kid, he was our family doctor. How fucked up is that?" His eyes are haunted, and I feel so bad for him. I have had a few months to come to terms with him being my dad, but this is all new information to Fraser, and to find out I'm his half-sister as well. It's all too crazy.

I give him a sympathetic smile. "Yeah, me too. Looks like he knew all along about the two of us as well."

"If this is true, though, we're family. We have each other." His eyes warm, and he offers a half-smile.

My eyes glaze over, and I try to blink away the tears. I hold out my hand for his, and he wraps his fingers around mine as we sit in total silence trying to think this all through.

"I always wanted a sister." He smiles over to me.

"I always wanted a brother, and now we have each other." I smile back.

CHAPTER TWENTY-SEVEN

INDIE

I'm still processing the fact that Fraser is my half-brother. It's so crazy, we have known each other a long time, but I see him so differently now.

I have gotten used to having Ryker follow me around when I'm out and about, but the rest of the time he keeps mostly to himself, just checking in on me throughout the day. He's not as scary as I originally thought, and after a few conversations with him, I've come to realise he's actually a pretty nice guy. Hard on the outside, but he's a softy. He has opened up about his family and how he came to work for Blake's dad in the first place.

I'm missing Elly. She is back to working on the styling business since her fall, but she is working from Fraser's place. He is being all protective of her, and this place is filled with way too much testosterone without her around. I can't wait for the day they will find Vinnie and my life can go back to normal.

I have spent most of my time painting. Something about all this craziness has me inspired with a new series of paintings. They will be perfect for the summer art auction that's only a month away. The colours are all shades of blue, turquoise, and deep purple in thick oil pastels. The people are dark and moody, and they make for the most beautiful compositions with the layering of colours. This is my best work yet. Today's painting is a woman's face close up. I have focussed on her eyes. She has one lone tear rolling down her face. The rest of the face blurring into a mix of layered colours in the background.

Ryker has been up here this morning and has just ducked down to his apartment to grab some lunch while I finish up here. Then we're heading over to life-drawing class for the afternoon. There's a knock at the door to my apartment, so I put down my paintbrush. Wiping my hands on the rag hanging out of my pocket, I notice there's paint all over my arms; different colours splashed all the way up. The life of an artist, I'm always covered in paint. The person knocks again. I go to the monitor the boys have installed with the security camera and check who it is. I don't recognise her. A well-dressed woman.

She knocks again.

"I'm coming," I call. Whoever it is, they're very impatient.

I open the door and a nice-looking lady in her late 20s stands in front of me. She looks fancy and from money, in a navy pant suit and white silk blouse, her blonde hair in a French twist.

"Sorry, love, I was looking for Indie Martin, the artist. Is that you?" She cocks her head to one side, looking me over.

"That's me, how can I help you?"

"I'm Mahalia Wintergreen. I own a design firm on the Gold Coast, and I've driven down today hoping to see some of your work. Sorry, I probably should have called first, but this is kind of urgent. Would I be able to have a look at some of your work today?" She offers a small smile.

I look down the stairs to see if Ryker is around. I've been on edge ever since Blake told me about Vinnie, and I know I'm too trusting of people, but if I know Ryker is around, then I can relax. He gives me a wave and a nod. "Yes, of course," I say, feeling slightly more at ease now. "I'll get the key to the gallery, won't be a sec." I go to the sideboard to grab the key for the studio, and she follows me into the apartment, walking straight over to the painting I've been working on.

"How much for this one, sweetie?" she asks, looking over the painting.

"It's not finished yet, sorry."

She looks disappointed. "It's beautiful. Do you have more like this? This would be perfect for what I'm looking for."

"I've just finished a whole collection along these lines. I'm sure there will be something in the gallery you will like just as much, or this one will be done in a couple of weeks, I just need to finish a few details, then the paint has to dry fully. I can have it couriered to you," I suggest.

"That's okay, I won't have time for that. Let's look at the gallery of finished work," she says, walking to the door.

I follow her, opening the door to the gallery. She walks around the room, looking over the paintings. "Do you mind if I take a photo of this one? Getting a second opinion from a designer friend of mine."

"Not at all, go for it. They're all on our website as well, if you want to send them the link."

She takes a photo of the painting and sends a message to someone.

"Would you like a tea or coffee while you wait for your

friend to reply?" I offer, hoping to make a sale out of this. After working at the café for so long, I can't help but offer coffee to everyone who walks in this place. That's why we had the coffee machine installed.

"Oh, a coffee would be lovely, darling, thank you. White, with one." This chick is a bit much, but if she's willing to spend the money to buy one of my paintings, then I'm happy to put up with it. She might end up being a repeat customer, and that's just what I'm trying to do at the moment, build up customers who keep coming back for something new each season.

I go to the kitchenette and make her coffee, then walk back into the room. The first thing I notice is the door is locked. That's strange. I didn't lock that when we walked in. Then I look over to Mahalia, and she smiles at me, but this isn't a friendly over-the-top smile like before. She stands with a gun pointed towards me.

My heart starts to race, adrenaline pumping through my body, but I'm frozen to the spot. My eyes flick back to the glass door. Ryker won't be able to see me from here, and if I scream, she's going to shoot.

"Do as I say and I won't have to use this, okay, sweetie?" she threatens.

Blake

I've been on edge all week. Theo didn't track Vinnie down and neither did Morgan. He's on the run and hasn't been spotted since showing up at Indie's studio.

I need to check in on Jenna, like I do every week. I look over my shoulder again as I walk into the library. Just making sure I'm not being followed. It's hard to know who I can trust at the moment, and who knows who Vinnie has working with him.

Jenna is behind the counter reading something, glasses on, hair falling around her face. This girl loves to read. She's always head down, glasses on, with some sort of book in her hand. But this looks like a piece of paper or a letter.

"How is our lovely town librarian today?" I smile over to her.

She jumps when she hears my voice, then smiles and folds the letter over, tucking it in her bag. Her cheeks are flushed like she's guilty or something. I wonder what that was about. "Doing well. How about you? Everyone's favourite builder."

"Just on my lunch break, thought I would check in on you."

She takes her glasses off, placing them on the counter in front of her, rubbing her eyes. "Has Drew sent you again?"

"Maybe." She knows he has. Every week he calls me to check on her, and I come into the library like a good friend to report back that she's fine, nothing has changed. He wasn't happy to hear about when Vinnie showed up and was close to getting on a plane home until I talked him out of it. He has a series of big comps and will be no help here if anything happens anyway.

"You can tell Drew, I'm just fine. Working hard, studying, and staying out of any trouble." She smiles sweetly.

I lean up against the front counter, trying to relax a little. My whole body is so stiff with anxiety at the moment, knowing I have all these people relying on me to keep them safe. I look around the library, and the more I think about it, the more I realise that I don't know how safe she really is here. If he works out this is where she works... I know she had given him a fake name and she changed her hair colour, but guys like Vinnie, if they want something, if they *really* want it, they will stop at nothing to get it. I take a breath and try to calm down. "How are you settling into your new place?"

"It's amazing, I love it. The neighbours are all so nice. There's this beautiful older lady in one of them. She's been cooking me dinners. She's really sweet. Used to be an artist. Your Indie would love her. She has so many wonderful stories about when she was younger and travelling the world painting. Looks like the one next to me hasn't sold yet, though."

"No, the sale on it fell through, so it's back on the market. I guess Ash is just waiting for the right person. I'm glad you're happy there. I'll let Drew know you're doing fine then."

That same blush is back on her cheeks and she shyly looks down, fiddling with the book in front of her. "Yes, please do that."

"See you next week, same time and place."

"I'll be here." She smiles a little sarcastically. Where else would she be, I guess? Until we track down Vinnie and deal with him, she's stuck just going to work and hanging at home. I don't think she minds too much; she seems like a massive introvert, and I'm sure she spends most of her time reading. It has taken her a long time to open up, but we have become friends now. She's sweet and kind. She and Indie have met a few times now as well. Indie understands why I just couldn't let Vinnie find her.

I walk out of the library smiling to myself. At least someone got a happy ending out of this fucked-up situation. And she seems thrilled with her new life.

From across the road, I see him. At first, I think I'm imagining it. He's been playing on my mind so much lately;

he must be a figment of my imagination. Why would he just be standing there in broad daylight?

I blink. It's him all right, Fucking Vinnie. The cocky bastard is up to something. He glares at me, his lips turning up at one side in a smirk. My heart beats faster as I feel the testosterone kicking in. Why is he here? What has he done? How did he find her?

Before he has a chance to do or say anything, I stalk across the street and punch him square in the jaw. He punches back, getting me in the gut, winding me, but I'm not going to let this slimy fucker get the upper hand. I punch him again, and he retaliates. Then I charge at him, knocking him to the ground. I have him by the scruff of his expensive shirt.

He laughs, actually laughs in my face. "You can do what you want to me now, Blake, but it's too late for Cassie—or should I say, Jenna—and your girl regardless. As we speak, she's in the hands of one of my guys, and that bodyguard you have for her, nowhere to be seen. You thought you could protect her, but you had to know your days were numbered. Now she's all alone in that apartment of hers, and you're here with me. She will disappear just like you helped my Jenna disappear." He spits blood in my face from his split lip.

Is he serious? My heart is hammering in my chest. I need to get to her, and fast. "You're full of shit. There's no one helping you." I shove him again.

"I guess that's a risk you'll have to take. You stay here with me and protect my girl from me, and while I have you distracted here, one of my men is picking up your girl right now. That's a hard one, isn't it, Blake? You want so badly to be the hero, but you can't save them all. Who do you pick?"

What the fuck is he talking about. He's got to be full of

shit. Ryker will be there; he will protect her. I throw one more punch to his smug face and he goes down cold.

I ring Ryker to see if everything is okay with Indie. The phone rings out. That's strange, he always picks up. I try again, and it rings and rings. Come on, fucker, pick up. Nothing. Shit! I try Indie's phone. It rings out as well. Why is no one answering? What the fuck is going on? Fuck! I'm going to have to go over there. I check Vinnie's pulse. He's out cold and can't do any harm while he's like this. I have to get over to Indie.

I call Jenna. The phone goes straight to voicemail. I leave a message and pray she sees it. There are two hours until she finishes up work, so there would be no reason for her to leave the building anytime soon anyway. "Jen, Vinnie is out the front. He's knocked out cold and the cops will be on their way, but don't leave the library until I get back for you. I need to go and get Indie."

I jump in my car and I scream out of the car park, wheels screeching. I call Theo. "Vinnie's out the front of the library. You might need an ambulance as well as a cop car, I knocked him out."

"What the fuck, Blake. I told you not to mess with him. I can sort this."

"There was no time to think. He has some guy going to Indie's place right now. I'm on my way there. But I can't get hold of Ryker, he's not answering."

"I'll send a car there as well. Don't do anything stupid, Blake. Help will be there soon."

My heart is hammering in my chest, I will not lose her today. I flick open the glove box and grab my gun, tucking it into the back of my jeans, just in case I need it. "Got to go, Theo."

I drive like a maniac to Indie's place and pull up out the front. It's quiet. Very quiet.

I run through the corridor and can see Ryker's door has been kicked in and lies on his living room floor. Fuck, this is bad. I take the steps two at a time to the gallery and push open the glass door. My heart skips a beat when I see her. "Lexi, what the fuck are you doing here?" She stands in the middle of the studio, gun drawn in my direction. I don't have time to pull mine.

"Oh, nice to see you again, Blake." She smiles over to me like this is any normal day and we've just bumped into each other out of the blue. I should have known right from the start she was going to be trouble. She has the fucking crazy eyes.

"What are you doing here?" I ask again, raising my voice louder this time.

She laughs and shakes her head. "You thought you were getting rid of me, sending those photos of you and your girlfriend all those months ago. But you were just making sure I knew who I needed to target. And when I ran into Vinnie after you dumped me at your sister's wedding, my plan kind of fell into place."

"Where is Indie?" I growl at her, getting more frustrated by the second.

"She's a little tied up, Blake. I thought I would wait for you here in case you had a change of heart. I really don't know what you see in her. She's very plain; a struggling artist. I guess it's kind of cute for a while, but when you could have a lavish life with me, why would you settle for that?"

Lexi has completely lost her mind and is somehow now working for Vinnie. She has a gun pointed at me.

"You're right, Lexi, of course you are. I have no idea

what I was thinking with Indie. You're much more my type, and when I go back to Sydney and take over from Dad, you can be by my side. Just let Indie go, you don't need her."

She walks towards me, gun in hand. "You think I'm stupid, don't you, Blake? I know it wouldn't be that easy to get you back. But if she's eliminated completely, then I know you'll have me back. And besides, I've made a deal with Vinnie, and he wants her delivered to him. So, for once just do what I say, and everything will work out for us. Okay, baby?" She is right in front of me now, and I could almost grab the gun.

But I don't know where she has Indie and if anyone else is here. I remember Dad's words: *This is about being the smartest, not the toughest.* As much as I want control over this situation right now, I need to be smart about it.

"Okay, Lexi, what do you want me to do?"

She smiles knowing she's won, and I have to do as she says. "Hands on your head so I can see them. You can say goodbye to her before we leave. You won't see her again after today, it's so very sad."

She walks behind me, and we walk towards the door of Indie's apartment. It's wide open, and their place is a mess. Indie didn't go down without a fight. "She's in her room waiting for Vinnie."

I get a cold shiver at the thought of that fucking creep with his hands on her. There is no fucking way that's going to happen. I walk through the door to Indie's room, expecting to see her on the bed or something, but the bed is empty. I can see rope where she must have been tied up. Where is she?

Lexi has the gun to my back. "Don't stop, keep walking." I search the room, trying to work out what happened here, then I spot her. I can see her reflection in the mirror, just barely. She's behind the open door. She has something in her hand. She motions with her head for me to get out of the way.

"What did you want to show me, Lexi?"

She walks into the room a bit further, assessing the scene. "What the fuck, that little bitch. I left her right here. She was tied up. Where is she?" There's clearly no one else involved here, so it's two on one now. I just have to get that gun before she realises where Indie is.

Lexi's not that smart, and I'm sure if I can distract her, we can get the upper hand in the situation. "If she's gone, don't worry about her. I'm sure Vinnie has already been to collect her. We need to make up for lost time, don't we?" I say, offering my sexiest smile, trying to distract her. "There's a bed right here, we could get started now."

She looks around the room again, then her eyes go to me. "Yeah, you're right. He must have come and got her already. So, what do you have in mind then, Blake?"

"Well, first you need to put down that gun. Going to be hard to fool around holding that, now isn't it, baby."

She tilts her head to the side, assessing me. "Not yet. First you can strip. Sit on the bed and take off your clothes for me, baby. I want to see that gorgeous body of yours."

"Okay." I sit on the bed and start to unbutton my shirt. Lexi's eyes are alight with desire, and from here I can see Indie clearly. She's not scared at all. She looks like she knows exactly what she's doing. She's just waiting for the right moment. I need to get Lexi closer to me. "Why don't you come a bit closer, Lex, and kiss me. You could help me undress; I want your hands on me."

A smile crosses her face, and she slowly walks towards me, gun still in her shaky hands. "Put the gun down, baby, and kiss me. You can relax now, you got Indie out of your way. It's just the two of us now," I say, reaching out for her and pulling her towards me. Her head tilts and drops to mine.

She kisses me, gun still in one hand. I let my hands roam up her body as I kiss her again, pulling her further into me. My hands roam over her body and to the gun. I take it from her hands as we kiss. I place it on the bed next to me, trying to gain her trust. I kiss her again, harder this time, making sure she's fully distracted. She has relaxed, her eyes closed, her body softening into mine. Her hands go to my hair, and I pull her in close. My eyes are open, and I can see Indie is about to move, so I moan loudly into Lexi's mouth. "Fuck, baby, I've missed you. No one kisses like you do."

She pulls back a little, looking back at me, and at the same time Indie whacks her over the head with the bedside lamp. She falls to the floor, a trail of blood coming from the back of her head. I reach for her gun, disarming it, and Indie collapses next to me. The tears she's been holding back roll down her face. I pull her into me.

"It's okay, Pix, I've got you. They can't get you now." She must have been holding it together until now. Her whole body is shaking. I hug her as tightly as I can, trying to calm her down.

INDIE

Blake kept saying this day would come, the day when Vinnie came for us all. I almost didn't believe him. I know I wasn't supposed to let anyone in unless we've done a background check, but she looked completely harmless, slightly stuck-up but nothing to worry about. Ryker even gave me the okay. How wrong could I be?

The words she kept saying to me will stay with me forever. The fear I felt when I thought I would never see Blake again. I know it sounds terrible, I've never inflicted pain on another person before, and I couldn't understand how anyone ever could—until today. Hitting Lexi over the head with that lamp and watching her go down was disgustingly satisfying.

I hug into Blake as tight as I can, inhaling his scent and feeling his warmth. I need this closeness from him right now like I need air to breathe.

We hear a noise as Theo runs into the room, gun drawn. His face is serious but softens when he sees us.

"It's okay, we dealt with her," Blake says, motioning to the floor where she lies. The girl so obsessed with Blake that she was prepared to hand me over to a mad man to get me out of her way for good.

"What happened? Who's the girl?" Theo points his gun in her direction.

Lexi starts to come to and looks around at us. Tears well in her eyes when she realises it's over and she lost. She rubs her head then looks at her hand covered in blood.

"Turn to face the ground and hands behind your back." Theo's voice booms through the otherwise very quiet apartment. She does as she's told. She's defeated. Theo reaches down and cuffs her, bringing her up to her feet.

We stand up together. I'm not ready to let him go just yet.

"Theo, this is Lexi. My ex. She has apparently been working with Vinnie," says Blake.

More tears start leaking from my eyes, as I have a flashback of him on the bed kissing her. I sniffle, trying to hold them back.

"Indie, are you okay?" asks Theo.

"Just shaken up a little. Don't worry about me, just go deal with her." I look at her, look through her. She seems so weak now. Pathetic, even, without that gun pointing in my face.

Blake turns to look at me. "How did she get in here?" he asks softly.

"She was pretending to buy some art. I thought she was legit. Ryker was around keeping an eye on me, then he was gone."

Theo clears his throat. "He was down at the station. Arrested for drug possession. He was set up. We're dealing with it now, but that's why he wasn't here. We still can't work out who on the force is working with Vinnie," says Theo.

"Did you get Vinnie?" asks Blake.

Theo shakes his head sadly. "By the time the car got there, he was gone and so was Jenna."

I feel Blake's body tense up again. "What the fuck, are you serious? He was knocked out cold, how could he have got to her so fast?"

"I don't know, but he has had a lot of help. The only reason she was out the front of the library was because the fire alarm was tripped and the whole building had to be evacuated. I have no idea how he got her without anyone seeing, but he did."

Theo's police radio starts to relay a message. *"We're on his trail. He's heading south on Beach Side Way towards the town centre."*

Theo talks into his radio: "Good, keep following. She's got to be in the car with him. I need to take someone into the station, then I'll be there."

The radio starts again, *"No sign of the girl, just two guys in the front. Vinnie's the passenger. Don't know the other guy."*

Theo nods and talks into the radio again. "She's got to be with them, she disappeared at the same time. Be careful, don't cause an accident, just follow and see where they go. I'm on my way."

"I'm coming with you." Blake turns to Theo.

Theo looks back over to us. "You know I can't take you, Blake. Stay here, look after Indie, she needs you."

I can feel how worried Blake is, how tense his body is. I should be worried that he cares so much for another girl, but I'm not. He's such a good person, he would care this much for anyone. "Drew will kill me if anything happens to Jenna."

"I will get her back; don't you worry about that. Stay here, and I'll keep you updated."

We watch Theo leave with Lexi in cuffs.

Blake looks down at me, pulling me in for a kiss. "I love you, baby, but I need to follow."

"I understand. I'll come with you."

"You're safer here."

A text pings on Blake's phone, and he pulls it out of his pocket to check. "It's Theo, he says the car Vinnie was travelling in has collided with an oncoming vehicle, just outside of the supermarket on Main Street."

"We should go make sure she's all right."

"You sure?"

"Yes." I take his hand, and we run out of the building and down the stairs to his car.

Ten long minutes later we pull up at the site of the wreck. I can't see Theo. There are ambulances and cop cars everywhere, and the road is blocked off in both directions. We park the car. It has started pouring with rain, so I chuck on my jacket and we make a run for it over to one of the cop cars, looking for Theo.

I look into the second ambulance and see Jenna. She's sitting on a stretcher with one of the paramedics. Thank God she's okay.

"Jenna," Blake calls to her, and she turns to look at us.

"Blake," she says, bursting into tears.

The paramedic calls us into the ambulance out of the rain. Jenna throws her arms around Blake. She looks okay. Her face is a mess with mascara running down her cheeks, and she's visibly shaken, but I think she's physically all right.

Jenna throws her arms around me. "Thank God you're okay," she cries. "Vinnie said they were coming to get you as well."

"What happened?" asks Blake.

"It all happened so fast. The fire alarm went off. We all evacuated the library. There was a police officer who asked me to come with him. Then the next thing I knew, Vinnie was there, and I was being tied up and shoved in the boot of his car. I didn't see the accident and the paramedics say it's lucky I didn't know to brace as it probably saved my life."

"I'm so glad you're all right," I say, grabbing her hand.

"Where is Vinnie and the other guy?" asks Blake.

She points to another ambulance. "They didn't make it. From what I've overheard, the guy driving, Matty someone, was high as a kite, and that's why they crashed. It was a head-on collision, and neither of them was wearing a seatbelt. Vinnie went through the front windscreen."

I shiver at the thought. What an awful way to die, even for someone like him.

"Talon," Blake calls out to one of the officers walking past, then turns back to us. "One of Theo's mates, he might be able to tell us more."

"Talon, what's going on? Where's Theo?" Blake asks. "He should be here by now."

"Hey, Blake. It's not good, mate. He's in there." He points to the third ambulance.

"I don't understand, he wasn't here when the accident happened."

"No, but the car they ran into… it's Fiona."

CHAPTER TWENTY-EIGHT

BLAKE

Today it's been a week since the accident, and it's a day you pray you never have to experience, burying someone so young with so much life ahead of them. The same car accident that saved Jenna, killed a friend, a part of my Byron family. Theo's beautiful fiancée, Fiona, was in the oncoming car. They raced her to hospital as fast as they could, but her injuries were too severe. She had lost too much blood, and she passed away. Fortunately, they were able to get their unborn baby out in time, a little boy that Theo called Jasper. He spent the last week in the hospital. He is cradled in Anne's arms today.

It's hard to watch Theo go through this. He was one of the good guys, fighting to help save a girl he didn't know. And he lost the love of his life. Life can be so cruel. I keep playing over what happened, wondering if we could have done things differently and how this would have played out, but in the split second I had to decide, I did what I thought I had to do. We all did.

Jenna is in hospital with a broken wrist and cracked ribs from the impact. The paramedics said her being in the boot of the car was probably what saved her. She couldn't brace for the accident because she couldn't see it coming. She's covered in bruises and an emotional wreck, but she's alive. She blames herself for what happened to Fiona. But it's not her fault. The blame is all on Vinnie, and he paid for it with his life.

Theo is a shell of a man. Completely devastated. Fiona was just in the wrong place at the wrong time. In her line of work, she could have been killed on any day, but on this day, she went out to grab some groceries and never came home. And now he is a single dad with a little baby to take care of.

Indie sits beside me, her head on my shoulder, sobbing, as we watch first Fiona's parents and sister, then the Walker family, one by one place white roses on her casket. Elly clutches her pregnant belly. She's been a mess since this happened. She and Fiona were really close. Fraser wraps his arm around her and takes her outside, she's sobbing so loudly.

Theo is last; his shaky hands bring the white rose to his lips, placing a kiss on it, then resting it next to her photo and bows his head. Tears roll down my face, and I let them. This is too much to watch. How did it all end up like this? The family makes its way out the front of the chapel as the curtain closes in front of the coffin. The rest of the mourners follow them out as music plays in the background.

Drew is the first one I see. "Drew." I wrap my arms around him in an embrace.

"Blake, Indie." He kisses her on the cheek.

"Are you home for long?"

"No, only three days, I have a comp next week I can't miss. I know Theo needs me, but I don't know what to say to him. How do you make this better?"

"You can't make this better, mate, but he has all of us

here to support him in whatever way he needs. Have you been to see Jenna?" Indie's eyes widen as she connects the dots.

"Yeah, when I got in yesterday. She's a mess, man. I don't know what to say to her, either."

"Yeah, I know. It's awful. I have organised a psychiatrist to see her tomorrow. Hopefully that will help a little."

"Thank you. You've been amazing looking after her. She told me everything you did."

"I'm glad she's okay, Drew."

Elly and Fraser have made their way over. Indie wraps her arms around Elly, and they both cry again.

I shake Fraser's hand and kiss Elly on the cheek. "I'm so sorry, Elly."

Fraser kisses Indie's cheek and squeezes her hand. "We're heading back to Anne and Jim's for the wake. You guys should come. I know Anne wants you there."

I still can't believe they're half brother and sister. "We will."

My phone rings, and it's Dad. "Sorry, guys. I have to take this." I walk away from the others.

I've talked with him a few times this week already. It was no lie, what Vinnie was saying. The same day it all erupted here, half of Dad's businesses were lit on fire. We assume by the Barrett brothers, but they haven't come forward to claim it as yet.

"What's the damage?"

It's not good. We lost two restaurants and a club. Luckily no one was injured; they all got out in time. Everything will be covered by insurance, so we can rebuild. It will just take a while.

"Fucking Vinnie. Still haunting us from the grave. What a nightmare," I say, running my free hand through my hair.

"Yeah, he's left us with a massive mess to clean up. I know you're not going to like this after the events of the last week, but we need you back here now. Things are getting messy with the Barrett brothers, and we need to deal with it."

I was expecting this, I knew it was coming. I had just been putting it off for as long as I could. "I understand. I have one last thing I have to do today. Then I'll be there."

"I'll send the jet. Bring Ryker with you, I've got another job for him."

"Okay. See you tonight."

"See you then, Son."

This isn't going to be easy. How do I say goodbye to Indie when all I want to do is stay and make her mine forever?

Indie

Anne has done a lovely job with all the food. It's always been her stress release, and she has outdone herself this time. The house is filled with flowers, and their scent travels through the air.

I can tell Blake is trying to hold it together; I know he feels like this is on him. He came to get me first. He was tricked, and Jenna and Fiona paid the price. But this isn't on him. He's a good man with a big heart who was just trying to help right some of the wrongs of his family's past. And this time, cruel fate had a different plan. Taking beautiful Fiona and leaving her baby without a mother.

Poor Theo. How do you recover from this? He didn't make it back to the wake, and Drew and Jim are out looking for him. He probably didn't want to face all these people when he's trying to understand how on earth this could have happened to the woman he loves. I know I wouldn't want to.

I sit down next to Elly with a plate of food. "I know you don't feel like it, chick, but you need to eat. Your baby needs you too."

"I know, but I can't stomach it. Oh my God, Indie, how am I supposed to have this baby? Fiona was supposed to get me through this, she was the strong one who knew what she was doing. I can't do this by myself, I need her. I know that sounds so selfish, but she was supposed to be the sister I never had and always wanted. We were going to do this together. I'm so angry that she's gone." She says it all without a breath, like the words are going to choke her, and if she doesn't get them out, she won't be able to breathe again. Tears stream down her face. I hold her hand and let her cry.

"Elly, you're going to be okay, I promise. Auntie Indie will help you in whatever way you need. I don't know much about babies, but for you I will learn. And you have your parents, and Fraser is so excited. He's going to be an amazing dad. You know he's got this; you just have to let him look after you."

"Auntie Indie. You really will be our baby's auntie, won't you? That's so amazing."

"Yeah, kind of still getting used to the idea. That dork Fraser I went to high school with is my brother, so weird." I laugh.

"It really is".

I throw my arms around her. "You got this, girlfriend. Now we just have to work out how on earth you help Theo through this."

"I have no idea, Indie. He loved Fi so much. You could see it every time they were in a room together. How do you ever pick yourself up and move on with your life? Now he is a single dad. How will he do it?"

"It's going to take a long time, but he's such a strong man, Elly. I'm sure with your family's help and support we can help him rebuild somehow, and he has that little boy to love, someone to do it all for."

She squeezes my hand. "I really hope you're right, Indie. I'm seriously worried for him."

Blake and Fraser have been talking for a while. I'm not sure what about, but every now and then they look over to us, and I can tell it's me they're talking about. Blake's about to leave, go back to the family business like he promised his dad he would. I know it. I can feel it. All week he's held me that much tighter, his gaze has stayed on me longer, and when we're in bed, he fucks me like it's the last time he's ever going to see me, his eyes never leaving mine. He hasn't said the words to me, but he's been saying goodbye all week. I know what's coming.

BLAKE

I watch her through the crowd, talking to her friend, and I think back to when I first met Elly. It feels like a lifetime ago; so much has changed since then. For all of us. These people have become my family, and it's killing me to have to say goodbye. Fraser promises me he will look after Indie, and I know he will. But how do I get the courage up to tell her I have to go now, right when she needs me here the most? We make our way back over to the girls, through the crowd of people gathered in the yard. Indie smiles over to me sadly, and I take her hand.

"Can we go somewhere to talk?" I ask, pulling her into me.

Her eyes rise to mine, and she tilts her head to the side, taking me in. "You want to walk down the beach?"

"Sounds perfect." I take her hand, and we make our way over to the beach. We walk for a bit in silence. I don't know where to start, but I know I need to. I've left this to the very last minute with her; my plane leaves in an hour.

"Indie," I say softly.

She interrupts me before I can speak. "Before you tell me whatever it is you're about to, Blake, I want to say something." She stops walking and turns to me, taking both my hands.

I nod for her to go on.

"I know this hasn't been a very conventional type of relationship, but the time I've had with you has been so wonderful. You make me feel alive in a way I never thought I could feel. I don't want to lose what we have. This is special. I know you have to go away, but I don't want this to end."

I pull her into me and kiss her perfect lips. "How did you know I was coming to say goodbye?"

"I know you, better than you know yourself."

"Probably." I laugh. "Even after everything you've been through because of me, you still want to be with me?" I say, a little unsure if I really want her to answer the question.

"I just know my life wouldn't be worth living without you in it."

I pull back and cup her face in my hands, looking into those beautiful emerald eyes. She blinks up at me, and a tear falls from her eye and hurries down her cheek.

"I can't end this, either. I don't want to. I'm in love with you, Indie. You're my person, and I will do everything within my power to come back to you as soon as I can."

"But you still have to go?"

"I leave tonight. In an hour, actually. I didn't get the call until today. They can't wait anymore, I'm needed back in Sydney. I have no idea when I will be back. I know it's a lot to ask but will you wait for me?" My eyes plead with her to say yes.

And she smiles a small, sweet smile. "Yes, of course."

"I don't know how long I will be, and we might not be able to talk much while I'm gone."

"Blake, I will wait for you forever, if that's how long it takes."

My hands go to the back of her head, and I pull her towards me, our lips meeting as we kiss.

CHAPTER TWENTY-NINE

BLAKE: ONE YEAR LATER

I've parked my car, and I walk down the main street of Broken Point. I've missed so much in the lives of the people I love, since I was here 12 months ago. Elly and Fraser had their little man eight months ago, and they recently got engaged. The girls' business is going from strength to strength. I couldn't be prouder of them and what they have created. I feel differently about the events of the past year still lingering in my thoughts. I'm hoping that being back here in some sort of normality, I can erase the darkness for good.

I wonder what Indie's doing right now. I stand out the front and look up at Indie's apartment, breathing in the salty smell of the sea breeze. I'm finally home, and this time it's for good.

My sister Amy's husband, Morgan, has taken over the family business now that Dad has taken a step back. Dad's getting on and didn't feel he could keep going in the same capacity. He's still involved—he will be till the day he dies, because he can't help himself—but the main responsibilities have been passed on to Morgan. He's now the king pin; it suits him. He's the kind of guy that was born to do that job and thrives on the power, just like my dad did.

Amy is just like Mum; she loves that lifestyle. The two of them make the perfect couple. I can't understand it, but it takes all kinds of people to make up this world, I guess. Dad wasn't happy that it wasn't me, but I think, after everything that has happened in the last year, he can see I'm not the right guy for the job, so he's shut up about it and accepted it.

I want to see everyone, and I can't wait to get back to work with the boys, but first I need to see her. That cute little brunette. She hasn't left my thoughts, not for a day. It's her I want to spend the rest of my life with. I knew that the first time I saw her when she ran into me, her red drink spilling down my shirt. The way her eyes looked into mine, I knew that was where I needed to be. All I've thought about is waking up to those bright, sparkling, eyes every morning, and falling asleep at the end of the day after making love to her, losing myself in her.

She doesn't know I'm coming back today, and I hope she's happy to see me. Twelve months is a long time to wait for someone. But, until we dealt with Vinnie's mates the Barrett brothers last week, there was no way I was risking coming home for them to work out she's someone important, so it was the way it had to be.

I take a deep breath and walk up the stairs to her art studio, red roses in hand. The gallery looks amazing, all paintings I've never seen before. She's been a busy girl. But I can't see her anywhere. I thought she would be in the gallery this time of day.

"Well, hello, sexy stranger in a suit. Are you here for the art?" I hear a familiar voice purr from behind me, and I feel the goosebumps scatter up my arms. I turn to see her standing there in her navy-blue painting overalls, her hair down, red lipstick on. She's better than I remember, and for the first time in my life, I'm lost for words. My heart's hammering in my chest. What if she doesn't feel the same anymore?

She breaks into a smile and runs straight to me, jumping into my arms, smashing her red lips into mine. Her legs wrap around my waist, and I drop the roses I was holding and wrap my arms around her, pulling her in as close as I can. She hasn't moved on, she still loves me. I will never get enough of her.

We crash into the wall behind us, knocking off one of her paintings, but she doesn't seem to care. We continue to kiss, desperate, hungry, hurried. My hands roam over her arse, and she bites my lip, pulling back to look at me, and there they are—those eyes— deep emerald pools, calling my name.

"I thought you were never coming back to me." She blinks up at me. Her voice is breathy.

I brush my hand over her cheek then down over those lush red lips. They part slightly, her eyes watching my mouth.

"Did you give up on me, baby?"

"Never, I would have waited forever for you, Blake."

"You won't ever have to wait again, baby. I'm never leaving your side." I pull her in for a kiss, my tongue swiping through her open mouth, gently stroking her tongue. For 12 months I've dreamed of this moment with her in my arms. I pull her into me, inhaling her scent. She's perfect, and it's so good to be home.

"Everything sorted?" she mumbles into my chest.

"I'm here for good this time, no going back."

"Good." She kisses up my neck. "You look so good in a suit, good enough to eat," she purrs into my ear, sending a tingle over my body. I'm so ready to show her just how much I've missed her.

"What? Better than the work boots?"

"I don't know about that, but you look fucking edible right now." She bites my neck playfully. There's my naughty girl, all ready to play rough.

"You're going to pay for that, missy." I slap her on the arse.

"I hope so." She giggles.

I carry her into her room and throw her down on the bed. "You have too many clothes on, they need to come off now," I demand.

She smiles broadly up at me, her face already flushed, her eyes glossy. She sits up on the bed, her eyes fixed on mine. She drops one shoulder strap of her overalls, biting into her bottom lip as she slides the other strap down her arm. I take off my suit jacket and place it on the pink velvet chair in her room. Then I drag her overalls down her legs to reveal lace panties in my now favourite colour, emerald green, gorgeous on her flawless tanned skin. I crawl over her, and she grabs at my shirt, her fingers fumbling to undo the buttons, making quick work of them and pulling my shirt down my arms.

She runs her hands over my body. "Mmm, you feel good." Her hands roam over my chest.

I drop down to her breast, sucking the nipple through the thin lace fabric, then sliding the bra straps off her shoulders. I push the fabric down her perky breasts and cup them with my hands. Rolling my thumbs over her hardened nipples, I bring my mouth down to suck on her. She arches her back and moans. I move to the other nipple, doing the same.

"God, I've missed you."

Her hands move to the back of my head, and she runs her fingers through my hair. "I've missed you too. It's been a very, very long year," she says, pulling my head back down to her breasts. I know she loves the way I do this.

INDIE

He's home, and two blissful hours later, we lie in my bed, our bodies still entangled. The light is starting to fade outside, and my tummy has been rumbling for a while. But I just can't let go of him. I can't believe he's finally back and in my arms again.

"Do you want something to eat? I can order in," I offer.

He pulls me back into him, holding me tighter. "Sounds perfect. I don't want to go anywhere tonight."

"Should I get some ice cream? Worked out so well eating it in bed last time." I giggle, remembering the mess. It took two washes to get the chocolate out of my white sheets.

"Whatever you feel like, baby. You know as long as I have my two favourite things, I'm happy."

"What's that?" I ask, playing dumb.

"You naked and junk food." He winks.

Twenty minutes later, our pizza arrives. We still haven't managed to hop out of bed, but when he hears the doorbell, Blake throws on his suit pants and strolls to the door to get our food. I could get used to this, Blake walking around my apartment, his hair a mess, no shirt; he is perfection. I pull my robe off the hook and make my way out to the kitchen, grabbing a slice of pizza straight from the box, while he is getting plates from the kitchen cupboard. I'm too hungry to wait. He places the two plates on the table, and I sit across from him, taking him in, enjoying the fact he is here, and we can do something as simple as eat takeaway pizza together. As I eat, he grabs my hand across the table, lacing his fingers with mine.

"Where are you staying now that you're back?" I ask.

"Elly and Fraser have offered me a room at their place until I get settled." He tilts his head to the side. "Or, I was thinking, possibly with a cute brunette I picked up in a bar a couple of summers ago."

"Is that right? She might let you crash on the couch, I guess. If you're willing to follow the house rules," I say, smiling smugly. There's no way I'm letting him stay with Elly and Fraser.

"What would those be?" he smirks.

"Let me think." I tap on the table, trying to think of something clever, but I have nothing, I'm too distracted by his sexiness. "Takeaway pizza at least once a week, your shout."

He nods. "I can do that, what else?"

"No food in the bedroom, especially ice cream."

"Probably for the best." He nods.

"Clothing is optional, especially when it comes to your shirt."

He smiles that cheeky smile, the one I love so much, where I know he's up to no good. "I can live with all those rules, on one condition."

"What?" I say, biting my lip.

"You accept the present I have for you." Now I'm intrigued.

"Okay," I say, a little unsure. He goes back to the bedroom and returns with an envelope. Very mysterious. "What is this?" I say, looking over the blank white envelope.

"Open it up and you'll see." He smiles, his eyes twinkling with excitement.

I rip open the top and peer in the envelope to see what looks like tickets of some sort. I pull them out for closer inspection, and my mouth drops open when I read what they say. "Is this for real?" I squeal excitedly.

He nods, and I run to him and jump into his arms again, screaming. I couldn't be more excited.

"Oh my God, I can't believe you planned this for us." Inside the envelope are two plane tickets to a romantic island getaway at Bora Bora, Tahiti, staying in over-water bungalows. My first trip on a plane, and I can't think of a more romantic place to go. I kiss his lips, and he draws me into his chest tightly, running his hands through my hair.

He pulls back to look at me, his expression a little more serious now. "There is something else I want to talk to you about." He plays with my hair, tucking it behind my ear. "You know how you said you want a big family." His eyes are warm and filled with love for me.

"Yes."

"Well, I was thinking we should get started straight away." That was not what I was expecting him to say at all. This boy is full of surprises today.

I slide out of his arms and take a step back to look at him. Is he for real? "Umm, maybe, but we're not married yet. I don't want to have a baby out of wedlock like all the other Martin women—you know, the curse."

"That's what I thought, so I took the liberty to book this as well." He hands me more papers, and I look them over, trying to make sense of it all.

"Elopement package?" I say out loud.

"Only if you want to. I haven't picked out a ring or anything. I wanted to see if this is what you wanted as well. I know I've been gone awhile, and you might have changed your mind. You might need more time. I don't know, I just thought..."

I jump up and down I'm so excited. Mr Romantic organising all this for me. "Yes, I want this. This is amazing, Blake. Wait, do we have time to order marriage licenses and all that?"

"There will be some formalities we need to organise to make sure it's all legal in Australia. And we need to get your passport sorted. But don't worry about all of that, I'll take care of it. So, if you are saying yes, when can I take you shopping for a ring?"

"You didn't actually ask me," I say, biting my bottom lip trying to be cute. He gets down on one knee in front of me and takes my hand.

"Indigo Violet Martin, will you do me the honour of spending the rest of your life with me as my wife?"

"How do you know my full name? I never tell anyone that," I say sarcastically, with a giggle, remembering how I gave him my middle name instead of my first on the night we met.

"I know many things about you, missy. Don't leave me hanging. What's your answer?"

"Yes, definitely, yes." He pulls me in for a kiss, and we collapse on the floor, tangled around each other again. I'm the luckiest girl in the world.

EPILOGUE
INDIE

THREE MONTHS LATER, WE ARRIVE AT THE MOST beautiful resort in Bora Bora. Our room is beyond amazing. It's the honeymoon suite, and it's a bungalow-type hut sitting out over the water. It has a white canopy bed and one of those glass-bottom panels that look straight into the lagoon. Just like I described my dream holiday to Blake the night I painted him. I can't believe he remembered and took note of my rambling. It's magical here. The air temperature is perfect, and I intend on spending all of my time in the water enjoying our honeymoon. But right now, I'm headed for the day spa, because today I marry the man of my dreams.

We didn't tell anyone from back home that we were going away to get married, except for Elly and Fraser, and unfortunately there wasn't enough time for them to plan to come away with us. But that's okay, I understand life is crazy busy with a one-year-old.

I walk into the day spa hut and hear the scream before I see her. Elly! She thumps into me, hugging me and screaming. "Oh my God, you're getting married today."

I pull back from her, and she's beaming with excitement. "And you're here to be my bridesmaid?"

"Of course, I couldn't let my best friend get married without me. Blake organised it all. He even picked the bridesmaid's dress, with Fraser's help."

"What? Those two in a dress shop! I would have paid to see that."

"It *was* pretty funny."

"He's organised everything, Elly! And thank God, because, well, we both know how good I am at organising things, especially at short notice. The only thing I had to do was my dress, and you already know what that looks like."

Elly and I had spent the whole day in Sydney. She had booked appointments with all of her favourite designers, because I had to have the best. But nothing worked, they were all too stiff, too fancy for me. Not my style at all. We were just about to give up, when we walked past a little shop with just one mannequin in the front and the most beautiful dress I have ever seen, by an up-and-coming dress designer. I knew it was the one, and when I put it on, the look on Elly's face told me all I had to know. It fit perfectly, and we bought it on the spot.

"Where is Coop?"

"The boys have him with them, and good luck to them, I say. The terrible twos have started early."

"Oh God! Poor boys." I laugh, imagining Blake dealing with a toddler throwing a tantrum. It will be good practise for him, if what he says is true, and he really does want a family.

"I know, right? Oh my God, Indie, you should see the little suit we got for him, it's so cute. I'm sure he will have it on for half an hour, then he will be covered in sand or food or something, but it's really cute."

"I can't wait to see him in it."

"Do you and Blake want kids? You would be such a great mum, Indie. All chilled and happy."

"Do you think so? I always wanted a big family, so I hope so." I look over to my friend. She has been a mum for a year now, and she's still the same Elly. I mean, sometimes it's a little harder to get hold of her, but she's still my best friend. "Elly?"

She raises her eyes to look at me. "Yes, Indie?"

"Can you keep a secret?" I ask, biting my lip so I don't let it slip yet.

She smiles broadly; she loves a secret. "You know I can, whatever you tell me I won't tell a soul."

"I'm pregnant," I blurt out. I had to tell someone. I hate secrets, and it's been killing me to have this one since this morning when I took the test.

She runs over to me screaming again. "Are you fucking serious?" She throws her arms around me. "Indie, this is so exciting."

"Just a little bit. So, you really do need to keep it a secret, not even Fraser. Understand? I only took the test this morning, and I will tell Blake tonight after the wedding."

"You told me before Blake?"

"I didn't take the test until after he left the room this morning. He doesn't want to see me before the wedding, and I don't think it's the kind of thing you tell someone over the phone."

"No, you're right. Plus, it's only fair, you knew about Coop before Fraser."

"True," I say with a nod.

She squeals again and grabs my hands. "Are you excited? You don't look scared like I was."

"I'm so excited, Elly, this all feels so right, so perfect.

Can you pinch me, so I know I'm not dreaming?" She pinches me on the arm and grins at me. "Ouch, I didn't really mean it." I laugh. "Okay, this is real, and I'm the luckiest girl in the world." I beam.

We've just finished getting our hair and makeup done and head back to the room. Elly is buzzing with excitement; she's like a little kid. I don't like my chances of her keeping this secret. I know she tells Fraser everything and is likely to blurt it out in the middle of the ceremony or something. But I had to tell someone, it was killing me. The florist has been and there are two boxes of beautiful white long-stem rose bouquets. No scent, but they do look lovely. My dress hangs in the doorway.

"Wow, Indie, I forgot how stunning your dress is. The lacework is exquisite."

"I know, I love it, it's perfect. Show me this dress they picked out for you." Elly holds up the garment bag, unzipping it, and revealing a beautiful knee-length, emerald-green, silk dress. "You guys did well, it's perfect."

"You know why he picked the colour, right?"

I shrug.

"Your eyes. Blake said that first night he met you he knew you were someone special when he looked into your eyes. He felt like he was looking into his future."

I have no words to say back to that. My eyes well with tears and I fan them away. "Elly, I can't cry, it will ruin my makeup."

"So emotional, Indie, so unlike you. Must be the—" She gestures to her belly, and I throw her dagger eyes to remind her to keep her mouth shut. "I'm not going to ruin the surprise," she tuts.

"Good."

"Let's get you into this dress. It's nearly time to go." She pulls my dress down from the hanger, and I take off my robe and slip it on. I stand and look in the mirror, smoothing out the intricate lace fabric, as she zips me up. I run my hand over my belly. It's so hard to imagine there's a baby growing in there. I don't feel any different. Not at all. I remember when Elly was pregnant, she was so sick she couldn't eat. I don't feel that. Maybe that's still to come. It's only early days, I guess. "You going to have another? We could be pregnant at the same time."

"Nope, no way in hell I'm going through that again. I don't care what Fraser thinks, we're done. Plus, I have a business to run," she says as she slips into her dress.

"Okay, we'll see."

She rolls her eyes at me. "As soon as you have one, Indie, people ask you constantly when you are having the next. It's painful. I love my little boy, but one is definitely enough for me." We stand side by side in front of the mirror. "You look perfect, Indie. Blake is going to jizz in his pants when he sees you."

I slap her across the arm. "Elly, I'm in a wedding gown, you can't say stuff like that. You've been spending too much time with Fraser; you sound like him."

"I do, don't I? That's scary," she says, pulling a face. "Come on, let's go."

I go to the dresser to grab the locket with Mama's picture in it, and as I do, I see a little white feather sitting on the dresser next to it. I smile, open the locket, and place the small feather inside. *Thank you, Mama. I knew you would be here with me today.* "Okay, I'm ready, let's go."

We link arms and walk carefully over to the beach, where the boys wait for us. The sand is warm beneath my toes, but there's a beautiful afternoon breeze keeping the temperature down. I can't help but wonder what it would be like to have my dad here to walk me down the aisle. But I guess I have something better: a friend for life in Elly, a half-brother in Fraser, and after today, a husband in Blake. This is my family. It might not be conventional but it's perfect, and I feel very blessed to have them.

"There they are. Man, we're lucky, Indie. How fucking hot do they look in suits?" says Elly, bumping me on the arm as we try to stay out of sight.

They look amazing, both in crisp white shirts with bone-coloured pants. They haven't seen us yet; they're talking and laughing. Blake looks relaxed and happy.

Elly and I wait for the music to start. I thought I would feel nervous, but I don't. This is it; he is my person. I have never been more sure of anything in my life, and I can't wait to marry him.

Blake

Today is going to be perfect. I'm marrying my girl in the most beautiful setting. The weather is ideal, sunny and warm, and I have my best mate next to me. We've been looking after Cooper all day. The little dude is a legend. He's cheeky and full of beans. I can't wait to have kids of my own, hopefully soon. They bring such a fun energy to life. He stands in between me and Fraser, and we're praying he doesn't make a run for it in the middle of the ceremony. This kid has some crazy amount of energy for a one-year-old.

Our song starts to play, and Elly comes into sight first, walking down the sand towards us in the emerald-green dress we picked out. It had to be that colour; it's Indie's colour.

Cooper can't contain his excitement any longer and pulls out of Fraser's grip, running to his mother. She laughs and picks him up, putting him on her hip, as she continues walking towards us.

Then Indie. She's breathtaking in an off-the-shoulder, ivory lace gown with a fitted bodice. Her hair is longer than when we first met. She's wearing it in soft curls swept to the side and, of course, red lipstick. Her cheeks are flushed and she's glowing. Her eyes meet mine, and her smile is carefree and happy. She makes it to the end of the aisle. I kiss her on the cheek and take her hands in mine.

The celebrant starts the ceremony, but I'm not really paying attention to what she's saying. All I can focus on is Indie, the vision in front of me, holding my hands. This incredible woman has agreed to spend the rest of her life with me. The vows go by in a blur. I say my part, but all I can do is concentrate on how beautiful she is and that she's mine forever. This is what got me through the last 12 months, the hardest of my life, knowing I had someone like her to come back to and spend my life with.

The celebrant announces us man and wife. I brush the stray hair away from Indie's face, and she smiles up at me. "Kiss me all ready, Blake," she says with a cheeky smile. She doesn't have to tell me twice. I pull her towards me and kiss her perfect lips, soft and slow. The others cheer, and Cooper wiggles out of Elly's grip and scampers over to Indie, hugging her legs. She gives him a high-five, and Elly collects him again.

. . .

We enjoy an afternoon of fine food and dancing at the resort with Elly and Fraser. They have said their goodbyes early, to take Cooper off to bed. The two of us walk back to the room hand in hand. The moon is over the water shining a silver shimmer. "This has been the most perfect day of my life. Thank you for agreeing to marry me," I whisper.

Indie stops walking, looking up at me. "Blake, I have a little surprise for you that might make it even more perfect."

"You have some super-sexy lingerie on under that dress?"

She smiles up at me, tilting her head in question. "You want your surprise to be sexy lingerie?"

"If it's on you, then fuck yeah. Stop stalling, Indie. What is it?"

She hesitates for a minute, holding my hand and giving it a squeeze. Then she looks up at me, her eyes shiny with excitement. "You might get that family a little earlier than you thought. I'm pregnant! Surprise!"

It takes a second to process what she just said. "Did you say *you're pregnant?*"

She nods. "Yes."

I pick her up and spin her around. "We're going to be a family."

I lower her back down onto the sand, and she says, "Yeah, I hope you're ready for it, Daddy."

"Sure am! This day just got even more perfect."

"I can think of one more thing that will top it."

"You read my mind. Let's get this sexy body of yours back to the room."

The End

ALSO BY A.K. STEEL

Always Fraser — Broken Point book 1

Eventually Blake — Broken Point book 2

Only Theo — Broken Point book 3 (coming soon)

If you enjoyed Eventually Blake, please leave me a review. Reviews really do make such a difference. Even a short one liner is a big help.

ABOUT THE AUTHOR

I'm a contemporary romance author of books with swoony men, twists and turns, and always a happily ever after.

I'm a busy mother of three pre-teens, who lives on the beautiful South Coast of New South Wales, Australia. I have always been a creative soul, with a background in fashion design, interior decoration, and floristry. I currently run a business as a wedding florist and stylist but have always had a love for reading romance novels. There's just something about how the story can transport you to another world entirely.

So, in 2020, I decided to jot down some of my own ideas for romance stories—always with a happily ever after, of course—and from that came my debut novel, *Always Fraser*. From that moment, I haven't looked back. Writing has become a part of me. I have a long list of stories plotted, and I look forward to being able to share them all with you soon. I hope you enjoy reading them as much as I loved writing them.

XX

For all the news on upcoming books, visit A.K. Steel at:
    Facebook: A. K. Steel Author

Instagram: aksteelauthor
www.aksteelauthor.com

ACKNOWLEDGMENTS

My partner, Kiel, you have changed my life in so many wonderful ways. Thank you for pushing me to start writing. Without your encouragement and love, I never would have put pen to paper and started this fantastic journey in the first place. I feel like I found myself this year, and I'm finally where I'm supposed to be. Without you, this never would have happened.

My amazing mum, Kay, thank you for your constant love and support. You read every word I write and have always been my number one fan. You put up with my meltdowns and endless questions, you are my best friend, and I'm grateful every day to have you in my life.

My dad, it's been seven long years since you left us, but the outlook you had on life still inspires me every day. It's the reason I believe that if you work hard enough, you can achieve any dream, no matter how impossible it seems.

My kids—Hamish, Marley, and Quinn—thank you for looking at me like I'm amazing and can do anything, even when I don't feel like I can. Everything I do is for you. And I hope I have shown you that with a bit of determination and hard work, your dreams really can come true.

Karen, my friend and mentor, you made this dream feel possible. Every time I thought I couldn't do it, you encouraged me to keep on going. I couldn't have done any of this without your knowledge and friendship.

Lindsay, my editor, thank you for your patience with a new author. Your knowledge and expertise have made this book what it is.

Sarah, for my gorgeous cover design, and your patience with my indecisiveness. I love the cover you created for me.

My beta readers—Elise, Shelly, Kirstie, Bek, and Francesca—thank you for your time, honesty, and support. Without you lovely ladies I wouldn't have had the courage to publish and share my story.

My proof readers Shelly and Kay, thank you for double and triple checking every word.

To my friends and family who have been so supportive along this journey—you have all been so amazing—thank you.

And lastly to my readers, thank you for taking the time to give a new author a chance, and making my dreams become a reality.

Printed in Great Britain
by Amazon